RUN FROM ME

WILDEST DREAMS

CRISTIANA JANELL

Dear Reader,

This novel contains adult themes and content that may be triggering for some readers. The setting is a fictional fantasy world that is oftentimes patriarchal and misogynistic. The authors chose this medieval setting to correlate common issues women face, even today.

Without spoiling specific events, triggers include but are not limited to: Blood play, cheating, domestic abuse, homophobia, human sacrifice, infertility, knife play, murder, pedicide, religious extremism, self-harm, sexual assault, sexual harassment, surgical gore, sword violence, torture, trauma, and violence.

There is a mention of a tannery on the island but no graphic descriptions of violence against animals. No horses or dogs are harmed in this book.

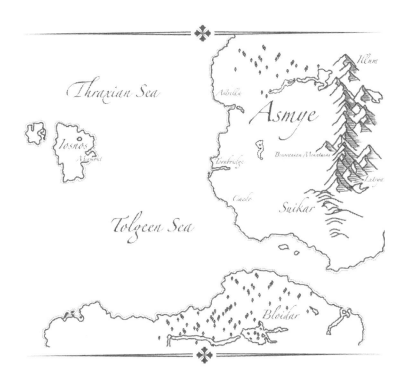

To Timber Timbre, my constant muse
To the Inner Circle *SPITS*WHORES
To my little family-Goodnight, I love you.
-Cristiana

To Taylor Swift, for everything, always
To Katrina, sorry you're second, you should've known
To the Inner Circle, this is about you, you know who you
are, I love you
-JaNell

PROLOGUE

Mountain peaks loomed high above the Monastery of the Adeshbu. Light snow fluttered softly around Luc as he ascended the steep stairs built into the mountain. The climb itself would offer no challenge to him. He'd run up and down these stairs daily since his arrival five long years ago. The trial was in facing the cold without boots or clothing. They only let him keep his britches.

Each step upon the cold stone burned into his skin and sent an ache to his bones, but Adeshbu training transformed his once-emaciated body into that of a great warrior. Every skill he'd mastered would come into play today. He couldn't afford to fail.

Mutters of voices yards behind him grew closer, edging the still, small voice inside Luc to press forward. The quicker he ascended, the more time to rest. The stairs, carved from the mountain face, were marked every hundred feet with an effigy to Adievasinis. Each statue showed another beastly enemy slain as the god collected his armor, piece by piece. Luc's eyes caught the flicker of firelight from the temple at its peak.

Luc crossed the threshold of the temple first. Adievasinis stood, frozen in stone, lowering his helm over his face. Ten Adeshbu soldiers stood tall as Luc walked to the center of the temple and knelt. The shelter warmed his blood as he waited for the other soldiers to finish their ascent.

"Only the strongest men are worthy of becoming Adeshbu." A helmeted elder with a black cape stepped forward as the men stood in line with their backs *straight and chins high. His voice commanded respect and inspired fear. "You have endured your training and survived when the weak could not." A horde of unclothed men stood huddled around a makeshift ring. An iron hook hung from the ceiling. The stone floor was stained with rust, remnants of champions past. Luc studied the blood streaks and where the textures bloomed.*

An ornately robed old man stepped to the center of the ring, unbothered by the filth covering his clothes. He held a text open but close to his chest.

The seconds felt like hours as his eyes studied each man, sizing them up like he could predict the outcomes.

"You are all here because you have pledged yourself to our powerful God, Adievasinis. Now, we will find how far each of you is willing to go for Him to choose you." The leather spine flexed as he opened the book. "Say these words after me. If God is strong with you, He will strengthen you." Piercing eyes studied the naked soldiers before them. A sneer crept across his face but he did not falter. God would weed out the weak. "I release pain. I feed death. I collect His debts." The old man's words awakened the temple and flooded into the crowd. A pulse echoed in the holy stone as if it might burst to life. Hums of power vibrated in the halls. "My blade is strong. I do not cast a second stroke. I am most merciful. Take my mercy, take it well." The book closed and, like a passing shadow, the life that vibrated around Luc and the other soldiers quieted.

Luc shuffled on the stone. His core was cold. They hadn't shut the temple doors. His shiver must have caught the old man's attention, for he walked right to him.

"You,"

Their eyes met.

"Father Trevarthan," Luc bowed his head.

"You are strong, son. Join me." Trevarthan stepped aside as Luc's strides carried him to the center of the stone. The statue of Adievasinis loomed above them. Luc stared into it with a silent prayer.

"To earn your armor, you must make a sacrifice to Adievasinis. You will wield no blade as you prove your worth." Trevarthan pointed at another man. "Come."

Luc stood across from his opponent, a man called Ferran. Luc would have considered him a friend, as much as one could be a friend when the future promised death. Little consideration was given to companionship or joy under Adeshbu rule.

Ferran brought his hand to his chest, rhythmically thumping it over his heart. Luc raised his hand, balling it into a fist, and pounded it against his bare chest with his eyes closed. Life had taken so much from him, surviving here had been exactly that. He wasn't sure if he even wanted to survive anymore, if anything would be worth it. He remembered her. He remembered their life before she was taken. He remembered his promise.

As Luc opened his eyes, Ferran came toward him with a hardy swing, Luc stepped back, avoiding the hit. He threw an uppercut into Ferran's stomach. Ferran grunted as Luc pulled back and landed another. Ferran wrapped his arm around Luc's shoulders, pulling him close so Luc couldn't get any power to his blows. Ferran hammered his fist into Luc's lower back. Luc winced as a sharp pain radiated inside his body. He caught his leg between Ferran's and tripped him. Ferran stumbled back but regained his footing as Luc caught the side of his face with a big right hook. Blood trickled from the cut on Ferran's cheek, warming the cold stone.

Equally matched, they brawled for minutes. They had trained alongside one another and sparred countless times. Neither seemed to gain dominance over the other as they ruthlessly fought. Father Trevarthan and the elders watched, sizing them up. Luc clenched his teeth as he threw jab after jab. Sweat stung his eyes. There were only two ways to leave this fight and Luc felt his strength dwindling.

Luc took a hit square on the jaw. Suddenly, his legs were heavy. He staggered and blinked as his vision clouded. Ferran cocked his arm back. Luc wanted to dodge it, but his body wouldn't move. Ferran's knuckles split the skin of Luc's brow, crumbling his opponent against the stone floor. Blood spilled from the cut, obscuring Luc's sight with red. Ferran jumped on top of him. Each punch buried Luc's mind deeper in a fog. Rust tainted his tongue. Terrified of the death that lingered so close, he reached out to Adievasinis.

Luc offered his life to the Blood God, begging for strength to fight back, to save himself. Heat rumbled inside his chest, a new power awakening. Another punch cracked against Luc's jaw, but Luc thrust his fist into Ferran's side. Ferran gasped as Luc hit him again. Luc seized Ferran by the neck. Inhuman strength burned in his arms and tightened his grip. Luc threw him onto his back, pinning Ferran. Luc pounded his hands into Ferran's face. Three hits caved in his nose as Luc's own bones fractured in his fist, the pain only amplified his bloodlust. Ferran's teeth cut into Luc's knuckles as they broke with each blow. Blood dripped from Luc's panting mouth. His hits were relentless as Ferran dipped out of consciousness.

"Stop," Father Trevarthan's voice was calm. Luc looked over his bruising shoulder, chest heaving as he sniffed. The holy man nodded, gesturing toward the corner near him.

He had fallen as Luc, as nothing, but he rose an Adeshbu. Onlookers chanted as Luc tied a rope around Ferran's ankles. The hook that hung from the ceiling lowered as another Adeshbu turned a crank. Ferran's body hung limply as the crank turned, raising the rope Luc hung on the hook. The black-caped Adeshbu presented Luc with a blade. Through a shattered face, Ferran begged indiscernibly as he met Luc's eyes, muttering weak pleas between groans. Luc's jaw tensed, but he did not hesitate. He drew the blade across the man's throat and stepped into the blood falling from Ferran's body. Blood soaked Luc's hair and poured across his body. The Adeshbu pounded their fists against their chests as Luc bathed in the blood sacrificed to Adievasinis.

"Kneel."

Luc lowered himself, Ferran's warm blood pooling around his knee. The Adeshbu lowered the helmet over Adon's crimson-coated skin. "and rise Ad Onondian, The Merciful."

CHAPTER ONE

King Rian watched his wife, her bare hand gripping the railing of the staircase of the ship that would take her from him. He wished she could see him. All that time, he had only tried to protect her, but her pride fought against him.

In the distance, Queen Ivy stumbled down the stairs. Her guard, clad in all silver, took his orders to keep her safe with the stoicism that the King had become accustomed to in the Adeshbu. Their armor covered every inch of their bodies, never allowing for recognition, save for the colored capes the four soldiers gifted to him wore. It also concealed all emotion. If this guard had a preference to stay in Asmye over the shores of Iosnos with The King's wife, he never made it known.

Rian watched as the guard caught his wife by the arm, steadying her back on her feet. Rian regretted never caring to learn his name, unable to thank him properly for carrying out his duty with honor and trust. Ivy brushed her long, dark hair over her shoulder and looked back toward the dock. Rian was relieved when her eyes met his, even by accident.

"Please," he had pleaded, desperate to hide the wobble of his chin as he begged his wife not to go. Over and over, he asked, yet her answer stayed the same. Rian would never forget how the light left her chocolate-colored eyes when he confessed his infidelity. No matter what he'd promised her since, she never wavered. Rian stared at his wife on the dock, silently praying she'd change her mind. He'd dive in if it meant she'd come back. Almost as if she heard the desire, his heart twisted with the clear shake of her hair in the wind. She made her choice. She left him.

An hour had passed, then two, then three. Rian sat atop his stallion, the sable fur that the colt was chosen for like black velvet under the king's matching cape. As the sun sank and dipped into the horizon, the horse and his rider faded into the colors of night. There was no crown to glitter in the starlight, only the gold of the ring he'd wear until the end of his days with or without her by his side. Hoofbeats clattered a dozen feet away before the thudding sound of boots met against the wood of the dock.

"Rian," Torin's voice broke The King's gaze from the dark gentle waves. Rian turned his head down to the right where his most trusted advisor and best friend stood beside him. His blue eyes pierced through the night up toward his King.

"Have you come to snark about her more?" Rian huffed. Torin rested his hand against the horse's flank. It was no secret that Torin and Ivy shared no love for each other. It didn't even matter if their King was in the room with them. Rian hated when they fought. He remembered gripping his wife's waist when she had once lunged at Torin, arms outstretched and poised to kill. The shrilling cries she gave to Rian after had cut him deeper, yet he had given her a reason. At this point, she had a million to leave.

"I come for you. It does no good for the country to see you like this." The townsfolk that gathered at the docks in the early afternoon had long departed. Once their beloved Queen had disappeared from view, they quickly dispersed back to their own lives. None dared to attempt to approach King Rian, not with Torin and the King's guard there, glaring at any and everyone he deemed unworthy.

"Like what?" Rian's quick movement unbalanced him on his saddle. His horse grunted and stamped a foot.

"If I said the word, I might catch the back of your hand." Torin sucked his tongue over his teeth. "We must remember our plan."

"Our plan?" Rian's voice hung on the word.

"Rian, she isn't coming back."

"You don't even try to hide the joy in your voice." Rian clenched the rein in his left hand until the leather gloves he wore crinkled.

"I care more for you than I do for her, yes. I will do what it takes to support you and right now, that means advising you to go home." Torin reached for the stallion's bridle, pulling his hand back when the horse snapped his teeth toward the advisor. Torin stepped back as the horse pinned its ears back.

"I will do what I must." Rian squeezed his heels into the horse's side and guided him to the left, toward Astrella. Inside its stony castle walls, Rian had born, lived, and died, only to be reborn again when she had awakened his heart with a tender kiss, saved him from a feverous plot, and destroyed him with deserved hatred. Now it would be his waking tomb, knowing it and his bed would be cold and empty when he returned.

CHAPTER TWO

A knock on the door startled Queen Ivy from her daydream. The lulling waves on the Thraxian Sea gave her comfort, allowing her to forget where she was and why. While her eyes were glazed over, she could pretend she was at home with her husband. She could even pretend he was kind. Instead, she sat alone at what was more desk than dining table as she was served dinner in Captain Vidal's quarters. It was nice enough, albeit plainness and practicality were favored over beauty and elegance. Maybe all that beauty she had become accustomed to back in Asmye was just excess. The Queen's Adeshbu bodyguard, Luc sat on the settee opposite her while a crew member quietly brought in her plate.

"Thank you." Ivy reached her fingers around the table as the ship caught a brisk wave, nearly knocking over the queen's wine glass. The sailor approximated a bow nervously before rushing out of the cabin. Ivy pushed the food around on her plate to find her appetite among the potatoes. Heartache would linger in her chest no matter how much ocean she crossed.

"Still hate eating alone?" He couldn't eat with her, not on this ship, not when they risked the crew seeing him without his helmet. Ivy wondered, now that they were running away, would he finally show his face?

"It never gets better." Memories of Rian leaving her to dine alone over and over fluttered in her mind. The same alone she felt in the years after her mother's death. This was the right decision. Leaving was all that was left.

Ivy looked up at Luc as he stood near the window. The sunset cast a soft tangerine glow, reflecting off his armor as he watched the waves. Ivy recalled her husband standing on the balcony, raven-dark hair bristling in the wind and cool, hazel eyes unfocused on the countryside as he was lost in thought. He lived a whole life without her behind those eyes.

"Somehow, it's lonelier than anything else."

Luc stood and walked around the desk to crouch beside her chair. "Querida," He touched her hand, swiping his long thumb softly along her deep bronze skin. "I wish you never to be lonely again."

Ivy sighed, "Just because we wish for things doesn't make it so."

There was a creak of metal as Luc scooted closer to his prize. "You change the tide by sheer force of will. You wished to run away, and here we are, far from that place." Ivy found her eyes looking anywhere but his visor until they fell upon her unadorned left hand. *That place* was supposed to be her home. "You said there was no other life when you are about to create one. As far as I'm concerned, the sun rises and sets for you alone." Luc pulled her attention back to him with a gentle touch of her chin. "I will always be with you, Ivy. You do not ever need to be lonely again."

Ivy held her delicate hand over his. Even in his best times, her husband had never spoken so sweetly as her new lover. A pang sank in her stomach. None of it would have to be this way, she wouldn't have fallen like this if he hadn't hurt her so.

"I cannot change the world or even my circumstances." She pulled Luc's hand away from her skin, tenderly squeezing it before releasing it from her grip.

"Then I wish you could see what I see." Luc stared at her fondly, gazing from behind the helmet at his Queen's beautiful face. Strong cheekbones sat high on her face, pushing her eyes into a crinkle when she let him see her smile. She wasn't smiling now. Instead, her teeth grazed her full bottom lip and her heavy brow furrowed as he watched her hands reach for her plate. Ivy held out a piece of bread for him.

"Eat with me."

"Querida,"

"Please?"

Ivy smiled when Luc pushed his helmet up, leaning in for a quick kiss against his soft lips before he was able to take a bite. Even in close quarters, she needed to feel him, to forget everything else.

Ivy leaned in, hoping to touch him again but restrained herself when she heard boots thumping outside. She let out a frustrated sigh, pursing her lips at the interruption. Luc nodded and stood, taking his post at the door.

"Who's out there?" Ivy asked, scanning Luc's body in that silver armor. A moment passed while they listened.

"Sailors. Some superstition about women on ships. One is bad, but three is-" Luc peered out a crack in the door and then stood up straight.

"Three is what?"

9

Luc only shrugged. "I won't repeat it."

Ivy's teeth clenched and tension seared in her jaw. *Of course.* Leave one pig only to find yourself on a ship with dozens. Ivy reached for her wine, downing the entire glass while Luc's back was turned. She held back a wince as the vintage burned as she swallowed. The Queen poured her next as laughter erupted from another room.

Luc pressed his hand on the small of Ivy's back before leading her to her chamber. She had declined the Captain's quarters, and while hers were not nearly as luxurious, it was comfortable, much larger than the bunk Ivy's maid, Madeline, and her beloved, Janelle would share for the week. Ivy considered going to visit them in their room, but something in her stomach twisted and she couldn't bear to see Madeline in pain so she asked Luc to take her directly to somewhere quiet.

Madeline's anxieties about the future were valid when Ivy considered what she had gone through for her own love. The pain and fear Torin had inflicted was barbaric. Lash after lash in the public square. Torin reported to The King that she had endangered The Queen at a servant's party. That wasn't true. Ivy sneaked out on her own. Torin likely knew that but punished Madeline for choosing a woman to love over him.

Ivy was grateful Madeline had chosen well. She couldn't have picked a better partner. Janelle's tender demeanor calmed her. It calmed Ivy, too. She would seek them out once they were settled. Maybe they all could find peace.

The quarters were as spacious as a queen could hope for on a vessel this size. The bed was hidden in a room that felt more like a big closet while the mattress was tucked into the corner under a low ceiling. The cabin was not luxurious, but some care was put into its appearance. Decorative crown molding elevated the look of it above a plain box. Heavy curtains were drawn across a small window that would let light leak in. Ivy squeezed the linen under her fingers.

"It's fine enough, I suppose." By no means was the room on par with the quality she had become accustomed to in Rian's bed, although the bedquilt was a vibrant fuschia weaved with birds and leaves. A small vase had been installed on the wall. Ivy skimmed her fingers along the bright wildflower petals. Marigolds and geraniums bloomed in orange, pink, and yellow, mimicking the sun that called them out from their buds. She wondered if they knew that soon they would wilt and die. Their fate was sealed when they were cut away from the soil that nourished them. They would likely not even survive the voyage and the thought panged in her chest.

Ivy's trunks had been shoved behind the couch in the main room, which was almost bigger than her bed. It creaked as Luc sat on it.

Luc leaned back against the cushion. "Might still be more comfortable than the hammock they hung in the corner in my bunk," he chuckled softly.

"I'm sorry." Ivy tucked her chin closer to her chest. Of course, she shouldn't comment on how drab her guest quarters were when her lover wouldn't even have a bed.

"Querida," Luc stood and walked toward her. He tilted his helmet up, and Ivy got a glimpse of his bearded chin before he pressed his lips against hers. His kiss melted her stress away, allowing her just to be.

"Close your eyes," Luc purred, and Ivy heard the thunk of Luc's helmet hitting the cushion. Ivy squeezed her eyes tighter as Luc's hand slid along her neck, drifting past her full chest, then around to meet his other behind her back. Ivy's pulse throbbed between her legs as Luc's tongue dipped into her mouth. He tasted like freedom. The day's worries melted away, and for once, no thoughts of Rian clouded her mind. If he could just keep kissing her, maybe she'd forget entirely.

Loud shanties were sung and hollered by inebriated crewmen outside in the corridor. Ivy was the first to step back from Luc, dropping her head to keep her eyes closed. Luc pulled her back in, stroking her neck under thick leather gloves. No one could see them, but they couldn't risk it. Luc's hand lingered at the small of her back, thumb petting over soft skin.

"I'll be right outside, Querida."

That word, it lit something inside her chest, like it meant she was safe. "All night?" Ivy whispered against warm skin. Luc tilted his head to press a soft kiss against Ivy's curls.

"All night."

Three hours passed since Ivy laid down for what she knew would be another sleepless night. Her resolve to leave Rian and the lush lands of Asmye weakened as hours ticked past midnight and a storm brewed above the ship, but now she had, and the thoughts that kept her up were anxieties she painted for what the future might hold. That and the uncomfortable nausea that pitted in her stomach as the ship made its way toward Iosnos. What would her father say?

The ocean ebbed and flowed under her bed. It was only the first night, and already, she was tired of it. Ivy loved the ocean but sailing, not so much. Wood creaked around her. Heavy footsteps of men walking on the deck pounded above her. Everything was musty, stagnant, and damp: the wood, the air, the smell. Ivy closed her eyes, amplifying the whooshing in her stomach as the ship swayed. She sighed. It was going to be a long trip.

Silently, she cursed herself for dreaming about Rian when sleep finally caught her. For every smile she stretched in memory, there was a bruise to match. Dresses and flowers would never cover the cost of his crimes. Ivy clutched her arms tightly around her pillow, angry with herself for having imagined Rian's body in her grasp. She should've spat in his face and left him to die from his poison when she had the chance. No one would suspect a woman to have saved him in the first place. By now, she could be the sole ruler of both Asmye and Iosnos, donned in her first gown not the color worn by widows. Instead, Ivy reacted, desperate to erase her guilt from the first night of her affair. No one would have missed him save for his whore. That could've been eradicated as well. Ivy huffed.

She didn't know what she would say or do about him when she got home. How could she tell her father she broke their deal? But how could her father have sold her to such a cruel man?

The truth was, it wasn't Rian's cruelty that hurt her. It was his love: wicked, awful, humiliating, beautiful, overwhelming love.

Ivy rolled over, wrapping her hands around her waist as she tucked her head into her pillow. She wished Luc could slide in behind her, touch her, comfort her. It might draw too much attention if she called him to come into her quarters. Voices carry, even on the sea. There was one week left in the voyage, too much time to leave Ivy alone with her thoughts.

Standing up was harder than Ivy anticipated. The constant ship rolling meant it was hard to find balance. When Ivy finally straightened her legs, she grabbed her green cloak and tucked her hair under the hood. It didn't matter that Rian had this made for her. It didn't matter that he embedded her wedding gown fabric inside it. It didn't matter that it smelled like his room. It didn't matter at all.

She twisted the door lock that Luc had insisted she secure and climbed the stairs to the main deck. Luc wasn't there like he had said. *It's late.* Ivy convinced herself he only told her that to make her feel protected when, in truth, there was nothing to threaten her. He probably supposed she wouldn't be stupid enough to leave her room.

The rich blue of the ocean under the moon was a monochromatic canvas of water and sky. This, she liked. Nothing but the sea stretched for miles and miles. Cold mist kissed her skin with the scent of fresh salt. The wind blustered through, caught by the massive white sail. Her hood fell, and her hair went wild. It was calming to her, the wind blowing away her anxiety while salt air reminded her of what was to come.

One of the deckhands shouted something unintelligible and called her name. Ivy whipped her head to see a large wave break against the ship's hull. The power of the wave knocked her legs out from under her before she could even try to brace herself, but an arm caught Ivy at her waist, pulling her against a hard chest to steady her.

"I got you," Luc's voice came from behind her. His free hand braced against a rope. The sensation brought Ivy back to the forest barely a week ago when he had fucked her from behind. Ivy felt a heat for him deep in her stomach but tried to shake it off.

"How long have you been there?" She couldn't help the mischievous smile that curled her lips. "I thought you said you'd stay outside my door all night."

"I've always got my eye on you." His hand ventured lower, exploring the shape of her waist. "Even under lock and key, you always find your way into trouble." Ivy bit down on her lip in an attempt to curb her appetite.

The ship began to steady and Luc loosened his hold to Ivy's dismay. She stayed there for a moment longer, almost leaning back into him before she remembered the Knights of Garreau were also on the ship. It was Rian's one insistence that Ivy had caved on. Ivy argued with him for an hour, nearly ripping out his throat about what concessions she'd make. If he'd gotten his way, Rian would have sent the whole of Asmye's navy with her. Truly, he didn't want her to go at all. She compromised at his sending all four Adeshbu with her, allies to survey Iosnos, and two Knights, his most trusted spies.

"You couldn't sleep?" Luc asked as Ivy tried desperately to find something else to focus on. She settled for shaking her head. There was no sense in telling him why. Luc looked over his shoulder, then reached for Ivy's hand. Ivy smiled but couldn't think of what to say. Her mind felt blank, but it wasn't. Ivy imagined cold steel embracing her skin while Luc's breath echoed in her ear. It had been days since she had tasted him. Running away to find time with a lover was difficult when The King was around. Her pussy clenched at the thought of the sweet pain of his thick cock pressing into her. She squeezed her eyes shut, pushing it all away.

"Come. I'll take you back. It isn't safe for you up here."

She couldn't see his eyes, but still, she could. He tilted his head to the left before leaning forward just the slightest. Ivy pulled away, weary of wandering eyes. She turned her face to look around the deck, catching the glint of another Adeshbu's armor near the bow. Rian's flag flapped in the wind as a bolt of lightning struck overhead.

Ivy made her way back below to her modest room, grabbing at anything that would support her. Luc tried to help, but she wouldn't let him. She was embarrassed, dumb, a silly girl making a fool of herself. Foolish and dangerous. Anyone could see them out on the deck. Anyone could give them away. Ivy retreated into her cabin, flooded with nausea and racing thoughts. She heard Luc's footsteps a few seconds later, slow and steady, then still, keeping guard.

Dinner the next night was served the same as the day before: alone in her quarters. Ivy had hardly expected the fresh and exciting confections Astrella always had to offer, but the reinvention of yesterday's potatoes left much to be desired. She'd only been gone two days. Ivy thought she'd kill for something fresh, even if it were just an orange. Just then, a chorus of laughter broke through next door and grew louder after something crashed against the wall.

"What are they doing in there?" Ivy leaned closer to her right, hoping to discern the noise. Luc sighed across the room.

"It's probably Adne peacocking and getting himself thrown around." Ivy couldn't discern in his tone if that meant something good or bad.

"Who?"

"You'll know him when you see him." Luc waved his hand in annoyance.

"Perhaps we should see then." Ivy stood, wiping her hand on a napkin.

"I don't think it's for the best." His body was now an obstacle in her path. "You don't want to get caught in the middle of men's silly disputes."

"Luc," Ivy picked up his hand. "I'm sure it's nothing dangerous. I can handle myself."

"We can't speak freely in mixed company."

Is it that we can't speak freely or that it is dangerous? Ivy sighed, pressing down the urge to engage and argue. "Speaking freely is not something we can do anywhere on this ship, not even here." Ivy softened her sad eyes up at him. "I should like a bit of fun."

His exhale gave her permission to push him out of her way gently. Her hand lingered playfully at his hip as she flashed a wicked grin. He snapped his hand up, locking his fingers around her wrists.

"Do you always have to cause this much trouble?"

Ivy smiled and nodded. What else was she supposed to do with her time?

"Can I join you?" The Queen stood in the open doorway as some crew members and the Knights held stacks of cards close to their chests. Everyone stared at her. The creaking of the ship only amplified the silence.

A red-caped Adeshbu rose to speak. His hand gestured fluidly when he spoke. "We would be honored to-"

"Now, Your Grace, you don't want to be among these ruffians." A black-caped Adeshbu interrupted from his post near the window.

Kieran leaned over to a nearby sailor at the table. "It's not like she'd know how to play in the first place."

Flames flickered in Queen Ivy's eyes. No man on this ship would tell her what she could or couldn't do. However, she knew that a real game was played long before the hand was ever dealt. She plastered a smile on her face and sat between two sailors.

"Deal me in." Sophie, Ivy's childhood friend, taught her how to bluff. That's all she needed. Ivy tossed a triumphant look over to her guard. His hip cocked to his side, nearly congratulating her with the gesture alone.

"Adon, please fetch my coin purse." Ivy hated using Luc's Adeshbu name, hated the way it stung like venom on her tongue. Yet, if she wanted to keep up their charade, she would have to play her part. She kept her eyes on the cards as they were dealt. "Fattening the pot will make things more interesting."

"I think you have already made things significantly more interesting, Your Grace." The red-caped Adeshbu organized the cards in his gloveless hands. "I could use a bit of a challenge."

"Easy to win when you hide your eyes, Adne," Kieran sneered. His stacks of gold coins looked diminished.

"It's easy to win against someone who can't hide a single feeling." Adne lifted the coins from one of his many stacks and let them clink and chime as they fell into a perfect stack. His crimson cloak suited the confidence of the way he spoke. "Look at you, cheeks flushed with embarrassment at your losses. Your eyes are panicked, desperately trying to make your cards work for you. Even your hands-" Kieran suddenly stilled his whole body as the room found him at the center of his attention. "-speaking truths. You hardly play the game at all. You're too afraid to lose."

Luc returned promptly with a small embroidered coin purse which he dropped into Ivy's delicate hand. "Let the games begin." She threw a generous bet into the pot.

Adne matched the Queen. The sailor to Ivy's left groaned and threw down his cards then left the table. Kieran matched Ivy and raised.

"It's rather early in our game for you to have so little, Sir Kieran," Ivy casually remarked. Quiet mutters moved through the room as King Rian's Knight flicked another coin into the pile.

"Thought you'd need us to take it easy on you."

Ivy drifted her eyes from the cards in her hand to the men scattered around the table. "No man makes anything easy on a woman, Sir Knight."

"Women cause enough troubles on their own," Kieran drew another card into his hand. His brow raised and his lip curved only for a second before he pursed his lips then drew them straight.

"In my experience, Knight, women make the world richer." Adne drew his next card. No emotion came from him behind the silver helmet. "They remind us of beauty beyond this life and give a poetic reason to sacrifice our lives."

Ivy scrunched her nose and gave a teasing smile toward the black-clad Knight as she danced her shoulders back and forth. If they'd been alone, she might have stuck out her tongue with pride.

"Ad Nekosen, need I always remind you not to goad?" Ad Baalestan's scruffy, smooth voice chided under his own helmet. His arms crossed over his armored chest.

"Your draw, my Queen," Adne nodded toward the deck. Ivy took her card and rearranged the stack in her hand. Adne leaned in closer. "It appears time for recreation and enrichment is not encouraged in Asmye as it is in others. Our friend has forgotten the pleasure of a good woman's touch. Perhaps his dick has shriveled to-"

Kieran stood from the table, his knees knocking into it as he stood and drew a dagger. Luc drew his sword, marching forward, placing his hand over Ivy's shoulder, and the tip of his blade at Kieran's throat. Adne raised his hands, not bothering to match the Knight's energy.

"Put your weapon away, Knight." Luc's chest heaved under the armor. Kieran looked between Luc and Adne, sizing up if it would be worth it to hear from Torin if he dispatched an ally. "Sit," Luc instructed. Kieran obeyed but kept his knife on the table to his right, far enough from Ivy that Luc took only one step back.

"I fold," Adne said. Even through the helmet, Ivy discerned a smile in his voice. He knew this wasn't his game to win.

Kieran snatched another card after the crewman to Ivy's right folded his cards, showing what could've been a winning hand if he hadn't been so frightened of the exchange. "Adeshbu, perhaps you could remind your subordinates whose throne they honor, whose rank to respect."

"That would be mine," Ivy sat up straight. She had left her husband, yes, but that was information only she knew, save for her guard. Ivy turned her head over her shoulder where Luc stood, relaxed as a stiff wooden board as he watched the card game play out. She took her last card. "You'd do well to remember that."

Kieran took the final card from the stack on the table and his eyes rolled back. He stared at Ivy, waiting for a sign, anything to give away what she held in her hand.

The Queen's eyes narrowed. "Come, Kieran, don't you want to play?" She angled her body so only Luc could see her stack." Dark curls fell over her shoulder as she looked up at him. He gave a short nod that he understood her hand. Ivy smiled and tossed another coin into the mix. "The pot can only get bigger from here."

Kieran rested his hand over his last three coins then tapped his finger on the wood as he stared at his card one more time."You play the hand you're dealt." Kieran threw his cards on the table as he folded. Luc relaxed his shoulders.

"I play the hand I want." Ivy carefully laid her cards out in front of her. She flipped the first. The room went silent as the men held their breath, anticipating the next card she'd flip."If you always play the hand you're dealt, you'll never get what you really want." Ivy turned the last card: a winking mourner. The room erupted as they realized the queen had held nothing. Ivy smirked.

"Oh, she's very good!" Adne clapped his hands together in admiration of the game she had played. He held up his cup in cheers, "To the Queen of Asmye!"

CHAPTER THREE

King Gerard's hand pressed Rian's shoulder down, forcing him to sit still. Rian didn't care about the punishment anymore. He just wanted to get away but he was too weak to fight his father's grip. Trevarthan pulled the boy's arm tight then pressed the tip of his silver claw ring into Rian's wrist. The little boy held back his tears as the claw drew out a thick stream of blood. Rian, no more than six years old, tried to yank his arm back, but the old man held it over an ornamental chalice decorated with a heart until it was nearly full of blood. His mother would have never allowed this. Elisa had protected him for months, but now Gerard had no opposition.

"Good, Rian, good." Trevarthan stared into the cup and let the boy's wrist go. Rian held his arm tight to his body, fearful he might get cut again.

"Holy Father, what do you see?" Gerard loosened his hold on Rian's shoulders as his focus shifted.

"Stronger than Emeric already. I'll need time, though, to be sure."

Gerard smiled. Rian squirmed away, running through the cathedral towards the doors.

"Boy, get back here!" Gerard's voice was firm, yet the child still ran. Two of his father's Knights stepped in front of the doors of the church. Rian tried to fight his way through them but one grabbed the small boy by the back of his shirt, lifting him off the ground. "Tristan," Gerard called, "bring him to me."

Rian flailed his legs and arms. He knew he couldn't win, but he would try all the same. He finally resigned when the young knight, decorated with thick muscle, dropped him back in front of Gerard.

"Sit. Do not disrespect me again." Gerard didn't need to yell. His menacing stare was enough. Fear held Rian's chest in its icy grasp. Reluctantly, Rian took his seat. Gerard's hand rested again on his shoulder, a warning. Rian winced, expecting his father to dig into the constant bruise from his strength, but now that the King had gotten what he wanted, the pressure never came. Rian watched the cup. The heart embossed in gold began to beat. The thump was painfully loud inside Rian's mind. He squeezed his eyes tight to keep them from playing tricks on him.

King Rian gasped for breath, lurching up from his bed. Sweat glistened on his chest and brow. The fire across the room had dwindled into embers, yet he still burned. He was desperate for fresh, cool air. He flung open the balcony doors, panting as he leaned against the railing. He glanced down at his forearm. Some scars had faded with time. Some had been reopened time and time again. The western wind carried him a cruel yet sweet kiss of lavender and salt. Rian stared off toward the coast. His eyes strained like, by sheer force of will, he might still catch a glimpse of his bride even as she faded away across the sea.

Wine flowed over his tongue from the bottle as he tipped it back. The vintage was warm and jammy. The heat of the summer months crept into Asmye's nights with every new sunrise. How many had he seen since she left? The cruel reality was of days falling wayside in her absence without motion. If he moved now, it would be an acceptance of the grief he couldn't bear to stomach. He learned long ago that love didn't die. You could bury or burn it like bodies, an attempt to smother it would turn it monstrous and vicious, but it was always there. He still carried his mother's love tangled inside his chest alongside his father's and even his brother's. He should have known better, shouldn't have let her see him, touch him so deeply. Rian chugged from the bottle in a futile attempt to drown the feeling, but it wouldn't be enough.

The sun broke over distant mountains, turning the sky a wash of golden-edged pink. Colette would come first, then Torin. They'd puppet him upright with their words and appointments. He'd haunt the halls alongside the memories and mistakes that wouldn't fade. A sad excuse for a King.

Rian drained what little remained in the bottle. His shoulder ached with Gerard's disappointment in the pathetic creature that his successor had become.

A short time later, King Rian sat on his throne, adorned in his most ornate clothing: black fabric embroidered heavily with gold filigree. A thick, shiny pelt hung over his shoulders, the fur draping around his left hand where the jewelry on his third finger caught the light. He didn't want to admit how much he missed her. The gold livery collar he wore to their wedding was strapped across his broad chest. Atop his black waves was his most impressive crown. Spikes of gold swirled up from his head. Rian watched as the artist's paint mimicked the deep ocean abyss from the large emerald stones in his crown. He remembered how his wife wore it that spring night. Rian clenched his fingers onto his broadsword, digging the tip into the floor beside his throne. As he twisted the pommel, the blade cast a sliver of light across the room. The artist sighed at the movement, focusing on a stable part of Rian to paint.

"This was to be our wedding portrait. What point is there if Ivy isn't beside me?"

"The world and our plans, your schedule don't stop just because she's gone." Torin was irritated at the inquiry. "And you speak half-truths about her. Won't tell me why or how. It is as if you believe there's a chance she will come back. If something has happened, I need to know. Arrangements must be made."

"It's not your business."

"Rian, *you* are my business. Your reign is my business." The King's advisor picked over the fruit on the side table. "There is nothing that happens in this country without my knowledge. At least, there wasn't before *she* came." Torin tossed a plump grape between his lips. "As far as the painting goes, I could make the proper inquiries to your territories or to Illum or Lutrya to see what they may have to offer as far as a more agreeable young girl of reasonable lineage to-"

"What of Lund's infantry?" Rian was desperate to change the subject. Losing Ivy was embarrassing, even if he never confessed as to why.

"They are...underperforming." Torin stood just to the left of the artist, who huffed as Rian continued to shift slightly in the throne.

"Your Majesty, you have to stay still," the artist pleaded.

Rian ignored him. "Underperforming?"

"They've made no advances. Suffered heavy losses." Torin spoke casually, as if lost lives meant little to him. "Lund very well may be an idiot. He has no talent for strategy." The war with Bloidar raged on. It should have ended with the aid of Ilum's soldiers, but there was no end in sight. Something edged it further.

Rian let out a low chuckle, "I'm not surprised."

"I think it'd be best to consider returning to the frontlines yourself. Take command of your allied forces. Show your strength."

Rian ran his fingers across his brow, considering the idea. He hadn't swung his sword since his injury. Too much time had passed since he last made payment to Adievasinis. That must be why his men were growing weaker. He needed to go. But what if Ivy came back and he was gone?

"Your Majesty! You have to stop moving!" The artist was frustrated, his tone inappropriately commanding of the King.

"I'm done for the day." Rian stood from the throne, shedding all the status accouterment from his shoulders as he walked towards Torin. "I'll consider it. Send Tristan to Lund. He can remedy the situation."

"And if Lund whines again?"

"Tristan will know to use force if necessary." Rian glanced at the painting. A vague shape of his wife's figure was blocked beside him on the canvas. The artist cleaned up his supplies, muttering something about discipline and debts. As he moved his paints, Rian noticed a stack of sketches. He took a step forward for a clearer view. He recognized Ivy's face sketched in graphite. "What are these?"

"I sat with the Queen for some studies before we started, Your Majesty." The artist took down his easel, snapping the wood pieces together, breaking the King's reverie. Rian flipped through the pages, seeing his wife's face in various expressions and poses half-drawn. As he turned the pages, one made him stop. Ivy's eyes were drawn in incredible detail. Light reflected in them, the grey looking nearly alive on the page. He stared into them, waiting for her to blink. Rian grabbed the stack of papers and tucked them into his coat.

The artist stuttered, claiming his work was incomplete, but Rian walked away with the sketches. Torin called after the King, then raised his hands in a forfeit. The gold coins twinkled in the artist's eyes as Torin produced them from a purse.

"How much?"

CHAPTER FOUR

"You fight well, Knight." Adne tossed aside his rich crimson cape and stretched his shoulders out. His build was sinewy, but his voice was decadent to the ears. Words danced off his tongue while the soldiers squared up for another round of sparring in the sunlight the next day.

Malcolm's straight teeth flashed at the compliment. He couldn't help himself. "High praise from an Adeshbu."

The trim Adeshbu hid his smile under his helmet as he spun the sword with flare. Malcolm dodged the advance, volleying back at Adne.

"Much more elegant than that big oaf I fought in the tournament."

"If I remember correctly, Tristan beat you," Malcolm smirked.

"On a technicality." They circled each other, sharing more banter than strikes. "But you, Knight, you're making me work for it."

Malcolm stepped forward with a combination of moves. The Adeshbu laughed with a chuckle as he blocked each of Malcolm's advances. Frustration trembled in the Knight's full lips.

"I'm not used to having to work for it," Adne said softly as he locked blades with Malcolm. "I like a challenge."

Malcolm's stomach fluttered as he felt the Adeshbu's eyes, looking over his rich umber skin.

"I would give you my name if you'd give yours, Knight."

The black-caped Adeshbu coughed a warning as he stood on the top deck, watching his men. His charge always walked the line and skirted the rules. It would not happen around him. He watched as a hand was raised toward him, waving him off.

"Malcolm," The Knight smiled, disenchanted with the Adeshbu malarky.

"Ad Nekoson-" he stood tall and drew his hand over his chest, an ode to Adievasinis. Then he tossed the sword up and spun around before catching the handle of the sword again and bowed. "-but you can call me Adne."

"Tricks don't win on the battlefield, Adne." Malcolm pushed forward, forcing Adne into a defensive position.

"This is not a battlefield, nor am I trying to win, at least not at playing swords."

Adne grabbed the blade of Malcolm's sword with his gloved hand, locking Malcolm's sword in a vice grip. Adne applied pressure and popped the sword out of Malcolm's hand, disarming him. Malcolm countered. He grabbed Adne and pulled his back to his chest. His arm tightened under the Adeshbu's helmet in a chokehold.

Adne couldn't help himself but whisper, "I could tell you liked to be on top, Knight." A blush warmed Malcolm's cheeks. Adne threw his elbow back into Malcolm's side, making the young knight step back. Adne smiled under his helmet while he waited for Malcolm to pick up his sword.

There was the shrill scrape of metal against stone. A black cape hung from an Adeshbu's shoulders as he sharpened his sword. "Ad Nekoson, why do you torture the boy? Clearly, he isn't your match." There was a relaxed coldness to his cadence.

"I don't know, Baalestan. I think he's a good match for me." Adne kept his focus on Malcolm, studying his shape up one side and down the other. He wished he could take off the stupid helmet. He could be much more persuasive that way. "A little short for a knight, though. I thought Garreau liked them big and brutish."

"The *King* likes them capable." Malcolm glared at the Adeshbu.

"I can see what he thinks of capability." Ad Baalestan continued to sharpen his blade without looking up. "Sends you away when there's a war to fight."

"You're here, too."

"I don't serve Garreau."

"Adeshbu are gifts to our King, right? Something to trade?" Malcolm stepped forward.

Adne put his hand on Malcolm's chest to hold him off. "He's trying to rile you."

"He insults my King, he insults me!" Malcolm's blood boiled.

"You insult me by thinking you are our equal. You fight for a King. I fight for God." Ad Baalestan thumped his sword over his own heart with a loud clang.

"He is *your* King, too."

"Only because he bends his knee at the same altar I do." Ad Baalestan sheathed his sword. Adne held Malcolm's chest plate to keep him steady. "Trevarathan claims he is touched by Adievasinis. If it is true, then he could be the harbinger that bathes the world in-"

"Your Grace." Malcolm lowered himself in a bow as Queen Ivy approached with Luc at her side. Her brilliant bronze skin glowed in the late morning light. Her thin green slip dress complimented her long brown curls, both catching in the wind. At Luc's insistence, she thought twice about the dress before deciding she didn't care about decorum. Many might think it inappropriate for a woman of any rank in Asmye, let alone a queen, to be dressed so freely. But she *was* free, and she wouldn't let any man dictate what was right and proper for her body any longer.

"Your Grace." Adne bent in a bow to Ivy, eyes dancing over her voluptuous shape, too. It seemed Adne could not control himself as he gestured toward her. "If it's not impolite to say, the sea suits you."

Ivy opened her mouth to express gratitude, but her words didn't even have a chance to leave her mouth.

"It is impolite, Ad Nekoson, for I know what you mean." Luc's voice was low and short; his timbre was of gruff propriety. He stood over his counterpart, calculating how far he might go to defend Ivy's honor.

"Your Grace." The black-caped Adeshbu hesitated before he dipped in a modest bow. "Ad Onondian," he nodded to Luc. Ivy almost cringed. It sounded worse when anyone else called Luc by his spiritual name. Silently, she counted out how many days were left until they reached Iosnos, until she could call him by his true name, until she could whisper it as he touched her.

"Ad Baalestan." Luc stood straight.

"Thank you," Ivy smiled.

Adne leaned back casually, tapping his fingers over the blade of his sword. A game came to mind. "Unless the queen is sparring with you in her free time, I doubt you're as sharp as you should be, Adon."

"You'd be surprised. She knows her way around a sword."

Warmth spread in Ivy's chest while Adne gave a deeper bow.

"Then show me what you've learned, and let us give the lady a show."

"I *am* aching for some entertainment." Ivy's cheeks turned rosy as her head tilted towards Luc. He couldn't deny her when she smiled at him like that.

"I suppose I could use the stretch." Luc stepped away from Ivy. His fingers motioned to Malcolm. Malcolm quickly took Luc's place at her side. Ivy restrained herself from rolling her eyes, but an irritated exhale left her mouth disguised as a hum. Could she really not be more than a few feet from an armed guard at any point? What could happen to her out on the open sea? Ivy hoisted herself up to sit on a crate to watch.

"So what did the queen teach you, Adon?" Adne circled Luc. Luc looked unbothered as he adjusted his sword in his grip casually.

"More than you can."

Adne chuckled, "Come on, then, old man, teach me something."

"Like The Queen taught you at cards last night?"

"If we recall the tale *properly*, I bowed out gracefully. It was your-" Adne pointed his sword toward Malcolm, "-comrade that came out short. We could be so lucky to take lessons from a teacher who is so beautiful and yet, so exquisitely ruthless." Adne inspected his blade and brushed off a dirt speck before turning to Ivy. "A Queen they will surely write volumes on for generations to come if her politics are anything like her mind at cards."

Luc puffed his chest when he saw Ivy smiling at Adne. She was not his to share. "You talk too much."

"One can't help but desire a little friendly conversation," Adne sighed and leaned in. "You know Ad Baalestan is no fun at-" Adne grunted as Luc walloped his chest with the flat side of the blade.

"I don't even need to look. You're so loud." Ivy could hear the smile in Luc's voice.

"For once, I'm speechless."

"A miracle," Ad Baalestan muttered.

Luc laughed. Ivy put her hand up to her face in an attempt to hide the pink in her cheeks. Luc and Adne sparred with more vigor. It was playful but brutal as they came at each other with familiarity. Adne mouthed off, throwing soft insults to bait Luc into lunging. Luc resisted the urge and made Adne do all the work by coming to him. Ivy supposed that was his style for everyone.

"So you've done this with the Queen," Adne tried to push Luc back. "Swordplay, I mean." They locked swords.

"He put up a fight," Ivy chimed in, remembering their first night in the old barn.

"How quickly did she put you on your back?" Adne grabbed Luc's blade. He used the leverage to pop the sword out of Luc's hand the same way he had with Malcolm. Luc didn't resist. He let the blade go and caught the grip in his other hand. Luc was quick. Adne froze at the touch of cold steel against the tender flesh of his neck.

"I put her on her back."

Adne laughed. Ivy's mouth went dry. She thought she heard Ad Baalestan's neck crack as his head whipped towards Luc. Luc dropped the sword from Adne's throat and stepped back, inviting Adne to continue.

"I didn't expect them to go after each other so hard," Ivy whispered to Malcolm.

"Adeshbu are even crazier than Asmyian soldiers," Malcolm lowered his eyes, studying the men in front of him. His mouth tasted bitter with jealousy as he watched the men fight. Ivy's eyes stayed fixed on Luc. It was all she could do not to drag him back to her cabin after he got a good swing against Adne.

"Perhaps you're not as rusty as I thought." Adne shook out his arms.

"You'd be better if you trained more."

"The sword was never my strength." There was a lovely melody to the way Adne spoke. Ivy didn't know if education or confidence enriched his syntax.

"All the more reason you should focus on your training."

"I'd rather refine my mind."

"The strength of your mind won't matter if you're dead," Ad Baalestan chided.

"I earned my armor the same as you!" Adne looked around at his fellow Adeshbu. "I have proved my worth."

Ivy leaned into her hand, bored of men and their cock measuring. Her spirits lifted when Madeline and Janelle approached with an open bottle. Ivy didn't even wait for a glass.

"You're looking well today," Ivy said as she helped Madeline sit on a chest, something to assuage the guilt of not visiting her room.

"I'm feeling well." The redhead took a deep breath in as she turned to look out across the sea. The pace of the ship was brisk, and the waves smoothed. Ivy caught Madeline smiling as Janelle's sand-colored hand briefly touched hers. The company of the ship was still too mixed. Ivy knew soon would be able to hold hands in the streets of Iosnos without fear.

A crewman called out from the crow's nest, "Siveryns at the bow!"

Ivy rushed towards the front of the ship. She grabbed a rope and leaned over the wooden railing. Her eyes rolled as Malcolm gripped his hands around her hips to steady her. Siveryns danced over and under the wake rippling around the ship. Their scales shifted between blue-green and purple as the sun shimmered around their fins.

"They're beautiful." Ivy had never seen them before. Bright eyes peered from under the water. Ivy gasped when she saw the purple-green scales shimmering as they jumped from broken waves. Their skittering squeals made Madeline giggle. Sharp tails cut through the water and a long snout led the school underwater before they burst in unison back to the surface.

"It's a good omen, Your Grace." The sailor Tai peered over the rail. "There's an old sailor story that they guide the waves to carry weary travelers home across the Thraxian Sea." He sat back on a crate and delicately plucked his fingers over his guitar strings. "Some speak of more superstitious and monstrous tales, but I've only ever seen them on days of good fortune."

Ivy hummed as she watched, transfixed by the playful creatures as the notes from Tai's guitar danced on the wind. She couldn't wait to get home, to breathe in the Iosnote air. She'd be home well in time for the Evane Festival. It was her favorite time of year.

"I've never seen anything like it." Madeline clutched her hand over Janelle's to the rail. They couldn't let go.

"Neither have I." Ivy turned her head to smile. "Saw it in a book once."

"You've seen lots of things in books." Madeline dropped her blue-eyed gaze.

"I suppose so." Ivy scanned her eyes across the horizon. "Doesn't amount to much out here. Just black ink and parchment."

"At least you know what you're looking at."

Ivy reached for her maid's hand. "Recognition is hardly understanding. If anything, I've yet to understand much of life or even myself. I look back-" Desperately, Ivy tried to push Rian's memory from her mind, "-clarity seems lost on me in the important moments. I would change so many things. It keeps me up at night: what could've been."

"What could be is far more of an exciting prospect. It's also the only thing we can have a say in."

Ivy's eyes flashed back to Luc. He had abandoned his training to admire the siveryns. She felt a softness in her heart as he looked over the bow. "You're right, Madeline," Ivy smiled. "It could be anything."

Bottles of wine passed between the queen, sailors, soldiers, and maids without hesitation. Chatter overlapped as they laughed. Ad Baalestan retreated below deck, exhausted by their cheerful nature. Luc found his way back to Ivy's side. He could hardly stand to be more than a few feet away from her. The guise of protection hid his true desire of closeness to hear every word that fell from her lips, to see the sun reflected in her eyes.

Adne grabbed the bottle from Malcolm's hand. He lifted his helmet to take a swig, revealing his dark brown beard and pink lips. A little wine dribbled out of the corner of his mouth. He caught a little smile drawn on his lips before he wiped away his spill and dropped the helmet back down.

"I thought you weren't supposed to show your face?" Malcolm asked as he took the bottle back.

Adne leaned in closer and tipped Malcolm's chin with his finger. "I won't tell if you don't."

The wind caught Ivy's hair and blew it across her face. Wine-drunk, she laughed and grabbed the hat off Tai's head before she tucked her wild hair underneath it.

"It's more becoming on you than me." Tai smiled and continued to play the guitar.

"Do I look like a wild adventurer on the high seas?" Ivy held her hand to her brow to look off into the distance.

"Undeniably."

Ivy reached her hand out to Janelle, bowing low in a gentlemanly way. "Can I ask you for a dance, my lady?"

Janelle put a hand over her cherub mouth to hide her giggle. As soon as Janelle's hand was in Ivy's grip, Ivy grabbed Janelle's waist to spin her in a dance. Janelle squealed with laughter as Ivy whisked her around the deck. Janelle's feet barely touched the planks as she followed Ivy's spirited lead. Janelle glanced down at Ivy's bouncing bosom.

"Janelle, are you staring at my tits?"

Janelle's round, green eyes were suddenly everywhere but Ivy's chest. "No!"

"I'd ask to cut in, but I doubt either would take me." Adne nudged Malcolm's arm.

"Who would?" Malcolm held back his smile.

Madeline bellowed with laughter as Ivy tripped over her own feet and almost toppled over. Janelle caught her as they unsteadily found their footing.

"Maybe too much wine?" Janelle asked.

"Maybe not enough!"

"Do you sing, Your Grace?" Tai asked as he twisted a tuning peg.

"Not well enough for an audience," Ivy blushed.

"Come, Your Majesty." Adne stood and handed her the bottle of wine. "Sing us a song."

"I couldn't," Ivy smiled shyly. Luc's stomach twisted in lust as he watched her play coy.

Adne sang:

A man's hunt for his pleasure
Can only be measured

Ivy pressed her lips together as she remembered the old shanty her mother had taught her when she was a child. The group laughed when they caught on to which song Adne chose. Of course, this is what he chose.

"Do you know this one?" Adne asked.

Ivy nodded and joined him:

When he lands at the docks
Pulls a maid from her frocks
And buries what he calls his treasure

Adne grabbed Ivy's hand and twirled her softly as they sang together. Ivy couldn't help the pure elation that flowed through her as they swayed to the music. She hadn't felt this much like herself since she left her home all those months ago. Perhaps just being closer to Iosnos meant she was already closer to herself.

The setting sun was warm, and Ivy lived to soak in the last of its rays. She laid down, her arm tucked behind her head as a pillow. Madeline and Janelle spoke softly while Janelle rested her head on Madeline's shoulder. Ivy stared into the sky as the afternoon sun began its descent in a deep orange and lavender haze. The view was framed by the masts and ropes of the ship, sails taut as the ship pushed forward with Captain Vidal at the helm. Tai snored, leaning against a barrel. The wine had caught up to him. Ivy had lost track of how many bottles they had opened that day. She didn't pause to question the cheer, only grateful for the respite from her own heavy heart.

Ivy had barely slept during the journey, so she welcomed its embrace when she felt herself drifting between asleep. Laid out on a blanket, she sighed, warm and relaxed. Her eyelids were so heavy, letting her float off into a dreamland. There was a fire crackling next to a soft bed, the weight of a dog on her feet. A soft hand rested against her swollen tummy. Warm lips pressed on her neck.

Her eyes snapped open. It was dark; the deep blue of the night drenched her eyes. Ivy thought she had only closed her eyes for a few minutes, but hours had passed. It was calm. The ship cut through the water swiftly. Madeline and Janelle were gone probably hours ago, based on how the moon hung high in the sky. There was a chill in the air, but as Ivy propped up on her elbows, she realized a cape was draped over her. Ivy blinked, adjusting her eyes, then felt the fabric. It was dark blue, almost disappearing into the environment. Shining like a fallen star, her Adeshbu stood with his back to Ivy and his helmet tilted toward the sky. His armor gleamed, almost twinkling in the starlight. His body leaned against a mast. His hip shifted to the right, and his shoulders dropped and relaxed. Ivy had hardly ever seen him stand so casually. There weren't a lot of threats to her safety here. No assassins to be found, and no attacks imminent. Maybe Ivy did like the ship. She felt safe, lost at sea. She rested on her back and closed her eyes again.

Someone picked her up. Ivy curled into his chest, half asleep as she held onto him. He was cold and hard, but Ivy didn't care. She was still half-dreaming. Little memories of her husband holding her flashed in the forefront of her mind. She didn't mean to, but it was so easy to remember when it was like this. Ivy clutched to him when he went down the stairs like losing her grip meant she'd float away. He lowered Ivy, but her arms clung to him.

"It's okay. I'm just putting you in bed."

Ivy groaned at his voice and loosened her grip, whispering her husband's name too quietly to hear. She jolted when she opened her eyes and her guard stood over her, brushing his thumb against her parched lips. Rolling over in embarrassment, Ivy buried her face in her pillow and felt her blankets settle over her.

"Thank you, Luc," Ivy whispered, praying he hadn't heard. She didn't even feel his lips brushing against her neck as she dozed back to sleep.

"I'll be right outside if you need me." Luc smiled, gently sweeping a wild curl away from her face before pulling the blanket over her shoulder. He closed the door quietly behind him.

CHAPTER FIVE

Father Trevarthan's shoulders hunched, a posture reflective of the age and pain in his back. His jowls hung loosely around his benign expression. Wrinkles pronounced themselves around his eyes as he tried to make out a word of the text. He dreaded the growing need for a magnifying glass. A knock broke his focus. The Holy Father pulled himself tall from his chair, flexing his shoulders. A deep inhale puffed his chest as his face adopted the appearance of a friendly old man. He adjusted his smile and cleared his throat.

"Yes?" He opened the door.

"Holy Father," Dieter, one of Rian's Knights, nodded respectfully. "I have what you, uh, requested."

Trevarthan's smile raised with a sinister gleam. "Lovely, lovely. You can bring him in." Trevarthan stepped aside. Dieter led a thin young man in by his shackles. His skin was smeared with dirt and grease. His beard patched over his gaunt cheeks, sidled under weak eyes that could barely open. "Sit him right here, son."

"You're sure about this, Father?" Dieter held the key to the shackles from the castle cells.

"Yes, we'll be quite fine on our own." The priest's pleasant demeanor was satisfactory assurance that Dieter unclasped the irons. "Thank you, Sir Dieter, for all your efforts to *rehabilitate* this young man. Soon, his sins will be forgiven." Dieter's eyes fell on the prisoner once more, a final glance before Father Trevarthan slammed the stone door.

Smoke ribbons curled up from the charred heart in the hearth and whispered to Father Trevarthan. The pop and crackle could be understood as long as he listened. The prisoner's corpse slumped in the chair. The man had begged repentance for all his crimes, and with a few holy words and the gift of his heart to Adievasinis, Trevarthan cleansed the man and offered him *true freedom*.

The hard bristle brush reddened his skin as Trevarthan scrubbed it in the basin. Sticky blood from the prisoner dried around his fingernails. It was unbecoming for a man of his piety to have anything other than clean hands. Cracked and chapped knuckles were preferred over blood-stained, at least in the eyes of his parishioners. Trevarthan dried his palms on a white cloth to be sure they were clean. The toe of his shoe dipped into the spreading puddle of blood but Trevarthan stepped back and wiped his sole against the stone floor. He lifted his robes as he stepped over the blood. Soon it would all be gone.

CHAPTER SIX

Ivy opened one eye, peeking at the ceiling of her cabin. Water. She needed water. She groaned as she sat up. She was wrecked and nauseous. Then she spotted it: a carafe filled with water by her bedside. Ivy groaned, lifting it to her lips to chug. She gained enough willpower to open her other eye. Another motion rolled through the ship and through Ivy's stomach. Light crept in through the gaps between the curtains, scalding her headache. A hustle of boots on the deck thudded above her. Ivy plopped back down on the bed, pulling the blanket almost completely above her head.

Luc was laid back on the couch. He must have fallen asleep there when he brought her back to the cabin. Why didn't he just come to lie with her? Luc lay there, unresponsive while Ivy crept past him. Halfway up the stairs, a wave rocked the ship. Blood drained from her face and twisted in her stomach. Ivy gripped the banister, letting the feeling pass before continuing her ascent.

The light of day was completely overtaken by green. Sickly, viridescent clouds hung all around them. The incoming storm was warm and humid. Lightning crackled far away, and thunder rolled around the water. It wasn't raining, but dew clung to Ivy's skin. Stagnant air blanketed them. The sails were limp, and the passive bobbing of the ship was miserable. Ivy stared at the horizon, tracking the ebbs and flows of movement, trying not to wretch. Her baby hairs clung to her forehead and the back of her neck.

The mood was as thick as the air. Something had changed from the day before. Suspicious eyes glanced toward the Queen. Sailors, soldiers, and crewmen seemed to consider Ivy's existence an insult. It was eerily quiet, save the murmurs scattered across the deck and wishing for wind. All joy from the previous day had been smothered out. Perhaps they were all as hungover as she was.

Her ears plucked discontentment out of the air as she walked along the portside.

"The siveryns were a warning. We were foolish to ignore it."

Ivy had read of siveryns since she was a child. They were harmless animals, not fantastical creatures from the unknown abyss. She rolled her eyes as she leaned her elbows against the railing. The water reflected the sickly hue of the sky. The surface was undisturbed and calm as they floated. Tai plucked at a string of his guitar. The twist of the tuning peg bent the note. Sharp and twangy, it set Ivy's teeth on edge.

"We shouldn't have women-"

Ivy pressed her fingertips against her eyes, drawing in a slow breath. *One, two.* It was sailor foolishness. That was all.

"Thraxus himself has denied us passage-"

It's fine. She shoved down the anger that brewed inside her with every whisper and sideways look. The mast towered above her with a loud creak to air its own grievances about her presence on the ship. Even Rian's flag sank without wind.

Luc approached Ivy's left side as she tried to find something to focus her eyes on. Luc's armor was covered in little droplets of water. He must have been burning up.

"Aren't you warm?" she said.

"I'm fine."

"Isn't it a sin to lie?"

Silence. Ivy smirked and looked down at her feet, pushing away her desire to ask for another of his confessions.

Captain Vidal approached. "Your Grace?"

"Yes, Captain?" Ivy straightened, trying to find dignity in her posture despite her wilting.

"We find ourselves delayed." He used his sleeve to wipe the sweat from his brow. "Doldrums are more unsettling to sea-weary men than any storm. Too much time to think."

"It seems to me that the thoughts are all of who to blame for the situation, and I don't ever think I've ever been quite so popular."

Captain Vidal gulped, "Sailors are men of superstition; you have to underst-"

"Oh, I understand, probably too well."

"Unfortunately, there isn't much I can do without wind. We must pray for this to pass quickly. Unrest grows with every passing hour. Days can turn men mad. Weeks will see-"

"Who should we pray to, then?" Ivy squinted as she stared at the sun. She knew Vidal was from Iosnos, the same as her. In fact, this ship and passage was a gift to The Queen on her wedding day. She had begged Rian to let her use this vessel instead of calling one of his warships back to Asmye. She couldn't imagine the cold she'd feel with his air surrounding her.

Captain Vidal stared at the Queen, unsure of how to respond.

"Thank you." Ivy managed a smile to break the awkwardness.

"Your Grace, would you like something to eat?" As Vidal described what they had prepared for the day, Ivy focused only on trying not to get sick as she listened.

"Are you okay?" Luc noticed the paleness wash over Ivy's complexion. He grabbed her arm and escorted her to a seat. Luc crouched down to get a better look at her face. Ivy waved her hand, trying to cool herself down.

She feigned a brighter expression. "My sea legs aren't so steady today, is all."

"Let me get some water. Stay here." Luc hurried toward the galley. As Ivy waited, she overheard Kieran's voice on the upper deck.

"We wouldn't even be here if it weren't for her."

"That's not true." Malcolm's tone was calm. "I've been planning on coming for weeks. King Rian wanted me to-"

"Well, tell me then, why aren't we on a military ship? Instead, we are stuck here without proper accommodation and a two-bit captain!"

"Calm down."

"Calm down?! I could faint from the lack of meat on this ship."

"The Queen preferred to travel on this vessel. It's just as fast, and it isn't wasting resources."

"Resources," Kieran sneered and took another sip of his wine. "Torin told me what was really going on." A knot twisted in Ivy's stomach as the Knights descended the stairs in front of her. She should have known Torin would not miss an opportunity to humiliate her.

"What does Torin know that we don't?"

"Torin only assumes," Malcolm interjected, "We don't know anything."

Luc startled Ivy as he came up behind her. "What are you doing?"

"Ssh!" Ivy waved him down, then turned back to listen. She tucked a tendril of curls behind her ear.

"Tell us," Adne insisted, "If you're so bothered by it."

Kieran sneered at the red-caped Adeshbu. He had not gotten over his comeuppance from the card game and he barely withstood sharing the same air with newcomers.

"Just that girl, she displeases The King again. And here she is, carrying on, drinking, and dancing with sailors. Have you ever seen such lowly behavior from a royal before? Torin was right about her."

"As if you didn't watch," Malcolm scoffed, then laughed. "It's Torin. What would he know about the Queen's private matters? She's the one that hates him!"

"You're not soft for her, are you?"

"I respect her. Is that too hard for you to comprehend? Blame the weather, not a woman." Malcolm clicked his tongue with disapproval. "Childish."

"I know that she's the cause of this!" He threw the bottle in his hands until it splattered on the planks.

"Do they think I control the weather?" Ivy grumbled.

"Stay here," Luc commanded Ivy. He moved too fast for her to say anything.

"Knight, watch your tone." Luc stood tall in front of Kieran.

"You dare speak to me like that?" Kieran scoffed.

"You speak ill of our Queen."

"Watch it, soldier. I don't share the same affection for the Adeshbu as Malcolm." Kieran flashed a drunken grin.

"Easy." Luc put aside the carafe of water he held.

"Do you think a night of playing cards and frivolity will raise your station any higher? That your proximity to my King's wife grants you any favor in my eyes?" Kieran pushed Luc's chest, and Ivy stood, watching through the slatted stairs.

"You don't want to do that."

"What? I'm not frightened." Kieran pushed into Luc's chest again. "Not of you, not of your helmet, not of that girl!" Ivy stared down at her feet. "And we're off to this godforsaken island, and she's just as bad as the rest of you."

"And what are we?" Luc dropped his hand to the pommel of his sword. Kieran blessed the last sip of wine he took.

"Adeshbu are cowards," he laughed, "Zealots with swords."

"We are soldiers of God." Ad Baalestan's voice boomed as he stalked forward. "The God of your king."

"You think I give a shit about what the King lets that old man fill his head with? Trevarthan is the worst of all of you. A fanatic, no better than a witch. You all make me sick." Kieran spat at Ad Baalestan's boots.

"Your time will come, Knight, and I will take pleasure in giving your blood to Adievasinis," Baalestan leaned in closer, "Yours, your king, and his pretty little wife. I'd take them all if it pleases my God." Ad Baalestan's voice sent a shiver down Ivy's spine. She stood, taking steps toward the altercation.

Luc grabbed Baalestan by the cloak. His voice was in a low growl. "Do not threaten her again."

"Taking our shit guard duties a little seriously, are we, Ad Onondian? You should be as disgusted as I am." Baalestan shoved Luc off.

"I've always known you were weak, letting a woman cloud your mind. I've heard you cleanse yourself of your ungodly thoughts." He leaned in and whispered, "How many lashes will the shame give you tonight?"

"Look at them," Kieran snickered, "They can't even get along within their own ranks, and they come to Asmye and feign to supplant us!"

"You all insult the King with this foolishness!" Ivy stood tall, emerging from the shadows, exhausted by the bickering.

Ad Baalestan laughed wickedly, "I insult the King? You parade around this ship like a common harlot." Baalestan stepped forward towards Ivy, who shrank with every step backward. "Is that not an insult? A woman of God would not insult her husband, much less *The King*, by acting like a whore!" He backed Ivy up against a corner, his helmet peering down toward her chest. He looked like he wanted to reach for her. Luc pushed Baalestan back and reached for his sword.

"Adon, no!" Ivy shouted. She spoke lower as his chest heaved in anger. If she stayed any longer, tears would fall. Luc's eyes did not leave his opponent. "I am unwell. Escort me to my quarters." Luc turned his helmet to her. Her eyes pleaded with him, begging to be rescued.

Luc turned back to the Knights and Adeshbu. "If I hear another ill word of the Queen from any of you, I will take your heads to the King myself." Luc loosened his grip on his sword and held his arm out for Ivy, pushing her toward her chamber.

"Where does your allegiance lie, Adeshbu?!" Baalestan called after him and laughed.

Ivy didn't bother shutting the door to her bedroom.

"What was that?" Ivy scolded. Luc made his way towards her, surprised when she held her hand against his chest.

"Ivy, I-"

"No!" She pressed him harder. "Why did he say that?" In her frustration, a tear formed. Is that what all of Asmye thought of her? That she was a whore? All the effort she expended to better the country was wasted in petty talk.

"He's overzealous."

"What do they know? Have you told them?"

"I would not let them disparage you."

"It seems they'll do it without permission," Ivy quieted.

"Not while I'm around."

"Does that make it better?" Ivy stared up at Luc. She didn't know why she was surprised. Her husband did terrible things to her. Why would she think he wouldn't let others talk about it?

"We don't need to have this conversation," Luc said. "You need to cool down. Drink something before you fall sick."

Luc took a step back and leaned on the doorframe, watching her. Pure heat overcame Ivy even in the dress she wore. Garments flew from her trunk as she rummaged through her things. Ivy pulled out a small red scarf. Ivy poured the water from the carafe into the cloth and held it to her brow. Cool water trickled back into her hair. The relief was instant. Ivy let out a deep breath, sighing, and pulled her skirt up around her knees. She kicked off her boots and rolled down her socks.

Luc stared at the long lines of Ivy's shapely legs. The dewy sheen on her skin caught the dim lamp light and led his eyes down along the thick, supple flesh of her calf. Ivy pulled off her stockings, exposing her ankles and feet. She exhaled the last of her frustrations and closed her eyes as her skin cooled. A small groan escaped Luc's chest as Ivy adjusted her seat and an inch of plush thigh peeked out at him. The noise called her eyes to look toward him. His wide, brooding shape filled the doorway.

Bravery, or maybe recklessness, washed over Ivy as she walked to him, looking deep into the visor of his helmet. She raised her hands to the cape fastened around his neck, unclasping it, and watched as it fell to the floor. She could see the beautiful shape of his neck now. He stood still.

"You can't tell me you're not warm." As Ivy pressed the wet cloth against his skin, droplets ran across his golden skin and behind his armor. He sighed with relief and grabbed her wrists, slowly drawing his thumb over her bare skin. "I knew you were lying," Ivy smiled at him and his stubbornness. He chuckled softly.

"It does feel really nice. Thank you." His Adam's apple rose and fell. Ivy stared at his skin. Strong elegant lines defined into a V leading from his jaw to his chest. She wished she could see more. Ivy felt him once in the dark, but what did it look like? She pulled at her bottom lip with her teeth. What did he look like? Her focus broke as his hand brushed a tendril of hair away from her face. Ivy looked up. The strong arched line of his helmet was plenty handsome for her. That was the face that had saved her, that had given his confession, that drove her wild with desire.

"Can I?" Ivy moved her fingers to the edge of his chest plate. Luc was about to stop her when her sparkling eyes begged for his permission.

"Yes."

Ivy unsnapped it slowly. He pulled off the pauldrons and other armor on his arms. His black undershirt clung to him with sweat. Ivy slid the cloth to the back of his neck. He tilted his head back, feeling the cool water drip down his back. He breathed loudly, and Ivy heard his hum. The collar of his shirt fell open, exposing just the tiniest peek of his collarbone. The slope of his shoulder curved down. Luc reached up, putting his hand over hers. His touch made her heart race. The sleeve stretched over his bicep. Ivy was jealous of every piece of his clothing that knew his skin better than she did. Ivy licked her lips.

"You looked so beautiful yesterday," Luc spoke softly, "bathing in the sun, unfettered by the world. I thought I had wandered into a dream."

Ivy took a tiny step forward. Her chest pressed against his. Only his undershirt was between them. She gazed up into the helmet.

"This is not a dream." His hands fell to her waist, resting against the curve of her body. "I am real and I'm f-" Before she could finish the sentence, his hands clutched at her dress, pulling it up. Patience be damned, he needed her. Ivy lifted her arms, letting the dress slide over her head.

"Close your eyes."

Ivy squeezed her eyes shut tightly. Luc leaned in, and she felt his lips against hers, tasting her. The ship shifted and threw her off balance. Ivy started to fall away from him. Her arms reached for her guard to steady herself, but he was already there, protecting her, holding her. "I've got you. You're safe."

Ivy sighed again when she heard his voice unfiltered. He whispered "Querida," and dropped his helmet at his feet. His fingers brushed her cheek. Ivy fought every urge to open her eyes. She had to squeeze them tighter.

The cool wet scarf draped over her eyes. The sensation made her jump. Luc tied it in a careful knot behind her head. Ivy hissed as cold water dripped down her cheeks. He pressed a gentle caress with his lips against hers. Ivy opened her mouth longingly, desperate to taste him. She pulled up at his shirt, feeling his warm stomach under her hands. His skin was plush and soft. Ivy cursed herself for comparing him to how Rian's hard body felt under her touch.

"I want you on my tongue," she whispered. Her mouth fell to his jaw, the flecks of his sparse beard under her lips. Her teeth gently grazed his jawline, biting at him playfully. He laughed with a low rumble as he grabbed her ass firmly in his hands. Ivy planted a deep kiss on his neck, licking his skin to taste its salt. She wanted every inch of him. Each ripple under her hand was a stroke on the canvas she painted of him in her mind. Her lips explored the subtleties of his flesh. Each new discovery of his body felt vibrant and rich. Ivy continued her descent, flicking his nipple with her tongue. She delighted in tasting him, letting her mouth linger over the ridge of his ribs. The nerves that always clouded her thoughts were gone. She was clear and present. She knew exactly what she wanted. If all of Rian's court thought she was a whore, she might as well not disappoint them.

When she reached the waist of his pants, she dropped to her knees. Luc tried to guide her hands, but she pushed them away, Ivy wanted to unfasten them by herself. His cock was hard in her palm as she pulled it out. Ivy leaned her head forward, skimming her tongue along the long surface until hair bristled against her mouth. Luc's fingers tangled themselves in her hair. As she pulled her tongue from base to tip, he took a sharp breath in.

"Oh, fuck."

Ivy wrapped her lips around his cock, letting her mouth salivate around it. His breaths were more ragged as she swirled tiny circles under the head. He was thick, filling her mouth. Ivy relaxed her throat, sliding him deeper. His hand held her hair back gently and he groaned. She wished she could look up at him, to have him watch his cock slide between her lips. She loved hearing his unfiltered voice at his reaction to her touch. Every breath and moan sent heat to her cunt.

"That's-" his breath caught in his throat as she found her rhythm,"-you're…you feel so good." His hips gently rocked with her. He stifled his moans, holding them with his breath. His fingers in her hair clenched as she increased her pace.

Something fell on the deck right above them. Ivy froze. The voices hovered only a few feet above her. Seconds passed like minutes. Ivy recognized one of them as Malcolm. Then Adne's voice came muffled through the floorboards. His boots stopped as they met with the shadow above.

Staring up at Luc from her knees, Ivy whispered, "Can they s-"

Luc's hand gripped over her mouth. The voices continued above. Ivy's ears strained to make out anything. Long seconds ticked by as blind and mute Ivy waited to hear if they'd been caught. Luc's hand pulled Ivy up, holding her tightly against him. The voices were so close. Luc was closer.

"You're safe." Ivy felt his exhale on her ear. His lips teased her skin. She bit her lip, trying not to make a sound. Luc bent down to her chest, sucking her breast into his mouth. His tongue teased her nipple. Between her legs, her pussy was throbbing for him. She squeezed her thighs and clenched, desperate to soothe the ache. His mouth released her breast, following its soft curve to her stomach, and drifted downward. She heard him fall to his knees.

"No, don't, they'll-"

"You only have to worry about being quiet." His hands slid between her thighs, guiding them wide and open. His tender grip pulled her forward and down onto his open mouth. The voices above them dwindled into soft moaning. Ivy could only guess what she overheard.

Weakness in her knees had her reaching out to brace herself on a post. All her focus was bent on not making a sound. The sounds of the knights still lingered above while Luc devoured the Queen. His mouth sucked hard against her clit until Ivy was light-headed. *Breathe. Remember to breathe.* The danger of the situation only heightened his desire for her. His grip was even more aggressive. His fervor to pleasure her was antagonizing. Holding everything in became excruciating.

Ivy's toes curled uncomfortably against the wooden floor. She could barely take it. Her cheeks turned red as she held her breath. How much longer could she hold herself back from crying out?

Bootsteps. They were walking away. When they had faded away, Ivy grabbed Luc's hair with a shuddering cry.

"Holy fuck," she let out a laugh as the tension spilled from her. He took that as encouragement and slipped two of his fingers inside of her. With pointed accuracy, he curled them. The pressure was even and firm as he massaged her. Ivy was already so close. Her leg muscles felt weak, but Luc held her up as she came, flooding his hand.

"You're so good for me," he whispered as she continued to come all over his hand. "I knew you liked the danger." Ivy gripped the beam as she tried to catch her breath. He pulled her away, spinning her body so her ass pressed against the beam. His lips craved her, kiss smashing against her. It only helped that it might keep her quiet. Ivy could taste her come, still wet in his mouth.

Luc hooked his arm under her thigh, opening her drenched pussy for him. He guided his thick cockhead to her slick, pushing into her slowly. Her jaw hung open in silence as a tingle flickered through her cheeks. His breath was slow and measured against her neck as he sank his entire length into her. Ivy held him there, digging her fingertips into his skin, and squeezed her cunt around him. Her fingers skimmed over his shoulders, tacky with sweat. He began thrusting. Her back braced and pounded against the beam. The wood creaked loudly, but Ivy didn't care.

"Don't stop," she panted as he kept his rhythm. Her fingers raked through his hair, twisting curls around her fingers. He kissed along her jaw. His hand slid around her throat, holding his lips against hers.

"I told you I'd never stop, Querida," Luc grunted lowly as he slammed into her. "You're mine now."

"Yes," she whispered, shaking against him as her leg went numb. Ivy gripped his shoulders for support. Luc took notice and lifted her so her legs could wrap around his waist. He held her with her back on the post and thrust his cock deeper, slamming his hips against her ass. His hand covered her mouth, stifling her moans. Ivy went blind and mute at his doing. Her pussy ached around his cock, flexing and gripping him tighter inside her.

Ivy tucked her head into the crook of his neck. His hand wrapped behind her neck, holding her close to him. He hit just the right angle, and she came again. Her cunt squeezed around his shaft, eliciting a rough growl from deep within him. He pushed her legs down from around him, resting her on the ground on her knees. Her head spun in a daze. Ivy reached her hands up for him for support. Luc took them and pushed them behind her back. His thumb pulled her jaw open, and he slid his wet cock along her tongue. Ivy moaned. It tasted sweet with a hint of his salt. He didn't hold himself back, fucking himself all the way into her throat. Ivy could hardly

41

breathe. Luc grabbed a fistful of her hair and rocked her head back and forth along his shaft. Ivy gagged and drooled around him, but he didn't care. He loved how she felt underneath him.

"You take me so good. Taste me." His words sank inside her as he shot his hot come down her throat. Ivy choked on an inhale and coughed, forcing it to dribble out of her mouth and onto her exposed tits. When he was done, Luc rubbed his come into her skin with his fingers, sliding them up until they were in her mouth.

"Did you swallow it all, Querida?"

Ivy nodded her head as her tongue lapped at his fingers. They were wet with sweat and the remnants of her first orgasm.

"Did you like that?" he was breathing hard, trying to keep his words quiet. Ivy had to take a second. Did she like that? Did she? He was rougher than she expected. Her Luc was so gentle with her. This was more like fucking her husband, doing whatever he wanted, and asking for permission later.

"Yes,"

"Say my name."

"Luc,"

"Did you like that, Querida?" He brushed stray, sticky hairs away from her face.

"Yes, Luc."

CHAPTER SEVEN

Malcolm hid himself away on the quarter deck away from the company of his fellow soldiers. They had dispersed after their squabble, retreating into their cabins and corners. Here was quiet and secluded enough for Malcolm. Kieran and he shared a cabin and his nerves were already shot without Kieran pouring more nonsense in his ear. He closed his eyes and exhaled. He loosened his belt and slid his hand into his trousers. He held his cock. There was nothing sexual in the touch, just a comforting grip on himself.

"Well, that's not quite how I expected to find you." Adne's voice cut through the quiet.

Malcolm startled, pulling his hand from his pants awkwardly. His dagger slid from his belt and thunked on the wood deck.

"God. Fuck! That was just-"

Adne put his hands up in a friendly surrender. "You needn't explain yourself to me. I am not your commanding officer nor am one to pass judgment on how a man spends his time." Adne glanced around them. "Even if the venue is in plain sight." Adne clicked his tongue.

"I thought I was alone." Malcolm picked his dagger from the deck. With flustered hands, he attempted to attach it back to his belt. "You Adeshbu are something else," Malcolm said.

"Me? I'm just doing the job. Baalestan is a kind of his own. He's the only one of us who chose this life for himself." Adne rested his palm on the ship wall beside Malcolm. Malcolm's anxious hands slowed as the Adeshbu got closer.

"Then what got you into this mess?" Malcolm gestured to Adne's armor.

"Trouble." Adne slowly pulled the leather gloves from his hands. His fair-skinned fingers were long and elegant. Most soldiers' hands were gnarled and with callouses and scars, but Adne's were almost delicate in their fluidity.

"I thought you were the trouble." Malcolm's gaze lingered on that deep dark line of his visor that should have been where he saw Adne's eyes.

"I only get into trouble when I see magnificent things like you and get caught."

"Yeah?" Malcolm swallowed the breath caught in his throat. Adne leaned forward and tilted his helmet before he pressed his lips against the Knight's. Adne pulled away to lick his own palm. His hand slipped against Malcolm's waistband before he slipped it all the way inside. Malcolm's soft hum was muted in the Adeshbu's kiss.

Malcolm opened his lips to taste more of Adne. Those long fingers wrapped around him in a sure grip, stiffening the Knight inside his pants. Long, slow pumps in Adne's hand had Malcolm struggling to hold back. Malcolm's fingers pressed hard into Adne's back as his pace quickened. Heavy breaths turned to soft moans. Malcolm's hands became desperate to feel closer. His thumbs kneaded into the Adeshbu's firm ass.

"Fu-fuck!" Malcolm moaned loudly. His breath shuddered with a laugh. "I am too quick."

"I knew you needed it." Adne's breath was low and heavy as he pulled his hand from Malcolm's trousers. "So tense, my sweet Knight."

Ivy begged Luc to stay with her that night. He escorted her back to the chamber foyer from her dinner with the captain. It seemed the Knights and Adeshbu no longer wanted to occupy the same space. She had hardly seen any of them since the skirmish. At least they were out of the doldrums.

"Please?" Maybe she'd had more than an extra glass of wine, but Luc should know that's how he should expect her by now.

"Ivy, you know I can't."

"Why not? You slept on the chaise outside my bedroom last night."

"There are too many people here."

Ivy huffed and stamped her foot, whining like a child. "I don't care about them."

"You should care," Luc said, resting his thumb and finger on her chin.

"We land in Iosnos tomorrow. Won't you at least be with me then?" Ivy opened her door and took a step inside. Luc followed Ivy into the doorway. "Please? I need you." She rested her hands on his hips.

"Of course, Querida, as long as you'll have me." His fingers hovered over her eyes, shielding her sight as he tilted his helmet up and kissed her. Ivy inched closer to him, wrapping her arms around his waist. Ivy nuzzled her nose up to push his helmet out of the way as she pressed into his lips harder. Ivy was drunk, and she didn't care. No one could see them.

"I always want you," she whispered, breathing into him. He shut the door behind him, closing them both in.

Ivy had managed to press herself against her bedroom wall with Luc close behind her. She promised not to open her eyes if she rolled over. Luc's helmet was within arm's reach, but she wanted to show that he could trust her. The bed was less roomy than how she wanted to spend their first night together, but she wouldn't complain about the strong arms wrapped tightly around her. Still, she could not find sleep.

"What do you think happened?"

"Hmm?" Luc hummed as he dozed.

"It sounded like Malcolm earlier." She couldn't stop thinking about what she had overheard.

"And Ad Nekoson," Luc's voice was lazy with sleep.

Ivy lay her head against Luc's bicep. "I thought homosexuality was a sin in your religion."

"Is it not your religion, too?" He drew his finger over her bare hip.

"I-" Ivy furrowed her brow. It was hers by marriage only. It was the reason she brought Madeline and Janelle on board with her. How could Adne and Malcolm get away with the thing they punished her friend for? "But they are soldiers."

"They are still men." He kissed the back of her neck and laid his head back down.

"Don't you think it's unfair? You get away with anything for being a man, but women are reduced to-"

"Be quiet. Ivy," Luc was desperate for sleep. "We can talk tomorrow."

Ivy didn't like to be told to be quiet, even if it was because she was disturbing his sleep. The phrase just reminded her of so many conversations where her voice wouldn't be heard. She let out a deep exhale. *He didn't mean it that way.* He would get an earful of her opinions tomorrow. She knew he would listen to all of them willingly. She pulled his arm tighter around her and prayed sleep would take her.

Voices called out their early morning commands, signaling to prepare the ship to dock. Ivy asked Adne to check on Madeline and Janelle, assuring that they were comfortable and ready to disembark. Ivy didn't want the Knights anywhere near her friends.

Ivy sank into her bedsheets, letting the waves rock and lull her into relaxation. She thought about Luc, how his warmth still lay beside her in the small bed. His scent lingered around her, mixing with the jasmine in her hair where his hands had tugged on her curls before he left that morning. A smile lifted her full lips up to her cheeks.

When her eyes opened, she stared at the wall where the wildflowers sat, taking real notice of them since the first day on board. Petals of pink and gold nestled over bright green stems. A moment passed while Ivy counted the days on board. Shouldn't the colors have faded by now? Even the leaves were plump and unfurled.

The Queen got up from her bed and trudged toward the bouquet. She lifted the petals of a geranium. Its orange color seemed brighter up close. Ivy plucked the flower and tapped the end of the stem. It was dry, yet still full-bodied, but how?

A voice bellowed high above in the crow's nest.

"Land, Ho!"

Ivy darted out of her room without stopping to put on shoes. She rushed to the bow of the ship to see Iosnos on the horizon. Her face sank. Her once-white shores were obscured with dozens of Rian's new warships. Gnarled metal and stone of new towers rose every two hundred feet along the coast. Banners hung with the brand of a bear's head. Large pikes gutted out of the teal waves off the shore to stop invaders from storming the island's beaches. Smoke rose from huge fire pits. The natural beauty of Ivy's island was being overtaken with defenses, defenses that she had wanted. Of course, she wanted to protect her home, but now that she saw it armored and overrun with the machine of war, regret weighed heavily in her stomach. Ivy heard something whipping above her. As her eyes drifted up to the top of the mast, she watched as Rian's flag, his sigil, loomed over them proudly. Iosnos was branded with his mark, his ownership, just like she was. Even here, she wasn't free of him.

CHAPTER EIGHT

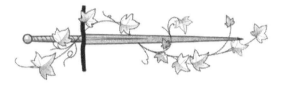

Rian sat on his father's right, eating quietly and staying mindful that his knife did not scrape against the plate. At thirteen, he'd become well-accustomed to how Gerard wanted him to behave. The King had been quiet while they ate. Rian thought he saw the whites of his father's eyes a few times, anxious that he might have something new to spew at him, but silence lingered until dessert.

"Pour my son a glass." Gerard motioned his knife lazily toward the empty cup by Rian's plate. Rian looked at his father. Lines creased Gerard's handsome, yet aging face from his small smile. "You've earned it, son. Tristan tells me you are dedicated to your training."

"Sir Tristan challenges me," Rian watched the servant pour wine into his cup. "I've learned much from him."

"And you excel at your studies." Gerard's stone-blue eyes crinkled with joy. "You give a father much to be proud of."

"Thank you." Rian couldn't help the pit of nervousness that jittered in his stomach. Compliments were few and far between when they came from his family.

"I have something I'd like to show you."

Rian followed his father to his room. He had hardly been here since his mother passed. Even though every reminder, every scrap of her, was gone, he could still feel the ghost of her embrace as he passed through the threshold. He watched as Gerard knelt, blonde hair wisping over his brow, and fished something from under his bed. He untied the leather straps and carefully pulled away the wrappings of fur.

"It took me almost a decade to find this." Inside lay a long sword. The blade was pristine and polished. "Aternous, the sword of Adievasinis. This blade was forged from the blood of a thousand men."

"Is this the-?"

Gerard balanced the sword on his forearm and showed the handle to Rian. His index finger pointed to a small vial of crimson embedded in the pommel. "Ouraina's own blood, still intact." Gerard was as giddy as his boy.

"But how did you find it? Was it not lost thousands of years ago?"

"Father Trevarthan used your blood to divinate where it was hidden."

"My blood?" Something inside the scars on Rian's arm fluttered like just the mention would open old wounds.

"Yes, Rian. This sword rightfully belongs in the hands of Asmye's Kings. It is your blood right to carry this sword when you succeed my throne." Gerard presented the ivory inlaid handle to Rian. "Would you like to hold it?"

Rian swallowed, then took the sword in his grip. He reminded himself to breathe as his arm tensed with weight. As his fingers adjusted, the weight dispersed. It felt so right against his palm, like a humming, telling him everything would be alright. It should have been too big, but the way his hand hugged the grip was like it had been made for him. His pulse thumped in his wrist, carrying the elation of holding the blade through his body. Gerard held out his hand to take the sword back. Rian hesitated. Nothing in him wanted to let go. With this sword in his hand, he could see himself, his potential, uninhibited.

"Rian." The king's sternness returned. Rian shook off his own thoughts as he handed the sword back to his father. Envy flowed through Rian as Gerard stared at the sword in his own grip. More than he wanted the crown or the title, Rian wanted the godly power in that blade. When he went to sleep that night, he dreamed of a way to steal it for his own.

King Rian hunched forward in a pew. His left hand clasped over his right but his fingers twisted the gold around his finger. His knuckles pressed deep into his forehead. He squeezed his eyes tight, focusing on the breath that filled his chest. It was empty. No warmth, no fullness.

"Please," he whispered. Was he always this empty or did she take a piece of him with her?

Footsteps lifted the King's head from his praying hands. The swish of Father Trevarthan's robes stopped when he saw Rian. Crimson splatters marred the crisp hem that floated just above the floor.

"My son!" The old man stepped toward Rian. "I see Adievasinis has already brought you to me. There is no time to waste now."

"Father," Rian rose from his seat. "I don't know what you speak of."

"Rian, you do, but you've let your mind become clouded. Distracted."

"But, I.. she left." Rian's earnest eyes looked for comfort in the priest. "I loved her."

"I know, my boy." Trevarthan placed his hand on Rian's shoulder. "Pain of a lost love is greater than its joy." Rian looked like he might cry. "Tell me, what are you willing to do?"

"Anything for her." The words raced off Rian's tongue.

"What about for yourself?"

Questions drew themselves across Rian's expression. "What do you mean?"

"Adievasinis has shown me the way for you to fulfill your destiny." Trevarthan's lips curved into a knowing smile. "Only if you are strong enough."

"How?"

"Where do you feel your pain?"

Rian looked up at the old man and drew his eyebrows together. "I don't understand."

"Listen to me! Tell me where it hurts."

Rian hand grasped at his chest. "Broken makes it sound so clean," he whimpered as his fingertips pressed into his body over his heart. "But it is torn, ripped, and messy. Like it could never be together again." His chin wobbled. "I would take the numb, dull ache of forever to not feel this way for a moment more."

"The pain in your heart will be your strength if you can wield it. Your prayers seek only to relieve it." His timber edged on condescension. "Do you even know who you pray to?"

"Of course I do." Rian stood. He would not tolerate this folly, not when there was so much else to worry about. He flipped his cape over the pew beside him and started down the aisle.

"You have a purpose, son," Trevarthan called after Rian, "your father's legacy." Rian stopped and inhaled. Trevarthan had not more than mentioned King Gerard in years. "Adievasinis set forth a vision for this world, and you've lost sight of it. What would your father say?"

"Do not bring up my father!" Rian stormed back to the man. Fire lit up within his veins.

"Then what about the girl?" Ivy's face flashed in Rian's mind, her smile when she outran him on horseback. He shoved it down deeper inside him. "I see it all, Rian."

"What do you see?"

"You know what you must do. Use your pain. Reforge Aternous. Adievasinis calls for it."

Rian's breath sharpened at the sword's name. The memory of how it was shattered. The last life it claimed. It was his fault. He knew that. He carried that guilt all of his days.

"Remember yourself, your father's purpose. Your purpose."

Rian's eyes darted over the stone floor leading up to the altar where candles burned. "How many will it take?" Rian's brows were straight and focused.

"At the very least, three hundred men by your own hand."

"And what of her? You said-Adievasinis said-she was the key."

"The key to unlocking your power. Desire and love are the cruelest feelings. Use your training. Harness your heartbreak. Make the sacrifices. Your destiny is waiting for you. Reach out and take it." Trevarthan's hand clasped tightly in a fist. "Only then will you find her again."

CHAPTER NINE

Ivy stared out the ship's port side as they neared the dock. She heard shouting from dozens of yards away. *Sophie*! Her heart beat faster as she tapped her foot, anxiously waiting for the deckhand to anchor them. Sophie slipped past the harbor guard and charged up the gangway, meeting the Queen in a fierce hug. Six months apart might as well have been sixty years between best friends. Sophie was scruffy and cute as a button. Cropped hair hid neatly under a cap, shading warm brown eyes, currently crinkled due to a wide smile. Her embrace crushed Ivy's lungs in the best way.

A smooth laugh sang behind Ivy, butting into their good time. Two hands separated the girls while an arm skimmed Ivy's shoulders and pulled her away. The other pressed Sophie a step back.

"My Queen," Adne's voice dripped with charm from behind his helmet. Ivy stared between him and Sophie, who raised her eyebrow with disdain. "It pleases me to see you smile. I do ask for your patience as I check your friend for small knives."

Sophie's face went stern as she took a half-step forward. "You think I would hurt her? She's my-"

"It's alright, Adne." Ivy stepped between them, more for the soldier's sake. She'd seen her friend fight and despite her short stature, she was a vicious brawler. "This is Sophie," Ivy laughed as she watched her friend bow dramatically. "I trust her with my life."

"That's not saying much," Ad Baalestan lumbered down the gangway, carrying his rucksack. Sophie watched Ivy's mouth twist while other sailors disembarked.

"They'll be fine. I've got it," Luc's voice came from the top of the plank.

"Well, then," Adne gave Sophie's shoulder a friendly squeeze before she shoved his hand away. "I hope you two have," Adne clasped his palms together in front of his chest, "the best time together." Then he strutted down the gangway and left them alone.

Sophie took Ivy's hand and leaned into her, then groaned out, "Are there always men around?"

"I've missed you." Happy tears brimmed in her eyes as Ivy laughed. It was good to be home.

"I've had eyes on every ship with an Asmyian flag since you wrote, and, finally, you're here! You look amazing!" Sophie pulled away from her hug to look Ivy over. "Did your tits get bigger?"

"Sophie!"

"What? Is this all too crass now that you're a *proper Queen*?" she drawled.

"You know better than anyone that there is nothing proper about me." Ivy raised a mischievous eyebrow, "And the tits," Ivy tossed a quick glance back to Luc as she pushed her chest out, "That's probably all the wine and cheese! As far as I can tell, that's the biggest perk of being a-" Ivy cleared her throat, *"proper Queen."*

"Did you bring any with you?" Sophie's wide smile showed off the adorable little chip that was missing from one of her teeth.

"Wine or cheese?"

"Yes." Sophie's nose scrunched. Everything about her made Ivy's worries disappear. "Although I might commit some mild crimes to get a line on a steady supply of that Asmyian wine. Do you know anyone who might have a connection?"

Ivy smirked and raised her hand back to the ship. "Captain Vidal?"

"Yes, Your Grace?" Captain Vidal stood straight up, halting his cargo check to give the Queen his undivided attention.

"Could you remind me where the wine we've brought will be delivered?"

"Yes," the captain nudged his elbow into Tai, who rustled through the pages of the manifest before handing them over. "We have several crates to be delivered to the castle and, yes, twelve crates for the Salt District care of Sophie Unstred at the Barricade."

"The Queen of Asmye!" Sophie sang and raised Ivy's hand in hers.

Sophie was tied to so many memories in Iosnos, most of them involving one of them getting the other out of trouble. Whoever started it merely depended on the day. Sophie gripped Ivy's face and kissed her cheek, but her expression changed as she looked over her shoulder at The Adeshbu.

"Who is that?"

"That would be my *personal* Adeshbu. He follows me everywhere."

"What's an Adeshbu?" Sophie raised a brow and leaned in.

"My guard. Rian, er, The King sent them to watch over us. He thinks I'd cause trouble. Can you believe it?" Ivy laughed when Sophie's brow lifted nearly to her hairline and her palms rested on her hips.

"Are they all your guards?" Sophie watched as another stalked down the gangway.

"Just that one." Ivy turned over her shoulder and gave him a quick wink. "Can't seem to get rid of him."

"He's standing there all cute. Why would you want to?" She reached a hand out. "Hi!" Sophie called to Luc. "I'm Sophie. The *Queen*," she said with an irreverent little voice, "and I are old friends."

Luc stood silently, raising his hand in a motionless wave.

"He's not much of a talker. You'll have better luck with a baby chicken." Ivy crinkled her nose at Sophie. As the crew unloaded the ship, Madeline and Janelle were coming down the gangway. Ivy waved her hand so they could come with them. Sophie turned to walk away from Ivy, but she turned and walked backward a few steps to look at her again. "It's hard to believe you're actually back. I thought I might never see you again." Ivy stared at her feet. She didn't know she would be back so soon, if at all. She supposed she might be able to bring Rian home once or twice in their lifetime; she had dreamt of showing him her island and everything she had ever loved. Darkness lodged between Ivy's ribs, knowing she'd never get the chance.

"I'm back," Ivy smiled as Sophie ran off to fetch the carriage. She made sure Madeline and Janelle would ride with them. They looked well. Anxious, but well.

Sophie gently bumped Ivy when she noticed how closely the maids sat next to each other on the roomy cushion. They looked comfortable, unlike Sophie squished against the window while Ivy was squished between Sophie and Luc and his giant suit of armor. There wasn't a chance Luc would separate himself from Ivy if he didn't have to. Ivy caught Sophie's gesture and subtly nodded. Love was love in Iosnos. It always had been. Madeline stared out the window the entire journey, asking Ivy any and everything about what she saw. The possibility of adventure glimmered in her eyes.

"Of course, when I'm not attending to you, Your Grace," Madeline swallowed. Janelle grabbed her hand as Queen Ivy smiled.

"There will be plenty of time for you to visit as many places as you like," Ivy feigned a smile. She didn't have any plans to ever leave her island again. Why shouldn't the girls make it their home, too?

Ivy lifted her eyes until she found her old castle. It sat high on a rocky cliff that jutted out from the island. It was hard to tell where the rock ended and the castle began but she could see the construction of a new tower rising up in a grand spike on the north side. Ivy sighed. Why did everything have to change?

"Everything alright?" Luc whispered over her shoulder.

"It's my home, but I feel like a stranger. I didn't expect time to stop when I left, but I didn't expect it to move so fast either."

"Time and memory can be cruel that way." Luc squeezed Ivy's thigh under the cover of her full skirt.

Ivy adjusted and crossed her legs. "I suppose it's a cruelty of my own making, expecting something that doesn't exist anymore."

The carriage stopped at the doors to her father's castle. Luc got out first, scanning the horizon, always wary of imminent danger. The only things coming for them were the carriages behind them filled with soldiers. He held out his hand to help as Ivy took the step down. When she took a step forward, he still held her in his grasp as he reached up with his other for Sophie, who shot an impressed glance at Ivy, wordlessly remarking on Luc's gentle behavior. Sophie was hardly a gentlewoman, though. Before the coachmen could start pulling the trunks from the carriage rack, she was climbing up to unfasten them herself.

The sandstone entry of the castle was warm and golden, fashioned into spectacular arches. A strong breeze blew and fluttered past the greenery covering the stone. The bloom of chlorophyll sated Ivy. Astrella never smelled this green. The grand wooden doors swung open and a parade of people emerged. Servants and staff came to attend to the cargo while a woman and two young women walked to the side, checking things off a list.

A tall man with a dark and warm complexion came out to greet the Queen. His hair was silver and black, combed back neatly, with his facial hair tidy and well-groomed.

"Princess! Excuse me, Your Grace." Russell smiled warmly, "Lovely to see you." He reached out, bending to kiss her hand. "Sophie, I should've known you would want to be the first to welcome our girl home." Sophie gave a quick curtsy of her own in her soft-threaded trousers. Russell was no stranger to her shenanigans.

"Uncle Russell," Ivy reached out to him. He held her hand in hers for a mere moment before she wrapped her arms around his neck in a warm embrace. Russell had been an advisor to the crown before his sister wed the King. Besides her mother, he was Ivy's first teacher, a kind, competent, and loyal man with empathy and ideas. "It's so good to see you."

"I'm glad to have you back. We could use another reasonable voice in court these days." His gentle, warm eyes were lined with years of service and dedication to Iosnos. Russell took her arm in his to escort Ivy into the castle. He raised a finger to two young women she didn't recognize. "Would you escort the Queen's companions to their rooms?" The women obliged and began to help Madeline and Janelle.

Russell looked to the Knights and Adeshbu. They were all postured and puffed chests. The tension over their altercation lingered in the air around them.

"Gentlemen, shall we take council before the day is out? There is much to discuss, but I'm sure you'd like a moment to refresh yourselves after the long journey." Russell was a true diplomat. He possessed dexterity in his words, guiding and controlling the atmosphere. "I'm sure a trip to the bathhouse would help ease any lingering weariness."

Malcolm nodded graciously. "Thank you, my lord."

Ivy turned to follow them. She needed a bath of her own. She was stopped by her uncle standing over her.

"Come now, Ivy." Russell held his hand gently over hers. "I'm sure you'd like to see your father."

Ivy should have assumed that these men would want to put her to work right away, but she was so tired. All she wanted was a hot bath and her nice warm bed. "I assume your bodyguard will be joining us." Russell looked back at Luc looming behind her while the other knights followed their escorts.

"Yes," Luc said, taking a step forward, annoyed that his presence was questioned. Ivy waved back at Sophie as she was carted off to see her father.

As they made their way through the halls, Russell lowered his voice, "I must forewarn, Ivy, he's not doing well."

"How bad is it?" Ivy was concerned. Through her father's worst years, she knew that at least Russell could keep Iosnos afloat.

"His tastes exceed our budgets. He will not heed any counsel on the subject or any subject for that matter. You know he's never been easy to follow, but our situation, under his leadership, Iosnos is rotting from the inside out." Russell glanced back over his shoulder at Luc before leaning in closer to her ear. "The drinking. It's worse now than even after your mother died." Ivy flinched at the mention of her mother. She shook her head.

"Didn't Sir Torin answer your letter, Uncle?" Even pretending to hold honor to that name made Ivy nauseous.

"Only to say that there will not be any additional funds until-" Russell sighed and looked his niece up and down. "well, it was conditional-conditions that we can't fulfill at the moment. But for now, we have enough to continue the builds through the next two months. Until then, I would just hope for your assistance with your father. His mind is elsewhere. He thinks but nothing of pretty trinkets and renovations."

Ivy swallowed hard. *From one broken man to another.* She approached the doors of his throne room. "I can help talk some reason into him."

"I certainly hope so." Russell pushed open the doors, and she took a deep breath in.

New crystal chandeliers shone brightly in the room. Ivy tried not to make faces as she looked at them, hiding her disappointment. A life she wanted to leave behind seemed to beat her here. King John Crestieene turned from his conversation and rose from his throne as Ivy entered.

"Daddy!" Ivy ran to him, jumping into his arms. Ivy was probably too tall to do so, but she felt like a child seeing him. He grunted as her body slammed into his. It took everything she had not to cry right there. He squeezed her tightly.

"My darling girl," His hairline receded in white in his old age, but it was still full. He made a handsome appearance, skin creased permanently with expression lines from worry or happiness. His eyes were shadowed by his dark, overgrown, and broad brows. He kissed her cheek, his whiskers scratching at her skin. Ivy could smell the wine, strong on his breath, even though it was only midday. Ivy chose to ignore it. "And where's your husband?"

"Rian sent me." *A lie.* Ivy straightened herself out. "I'm here on his behalf to help oversee the new defenses." *Another lie.* "I bring his Knights, Malcolm and Kieran, as well as the Adeshbu."

"Ah. Well, that is a disappointment." He returned to sit on his new throne. "I had desired to speak with Rian directly. Has he at least sent Sir Torin?" There was a soft scoff in his voice as if Ivy's presence was a slight.

Ivy wanted to scream at the mention of Torin's name, but she suppressed the urge. "*I* am here. You could speak with me."

King John chortled, "I don't think so, dear." He held out his chalice to be refilled with wine.

Her warmth towards him evaporated. Ivy took a deep breath, trying to shove down her feelings. Could he not wait even five minutes before diminishing her spirit?

"I would like to help with whatever I can while I am here."

"That's unnecessary." He tipped his chalice back to his lips. "Russell, how long have you been coaching her for this to be the first thing she says to me? At least try to be subtle."

"I haven't. She speaks for herself."

"Sure, she does." He was so dismissive.

Ivy took a step closer. "Daddy, what's going on? I saw the construction. Everything's different."

"Everything is proceeding. We are being taken care of. It would serve you well not to ask so many questions." Dark eyes bore into her and she was afraid, reduced back to the girl who was punished for being her own person at fourteen. "You'll join me for dinner tonight." John nearly laughed as he kissed her cheek and spoke softly to her. "In the meantime, there is one thing you can help me with."

Ivy steadied her anxious breath. "What is it?"

"Send a pretty note to your husband."

"Why?" Ivy looked back to Russell, who swallowed a shallow breath.

"His funding, my dear." John's smile stretched into a thin line as his brows creased. After all, they had an arrangement. "He gets you. I get the gold." Was there nothing more important to this man? Ivy had not been in her home a full hour, yet she was no longer as shiny as the idea of her husband. John grabbed Ivy's hand, sliding his thumb over her bare left finger. Ivy's heart quickened as she awaited what was sure to be her father's wrath. To her surprise, he withheld.

A knock banged on the wooden door then a steward bustled in, kneeling to the king. "Your guest has arrived, Your Majesty."

John nodded, then turned toward his daughter, giving her jewelless hands another squeeze. "Bring him to me by whatever," he looked her up and down with a smug expression on his face, "bait or lure you possess."

Ivy took a step back as her father released her.

"Straighten yourself out, darling, we have company for you to receive," John cleared his throat.

"Daddy, I'm not ready to meet anyone. It's been a long-"

"Ssh, Ivy," John waved her down.

"Can't I take a moment to prep-"

"No. You're here now. We will do it now. She's been waiting for you." Ivy took a half-step back and bumped into Luc as her father lowered his voice. His tone reminded her of Rian. *She?*

"Your Majesty, the Queen must be quite tired from her long journey," Russell's voice was submissive, "could we not at least provide her with a seat?"

"No. There is only one sitting monarch in Iosnos. She can stand." Harshness rasped in John's voice. "It is only a courtesy to her husband that a woman is allowed on this dias at all."

Ivy took a deep breath through her nose. It wasn't unfamiliar. She turned away from her father and brushed her hand quickly against her cheek to catch a tear before it fell. She glanced at Luc. It was subtle, but his nod comforted her in the smallest way. Ivy pushed her shoulders back and lifted her chin before the doors opened.

"The Holy Priestess of Adievasinis, Natassa Senna," The page announced loudly at the back of the room when the doors opened.

White robes skimmed over the floor. The light shined at her back as she stepped through the rays of light, casting her silhouette through the layers of ivory fabric before the door closed. A veil draped with gold chains from a delicate headpiece lay over her yellow hair. Natassa's head lowered

57

in respect to the King of Iosnos as she briefly curtsied. The gesture was cut short as her blue-eyed focus turned to the Queen of Asmye. The priestess' gaze burned with the cold beauty of gray stone beneath seawater.

"Your Majesty," Natassa's lips hugged the words as her curtsy dipped low, "It is an honor to welcome you back to Iosnos."

"Thank you." Ivy gave a small smile.

"I am the one who should be thanking you. Your acceptance of Adievasinis has allowed His teachings to flourish here in Iosnos. While modest in comparison to the great cathedrals of Asmye, our church grows strong with new converts. I humbly invite you-" Natassa tilted her head toward John, "-and your family to partake in the faith with us. I have much I'd like to discuss with you, Your Majesty."

Ivy all but groaned. She wasn't ready for a sermon. "Thank you, Natassa," Ivy swallowed. "We will be by soon." She tossed a glance at Luc, who could discern the lie on her lips. "I'm sure you've learned I've only just gotten home this morning, and I should like a rest."

"Of course," Natassa kissed the Queen's hand once again, then turned it in her grip. Natassa's soft pale finger traced the scar on Ivy's palm. Her hand clasped over Ivy's as she took one step closer. She lifted Ivy's hand and drew a line over her skin with her fingertip and gasped. Ivy pursed her lips but didn't pull away.

"Your Grace, if I may…"

Ivy didn't move. A shudder ran down her spine as Natassa's finger followed the vein in her wrist up to Ivy's shoulder. Natassa paused then connected a line across Ivy's chest and flattened her palm on Ivy's breast over her heart. Ivy stiffened, peering around as a roomful of men watched her. Natassa hummed.

"She can bless your family."

"She?" Ivy stared at the woman. Natassa couldn't have been much older than Ivy, but she spoke with such confidence.

"Don't you believe in Ouraina's power? Tell me. What are your teachings in Asmye?" Natassa's eyes held Ivy's gaze like she was reading each of her thoughts. Her grip tightened on Ivy's wrist. Ivy could only stare while Luc studied the priestess. Natassa took a step closer, resting her hand on Ivy's stomach. "If you believe, Ouraina can gift you with life."

Ivy's heartbeat quickened. There was no way she wanted this. She was gone. She left Asmye. She left Rian. There was no purpose in what this priestess suggested.

"You take too many liberties with your familiarity." Ivy pushed away Natassa's hands. Months of failing to conceive fell in memories like bricks upon Ivy's shoulders. She had hoped to be rid of them as she was rid of her husband.

"Your Grace, I only mean to help."

Luc coughed somewhere behind them.

"Your help was not asked for nor desired. Please leave." Ivy tried not to cry. How could her father invite this into her home?

King John pushed himself out of his chair, reaching for the Priestess. "There will be none of that, darling. Our guest is-"

"My help is needed, is it not? Your father has informed me you haven't been able-" Natassa looked Ivy up and down. She wasn't finished with her testimony. Ivy threw her hands up. The king tried talking Ivy down, but she wouldn't hear it.

"Adeshbu!" Ivy called, "Escort her out!"

Luc stepped between the Priestess and his Queen. He hesitated, concerned to dismiss someone of his own faith, but between Ivy and his god, only one ever showed him Heaven. Natassa picked up her skirt and held her hand up.

"I'll go."

Luc held his hand over the pommel of his sword as the Priestess shuffled out the way she came.

"I apologize, Your Grace. I pray we will meet again."

As soon as the doors closed, Ivy turned to her father, in tears. "How dare you disrespect me like that."

"I disrespect you? Girl, you forget where you stand. You're a long way from home."

Ivy scoffed, "That's clear." She waved her hand to Luc as a gesture to leave. Wasn't this supposed to be home?

John grabbed Ivy's wrist mid-air. "Do you need to be reminded of your place?" His grip burned as it tightened. "Or can you behave?"

"Daddy, stop!" Ivy yanked her arm back, but John, even in his old age, held firm. She didn't see Luc unsheathe his dagger behind her.

"John!" Russell rested his hand on Ivy's shoulder as a comfort. "Your daughter is tired. We have overwhelmed her," Russell intervened, then stood in front of the Queen, holding her chin up with his finger. "Perhaps we should save the rest of your visitors for another day." His eyes shone with compassion.

John released Ivy's wrist and waved his hand dismissively. "Darling, that's enough of this foolishness. You know your duty best." He gave a forced grin and reached his hands out for his daughter. Ivy stood like a statue, humiliated in a room full of men. She exhaled quietly, forcing the crimson out of her cheeks. She stormed out of the room with Luc trailing closely behind.

Nerves jittered in Malcolm's stomach as he sat in the council chamber. He was still green when it came to matters of politics. His intellect was capable of keeping pace with any conversation, but he feared his own

tongue. What if he misspoke? What if he jumbled the words? What if he-
Malcolm's thoughts were interrupted as an Adeshbu accompanied Russell
into the council chambers.

"I see someone is eager to get to it." Adne's glove landed on
Malcolm's shoulder before he took the seat beside him.

Malcolm managed a small smirk and felt a different kind of jitter in
his stomach. "There is much to be done."

"You're right about that." Russell took a seat at the head of the table
while the rest of them settled in. "Let's dive in, gentlemen."

"How many trained men do you have at your disposal?" Ad
Baalestan's deep timber demanded the respect of the room. Russell looked
surprised at the sudden shift.

"There are thirty-two full-time guards for the castle. Additionally,
we have sixty city guards that patrol in shifts. We have a small militia, but
they aren't formally trained."

"Well, that will need to change," Ad Baalestan sighed, "We are
working at a disadvantage here. Far too few men. Russell, can you bring in
the captain of the guard?"

"Yes, I'll-"

"Good." Ad Baalestan didn't wait for anyone else to give opinions.
"We will call on the militia," Baalestan looked toward his own men.
"Recruit whoever we can. I'll oversee their training. Ad Nekoson, I want
you to survey. Use that mouth of yours to charm whomever you need to get
information. These smugglers will have friends in the city."

"So do I," Adne said with a smile in his voice.

"Is that right?" Baalestan urged him on.

"I've been to many places in my travels. I'm certain someone I
know knows of someone else and someone else…" Adne lifted his hand and
waved it in a circle.

"Seems fitting whatever trash you keep company with would end
up on this godforsaken place," Kieran piped up.

"Cool it," Malcolm couldn't help the boom his voice made.

"Otherwise, why would they come here?" Baalestan stared the man
down.

"Now, I'm not so sure about that." Russell raised his hand. "But we
are in need of you gentleman on the island. Your skills and experience
outweigh most of my militia and we are forever grateful to you and The
King for your services."

Adne nodded his head in agreement, then leaned back in his chair.
No one spoke for a long moment.

"Ad Viena, you'll stay with me. Work on the training and strategize
how to clean up this mess."

Kieran snarked, "Aren't you going to bark orders at us, too?"

"No." Baalestan didn't even turn his head to look toward the knight. "Ad Onondian will continue with the Queen."

"It is a waste of your talents, Adon." Adne leaned back in his seat, raising his arms behind his head. "Don't you desire something with a little more bite?"

"The Queen bites plenty from what I hear," Kieran grinned playfully. Luc tensed in his seat, turning his head slowly toward the knight. Kieran chuckled, "Never seen the King so worked up and miserable."

Malcolm groaned, "Might as well get out the needles and thread if you insist on gossiping like maids."

"Come on, Knight. Poking at the royals is part of the fun." Adne's cadence could make anything sound reasonable. "Makes the days go down a little smoother." Adne leaned closer to Malcolm. "Just like the Queen herself. Perhaps that's why the King is in such despair. I've heard that she likes to take it up the-" Adne whistled a sharp high note, gesturing with his fingers.

Luc gripped his knife, ready to lunge across the table. He chewed his lip under his helmet.

Russell stood suddenly, slamming his palm against the table. "Perhaps it would suit to remember that besides being your Queen and the sole heir to Iosnos, Ivy is also my niece. You will treat her with respect."

The air was sucked from the room. Adne sat straighter in his seat while Luc relaxed. Eyes stared at the table, avoiding Russell's feracious gaze.

Baale cleared his throat, "Russell, I'll also need maps, city plans, whatever you can dig up."

Russell sank slowly into his seat as the tension started to unwind.

"King Rian asked us to oversee the construction of the ships and the new port accommodation," Malcolm spoke with confidence. "We can assist with the training and patrols. Is there much of a population outside the city?"

"The rest of the island is only farmers and small villages."

"Then we can concentrate our efforts in the city," Malcolm asserted, "but we will need to see the rest of the island. It is completely vulnerable."

"What do you think we will be training the men for?" Ad Baaleston snarled.

Malcolm chose to ignore the comment. "I'll need to speak to whomever you've contracted the construction. The King desires a large fleet, and what I saw as we landed was not sufficient. I'll send to Asmye for more men if need be: builders," Malcolm looked to Baale with a straight face, "soldiers, too. We are on the same side here."

Malcolm was quite pleased with himself as he left the council. It wasn't a perfect performance, but he'd held his own and made a decent impression. At least not the same one that Adne did. Malcolm jogged two steps to catch up to Adne and walked beside him through the corridors.

"Ah, couldn't get enough of me, could you?"

"I think everyone had more than enough of you." Malcolm grinned and followed Adne's path "Use that mouth? How exactly do you do that when your foot's inside it?"

"I was trying to be friendly." Adne shook his head softly. "There isn't a lovelier woman than the Queen. It was a compliment, really. Some of the best people I know take it up the bum." There was a sincerity in Adne's voice that Malcolm was growing fond of.

"Old friends?"

Adne raised his arm, cutting Malcolm's gait off at the shoulder. "Are you curious, Knight?"

"No, uh, I only meant-" The two stared at each other, although Malcolm could not see the other's eyes.

"Calm down, Knight. You need a bit of fun in your life."

"And you think you're fun?"

Adne gave a quick whistle then Malcolm heard his lips smack. "You have no idea."

Dinner was less than eventful. King John drank more than he spoke, which was quite a feat, considering he never shut up. It was surprisingly easy for Ivy to fall back into old habits, tuning him out the same way she did as a child. Russell shot Ivy concerned glances like it was her responsibility to fix it. Always another man to fix. Fine. Ivy couldn't fix Rian, but maybe she could fix her father. No, she *would*. Her people depended on it. At least there would be one kingdom that would benefit from her presence. Ivy swore it.

"You'll need to be watchful over the southern sector, dear. I know how you like to wander. Some riffraff is setting up a camp. You should have your husband send more men to police the city."

Ivy swallowed and shifted at another mention of Rian. She couldn't understand it. It was like the second she left, her father only saw her as a token, a bargaining chip for something better.

"Have you spoken with any of them, Russell? Are they dangerous?"

"We would benefit from the aid of more soldiers, Your Grace." Russell looked down at his plate like he hated asking. Ivy nodded and downed the full glass of wine in front of her.

Ivy sighed, "I'll see what I can do." Without another word, she stood, kissed her father's cheek, and left. Luc, who was leaning against the wall opposite her, stood straight to his feet and followed her out.

"I can speak to the others," he said once she was out in the hall. "There's already talk of a militia forming."

"What for?" Ivy stopped.

"Protection."

"For Iosnos?

Luc swallowed, "Of course."

Ivy wasn't sure that she totally believed him, but it was better than the alternative. They walked toward her room, but she kept going once they reached the door. Ivy grabbed his hand, pulling him in behind her.

"What are you doing?"

"I just want you close to me tonight." It was the truth. Ivy didn't even want to fuck him. At least, she thought she didn't. She told herself she just wanted the comfort of his arms. "I'm just-" Ivy felt a lump in her throat, "-this day has been so fucked. I'm so disappointed. I thought it would feel different to be home." Ivy wiped a tear from her cheek.

"You are The Queen of Asmye. You outrank him, you know."

"He is my father."

Luc closed the door behind him and embraced her. His hug swallowed her up. All the pent emotions of the day flowed freely until she was sobbing against his chest.

"Let it out, Querida, It's going to be okay. I'm here," he whispered as he held her. His hand brushed softly over her curls.

"I'm sorry," she whispered into his shoulder.

"Don't be sorry. You're allowed to feel." His words were warm. When she caught her breath, Luc helped Ivy undress and opened the sheets so she could slide in.

"Will you stay with me?" she asked, sliding back to make room. Luc looked around like they were being watched.

"I don't know if it's wise. You need rest."

"Please?"

"I should take a walk first. Make sure no one is coming."

"No one's coming, Luc. Nobody cares." Ivy rolled onto her back, covering her face with her hands. "I'm not what anyone is concerned about. The only people in this castle who speak to me only want to speak to my husband!" Ivy pressed her palms over her eyes, pushing any tears back into them. She was too upset to care about how she was embarrassing herself or to at least censor mentioning her husband around her lover. His silence said so much.

Luc stood there, debating. Then he walked away from her.

"Where are you going?" Ivy asked, sheepishly pulling the bedsheet to her chest. Luc didn't go toward the door. Instead, he blew out the few candles decorating Ivy's bedroom. Ivy lay there a long minute in darkness before she finally heard the snap of Luc's armor being undone.

"There are many words in the book of Adievasinis about temptation and influence. I find myself succumbing to yours easily, Querida." Ivy reached her hand out in the dark, silently begging for him to take it. "I cannot break my oaths, but I will bend them." Luc brought it to his face and tipped up his helmet to kiss it. Ivy desperately wished to see a glimpse of his chin.

"I have broken every vow I made to my husband and still I cannot hold your hand or see your face," her exhale was as weary as her words.

As soon as Luc lay his head on the pillow, Ivy rolled onto her side, clinging to his skin. His right arm encircled her, tracing lines up and down her back. Her heart pulsed inside her chest. She wished it was the closeness of Luc, the thrill of laying with him like he was her husband. Guilt coursed somewhere inside her. Ivy pushed it away with a sharp exhale like Rian would shoo and begone forever. At least he would that night.

"I'm sorry," he spoke at last, "I know this is difficult for you."

"I'm sorry, too. Thank y-"

"I think it's best that we don't speak of him."

Ivy opened her eyes in the darkness and could only nod. How could he know what she was thinking? She tried to swallow quietly. She knew he was right. She just didn't want to be told to do anything else today.

"Will you touch me?" Ivy whispered. Luc was quiet. Maybe he was sleeping already. She was sure the journey exhausted him, too. Worse, he had to put up with her.

"Can you stay quiet?" Luc challenged her. She could hear the joy in his voice. She needed him, needed to feel him, to forget about anything else. She wanted nothing other than to live in this moment with Luc's arms tracing her body.

His kiss lit a spark in Ivy's chest. She pulled his head down so she could taste more of him. His body rolled on top of hers. The cool night air brushed against Ivy's breasts, causing her to gasp until Luc's warm hand caught her nipple and squeezed.

"Please," Ivy's teeth nibbled against Luc's neck. Delusion swirled around her that life could actually be like this. Life without Rian could be pleasurable.

More pleasure came when Luc grabbed Ivy's hand and wrapped it around his cock. His moan bellowed in her ear as he kissed her collarbone, praising how good she felt on his skin.

"Keep going," he grunted, lifting his body up on one hand as he brought the other to slide between Ivy's folds. "You're so wet for me, Querida."

Ivy curled her toes at just the mention of Luc's name for her. Nothing had ever made her feel so special. She moaned as Luc pushed a finger inside her.

"I thought you said you could stay quiet," he nipped at her breast.

"I can't help it," her voice wavered between a giggle and a moan. "You feel so good."

Luc grinned and kissed his lover in her bed. Ivy let her hips fall open and raised them, daring Luc to fill her up more. He answered by swatting her hand away from his cock and shoving the head inside her. His hand immediately covered Ivy's mouth as she whined while he inched further and further until his cock brushed against her walls. Her breath was hot against his palm. Slowly, he thrust deeper. They couldn't risk the sound of slapping skin as much as he wanted to really fuck her. Everything Luc wanted was right here, lying underneath him, giving him everything she had right back to him. Her nails scratched along his back as she held him close. She was frantic, biting her lip to quiet herself while her hands explored bare skin.

Love or something ignited in Ivy's veins. Caution seemed to fall away as need overwhelmed restraint. She couldn't get close enough to Luc. His hips beat against her, driving her crazy.

"Please," Ivy breathed. Luc grabbed her face with one hand and kissed her mouth. She could feel his lips tighten in a grimace as he moved faster. She guided his hand to her clit and jolted when his thumb pressed in.

Ivy's body went rigid. Her lungs held back every muted scream and breath. Her head went woozy as it hit. Luc fucked her harder through her orgasm and met his peak moments after like he was barely hanging on. He collapsed, half on top of her with panting breaths before he wiped away the come on Ivy's stomach.

After a few moments, she slid her hand across his chest, hugging him tighter to her. He stirred only to rest his left arm over hers, holding her hand gently. He squeezed her hand three times and turned to kiss the top of her head. Ivy could feel his breath in her hair. The moon hung in the sky but on the other side of the castle. There was next to no light in her room. Ivy tried imagining his face but didn't dare look up. Luc lay on the bed with her, just holding her, comforting her. This was enough.

"Querida,"

"Hmm?" After she answered, Ivy tucked her face into his chest, pressing her lips against his skin.

"Tomorrow, I want you to show me your island. Just you and me."
Just you and me. Yes, that was enough.

CHAPTER TEN

"Did you enjoy my gift?" King Gerard asked as he sat back on the luxurious chaise in his tent at the encampment.

"Very much, Father. Thank you." Fifteen-year-old Rian gave a breathless smile.

"Were they agreeable?"

"I'd say so." Rian held his hands behind his back as he stood with his back straight and his chin high.

"Good." The King stood eye to eye with his son. In his youth, Gerard's hair had glimmered with copper blonde, but age had darkened and dulled the King. "I need you fresh. Hopefully, you haven't exhausted yourself too much, but a well-practiced whore can clear the mind."

"I shall sleep well tonight." A smirk crossed the young man's face.

"You're a man in more ways than one now." Gerard let out a soft groan as he sat back in his chaise. "Use them for what they're worth. Strategy will come easier to you with unfettered thoughts." Gerard scratched his fingers against the unkempt stubble that lined his chin. "You've fought well in this campaign. It's apparent to me that you've taken your training with Trevarthan seriously."

"His lessons have been enlightening. I feel close to Adievasinis and close to the power He gives me."

"You're a good boy, Rian." Gerard held the back of Rian's neck affectionately. "Smart." Gerard patted him on the shoulder. "I worried after your mother-" Rian flinched at the memory of her lifeless body falling before him when he was just a child. "-but you have proven yourself to me." Gerard managed a smile that somehow didn't curl his lips at all. "You have

yet to take your place in this world, but you are well on your way. Trevarthan has seen the promise the future holds; I see that in you."

"Thank you, Father."

"Let this be a lesson to you."

Rian's eyes followed a servant around Gerard's luxurious tent as he poured wine for them. The King took the cups from the servant and held one out for Rian.

"Always pay for cunt on principle."

Rian couldn't help but lift his eyebrows in shock. He took the cup and sat on the chair opposite his father.

"You may think that you're handsome enough to bed any maid or lady you come across, but if you don't pay, it will cost you tenfold in other ways."

Rian nodded.

"You'll be the king one day, and you will marry. Believe me, you'll pay for that cunt, too." Gerard downed his cup of wine. "Until then, never finish inside them. You don't want some half-breed lowborn laying claim to the throne." He held his cup out to be refilled without turning his eyes to the man who held the bottle.

"Of course, Father," Rian added this to the mental list of wisdom his father bestowed.

"Women are far more challenging opponents than any man who wields a sword." Gerard sniffed deeply and cleared his throat.

"I find that hard to believe." Rian let out a soft laugh as he sipped from his cup.

"Believe it, Rian. They weaken your mind, manipulate you with pussy and pretty words." Gerard's hand lazily motioned as he spoke between sips. "They are who you should really fear."

"I think I would know-"

"You won't know. They do it so subtly, making you think the ideas are your own. They are cunning." Gerard leaned forward towards his son. "Women are never to be trusted. Whores are more trustworthy than wives. If you pay them well enough, they will only open their mouths for your cock. Look at what your mother did to me."

Rian had heard his father's mutterings of that treasonous bitch countless times. The emptier the wine bottle got, the looser Gerard was with his hateful words. Rian looked at the ground in front of him. "Have you heard any news of Emeric?"

"No. Nothing for a few years. I fear the worst."

"You think he is dead." Rian swallowed hard at the thought of never seeing his brother again.

"Much worse. If what they tell me is true, he fights with Bloidar."

"Then shall we discuss strategy?" Rian, desperate not to speak of the family he'd lost, put down his cup to look at the pieces on the map. "We

are holding the southern territories. Leaston, Caedo, Khassian - the rebellions have been quashed. Nothing more than rabble. But, Suikar, they have been funneling in Bloidarian legions from the Tolgeen sea."

"And how shall we proceed?"

"We haven't faced an organized uprising since you first took the country."

"Go on, son."

"Bloidar outmatches us in numbers. They will always have that advantage, and they have risen the Suikar militias from the ashes and united them under one banner."

"Yes, but numbers don't win wars. So how do we win this one?" Gerard grinned as his son confidently pitched his strategy.

"They expect us to meet them in formal combat. We simply will not. We can break them. If Bloidar has called all the capable men to march on Asmye, the villages, farms, and cities will all be vulnerable. You took Suikar once in an honorable way, and now they march against you aided by your greatest enemy. Punish them. Destroy its people."

"And how do we do this?" Gerard's heart swelled as he finished another cup of wine.

"You will distract them. Pull their armies away. I will take fifty good men, and we will burn the countryside. They will bend quickly once you've gutted their heart."

"It seems you'll be the one doing the gutting." King Gerard stood and rested his hand on his son's shoulders. "Your time will come."

Rian shifted his weight into his stirrups and leaned forward in his saddle as his stallion leaped over a fallen tree in their path. A smile pulled at the corners of his lips. He had run nearly side by side with him the whole way. He hadn't ridden like this since, well since - the smile disappeared as quickly as it came. Ivy had tried to tell him that day in the greenhouse. Tried to tell him that she loved him, but he stopped the words from falling from her soft, kiss-stained lips. What he would give just to see her lips again, to run his thumb across them and feel her breath when they parted. An uncomfortable ache pitted in his groin and snapped his focus back to his ride. His horse threw his momentum into his stride as he climbed a steep hill. Rian pulled back on the reins as they breached the crest of the hill. He cooed a soft praise to his horse as he stroked his shoulder. His hound Basker prodded up and trotted to a stop, grey hair wind-whipped back. The dog ran beside the King for nearly the entire journey. Golden sunlight blazed as he squinted to make out the horizon. Hoofbeats from behind him came a few minutes later.

"I thought maybe you had fallen off," Rian held back a chuckle as he turned to see Torin with a sweat-drenched brow and heavy breaths.

"Almost." Torin struggled with the words through his panting mouth. "We haven't ridden that path since we were stupid boys and we probably shouldn't if we desire to keep our necks unbroken."

"Are we not still stupid boys?" Rian playfully shoved his advisor's shoulder. "Oh, come on. You said you wanted to go for a ride to clear my head and 'save you from another afternoon of morose conversation.'" The truth was, Rian needed the distraction. Father Trevarthan had more than suggested Rian's next step but he feared what could happen should he travel that path.

Torin cleared his throat. "I didn't realize the alternative included the potential of imminent demise."

"Where's the fun if it's not a little deadly?" Rian sucked in a breath with gusto. "Makes you feel a bit more alive."

"Sure." Torin awkwardly adjusted his britches that had bunched in his saddle. "Can we have this conversation in the shade of the lunch tent? I'll be more cooked than our chicken if you insist on keeping us dallying in the sun for much longer."

The tent had been lushly set. Expansive shade covered a richly woven blue carpet adorned with fine dining wear and a generous lunch feast for the two men. A bed, lush with pillows and fresh linens, was made for the King in the far corner. Basker sauntered right to it after lapping up a full bowl of fresh water. Rian dismounted and barely looked at his servants as he handed off his reins and riding gloves. Torin was quick behind him.

"Colette roasted the chickens herself just the way you like, brother." Torin patted Rian's back and smiled broadly. Rian returned the smile, his worries suddenly much further away.

Rian sucked his bottom lip into his mouth, savoring the flavor of the chicken he had just swallowed. He licked his pinky before the juices could tarnish the golden ring adorning his hand. His head tilted back in exaltation.

"Fuck! Maybe we did break our necks getting here," Rian laughed softly as an easy warm happiness held him or maybe it was the second bottle of wine they had just finished.

"Compliments to the cook. King says, 'Divine!'" Torin elicited a hoarse honk of a laugh from the King. The advisor listened as Basker smacked on his meat under the table. "How long has it been since she's cooked for you?"

"Not since my seventeenth birthday." Rian's eyes had a soft sleepiness in them as they searched through hazy memories. "You remember that one?"

"How could I forget?" Torin's sharp features dulled with nostalgia. "You wore this new green cape." Torin chuckled under his breath and motioned to his chin. "You had the most horrid little beard."

"Colette made me shave."

"Made you?"

Rian giggled, lines creased deep in his cheeks. "Shall I say, it was strongly suggested..." Rian self-consciously touched the unkempt beard that had started to darken his jawline. "She set my breakfast plate with a razor and cream and stood there-" Rian shook his head softly, "-She didn't say anything, just stood there quietly until I was done."

"Someone had to look out for the security of the nation."

"Perhaps I should give her *your* job, she sees everything." Rian had a laugh to hide the gut punch his memories played in his mind. Of course, Colette saw everything he was. She also saw everything he wasn't. Yet, her loyalty remained with the Garreau line, even if it had meant hiding the truth from Ivy.

"She sure does," Torin laughed at the joke. "How else would I get her to make her roasted chicken? Had to try everything to cheer you up."

A quick brush of the napkin over The King's chin covered the frown he carried with him in his waking moments. He still had never confessed to Torin that Ivy left him for good. It hurt too much to consider saying out loud. Torin hated Ivy anyway. Why open himself up to hear only "good riddance" and the incredulous look that would be on his friend's face, asking how The King *let* her go in the first place? His agreement with Iosnos depended on their marriage, depended on their legacy. It was doubtable that Ivy carried his child with her across the sea. If he was wrong, surely she'd write to him. Maybe she would even come back.

"Thank you," was all Rian could say. He picked up his cup and a piece of the chocolate cake on the table before trotting to the comforting nook in the corner. It had been a long day.

Rian raised his cup of wine before he drained his cup and relaxed back in his pillows. He let his eyes fall closed. Tension loosened in his shoulders. The only thing that would make this better was his wife. The way her fingers would casually stroke through the hair at his temples. The gentle drag of her nails against his scalp. Her laugh would fill his ears when he couldn't keep his hands off her and he'd utilize this bed for a more gluttonous purpose. That would mean he was truly in heaven.

A delicate hand slid across his chest. She always knew just how to touch him. His lips parted, desperate to taste her mouth again and again. Warm lips brushed against his neck. He remembered a night when she had bit him there. He liked that, too. Another hand pulled up on his tunic and brushed fingertips against the trail of hair between his hips. A kiss deepened against his pulse. Rian's face turned to find the kiss, desperate to taste Ivy again. His heavy eyelids barely opened then widened as he realized the woman lying to his right was not his wife. Honey blonde curls bounced as the girl in front of him smiled but there was no trace of innocence in her soft eyes. His head pulled back to find another woman to his left working on the laces of his trousers. Rian's hand clasped around her wrist and wrenched her away until she caught herself on her knees. Torin sat across from him on a cushioned settee with a dark-haired beauty straddling his lap.

"What are you doing?" Rian snarled.

"I'm about to fuck this whore." Torin slapped his hand across her plump ass then gripped his fingers into her roughly as he stared at Rian. The girl clung her arms around Torin's shoulders as she looked back at The King.

"I didn't ask for whores." Rian spoke through clenched teeth.

"Well, I judged you needed one and Danielle wasn't available, called out to the sentries, you know. Wonder how she's faring out there. Although, perhaps, the ruttings have ruined that royally favored pussy." Torin crinkled his eyes as he grinned. "So I figured four or five fresh cunts would suffice for the afternoon." Rian surveyed the tent and saw two more women, barely covered with soft, drapey fabrics around their bodies. The rage that stoked inside his stomach was something he had not felt in years. "Now shut the fuck up and bury your cock in something." Torin bit at the girl on his lap's waist with a growl. "You'll feel better."

"I'm married!" Rian shouted as the whore on the floor scurried away from the King to stand awkwardly half-clothed in the tent behind the other girls.

"Oh, I know." Torin didn't take his eyes off the naked breasts of the girl grinding against his trousers. "I've had annulment papers drawn up."

"What?!" Rian was too stunned to move.

"What? She failed to fulfill her side of the bargain. It's a clean end. You can't imagine the dozens of letters her father sends a week." Torin rolled his eyes. "You'd be free to remarry, whoremonger at your leisure, or whatever else you wish." Torin twisted his finger in his whore's dark curly hair. "I'll even lend you this one if you'd like, she has the look you've grown fond of these last months." The girl held back a giggle, simply too pleased to be in the presence of the power behind Asmye.

"You will stop at nothing to destroy her even after she's gone," Rian scowled as he stood. "Maybe she was right about you. You're sick, Torin." Rian tucked his tunic back into his pants. "There's nothing good in you."

Torin laughed as he stood, pushing the girl off his lap roughly until her hips thudded on the ground. "Good? You want good? How far have you fallen? Good is for farmers and fishermen. We are the bad men who do what needs to be done so that the good people can keep their hands clean of the blood and shit we dig through for them. You are a bad man, Rian." His words were bitter with anger. Torin stalked forward with a keen-eyed predator's gaze. "A bad man who needs an heir to secure his line. Your sentimentality for a piece of pussy with a pretty face is weak. The Rian I knew, the King who would bend the word to his crown was not *good*. Neither was his father."

"Leave him out of this!" Rian shouted but Torin pressed on. Basker rose to his feet, hackles raised as his master's rage grew. Basker had been around Torin nearly as much as he'd been around Rian, raised as a pup, but he only obeyed one.

"Chicken, wine, whores, I don't care what it takes but I need you-" Torin shoved Rian, "-the fucking King to act like you give half a shit about anything besides your own self-pity. Do something, anything besides pining for some weak-lineaged girl. It's disgusting how pathetic you've become."

Rian pushed Torin until his back hit a tent pole. Rian grabbed a fork from the table and pointed it toward the endless cold blue of Torin's right eye. "You want to say that to me again?"

Torin smiled, "Your Majesty, so nice of you to join us."

Rian mouth twisted with anger. He had fallen into Torin's trap. What would Ivy think? He dropped the fork, letting it clatter against a plate, then folded his arms.

"Do you have a point?

"You read Tristan's message from Suikar. What shall we do?"

Rian pinched his brow, honing in on the only thing his father did well: strategy. "I'll go to Suikar. You'll attend to our interests in Tornbridge."

"Very good," Torin smirked and Rian dropped his hold on his advisor's chest. "I'll make the necessary arrangements."

The King gathered his gloves from the servant and headed toward the tent exit.

"Rian?"

The King's large hands clenched the tent flap and barely turned his head back to his advisor, yet he said nothing.

"Sign the papers. Let's move on."

Rian took a step back into the covering. His sea-glass eyes darted between the whores and servants in the tent. Rage flickered in his soul. Torin was right about one thing; he couldn't afford to be perceived as weak. He lifted his finger and pointed at every single person in the tent, save for Torin.

"Take care of this, will you?" Rian mounted his horse and snapped for Basker to follow. "I have a war to win."

An evil smile slowly crept across Torin's lips, igniting a fire in his pale blue eyes. "Yes, Your Majesty."

CHAPTER ELEVEN

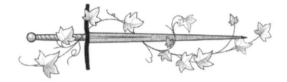

Ivy watched over her shoulder as her father's castle dwindled from sight. The more she walked, the smaller it appeared, along with her desire to stay within its walls.

"Is everything alright?" Luc asked as he stared at her subtle grimace. Ivy dropped her expression.

"Everything's fine." She turned back to the path. "It's not too much further."

The lightly beaten path wound between trees and past a small brook before leading them to their destination. As they approached, rose bushes bristled as Ivy brought her fingers over them. The lilies surrounding her mother's grave were wilted in brown. The headstone was covered in dirt and neglect. Ivy raised her hands to cover her mouth.

"What is this?" Luc asked.

Ivy's chest heaved as she looked around. All the flowers, everything from the garden she had planted for her mother, it was all dead. Disappointment suffocated her.

"Let's sit." Luc guided Ivy to the grass below them. Tears brimmed but she would not let them fall. "What is this place?"

"This is where my mother is buried." Her shoulders dropped as she leaned her forehead on his chest. He held her there in silence. Ivy stared off at the coast in the distance. A breeze blew gently, whipping her hair in front of her face. Luc's arms were strong around her as his fingers brushed through the ends of her hair.

"I just hoped he would've kept this place up." Ivy swiped a stray tear away. "Or at least my uncle would have come by to visit."

"I'm sorry, Ivy."

"You know, he never even appointed her as Queen of Iosnos?" Ivy plucked grass from the earth beneath her. "He only had her referred to as Consort." Ivy tapped her foot against the ground, rage and disappointment swirling inside her. She didn't know why she thought of it. Maybe the hurt reminded her of her first week in Asmye. Rian called her Consort once and it nearly broke her, although she'd never admit it.

They sat in silence for a while as Ivy stared at the covered headstone.

"Her name was Ophelia?" Luc broke the quiet with a soft whisper.

"Yes," Ivy sniffed. *He remembered.* She couldn't ever remember telling Rian her mother's name. Then again, Rian never asked.

"Will you tell me about her?" Luc asked.

Ivy smiled. "She was a patch of sun on a cold day, warm and comforting. She seemed to have endless amounts of love, no matter how sad she was," Ivy swallowed. "She *was* sad. I didn't have words for it when I was young. I only thought she was tired."

"Can I- would you mind if I asked how old you were when you lost your mother? I don't want to be rude, but-"

Ivy lifted his hand and pressed her lips sweetly against his knuckles. "It is not rude to be curious or want to learn. It is not lost on me that we barely know each other." She looked away, searching her memories. "I would have been...eleven, I think," Ivy cleared the uncomfortable lump in her throat. "It was sudden. She kissed me goodnight and then I just never saw her again."

"What happened?"

Ivy took a quiet moment. "I don't remember much. It's all a little hazy."

"You don't have to."

"I can tell you what I do know." She swallowed her panic and it lingered in her chest. She couldn't look at him. If she saw him look at her she might fall apart. "Um," her lips smacked a little as she rubbed them together. "Raiders. For years they caused trouble. Pillaging ships in and out of the harbor. Small parties would rob the people in our city but it was manageable." Ivy recited the story as if it wasn't hers. Just a series of facts that had been repeated to her. "Then one night they burned the city and tried to take the castle." She rushed through her words. "They took her as a bargaining chip, and when he didn't adequately meet their demands, she was killed." Her nose twitched as she restrained herself from her own emotions. His finger under her chin turned her back to him. Her eyes were glossy.

"I see how you hide your pain."

"Rian says it was my father's fault, that he didn't protect her," Ivy's lip trembled, "that he couldn't protect me."

"I will always protect you, Querida."

74

Janelle stirred under her lover's touch. Her soft groan warned of needing just one more hour.

"The sun is high!" Madeline squeaked. She was healed and impatient to discover all the paths of her new home. If what the Queen told her was true, Iosnote markets were even wilder than Asmye's. She was desperate to connect to the worldly bounties. Queen Ivy had left before dawn, it seemed. Madeline wasn't there to help her dress, and she wasn't sure who did. She hoped she wouldn't disappoint the Queen, but without Colette, the days in Iosnos flowed unstructured and uncomfortably chaotic at times.

"And so are you if you think I am ready to leave!" Janelle tossed the quilt over her eyes. It was true, the sun *was* high and shining right in her face. She curled over to her side and buried her face against Madeline's rib to block out the light.

"I've spent more than enough time in this *very* comfortable bed. I want to be out!" Madeline poked her. Janelle fought her leg from the blanket and trapped Madeline's arm between her thighs. "Come, let's find something to eat."

"I'm tired!"

"Then we should stay."

"Really?" Janelle peered out from her cover. Wonder and joy sparkled in Madeline's eyes. Janelle knew that the sun would darken the freckles that dusted over her fair skin. It would only make the redheaded maid she had fallen so madly in love with more attractive. A smile stretched Madeline's pink lips taut.

"No," Madeline stood and yanked the blanket away, revealing her lover's naked form. "Come, the sun will warm you and energize you like a flower."

"Am I a flower?" Janelle pined. Madeline dropped the blanket on the floor but kneeled on the side of the bed, leaning down to press a kiss against Janelle's forehead.

"You are as beautiful as a rose," Janelle kissed her mouth with fervor, "and as prickly as the thorn in my side you so often insist on being." Janelle went to push Madeline's arm away with a laugh, but her beloved caught her lips in a kiss before insisting, once again, that she get up.

The Queen *was* right. Merchants bustled to and fro, peddling everything from spices and herbs to meats and flora. Madeline stopped at nearly every booth, excited by the money in her pocket for once in her life, and Janelle's fingers intertwined with hers where all could see. Hardly anyone batted an eye at them, save for the polite stares of passersby each time Madeline gushed over how delicious the confection samples were.

"Do you have to try everything?" Janelle laughed.

"Yes, I do!" Madeline licked salt off her finger. "How will I know what I like if I don't try it all?"

Janelle smiled as Madeline, rosy-cheeked and bright-eyed, dragged her through the crowd, always hunting for the next treat. Madeline hadn't told her what they'd really come for. After almost an hour of searching, Madeline stopped.

"This is it!"

"What is?" Janelle's round, bright eyes narrowed as she studied the booth before them. "It's chocolate. You've had at least six others on the way here." She raised her hand to wipe a crumb off of Madeline's lip.

"*Chérie,* I've been waiting since we got here to tell you of these." Madeline paid the vendor from the purse Queen Ivy gave her and took Janelle's hand again, leading them toward a canopied bench. "The Queen showed me these once, back at home." Madeline opened the flimsy box to reveal a dozen dipped and decorated chocolates. The warmth from Madeline's hand melted the coating as she held it to Janelle's lips. "Try it!"

Janelle held out her tongue and bit into the truffle. Her breath stopped as she closed her eyes and hummed. Sticky lips met hers as Madeline darted her tongue to where the chocolate glazed her mouth. Janelle laughed and pushed her back.

"I need another."

"Was it worth getting up for?" Madeline's blue eyes crinkled when she smiled as the girls kissed again. They only turned when a man started shouting.

A gaunt man stood on a bushel overturned in the center of the square. He held a text under his arm and raised his hand to reach toward Heaven.

"Rhyzden, God of the Ocean, smothered out the great fires that once erupted and consumed our land. He has given us the bounty that we feed our children, the sandstone we build our homes with. He has brought the ships that grow our city! We have honored Him for centuries on this island! He is the true-"

At first, the crowd stopped to listen but quickly dissipated when he started threatening what could become of their souls if they did not heed his word.

"Blindly, you follow another with promises of wealth and prosperity! That witch is nothing but evil! Why do you so quickly forsake the God that has blessed these lands? You will fall if you so recklessly abandon the truth for this blood god-"

Madeline and Janelle shared a look as they listened in. Adievasinis was the God of Asmye, the most prosperous kingdom since the gods abandoned soil and water for the sky. How could this man say they were not also blessed?

"Fuck off!" A stout man with muscles kicked the bushel, knocking the preacher off balance and onto the ground.

"Freddie, quit!" Two men with the bully pushed him down the alleyway. Madeline swallowed. She didn't expect to see such a display in the streets. The preacher cowered and grimaced. Fear froze Madeline. Janelle's hand left Madeline's grip as she got up.

"Here, let me help you." Janelle's dark hair fell in her face as she reached down toward the preacher. The market bustled around them. The man rose and Janelle dusted off his clothes while he kept carrying on.

"Be wary, young one," The preacher held Janelle's hands in his. "This new god does nothing but bring terror. Protect yourself!"

"From what?"

"Blood will run across stones, grass, and sea. He calls for it. He *aches.*"

Janelle tried to maintain a neutral face but the man's words sunk deep into Janelle's mind.

"Are you alright?" she asked again and again until the man nodded. He thanked her and pressed his palm against her forehead. He whispered something she couldn't discern and walked toward a pub on the corner. Janelle watched him for a few steps then walked back to Madeline.

"You shouldn't be so trusting." Madeline's nervous eyes looked around them. "He could have hurt you."

Janelle shook off whatever shudder she held in her shoulders. "I will not live my life afraid." She touched Madeline's rose-tinted and freckled cheek. Her soft hand brought Madeline's focus back to her joy. The life she had always wished for became more real with every passing day. She didn't know of all the Gods or their heavens, but this, with Janelle, was paradise.

Meelaflowers leaned out to open their faces as they reached toward the sunshine. Deep crimson star flowers faded to an incredibly rich cobalt blue along their edges. They loved the climate in Iosnos, growing wildly all over the island. Ivy picked their buds, looking for the flowers that had just begun to curl. That is when they'd be the most potent.

Sand and grass were soft beneath her feet. That hadn't changed. Being barefoot was how she preferred to be. Here she was, at home with *him,* with Luc. After a couple of hours of walking far away from her father, the city, and the calls of duty, Iosnos finally felt like home. Sunshine kissed her shoulders. As Ivy walked through the overgrown bushes of meela, she looked up at him. He looked so handsome in the sun, his armor practically glowed in this light. A gentle pain rippled through her stomach when she realized Luc couldn't feel it on his skin the same way she did. His gaze stared out at the beach.

Waves gently pushed against the tide pools before they retreated into the endless blue-green. Ivy plucked a few more buds for her harvest before she walked over to her guard. Her arms slipped under his to hug him from behind. Ivy pressed her chest against his back. Luc's arms rested atop hers, holding her hands in his gloves.

"Hi," she whispered, leaning up to peek over his shoulder at the beach in front of her.

"Hi, yourself." His helmet turned back just a little towards her face.

Ivy smiled up at him. "I think it's a little warm for these." Ivy tugged on his gloves, pulling them off his hands. Ivy let the worn leather fall to the sand, touching his warm olive skin in her hands.

"That sun feels nice," he hummed, then she massaged his palms. "You feel nice."

"It would feel nicer without all this," Ivy pressed her hands against his chest plate.

"Ah, I see what you're getting at," he said with a knowing grin.

"I just want you to feel the sunshine on your skin." Ivy played innocently. "How long has it been since you've felt the sun...unencumbered?"

He sighed, "Too long."

"The west shore is completely wild, untouched. No one will bother us here. Just...leave your helmet on." Ivy tugged at the clasps on his chest plate.

He laughed, "If you insist."

"You know what would make this perfect?"

"What?" Luc asked as he dropped his thigh guards into the sand.

"If we had something to light this meelaflower with." Ivy held the cigarette she had rolled that morning in her fingers. Ivy had tucked it against her breasts in hopes she'd find occasion to smoke it. "I found my old stash when I was getting ready this morning. Didn't even consider how I'd light it." Ivy laughed at herself, looking up to see Luc. He already looked naked just without his armor. The wind blew his undershirt tight against his body. Seeing the shape of his chest and shoulders beneath the black shirt was enough to make her lust rise.

"Well, I might be able to help you there." He reached down amongst his things, pulling out a tiny striker. "I got this after I had to make that fire." Ivy remembered the night in the barn, the first time Luc had taken her. "I figured it might come in handy." He held it up as she put the cigarette to her lips. He struck it three times until the spark caught the edge of the paper, lighting a flame. Briefly, it ignited and then mellowed into a smoking ember. Ivy pulled in a drag. The smoke filled her chest. Ivy closed her eyes as she held it in, then opened them as she let it drift from her lips.

"Did you anticipate needing to keep me in another barn all night?" Ivy hummed.

"I know you, Your Grace. I wouldn't be surprised what trouble you got us into." Luc brushed his bare fingers against his lover's cheek. "That good?"

"Yeah," she smiled, "do you want some?" Ivy turned to look at him. The glow around his helmet looked heavenly in the sun.

He was quiet, "I've never done that before." His helmet hid his embarrassment, but the waver in his voice gave it away.

"If you want to, you should try it. It's wonderful. Just makes everything more..." Ivy breathed in, searching for the words. She bit her bottom lip like it would help her concentrate, "...vibrant. Present."

"Not dumb like wine?"

Ivy laughed, "Well, a little dumb, but in a good way."

He looked around. His vigilant scanning was a tell-tale sign that he felt unsure.

"You don't have to-"

"I want to, just need to make sure you're safe." His helmet finished its slow surveillance of the surrounding area. He was satisfied. "Okay."

Ivy took a deep drag on the cigarette. Her hands went to the sides of his helmet, drawing it close to her face. Ivy tilted her head as her lips released the smoke under the edge of his helmet, billowing up until Luc breathed in deeply. A small cough caught in his throat. He tried to suppress it, but he was unsuccessful.

"That happens to everyone," Ivy smiled.

"I don't see you struggling," he groaned between coughs.

"I am an expert," she laughed and shot him a wink.

Ivy took another light drag for herself. She really felt it now. The tension melted away from her shoulders. Her mind cleared of the excess chatter of her thoughts. Luc pulled his shirt off. He sighed as the sun lay against his bare chest. Her heart raced as she looked at him. He was even more beautiful in the daylight. Ivy didn't want to look at anything else now that she saw him.

"Come here," Ivy pleaded as she sank into the sand.

Luc noticed her staring. He giggled as she pulled him down to sit next to her. Ivy felt an embarrassed blush rosy her cheeks as she giggled back at him.

"More, please," he asked sweetly.

Ivy pulled in on the cigarette again.

"Close your eyes." In the darkness behind her eyelids, she felt his mouth against hers. Her lips parted with the smoke dancing within. Ivy blew gently, letting him draw in her exhale, sucking the smoke into his lungs. The stubble on his chin scratched against her jaw. Her hungry lips consumed his open mouth in a kiss. Luc's hand on the back of her head pulled her deeper into him. Ivy tasted the lingering smoke on his tongue, moaning deeply. Her whole body tingled for him. Her senses screamed out in ecstasy at his every touch.

He pulled away, sucking in a deep breath. Ivy heard the helmet drop back down, "Open."

Her eyelashes fluttered. Ivy kept her eyes locked on him as she stepped back toward the waves. They called to her. Ivy lifted her dress over her head, showcasing her bare body beneath it. The sun hung behind her head like a halo shining into Luc's face.

"Come here," she smiled, taking slow small steps backward. Ivy tied her scarf over her eyes.

He leaned down, keeping his eyes up on her as he pulled his boots off. His hands struggled to unfasten his pants; he was distracted by Ivy beckoning him. He got one leg off, and Ivy started running blind toward the ocean, laughing.

"Wait!" He called after her. "That's dangerous!" He almost tripped as one pant leg caught around his ankle.

"I'm in need of saving then."

Once he was free, Luc took off after her. His helmet landed with a soft thud in the sand. The water was warm. Foam crashed around her body. Waves splashed against her bare chest, contrasting with the touch of the sun. Maybe she got ten good strokes into the water before she squealed out in laughter when he caught her. Luc pulled Ivy to his chest, and she wrapped herself around him, kissing his shoulder.

"You know, this would be so much better if you took this off." Ivy tugged at her blindfold, but he stopped her.

"Don't push it or I'll leave you to float away." He ran his hands over her legs underwater, feeling the motion and friction of her skin against his. He felt perfect in her arms. The world outside of this moment fell away. Like children, they splashed in the waves, chased each other, and embraced. They stole kisses with closed eyes.

After an hour or so, the current tired them out. Luc lay down in the sand. He rested his head on his bent arms. Ivy lay on her side, tracing her name into his back beneath the sun. She pulled her blindfold off as she felt scars beneath her fingertips. Lines drew across his skin the same way Madeline's lashes had been etched in hers. Ivy opened her mouth to speak but couldn't find it in herself to ruin the moment. The water lapped at her legs as he twisted around to lie on his back. Ivy could only stare as his chest moved with each of his comforting breaths. As she lay beside him, her hand reached down to tangle his fingers in hers. The sun was bright, and she draped her arm over her eyes. Luc squeezed her hand tight.

"Yeah, that's nice." Luc let out a contented groan as the sun touched his face. Ivy smiled as he spoke. Ivy knew the joy of that freedom. Silently, she wished to always be like this with Luc: free. Lying naked with this man on the beach was the closest she'd been to some kind of Heaven. The meelaflower danced in her veins, making her so happy she could cry.

"What color are your eyes?" Ivy asked.

"Brown," Luc answered without hesitation.

Ivy hummed. He traced his thumb over her hand. "What is it?"

"I like brown eyes." Ivy imagined what shape they might be. Were they open and wide? Did they curve like the shape of a half-moon? Were they young or old? Ivy knew they'd be kind. Either way, it didn't matter. Ivy may never see them. His heart was what she was falling for. His soul was what made him so beautiful.

"My eyes are still closed." Ivy rolled onto her side to face him, snuggling her body against his. Sand clung to the wet skin of her back. His hand gently dusted it away.

"The tide is coming in," he whispered into the top of her head. Water reached further and further up their bodies as they lay there.

"Tell me about it," Ivy chuckled to herself.

"What do you mean?"

Ivy put his hand between her thighs. "It's not the only high tide." Luc's fingers caressed her pussy. He felt the ample wetness as he gently stroked her. His touch just teased her as she pressed her lips against his chest. Ivy moaned as he grazed against her clit.

"Put your helmet back on."

Luc pulled his hand away from her. "Open your eyes."

Ivy climbed on top of him, straddling his half-hard cock. Her hands pressed against his chest. Even if she couldn't see his face, she wanted to look at him when she made him come. A wave splashed against her.

"Don't drown," Ivy laughed as she began sliding her slick cunt against him. Luc groaned as he stiffened.

He slid his hands up her sides. "Put it in, Querida."

Ivy reached between her legs, positioning him against her cunt, then slid down onto his shaft.

"Oh, fuck," he moaned out as she took his full length into her. Ivy steadied her breath as she began to slowly lift her hips up and down.

"How's that feel?"

"Ivy, you feel amazing. Just like that." He grabbed her breast and circled her nipple with his thumb.

"Is it me or the meela?" she teased, kissing his shoulder.

"It's you. It's always you." His hips rose to meet her motion. A wave crashed against her back, but her rhythm stayed unchanged as she shuddered. Her fingers gripped his chest as she stared down his body. His soft tummy pressed against hers. Ivy wished she could see his face as his growl rumbled against her palms.

Ivy increased her speed, with her thighs beginning to quiver. *Fuck!* She was already so close. The meelaflower had heightened her sensitivity.

Ivy dug her nails into his chest, eliciting a moan filtered behind that helmet. Her momentum started to waver as she felt unsteady. Luc's cock twitched as she clenched around him.

"You look so beautiful," he panted as he fucked into her harder.

"Luc-" Ivy could barely get the words out "Luc, I'm gonna-"

"Come!" His hips pounded her upwards. His hands on her waist kept her from collapsing, holding her in the perfect position as he pumped in and out of her. Her hands grabbed onto his forearms. The muscles in them flexed hard as he gripped her tighter. He was grunting with every stroke. Every part of her was vibrating in release, losing all control as she came. It was so intense Ivy thought she might burst. Every place his body touched flashed like lightning, overwhelming her in a flurry of pleasure. A flood flowed from between her legs, spilling from her all over his cock.

"You are so good for me," he cooed as Ivy shook on his cock. He stopped thrusting. He held himself deep inside her as she quivered on top. The spray of ocean water against her spine jolted her as she sat on him. Her thighs clenched against his sides for support.

He sat up, hugging their chests together, and waited for Ivy to catch herself. "I'm going to keep going. Is that okay?"

Ivy hummed, nodding her head. Luc started slow again. Ivy gasped with every thrust. Ivy stared down at his chest at the red scratches she left on his skin. His perfect stomach brushed against hers. Ivy loved how his skin felt so soft against her like his body could swallow her in comfort and safety. His shoulders looked bronzer after being in the sun for a couple of hours. They heaved up as he fucked her. His breathing was heavy.

"Are you close?" Ivy pressed her lips to his neck.

"Yes," he groaned out.

"Luc, I-" Ivy moaned as his speed increased just at the mention of his name. " -I, I need to kiss you. Please," Ivy closed her eyes and pushed his helmet up until it dropped beside him in the sand. Her lips crashed into his. Ivy craved his mouth. He fell back onto the sand, pulling her off his cock. His fist pumped twice then she felt his hot come drip down her ass. He moaned into her mouth as he came.

"That felt so amazing." His chest rose and fell beneath hers, heaving with pleasure.

Ivy hummed, satisfied, relaxed. "You should smoke with me more often."

They lay there in silence for a long while, listening to the waves splash against the shore. The sun tingled against their skin, washing them in warmth. Ivy didn't stir when Luc brushed his hand against hers in the sand.

"I lost my mother young, too. A fever took her when I was six."

Ivy turned her face toward him and returned a kiss against his side. "I'm so sorry, Luc. You were so young. What about your father?"

"I never knew him. She was all I had."

"I feel just awful. I had no idea." Ivy shook her head. "To be on your own like that. I can't imagine what that must have been like."

"It was hard. I'd steal trinkets, pickpockets in our town and sell them for pennies. We'd have to hide them from the mistress at the orphanage or she'd take them for herself. It was the difference between starving and surviving."

Ivy's brows gathered in sorrow as she listened. No matter her hardship, she had always been cared for. She had food, a nice bed, a comfortable life. Her own hurt seemed so quaint.

"When we got older, she sold some of us to the workhouses. I got out. Stole what I could. There was a man who'd hire me sometimes. I was good at it. It's easy to go unnoticed when you're nothing to people."

Every word was a punch to Ivy's heart. Luc said it so casually. A long-accepted truth. His voice didn't waiver or falter. Was there pain in his eyes?

"I tried to find honest work, but the town had dried up. Then Adievasinis found me in all that misery and for the first time in my life I was worth something." Luc paused. His back seemed to straighten with pride. "I commanded respect. I was no longer eating from someone else's plate." His chest puffed. "And now, I hold the Queen's hand." Joy radiated in his voice.

Warmth tingled in her cheeks as her sorrow softened into affection.

"And she looks at me *that* way."

She beamed. Luc traced his thumb across her cheek and along her jaw. A growl purred in his throat when he brushed his thumb down her bottom lip.

"And I know the sweetness of her lips." He exhaled. Ivy's chest heaved with longing. He watched her, holding her in suspense about what he might do next. "And she's mine now."

CHAPTER TWELVE

Sweat collected on King Rian's brow as he rode across the border from Asmye into his territory of Suikar. The rolling green countryside gave way to golden wheat fields and red stone mountains that jutted in eerie yet impressive shapes. The sun stood high and center, bathing his small company in the intense midday heat. No flags or sigils decorated their party. Too dangerous. Dangerous enough that the King rode in a manner of disguise, his black hair tucked beneath a dark hood and his face concealed with a scarf.

Rian led the company under the shade of a wide blue palo tree. He dismounted and ran his hand along his stallion's shoulder and under his tack. Sweat moistened his hand. Rian pulled down his mask that covered pink-flushed cheeks. He poured water into his cupped hand for Basker. The hound happily lapped. Rian sipped from his canteen, desperate to quench his parched lips.

The shade was needed relief for the company. Three long days of fast and light travel had left them weary. The intensity of summer's heat would only grow the further south they went. It was something his wife might have loved. One in his party began digging in the soft earth until he hit groundwater. The men were relieved and quickly shed their layers and the tack from the horses.

"Maren, take the first watch. The tree should provide ample vantage."

"Yes, Your Majesty."

Rian nodded and unbuttoned his pourpoint. A gust of wind cooled the sweat on his back in his tunic. He stretched his head and shoulders back until there was a deep crack in his neck. His chest swelled with a deep breath as he rummaged through his rucksack for the book Father Trevarthan had given him.

The horses gathered around the newly dug oasis for fresh cool water. Rian managed a half-smirk as his bossy stallion nudged one of the soldiers out of the way for a premium shaded spot to roll and lay. Rian found his own site to rest, and Basker stretched out beside him.

A page was bookmarked with a sketch of his wife. Rian's eyes caressed her cheek the way he longed his fingers could. He tucked it safely away while he read. This ritual Father Trevarthan walked him through was simple enough, but he couldn't help but study the pages again and again. The cost of reforging his father's blade was high; he couldn't add to it with clumsy mistakes.

The mattress sank under Malcolm as he sat. The hazy light streaming through gauzy curtains was thick with perfume and incense. "Why, exactly, are we in a whorehouse?"

"Always in such a rush, Knight." Adne leaned against the patterned wallpaper. "'Why? How? Who?' You have much to learn about asking the right questions to the right people." Adne pulled his leather gloves off. His fingertips lingered over a bit of purple velvet that draped over a credenza.

"I can't imagine the right people are here." Malcolm's belly ached, thinking about how the Adeshbu had once touched him. He looked around at the finely decorated walls and luxurious linens. "It is a nice whorehouse, I suppose."

"Have you been in many?"

Malcolm laughed nervously. His dark full lips parted to speak when the door opened.

"Ah, hello, lovely!" Adne exclaimed as he turned to the woman entering the room. She was buxom and fair. The deep berry linen that floated over her thick hips and plump stomach brought out the natural flush in her cheeks and lips.

"Who's the stiff?" she asked as the dark-plated soldier stood from the bed.

"Look at you." Adne wrapped his arm around her waist. "Ourainia herself would be jealous."

"Your tongue is wasted on pretty flatteries when you pay," she giggled with a sweet melody.

"My tongue is never wasted on you, love." Adne pulled her closer. "But I must introduce you to my friend, Malcolm." Adne's arm outstretched toward the young knight. "This is Endaya. The proprietor of this *bustling* establishment. We are quite lucky to have her attention."

"You'll pay handsomely for the luck," Endaya smugly smiled.

"Don't lie." Adne ran his hand over the madam's shape. "You can't keep yourself away."

"Whatever you need to tell yourself." She pressed her bosom against Adne.

"What would help me is if you could give me a few more details about the raiders." Adne's playful voice turned more somber.

"Oh, I had hoped you wouldn't be so boring this time," Endaya smirked, then tied her robe tighter over her chest. "Some things have happened since you visited me last." She sat on the edge of the bed, staring at the floor. Malcolm's eyebrow raised as the madam implied familiarity. He clenched his jaw, avoiding eye contact with Adne.

"Tell us, sweet," Adne knelt before her. His friendly touch was only that. "Just between us, that's why we are here," Adne turned his head toward Sir Malcolm, "The *gracious* King Rian has sent a small group of reinforcements to protect the island."

"And the Queen," Malcolm reminded.

"Yes, yes, she's here, too, and she is stunning." Adne stood. "If you could tell us what you've overheard."

Endaya's big brown eyes looked away from the soldier before her. Her fingers twiddled. She took a deep breath.

"I know it is not without risk for you or your business," Adne spoke softly. "We are here to make it safer. Safer for you and your girls."

"I learned a long time ago how to keep my girls safe. Don't patronize me with false promises. I take the risk on my own." Her full cheeks puffed with an exhale. "There's a tavern on the outskirts of the city's eastern edge near the tannery called Port Cane. They paid for three of my girls to visit them there."

"Is that normal?"

"For high-paying regulars, it's something we offer," she sighed. "The one that came in, Freddie, he's been in a few times. He can be rough and ill-tempered, but he tips generously. The girls don't care for him, even with the gratuity."

"I wasn't aware whores had to like their patrons," Malcolm snarked.

"And do you enjoy murder and maiming or is it your job?" Endaya bit back at the Knight. Malcolm apologized and Endaya continued with Adne's reassurance. "Freddie came in and said his boss wanted to hire a few girls for a long night. Sounded like a party of sorts. He picked the girls. We agreed on a rate. The next morning, only gold came back." The mourning in her eyes said what she knew but could only assume.

"Have you told anyone else?" Adne grabbed Endaya's hand.

"I'm telling you."

"Do you know anything else about them?"

"The one running things. They were calling him 'The Rex.'"

"Thank you." The sincerity was apparent in Adne's voice. "And I'm sorry you lost your girls."

"Don't be sorry. Put an end to it." Endaya took a deep breath and cheer flushed back into her cheeks as if it was a familiar mask she wore. "Now, don't go charging in there all shiny and ferocious. Men like you stick out here."

"Men like us?" Malcolm sneered.

"Yes," Endaya snapped back.

"We are here on orders from the King. What kind of man is he?!" Malcolm's chest puffed under his armor. Endaya only laughed.

"I've heard plenty of what kind of man he is." Endaya wiggled her fingers close to her face. "Spies everywhere." Adne rested his hand on Malcolm's stomach as he lurched forward.

"Thank you, Endaya," Adne brought her attention back to him. "Anything else worth telling me?"

"Not much, but I wouldn't be surprised if they run more than a single tavern in Iosnos, Adne."

"Who else knows about this?" Malcolm asked.

"They have been here for years, Knight," Endaya laughed, "They are comfortable."

"Thank you," Adne dropped a jangling pouch into Endaya's hand. "It's always a pleasure, Madam."

"Likewise, Adne." She dragged her finger down his chest plate. "The best quality a man can have is his *generosity*."

Adne leaned in to whisper something into the Madam's ear. She nodded. Adne bowed and waved his fingers as she left the room.

"Are you always so informal with an informant?" Malcolm's eyes narrowed.

"Pulling off someone's fingernails is one way to get information, but honestly, I never had the stomach for things like that. It suits me much more to be friendly."

"You seemed more than friendly." Malcolm knocked his shoulder into Adne as he passed him.

"Forgive me, Knight," Adne shut the door as Malcolm tried to open it. "For a moment there, it almost seemed you might be jealous."

"And if I am?" Malcolm's lips pursed into a pout.

Adne touched Malcolm's arm. Malcolm pushed it away as his nostrils flared.

"Okay, then," Adne sighed. He grabbed Malcolm and threw the knight down on the bed, pinning him to the mattress. "you have my undivided attention."

Malcolm tried to push back, but the Adeshbu had his wrists tight in his grip. "Why do you insist on being this way?"

"Why, why, why, why…always the why. It has the desired effect." Adne rubbed his body against Malcolm's stiffening cock. "At least, it feels that way to me."

Malcolm groaned at the friction. This is what he wanted, after all. His desire had become unbearable. What is more enticing than a mystery and a man like Adne was nothing but.

"If I let you go," Adne panted, "are you going to fight me, Knight?"

"No."

"Good." Adne released his grip. Malcolm desperately grabbed Adne's body through his layers with his newly freed hands. He groaned, frustrated by the armor between them. "Slow down. I paid extra for the room because I want to take my time with you."

Warmth tingled in Malcolm's cheeks as he stared up into Adne's helmet. He wrapped his arm around Adne's slim hips and flipped the Adeshbu onto his back. His fingers were well acquainted with taking off armor. Nimbly, he unclasped the chest plate, and it clanged loudly as it fell to the floor.

Adne laughed, "Have you done this before?"

"Of course." Malcolm pushed up Adne's tunic and kissed the dark hair that trailed up Adne's stomach.

Adne moaned as Malcolm's kiss deepened against his chest. "With a man?"

"I prefer men." Malcolm grazed his teeth against Adne's side.

"Here I mistook you for, ah-" Adne's breath sharpened as Malcolm yanked down on his britches and released his cock. Malcolm's lips were achingly close as his exhale made Adne's thighs quiver. "-I seem to have lost my thought."

"I should have known there would only be one way to get you quiet."

"If I'm quiet, you're doing something wro-" Adne gasped as Malcolm teased him with a long, slow lick from base to tip. Adne slammed his palm against the headboard to restrain himself. To tease had only brought Adne pleasure and power. To be teased was sweet misery. His hips raised, hoping to find a satiating touch. The knight defied him, moaning deep in his chest as he sampled the Adeshbu's body.

Malcolm slipped his fingertip over the wetness on the head of Adne's cock. The tiniest touch made him writhe. Adne cursed when Malcolm's lips dipped to wrap around his balls. It delighted him to give Adne the same gentle torture he'd felt for days.

Adne pinched his own pink nipple. He didn't know how much he could take before-

Malcolm kissed the head of his cock. Adne's feet tensed in anticipation. A man hadn't ever made his mind this willingly desperate.

"Please," he whined.

Malcolm took the head into his mouth. Slowly, he slid Adne deeper into his throat until dark hair bristled against his lips.

"Oh!" Adne reached down and gripped the back of Malcolm's neck. "You are stunning." Adne fucked his hips up gently. Adne admired his paramour's umber figure under his touch. Broad shoulders and rippling muscles stretched over his lean figure. Adne's heart swelled when Malcolm's ass arched like he was a sensual display just for him. Tears welled in the knight's eyes, but he didn't pull away. His thumbs dug into Adne's hips.

Malcolm gasped for air when he came up. Adne's grip stayed tight as he pulled the knight up from between his legs. Before words, protests, or consideration, Adne pushed his helmet up and off his head. Malcolm didn't get a chance to adore him before his mouth was consumed with hunger. Adne trembled as he sucked hard on Malcolm's bottom lip. He pulled him nearer, opening his mouth so his sweet knight could taste his tongue. Their hips ground together. Friction couldn't ease the ache that burned between them. Adne's hands slid down Malcolm's muscular back and under the waistband of his trousers. Malcolm's ass was more than a handful. The knight nipped at Adne's lips when his finger tickled his rim.

Malcolm gazed down at the Adeshbu's face, taking it in for the first time. Adne leaned up, and Malcolm grasped his throat and pushed him back into the pillow. His thumb followed the sharp line of his jaw, obscured by a dark beard. Pink lips drunk on kisses. The Adeshbu's complexion was pale but not sullen. Their skin colors couldn't contrast anymore. It should have been illegal to hide such fine features under a helmet, for he was, objectively, a very pretty man. Disheveled brown hair wisped over his dark eyes. Malcolm tried to look deeper. Adne tried to turn toward the pillow to avoid the longing in Malcolm's eyes. Malcolm held him there.

"I want to look at you." He dived back into their kiss. "Undress me." Adne blushed and then complied, stripping away everything between them.

`Sunlight streamed through the sheer lavender curtains, casting a hazy glow over the lovers. Their eyes hadn't broken contact in minutes, but it might as well have been hours.

"I see you've lost your spunk without the protection of your helmet, Ad Nekoson."

Adne's white teeth shone from a grin. "I can show you spunk, Knight." Adne spit into his palm twice, then quickly grasped Malcolm's curved cock. The Knight groaned and buckled on his knees, dropping his hands on either side of Adne's hips.

"I thought you'd done this before," Adne teased. Malcolm growled, then took him in a kiss. Adne's hand rested against Malcolm's jaw, delighted in how it clenched when Adne nibbled his full bottom lip. "I need you." Adne pushed Malcolm on his back, never letting go of the grip he had in his right hand. Adne bent over to slide his tongue over Malcolm as he throbbed.

"What are you waiting for?" Malcolm reached his hand out to Adne's arm and drew him closer until they were chest to chest. Malcolm ran his fingers through Adne's thick hair and only pulled him back to entangle their tongues one more time. "Get to it," Malcolm ordered.

Adne straddled Malcolm's hips, reaching behind him to give Malcolm's thick cock one final squeeze with his hand. He exhaled through pinkened cheeks as he lowered himself, inch by inch, around Malcolm. Both soldiers had seen their share of devastation and pain before, but nothing wrecked them like this.

Adne fell forward as Malcolm thrust deeper and deeper. His whines elicited a knock on the door. The knob creaked as it twisted. Without consideration, Adne reached down to his pile of armor and fished out a small knife, throwing it against the door and its frame, blocking out the curious party on the other side.

"I'm impressed," Malcolm brushed a tendril of Adne's hair from his brow before leaning up to kiss his collarbone. His hand slid down Adne's solid but soft abdomen and teased his cock with a gentle touch.

"Fuck me, Knight." Adne sank deeper, anxious to release. His hips bounced in time with Malcolm's as they both reached their peak. Malcolm's hand squeezed and tugged harder with each pull as both soldiers groaned at the other's pleasure. Adne slapped the mattress beside Malcolm's head and finally spilled out over Malcolm's hard stomach. Adne's clenching drove Malcolm wild, inviting him to let go. He held back a wince as his engorged cock shot out his come inside Adne.

It was a long moment before either could speak again, but of course, Adne was the first to break the silence.

"You impress me, too, Knight," Adne sighed, then hopped up from the bed. He inspected their mess and then dropped more gold coins on the credenza. Malcolm stared, incredulous at the display of energy.

"What? It's good for business," Adne smiled.

Under the blanket of the deep indigo night, Rian arrived at the Suikar encampment. Firelight danced along the canvas walls, casting shadows of the men against them. Men stood at sudden attention only to dip low in respect to their King. Rian's boots scraped with each long step. His chin was high, and his eyes stayed undiverted from his destination. Their quickened heartbeats thumped with fear. Rian could feel it in his fingertips. His men didn't love him. They were terrified.

"Welcome, Your Majesty." Tristan's massive frame ducked through his tent. Short, wispy light hair poked from under his helmet. Soft features often misguided his prey from when he could lure them into a trap. His methods and strategies had pleased King Gerard enough to promote him to general when he was barely a man. He kept Rian's respect and loyalty, even from the new King's boyhood. Tristan was there, that fateful night in Bloidar. Rian would always love him.

"Sir Tristan," Rian smiled as he grabbed his General by the forearm for a firm shake.

"Come, sit. You've had a long ride. Water or wine?" Tristan asked as he held the screen of the tent open for Rian.

"Water."

"Ice?" Tristan asked with a smirk.

"You've found ice?" Rian tilted his head.

"The Suikarians are a clever people, Rian." Tristan handed the cold cup to the King.

"Not clever enough to know their efforts are futile." Rian sipped his water. The crisp liquid reached down inside him, quenching his thirst but not his desire.

"They do hold on tightly to their grudges." Tristan relaxed in his seat.

"They had many chances to cooperate. They choose violent means." Condensation dripped against Rian's fingers. "They still choose them."

"You've managed to hold the territory for fifteen peaceful years-"

"Peaceful?" The line between Rian's brows deepened.

"You'd blame the farmers and the merchants for the radicals? The Dureto sect has never represented all of Suikar."

"The Dureto have grown their numbers. I have to cross my own borders like a bandit for fear of their watchful eyes in Suikar. They are an infection; if we don't eradicate it, it will fester and grow until we lose complete control." Rian finished his water. "The Bloidarians smuggled their assassins in through Suikar because of the Dureto. They passed into Asmye unchallenged. Clearly, we have not had a firm enough grip."

"This is not an enemy we cannot meet in open battle." Tristan rubbed his beard.

"It's not a battle I want." Rian sucked a drop of cool water from his fingertip. "I want prisoners. I want fear. I want the air rank with it," Rian smiled, but it could have been mistaken for a snarl. "And I need you to send a thousand men to hold Tornbridge on the western coast. We've heard whispers."

"We?" Tristan raised an eyebrow.

"Torin's little spies." Rian tried to relax his jaw but the tension tightened. "Bloidar wants to come from all sides, and they intend to fuck me when they do, and I don't intend to be fucked by anyone besides the queen."

"So Lund holds Caedo in the east." Tristan scratched his cheek. "Tornbridge gets fortified in the west, and I've just gotten word from Iosnos."

Rian's mouth went dry.

"Malcolm has requested men and supplies in Iosnos. Supplies for ships." Tristan refilled their cups. "We need to launch your fleet to patrol the Tolgeen Sea. Our borders are too vast to line with men, and Bloidar will spread us thin if we fortify every castle Torin hears rumor of being taken."

"Men, tools, weapons - I agree. Send Malcolm whatever he needs. We can no longer wait on our heels, fat with wealth, while our enemies come to us." Rian pressed his lips together before standing tall. "Is that all that you've heard of Iosnos?"

"That and the Adeshbu are difficult, but they are making headway in securing the island."

Rian nodded, disappointed. "Good. Iosnos will need to deliver on its potential." Rian's eyes went unfixed as he stared past Tristan at nothing.

"Rian, is everything alright?"

Rian snapped back into focus, staring down the General.

"Your Majesty,"

"I need prisoners. How many do you have?"

Tristan's mouth twisted into a wicked grin.

Ivy hesitated before she tapped her knuckles on her father's door. He had called for her to visit him there but still, it had been so long since she felt close to him.

"Come in, darling," John hoarsely called. Ivy opened the door to see him lying, propped up over thick pillows on his bed. The old king coughed into a handkerchief and waved his daughter in.

"Are you unwell?" Ivy asked, concern creasing between her brows.

"It's nothing. Just a bit more malaised than usual this morning." John tapped the bed beside him. "You've been gone for months. Can't I enjoy time with my daughter?"

Ivy swallowed the caution in her throat. There would be something. There was always something. "And the cough?" Ivy sat across the blankets of her father's bed. Her fingers found the edge of one of her mother's afghans draped across her father's lap. Time and use had begun fraying one of the edges.

"When you are old, you will understand that not all coughs are sicknesses," John chortled. "I am, unfortunately, very old."

"Not that old," Ivy smiled and relaxed to lean down on her arm as they talked.

"Give yourself a few more years and suddenly, you'll find yourself aching and groaning. You'll see your reflection in the mirror and while you-" John tipped her chin. "-may still be as beautiful as your mother, without line or crease in your skin, you will feel so much older than you are now." There was a clarity in his eyes. He hadn't yet dulled his facilities with wine and kindness sparkled under his brows.

"It will be good to be older. Maybe even wiser."

Ivy kept it to herself that she wondered when the time would come that her father would show great wisdom. Maybe the Crestieene line ran out all those years ago. Still, it didn't matter. She would take a moment of reprieve to feel like an honored daughter. A servant interrupted their quiet company with lunch. Plates of fresh steaming pork picadillo served over rice filled the space with fragrance. Ivy cringed a bit at the sound of his glass being filled with wine. Ivy pondered when his kindness would be washed away by the bottle as the two sat and read for a while.

"She picked out your name. Did you know that?" John finished his third glass.

"I figured as much."

"If I had, you would have had something far more traditional." King John looked up from his book.

Ivy flipped a page. "Princess Beatrice or Margarite probably wouldn't have suited me."

"Not at all," John chuckled. "I asked her why she would name our firstborn after something so common as ivy."

Ivy made a face.

"She told me, 'Ivy isn't common, it's pervasive. It persists through the adversity of winter and grows in the harshest of conditions. Crawls over rock and tree and stone and makes the world more lush and beautiful. It fills up every space it can and transforms it.'"

Ivy stared at her book but was no longer reading. An image flashed in her mind of the time she spent with her mother in the wilderness. Iosnos was beautiful, sure, but there was no beauty Ivy thought greater than her mother Ophelia. Ivy shut her eyes tight.

"Your mother said no other name would do, for there was no part of her that wasn't you."

Heartbreak ripped at her chest. The old wound of her mother's death had never healed. The feelings only tangled into an unsolvable mess that she buried deep within. "I so miss her." Ivy tried to keep her tears at bay.

"I do, too, darling. But she's not something we can get back." John refilled his glass. The bottle clanked as his unsteady pour wobbled over the rim.

"But we can hold onto her."

Ivy would. And Ivy had. Not a single day that passed had Ivy not thought of her mother and how she would have melded into Ivy's everyday

93

life. She sat and considered. If her mother had been there when she was sold to Rian, she would've begged her mother to join her. What would Rian have thought of that? Would John have let her go?

"No," John said when Ivy asked. "I would've kept her by my side until Adievasinis took her from me."

"Adievasinis?"

John raised an eyebrow. "Don't pretend you know not of your husband's god."

"I don't pretend at all. I merely wonder why you bring either that god or my husband up in conversation." Ivy shifted on her bent knee as she felt the energy shift in the room. What was once light and connective now felt heavy and hollow.

"You don't believe, do you?"

Ivy only shrugged.

"I don't either," John said with a smile. Ivy furrowed her brow.

"Then why-"

"I am doing my part." John tilted his chin down along with his tone. "I have put on these airs for the island. Let the people see my support for your husband. And now it is your turn."

"My turn?"

"An heir."

Ivy stilled before her father. A cool wave of horror and annoyance washed over her.

"Ivy-"

"Don't say it, Daddy."

"It is a wife's duty to be by her husband's side."

And there it was. Between the wine and the guilt, Ivy was not inclined to fight. She'd done enough for a lifetime with her husband. Any time longer spent in this room would surely turn sour. Ivy shut her book and nodded at her father.

"Sophie's waiting on me." Ivy hopped off the bed and strode out the door.

Luc stayed with the group, although he was further back than Adne and Malcolm, way up ahead. Madeline and Janelle wandered sideways to and fro, slowing everyone down as the redhead simply must inspect every plant that they passed. The Queen was no help keeping up the pace, and she knew every name for every leaf to educate her friend. She also hung her arm around Sophie's shoulders, walking in step and whispering so low that Luc could not hear, except when she laughed. Oh, how he loved that laugh. In his jealous mind, he believed it was his to elicit from her.

"Come, Ad Onondian," Adne sang from the front line. The hill they climbed was nearing its peak, step by step. The cliffs near the Tolgeen Sea gave a near-perfect vantage of the entire island. A smoke cloud billowed from the far side of the island.

"That's the tannery," Sophie explained to Madeline. Poor thing had hardly explored more than a mile from Astrella in all her life. While Iosnos made her feel like she didn't know left from right, she was inspired to swallow every bit of knowledge the island offered.

The ivory blanket caught the wind as Madeline shook it out. Janelle caught the other side. The basket pinned the blanket down in the lush grass. The food the girls laid out was simple but easy to carry. Luc grabbed his bread and an orange, then walked away from the crowd so he could eat. Adne had gone the other direction, but the Knight Malcolm didn't look to be too far behind.

Ivy stared after Luc as he stalked behind a tree. He'd been on edge ever since Sophie had arrived that morning. It was a good thing he had left her room before dawn. Even though her room was darker than she would have liked, holding Luc close to her each night was worth it. Ivy used to watch as the moon hung in the sky when she was in Rian's bed. The light brought hope and peace when all was well. But that was gone. It grew easier, the pain in her chest, when she felt his arms encircle her under the sheets.

"How long does it take to walk across the whole island?" Madeline asked, shoving another grape in her mouth.

"About half a day if you're focused. Most of the population is in Mermont. That's what the city is called," Ivy smiled. "There are small villages that the farmers informally organized. Most of it is still wild. At least, I hope it is." The whole reason Ivy had arranged this excursion was to survey and take note of the changes. "It's all beautiful, though."

"In our youth, we would run or ride everywhere. The wilder, the better." Sophie nudged Ivy. "This one loved to get me into trouble."

"I did not!" Ivy protested. "You were always the troublemaker!"

"Hardly! She couldn't wait to risk it all for a quick thrill." Sophie made a face at her friend. "Just because I was your scapegoat to your father doesn't make it true."

"Well," Ivy scrunched her face, "maybe you're right."

"I'm always right."

Janelle laughed, refilling her cup from a bottle of Asymian wine. She lifted in a wordless offering to the others.

The girls finished their lunch and then lay on the blanket, staring up at the sky. The lush greenery around them provided a soft bed as the sun warmed their skin.

"I missed this," Ivy sighed and raised her hands over her head. Her chest pushed forward with each breath. Suddenly, a shadow cooled over her body. She opened her eyes to see Luc hovering over her.

"We cannot stay here all day," he said.

"We can stay longer than this," Ivy smiled. It was all she could do not to reach out for him, to pull him to lie next to her. She ached to be able to touch him, but it was not safe there. Something in his stature suggested frustration, but it would not bother Ivy today. Here, she had her lover, her best friend, and the Iosnote summer to distract her from everything else.

What seemed like only moments later, Adne called out that the cavalry was arriving, and then the men laughed.

"Baalestan will love having someone else to boss around."

Ivy picked herself up from the blanket and stared out at the coast. Asmyian flags above broad ships flapped in the wind as they entered the bay. A pit sank in her stomach.

"What does this mean? Is the King here?" Madeline held Ivy's shoulder, but Ivy kept her eyes fixed on the black bear sigil that teased her.

"I didn't know he was coming." The Queen kept her face stoic. She thought she had escaped, but then she questioned if she even wanted to.

"I'd like to meet him," Sophie gave Ivy's hip a bump with hers. "If he's half as handsome as you write about, then I'd-"

"Sophie!" Ivy gripped her friend's wrist. She didn't turn her head for fear of seeing Luc's body language shift. Evidence of her affair littered her room and her body. "There is much to be done," she breathed. "I need to go back. I need to change. Madeline!" Ivy stormed back to gather the blanket, anything to keep her hands busy. "I will need you, as soon as we get home, to press that blue dress. It's his favorite."

"Yes, Your Grace." Madeline looked at Janelle, disappointed their day had to end so early. The blanket rumpled as they shoved it back into the basket. Luc didn't bother to help.

"Will I have time for a bath?" Ivy asked aloud. Already, she felt dirty. She should ask for her sheets to be changed, too. "How long will it take him to tender?"

"I don't think you have to worry about that." Adne raised a scope to his visor and shook his head.

"What do you mean?"

"He isn't here, Your Grace," Adne spoke. Sophie stared at her friend, sizing up her reaction.

"Let me see." Ivy reached for the scope. The King's personal banner didn't hang on the mast. She wasn't sure, then, if she should rejoice or cry.

"He sent soldiers, Your Majesty." Adne nudged Malcolm's shoulder. "Looks like he answered your query. You're moving up in the world."

Ivy glanced up at Luc. Even behind a helmet, his eyes bore into her, and she knew the mistake she made.

"You should head back," Luc spoke to the other men. "There's much to be done," he teased. "I'll stay with the Queen and her companions."

"Don't you think I shou-" Ivy started.

"They can handle it," Luc interrupted. "The only thing you should worry about is enjoying your day." Ivy swallowed. She could see the lie clearer than she could see his lips through the helmet.

Luc allowed her a moment to watch through his scope as the ships took anchor off the coast. They were too large to dock in the harbor. Tenders dropped, filled with men and crates. Their arrival drew a crowd of Iosnotes. It was a spectacle. She couldn't blame them for their curiosity. Everyone wanted a taste of Asmye.

The sunrise washed the Suikarian sky in shades of orange and purple. A braided rope secured the prisoner's ankles as he lay on the ground. Coarse fibers reddened the skin beneath them as the knot tightened. King Rian nodded as a soldier tossed the rope over a tree branch and then pulled. The branch creaked as it adjusted to the weight of the man now hanging under it. The prisoner stuttered through the gag while blood rushed into his head. Shades of maroon deepened in his face. Rian kicked the basin into position under the prisoner, sizing him up for the kill. Rian's squire held the wooden box, inlaid with velvet. He slid his tongue over his teeth as he lifted the lid. Shards of his father's blade gleamed as Rian carefully removed the pommel with a sharp edge still attached. He polished it with an ivory cloth before the words he practiced flowed off his tongue.

"Adtinq valas berain tometerrian." His worry eased, and his eyes closed as his need came into focus. This is how he would win her back.

"Hold him steady," Tristan commanded his soldiers as the prisoner squirmed and shook. He honored Adievasinis in blood, too.

Rian's fingers gripped against the prisoner's hair, ripping at his scalp to hold his head still. He repeated his words, an unbroken circle of prayer. The beat in his prey's chest panicked as the blade sliced through the flesh of his neck. A crimson spray cast across Rian's face and chest. He closed his eyes as a surge of strength quickened his own heart. For a fraction of a moment, Ivy's face flashed in his mind, like this was all for her. Rian stretched his head back and tilted his face toward the sky while clouds covered the sun. His lips quivered at the release as he shook his head. He would not see her again. The potency of his kill, his sacrifice, lasted only an intoxicating few seconds as the blood drained into the basin. Rian pulled back on the man's head to ensure every drop had been drained.

"I'm ready for the next." Rian wiped the blade clean.

CHAPTER THIRTEEN

The sheets draped around Ivy's hips. Half awake, a chill whispered up her back. She reached for her lover, arms outstretched to Luc's side of the bed, only to find emptiness left behind. The morning was still young. Even moments before, she would have sworn she heard his breathing and felt his weight sink into the mattress beside her, but reality was less kind.

Just like every morning since they arrived, she awakened to find herself with only the ghost of their nights. Ivy squeezed Luc's pillow close to her chest and drank in the notes. The scent of his sweat evoked his taste on her tongue. She grinned. If he was a ghost, then he was haunting her body, the soreness in her pussy, and the love bites on her breasts. A tightness lingered where he hadn't wiped away his come. And she haunted him right back in the scratches she left on his shoulders and the teeth marks embedded in his neck and tummy.

Eastern sunlight cast over Ivy's pillow. She pulled the blankets over her body and squeezed her eyes tight. Maybe she could trick herself into not feeling quite so alone. Half of the reason she was even in Iosnos was to be with him. The other half was still too painful to think about. There had been mornings Ivy awakened without Rian. She couldn't decide which hurt worse.

Little had turned out how she fantasized since her return to Iosnos. Her thoughts of ease and peace were nowhere in actuality. Moments outside of her bed with Luc were nothing but stolen touches, nothing of consequence. And he wouldn't take off his helmet for her. Ivy wouldn't care what he looked like. She saw him straight through to his heart. It was that he didn't trust her. Maybe he loved his god more than he loved her. Rian did.

What if something went wrong? She couldn't possibly go back to Asmye, not ever. Even if she wanted to, how could she believe Rian would let her? For all she knew, the marriage was already annulled. It was all a matter of time before she disappointed her father again. She had to make it work with Luc. She couldn't be disowned and exiled without him. But then, he wasn't even there. She was on her own. It was a hard-admitted truth to fear how alone she could be in the world. Hollowness hit the valley in her chest. She shivered, moistening the pillow under her cheek.

The warm sun of Iosnos had blazed high above as all the people who sought relief played in the waves of the ocean. Queen Ophelia sat, closely watching her baby build something indiscernible in the wet sand with another little girl. But Ivy was hardly a baby anymore. At almost six, little Ivy was already confident and outgoing. Her sharp mind was matched by a sharp tongue that tended to get her in trouble. Ophelia hated to dull it in any way, but Ivy was her responsibility, and that sharp tongue wouldn't protect her from the men who hated to see a girl use it. She hoped the world might be nicer to Ivy than it had been to her.

Ivy turned towards her mother. Her wet, wild brown curls clung to her bronze skin. Ophelia smiled wide at her daughter. Sand stuck to Ivy's feet as she ran. Ophelia caught her when she leaped into her arms.

"Mommy, did you see what I built?"

"I did. Who's your friend?"

"That's Sophie! She's loud," Ivy smiled. A tooth was missing from her grin. "I like her!"

"Louder than you?"

"Yup!"

Ophelia raised her eyebrows. As if that were possible.

"She says she is coming back tomorrow. Can we come back tomorrow, too?"

Ophelia smiled and waved at a portly woman further down the shore. Sophie's mother, she presumed. "After your lesson with Uncle Russell."

Ivy pouted at the idea of her daily lesson. "It's so hot." Ivy grabbed her mother's hand and yanked. "I want to go swimming."

Ophelia pulled her dress over her head as Ivy led her into the water. Ivy paddled and dunked her head under the water, emerging with strands of hair pasted to her face. Ophelia proudly watched her little girl, a true islander in so many ways. The only quality of her father Ivy possessed was his stubborn nature. Ivy spit water at her mother through the gap in her teeth. Ophelia laughed and splashed Ivy back. Ivy squealed and dipped back below the waves.

"Don't go too far!" Ophelia shouted as Ivy swam in circles around her.

After the sun started its descent, Ophelia held Ivy's hand as they walked up the long hill to the castle. She took a deep breath, bracing herself for returning home.

"Mommy?"

"Yes, darling?" She dug into the bag slung around her shoulders.

"Why do you have such sad eyes?"

Ophelia feigned a smile at her daughter. A six-year-old had no business troubling herself with relationship concerns. Her father was waiting for them to sit for dinner. "I'm just tired, my love."

"Your Grace?"

Ivy blinked open her eyes. Madeline's voice, followed by her shape, came into focus. It was so strange how Ivy felt like she could sleep through anything.

"You missed breakfast. I thought you'd want me to wake you."

Ivy rubbed her hand across her puffy eyes and let out a groan. It was mostly a happy memory of her mother she'd remembered. At least there was Sophie.

"Are you sleeping well?" Madeline pulled back the curtains to let in more light. "You've seemed tired since we arrived."

"I'll admit to missing my bed in Astrella. The King does have fine taste in linen and mattresses."

"I'm sure he'd send whatever you asked for. He'd want you to be comfortable while you are away. Have you heard from him lately?"

"No," Ivy said a little too quickly.

"I'm sure he's destitute without you," Madeline smiled and put her hands on her hips, studying the room for where her supplies were in this new castle. The pose evoked Colette, but Madeline seemed unaware, and Ivy resisted the urge to point it out. Madeline opened a drawer and unfolded a dressing gown. "Would you like me to lay out a dress for you? Help you this morning?"

"No, you don't need to worry about me," Ivy yawned. "You should be out enjoying yourself."

"It is still my honor to aid you, Your Grace," Madeline winked as she tidied up small things. She groaned as she reached under the bed, picking up the dress that Luc had pulled off Ivy amidst a fit of passion. Madeline inspected the garment closer. "Did this tear?"

"I must have been careless." Careless wasn't a lie. *A ripped dress. Rian could tear anything with his bare-Don't!* Luc was fine. She was fine. Ivy sighed in frustration.

"I'll get it mended and washed right away." Madeline dropped it into her basket at the foot of the bed. "Can I at least help with your bath? It's warming in the next room. I've already added those rose petals you like." Ivy stretched while she considered the offer and noticed the violet marks Luc's kisses had left behind. She crossed her arms to hide her body.

"As long as it's hot, I can do the rest myself. Thank you, Madeline."

"Just call if you need anything." Madeline turned back to the Queen.

"I hope if I do, I won't be able to find you," Ivy smirked. Madeline straightened a blue-jeweled necklace on the Queen's vanity. Busy work. "Go! No need to lock yourself up in this old castle."

As soon as the maid cleared the room, Ivy collapsed back into bed. She was a mess. How long could she live half in the dark?

Thank the heavens Luc wasn't careless enough to leave the love bites anywhere her dress wouldn't conceal them. The bright mustard fabric outshined the dark hollows that lingered under her eyes. She doubted anyone would notice her tiredness once they saw the dress. A brass loop gathered the deep yellow linen under her breasts, showing off the supple shape of her waist, back, and chest. Colette would never have allowed Ivy to dress this way. The ladies in Asmye would scream if they saw the Queen in this. That delighted Ivy. Lavender sang as she dabbed a little of her new oil on her fingers. The scent mellowed as she tapped it on her neck. The notes of lemongrass and bergamot started to ignite as she primped her curls in the mirror.

Luc would certainly appreciate the dress today. Ivy wondered why he hadn't just come into her room yet. She adjusted herself quickly and raised her cheeks in a saucy expression as she opened the door. Her face dropped when Kieran turned to look at her.

"Where is my guard?"

"He's off to the service with the other Adeshbu, Your Grace."

"Don't you have more important th-"

"He insisted one of the Knights keep watch. Seems he has little faith in Iosnote soldiers." Kieran snarked, "One of the few things we agree on."

"You're dismissed." Ivy pushed by the Knight. Her cheeks puffed as she attempted to exhale her annoyance. Or was it disappointment? It was hard to tell.

Archways opened toward the Thraxian Sea, a view Ivy had been fond of since she was a child. The beautiful stone was laid on top of itself in abstract shapes, holding the walls of this castle for hundreds of years. The servants kept up appearances, hanging bouquets of flowers opposite the sconces to bring the beauty of Iosnos indoors. Gulls called above the fishermen's boats as they pulled up their nets and traps. It was an industry she'd never have to worry about in Iosnos. If her father's line ended with her and his castle crumbled like sand hundreds of years from now, her people would still fish these shores.

"Good morning, Your Grace," an alluring, high-pitched voice sang. The Queen twisted her neck to see the priestess her father ambushed her with, floating in white robes behind her down the stone corridor.

"Good morning," Ivy let the words hang as she looked around. Had Kieran really not followed her? Luc would be furious when she told him. The small woman bounded toward her. Ivy couldn't remember her name. With all the information from that hectic day, what to call the woman who only cared if she conceived was the last bit of knowledge to hold onto.

"Natassa, Your Grace," she bowed her head, concealing her bright complexion under a hood in the shadow.

"Yes," Ivy gave a curt smile and continued down the hallway.

"We missed you in the congregation this morning," Natassa called after the Queen.

Ivy stopped. "Congregation?"

"Yes, Your Grace. I delivered Ouraina's message this morning." Was it over? Why hadn't Luc come back for her? "I'm glad I found you. I hoped I could give you a piece of Ouraina's love and wisdom."

"What could *you* give me?"

Blue eyes shone brighter as a smile rippled across Natassa's cherry-cheeked face. "Of course, you are already blessed by the gods, chosen to bring life into the kingdoms."

Ivy covered her stomach with her hand as Natassa looked over her body. Dark fabric ruched under her fingers. There was nothing there. She knew it. Still, she didn't like prying eyes.

"You protect yourself with your husband's power."

"I beg your pardon." Ivy shook her head.

"Your hand," Natassa grinned again, "is that not where your husband bled into your skin?" She reached for The Queen's hand and raised her palm. The thin line of a scar nestled between the lines of life and fate in her skin. During their wedding, Rian cut her palm with his blade. When she was too nervous, he cut his own and then pressed their hands together. Father Trevarthan said it was a blessing, something to unite their kingdoms and to honor Adievasinis. Ivy gulped. She tried not to pay attention anymore to the marks Rian left on her body.

"Doesn't it make you feel closer to him?" Natassa skimmed her thumb against Ivy's pulse in her wrist.

A few weeks had passed since Ivy decided to leave her husband. Closeness wasn't a way she could describe how she felt about him. Whatever they shared was broken. He hadn't even written. If she thought about it too long, she could consider what or whom Rian might be doing in her absence, and that would be too much to bear.

Natassa watched Ivy's expression sour. "It must be hard to be so far from him." She reached out with a comforting touch to Ivy's shoulder. The Queen could only hum. "Father Trevarthan sends word."

Ivy hid a flare of disgust. Trevarthan had never been at the top of Ivy's list of friends. Her husband spent more time with him than anyone. "Word of what?"

"The King spends his days in agony, missing his beautiful wife who brings him nothing but joy." Her tone rang with a lightness, something hyperbolic to comfort Ivy on her supposed diplomatic mission. "He is away from Astrella now. Adievasinis has tasked him with great responsibility." As Ivy's brow furrowed, Natassa leaned in to reassure her. "Fear not. He will protect The King." Natassa raised her head toward the sun shining in the windows, shaking her hood free to show off scraggly blonde curls. Hope hid in her eyes.

"Where is he going?"

"I'm sure you know well that these men don't tell us women everything." The priestess gave Ivy a friendly jab. "We must pray for Adievasinis to bless our King with wisdom and guidance."

Natassa's head bowed quickly, whispering something the Queen didn't understand. Ivy followed in respect. Even after everything, she didn't wish harm on Rian or their people.

"Ow!" Ivy shook.

"What is it, Your Grace?"

The scar embedded in Ivy's palm throbbed, beating blood up to the surface. Ivy winced, but Natassa stared in awe. Vines that grew over the stone archways furled their leaves like a gentle wind carried over them.

"Ouraina," Natassa purred as she took in the sight. She grabbed Ivy's hand, drawing a line up her arm with her finger, then over her chest, and down to her heart. She did not ask permission to reach for Ivy's stomach but began praying again. Ivy squealed in pain again as something poked from inside her skin.

"Do not touch me," The Queen commanded.

"But, Your Majesty, it is only Ouraina's gift. She reaches out only in love."

"It hurts!" The cut on Ivy's palm opened and pooled blood cupped inside her hand, pulsing in time with her heart.

"My Queen, there is a ritual I can help you with. If it is completed, you will be the way for-"

"No!" Ivy struggled as Natassa gripped her shoulder, still holding on strongly to the Queen's wrist.

"Ouraina only knows peace. I can help you."

"Get off me!" Ivy pushed as hard as she could. Blood stained on the white cloth as Natassa stumbled back.

"What is this?" Luc appeared in the hallway. Ivy's breath was unsteady as she looked into her palm. Blood smeared her skin in a long line. Panic overtook her expression.

"She cut me." Ivy held out her hand to Luc. "I don't know how she did."

Luc ripped his cape, tearing a piece off for Ivy to hold against her cut.

"Your Majesty, I did no such thing." Natassa stepped further back as the Adeshbu's gaze locked onto the priestess. "I only prayed. That is all."

Ivy wiped at the blood. It smeared, but underneath, there was no cut. Her scar remained intact, only marred by the reddish tint her blood left behind.

"Adon," Ivy felt faint. She felt it. It was there. The blood was there. "Come here, please."

Luc stared at her palm. "I-" His breath was heavy. He looked over Ivy's arm, inspecting it for cuts. "I've never seen anything like this."

"It is a blessing," Natassa spoke softly. "A revelation. Adievasinis and Ouraina show you favor." She dropped to her knees before Ivy.

Ivy wanted to be angry. How could she not be? Awe or something like it overtook her. At her feet, the priestess prayed. She had only witnessed such displays at the feet of saints. She had no faith, but it was getting more difficult to deny Adievasinis' power.

Night fell in the Suikar encampment. The sacrifices gave Rian a fleeting high. He craved more. Only thirteen had been given to Adievasinis. Drops in the bucket compared to what he needed. Tristan assured him that all the vital information had been drained from them long before their blood.

Rian rubbed his eyes. It was late, yet sleep seemed far from his grasp. He scribbled some words on a piece of parchment. The slant of the letters was sloppy and tired. The quill scratched at the paper. Basker raised his head from Rian's bed, noticing something the King couldn't. The hound leaped off the bed and trotted out of the tent. Rian shrugged. He wasn't the only one that was restless.

There was an ache in Rian's hand and arm where he wielded Aternous. He flexed his bare hand as soreness radiated up his shoulder. Long days of fighting had yielded a similar pain, but in recent days, he had done so little. Why was the cost so high?

Basker barked, distracting Rian from his thoughts. There was yelling in the distance. He reached for his sword.

"Dureto! Dureto!" A soldier shouted from outside.

Rian stepped out of his tent only to jump back and out of the path of a horse galloping by. Flames engulfed the far side of the encampment. Chaos scattered his men, making them easy targets for the Dureto's skilled soldiers. Their cavalry weaved through the camp, taking heads from drowsy men. Rian took down who he could, but they came from all directions. Rian turned just in time to see a man leap from his horse, tackling the King. Rian twisted the soldier's neck with a loud snap and pushed the body aside.

Tristan yelled orders at his men. He swung his axe high, knocking a Dureto soldier off a horse and caving in his chest.

"Take them down!" he bellowed. "They don't have the numbers!" An arrow clipped Tristan's shoulder. The archer pulled back for another shot at the general. Rian stood and threw his broadsword. The blade sliced through the thin night air and planted itself through the archer's chest with godly precision.

"Throwing a broadsword," Tristan smiled at the King, "Who taught you that?"

"Certainly not you," Rian snarked. A powerful high pulsed through him.

"In formation! Line the camp!" Tristan yelled as the Asmyian soldiers got their bearings. The threat passed, and the remaining Dureto soldiers scattered.

Rian walked toward the body of the archer he killed, rolling him onto his back with his boot. Basker followed behind, snarling with blood-stained fur from his own kills. Blood trickled from the Dureto soldier's mouth, and an unbroken stare from the archer's lifeless gaze. He clutched the bow in his cold hand. Rian stepped his boot on the man's chest as he yanked his sword free.

Ivy flexed her hand. The pain from her phantom cut had subsided, but the eerie feeling lingered. The blood was real. It washed away in a basin, clouding the water with a tinge of pink. She squeezed her fist tight as she tried to make sense of it. Luc's presence was soothing as he walked closer to her.

Russell shuffled through the hall, concerned with the papers in his hand. His pace was confident, even with his eyes fixed on the words. The scene was something Ivy was familiar with.

"Some things never change." Ivy gave Luc's side a playful jab. Her words made Russell look up.

"It's more akin to the work never stopping." Russell stopped in front of Ivy and leaned in to kiss her cheek. "Good morning, my dove, and where are you off today?"

"I'm not sure," Ivy sighed frustratedly at the floundering nature of her schedule. "Perhaps I shall track down Soph." Ivy glanced down at the papers in Russell's hand. "What are those?"

Russell looked between his princess and her guard. "Why don't you walk with me for a moment?" He nodded his head in the direction of the council chambers.

"Of course, Uncle." Ivy waved to Luc over her shoulder.

"I feel as if I've hardly had a moment with you to myself." Russell guided Ivy with a hand at her back. "It's my fault, really. So wrapped up in all these-" Russell searched for the word, "-matters."

"Is something wrong? Anything I can help with?" A guard opened the council chamber doors for them.

Russell's face dropped. "You know I would, but your father's been quite cle-"

Ivy waved her hand for him to stop. "Don't." She plopped down in a seat at the large wooden table, a seat she had sat in many times before. Never in council, but Russell had sometimes given her childhood lessons on politics, trade, and the like at this very table. Her finger trailed over the woodgrain. Her marriage contract had been signed on it, too.

"One day, I hope I will have the honor to take my direction from you, Queen Ivy of Asmye," he reached for her hand, "and Iosnos."

Ivy's chest filled with warmth. "Thank you, Uncle."

"But until that day, I must make the necessary concessions to your husband and make your father believe they were his ideas, or at least to his direct benefit."

Ivy sighed, "Has he no interest in actually doing the job he is so attached to?"

"For all his faults, I think he did try in the beginning." Russell organized his papers on the table. "I would have audiences with your grandfather seeking change, and I'd get nowhere, but John came to me: a new King to our little farm." Russell looked like he was still in disbelief. "He sat at my kitchen table and offered me the chance to get my hands in the mix."

"Oh, my father left his castle? I've never heard of such an event." The words tasted of Ivy's own bitterness.

"He was a different man then. If you could have seen his face glow when he saw your mother. I've never seen a man fake such an interest in tea just because a beautiful woman poured it for him."

Ivy's eyes lit up. "Did she share his affection?"

"I won't lie to you, Ivy. It was no great romance. Not like you and your husband from what I've read in your letters." Ivy swallowed. She had only written him good things about Rian. Why should he suspect any differently? "Your mother understood what she was doing, and there was love in it. And then *you* were in it. That was enough for her."

Ivy shrunk into her seat. It was heartbreaking that her mother didn't know love like she had deserved. "I worry I might end up like her. Another woman trampled under men and their legacies."

"I don't think that will be your fate."

"Fate, premonitions, foresight." Ivy shook her head. "It feels as if I have been assigned these things against my will. The world would like it very much if I took it without question. I can't do that anymore. Not for someone else's benefit."

"Has something happened?"

Ivy waited a moment. Russell stared at her with concern. Ivy's mouth went dry. If no letter had come about an annulment, the safest thing she could do was be silent. "It's nothing. As my father would say, I have a flair for the dramatic." She glanced at her uncle to see if he believed her. "After all, I'm home in Iosnos when she is most beautiful. Why shouldn't I be happy?"

"It is a happy time," he nodded. "We are fortunate to have you back for your birthday and the Evane Festival. I remember when you were small; you were convinced that the ocean made the lights dance for you."

Ivy laughed, "Do they not?"

Russell grabbed her hand and gave it a kiss. "They are brightest when you are watching." The twinkle in Ivy's eyes faded when the council doors opened.

"Lord Russell," Malcolm spoke as he entered the room. He bowed his head when he saw Ivy. "My Queen."

"Yes, Sir Malcolm." Russell turned away from Ivy.

"We've just had a ship in." Malcolm lifted letters in his hand. "News and orders from Asmye."

"Asmye?" Ivy stood, "Is there anything for me, Malcolm?" she asked with hope.

"Nothing, Your Grace." Malcolm passed the letters to Russell.

"Ah." Ivy pressed her lips together in an attempt to hide her feelings. "I shall be off then." The men nodded in a show of respect. That's all it was, a show.

CHAPTER FOURTEEN

Ivy admired a freshly unfurled leaf from the monstera she had planted from a cutting right after her arrival to Iosnos in the castle garden. The small clipping had thrived, shooting up thick green stalks that ended in large irregular leaves. Ivy put her hand against the soft delicate skin of its newest frond. Its color was lighter than the older leaves and the edges of it still curled slightly, as if it had yet to stretch in its full salute of the sun. The baby leaf was longer and wider than Ivy's hand. It pleased her to see it doing so well.

"I didn't come here to stare at the plants!" Sophie shouted from the chaise where she lay.

"You can't bear a few minutes of me checking on my garden. Are you so desperately needy for my attention?" Ivy continued to check the progress of her monstera.

"Every moment of every day," Sophie whined. "Your plants will still be here tomorrow, but I will have to go to work."

The cutting Janelle had planted just to the right was only about half the size of Ivy's. Ivy scorned herself for the prideful feeling it gave her, but she couldn't help that there was just something about her touch that made a difference. It had to be knowledge her mother had given her. Ivy wiped her hands across her skirt before she lay down beside Sophie.

"So," Sophie declared suddenly. She and Ivy lay back on opposite cushions, only their faces turned toward each other as their feet splayed in opposite directions. Ivy plucked an orange slice from Sophie's palm. Branches and leaves hung over them, fluttering amidst the breeze through the open garden gate. "Now that I finally have you alone. What really happened in Asmye?"

The orange in Ivy's mouth turned sour. Tartness vibrated through her as her mind flashed over the moments that led her here. Ivy swallowed.

"The King sent me here to deal with my father," Ivy paused. Luc waited outside the conservatory while Ivy tried to relax on the other side of the door.

"Bullshit." The accusation hung in the air between them, Sophie unsatisfied with her friend's response.

Ivy brushed a piece of pith off her bodice and watched it crumple on the ground. "I see you think there is no need for decorum."

"You're at home. Talk to me."

"I've been told there are some financial concerns. Rian thought it best that I oversee them on his behalf. A sort of liaison between-" Ivy wanted to stop talking, but she spilled erroneous details of invented conversations. It was better than telling the truth. The concerned crease between Sophie's brows didn't allay the nerves in Ivy's chest.

"You know, you can always tell me anything, especially the truth." Sophie reached for Ivy's hand. "Are you and Rian okay?"

"I'll bet he's just fine." Ivy's lips tightened. "That priestess mentioned that he was away from the castle. The Holy Father sent a letter."

"That creepy as shit old man you wrote to me about?" Sophie rolled over to one side and rested on her elbow.

Ivy had a laugh, "That would be the one. I suppose he thinks he's charming. Rian certainly seems to think so. Sometimes, I think he wants it for me and Rian to work out more than I do. It's the elevation of his religion over me that bothers me the most." Ivy looked toward the door, hoping Luc might have heard.

"We've had some of that since you left." Sophie plucked a piece of grass from the ground.

"What do you mean?"

"Your dad's getting into this religion thing, too."

"What do you mean?" Ivy repeated as she rolled to her side.

"He's not forcing it but it's clearly been endorsed." Ivy tapped her fingers on the ground, scanning the dirt as if it could speak to her. "It's as fashionable as Asmyian wine or painting your lips red - although I think that one could be blamed on you. That priestess, whatever her name is-"

"-Natassa." Ivy's heart pounded in her chest as her eyes drifted to her hand. She closed her fist to hide the scar on her palm. "Can I tell you something?"

Sophie turned to The Queen and rested her head on her propped-up hand. "Anything, always."

A small twinge of panic settled in Ivy's chest. Her father's plan to convince the island of Rian's religion as a good thing or something to be welcomed was working. If he convinced Sophie that he was sincere, there was no telling who else could be a believer now. Ivy pursed her lips to the side, swallowing the truth. She couldn't tell Sophie one thing without telling her everything. "Actually, I'm sorry. I interrupted you. What were you going to say about Natassa?"

If Sophie noticed the subject change, she didn't let on. "Just that she's been seen in the castle. Word is she has the King's favor and speaks as if she has the authority of the court."

"Is that true?" Ivy leaned in.

"I don't know. Is it?"

The two locked their eyes in a stalemate. Sophie's raised eyebrow forced Ivy to speak. "Rian doesn't tell me much of what he does with Father Trevarthan." *Or anyone else, for that matter.*

Sophie paused and pursed her lips, recalling what Ivy said about the old man before. "Why wouldn't it work out? And why would you get information about your husband from some old priest?" Sophie was too good at catching the truth.

Ivy lay her head back on the pillow and fiddled with the flower stem in her hands. *Because he's a monster.* That's what she wanted to say. "You'd have to ask the King himself. Obviously, he can't be bothered to write me."

Sophie rolled flat on her back, deciding which words from her friend were false. "You wrote such nice things about him," she hesitated and narrowed her eyes. "In fact, you wrote only nice things about him. You're hiding something from me, Ivy. What happened?"

Ivy huffed, "I'm not hiding anything."

"Did he do something?"

Lie better. Ivy could think of a dozen things he'd done to her off the top of her head. Intertwined with those, though, were those moments of intimacy and power that she'd been empty of since she left the Asmyian shore.

"He's obsessed with his war. He has plenty of control over the world, but it will never be enough for him." Tears started to form in Ivy's eyes. "And all I do is wait in his bed to perform my duty while the world cares only about him. My whole life is only an afterthought in the wake of kingly decisions," The words came quicker and quicker. The leaves underscored her words as if Ivy's agitation itself rustled through them. "As if I would simply disappear, turn to mist if it wasn't for my relation to weak, vain men with delusions of grandeur. I mean no more to them than any other pretty trinket they possess. I am sick of being reduced to chattel!" Sophie watched Ivy cover her face with her hands, palms pressing against her eyeballs. "And yet they go on and on about their God and destiny, filling their vaults with gold and treasures from the far corners of the world. As if nothing else matters. Running amok while I am a prisoner inside my own head."

Sophie sighed, "Finally, a truth, even if it is vague. I ask for the truth out of concern, not curiosity. I see you clearer than almost anyone. You don't need to hide from me."

"I don't want to keep secrets from you. I feel my thoughts are not even my own anymore! Every word from my lips has me tied in knots."

"Is there anything good to tell me of your husband?"

Ivy paused. Of course, there was. Ivy spent many happy days with Rian at the jousts, at the beach, in bed. But there were many painful days, too. "I just don't think I'm good at being a wife. I didn't ask for this!"

Sophie reached for Ivy's hand. She had avoided that fate longer than her friend, a small victory of being a peasant. "Being kept has never suited you, but I bet he just wants to keep you safe."

"By hardly allowing me out of the castle?"

"Isn't it cold there? Why would you want to leave anyway?" An attempt to diffuse Ivy's anger.

Ivy pursed her lips. If she hadn't told Sophie the truth, she couldn't be frustrated that she didn't understand. "You know, he told me once of Lutrya and their *beautiful libraries*. He promised he would take me, but all he does is leave me inside stone walls, and I can never guess if he's coming back."

"It's barely been half a year, Ivy. You have plenty of time to spend his money."

"There was one time I thought he was dead," The mood shifted and a stone's weight sank in Ivy's stomach as she remembered his injury and how she threw herself over his dying body. She could still hear his screams as his whore stayed by his side. Sophie didn't need to know that yet, not until Ivy knew she was safe in Iosnos, when the ships stayed away.

Ivy recanted the story of Rian's recovery. Nausea swirled her stomach as the putrid smell of poison wafted in her memories. The lengths she went to. The sleepless nights. All while she was too blind to see the lies he paraded around her. It didn't matter to her that Colette said it should be expected. Rian was hers. And she wanted to be his. The wound was still seared with that pain in her heart.

"You never told me any of that," Sophie was as solemn as Ivy had ever seen.

"If my letters ever got into the wrong hands, who knows what would happen?"

"But you've been here for weeks and never said anything."

"I don't like to think of it."

Sophie watched Ivy bite her lip and turn her head. "You're worried for his safety? While he's gone?"

Ivy inhaled. Maybe she was. Her fears for Rian and of Rian blended so well; who could tell where one began and another ended? All she had wanted was to leave and find her freedom, find herself again, but nothing made Ivy forget her husband.

"It's okay to worry. It's what wives do." Sophie's tone lightened, then sobered again when she looked over at Ivy, eyes glassy as she stared at the ceiling. "Has he told you he loves you?"

A blink loosened a tear as Ivy recalled Rian begging forgiveness for his infidelity while claiming how he prized his wife. "He has."

"He'll come for you, then."

Ivy forced herself to hold back a laugh. "He never has before."

Near sunrise, Rian pushed aside the heavy cream canvas and walked into the medical tent. Those who could stand were quick to show their respect to the King. The others were lined up in their cots, broken and bandaged. Nurses scurried around, tending to the men and their wounds. They were so busy looking down at their patients, that hardly any of them raised their heads to notice, much less to honor their King. Tristan sat in a wooden chair, half-stripped of his clothes with his chest and belly out. Blood smeared down his arm. He held a bandage over his wound. A nurse walked by, and Tristan raised his hand to get her attention but got passed over.

"Can't be too bad with the way they ignore you," Rian chuckled.

"You'd think I'd be used to being ignored by beautiful women," Tristan grimaced as he pulled away the bandage to look where the arrow had cut him. "Why are you here? You don't even have a hair out of place."

"Is the King not allowed to ensure his General is well?" Rian sat in a chair across from Tristan. He spoke quieter, "My father always said making an appearance raises the soldier's spirits after a loss."

"I didn't think we lost." Tristan cocked a half-smile.

"They caught us with our dicks in our hands." Rian shook his head. "How did they even get that close?"

"Your Majesty, we have watchmen, dogs, spies."

"Why didn't we know?! How did they even know I'm here?"

Tristan's eyes narrowed. "You think there's a man inside."

"Ah, glad you decided to join us, General," Rian affectionately snarked. "We need to tighten our communications."

"Who can you trust?"

"Torin, Malcolm, Dieter's a fuck up, but he wouldn't go against me. You, maybe." A dimple sank in Rian's cheek with his tilted smile. "My wife." Pain shot across the king's face. He loved her as much as he trusted her. "Father Trevarthan. If we are getting specific, the head of household staff."

"The inner sanctum, then?"

"Although, they would all know how best to leave me vulnerable." The only one he could potentially believe would seek to hurt him was Ivy. Her face, scorned and hopeless, had seared into his heart. He hated that he had caused her pain. Would she have sought out Bloidar for revenge? *No.*

Rian looked up at the nurse walking by. Blue eyes caught his. One of her blonde hairs fell out of its tie and haphazardly clung to the glisten on her neck. The dew on her lips enticed him, asking him to take another bite. He found himself tempted even in the worst moments. He hadn't touched her in so long. He hadn't even wanted to. But it was hard to deny out here when only Adievasinis knew what might happen tomorrow.

King Rian found his wedding reception dull, with hordes of requests coming from the crowd. He should have known people would use any moment, even his wedding, to try to get something from him. Danielle caught Rian's eye over the soft curve of her shoulders. He had felt the creamy silk skin under his hands countless times, but with preparations to wed his new bride, it had been too long. Rian's mouth watered at the thought of wrapping that golden hair in his fist, of taking her again. Danielle glanced forward, tilting her head toward the empty hall. The blue in her gown unmistakably matched the longing in her glassy eyes. She looked deceivingly innocent as silk butterflies and flowers decorated her cinched waist and ample bosom. Without a look at his bride, he followed her into the hall.

Rian loved the way her mouth fell open as she moaned. Danielle sat atop a credenza with her dress pulled up over her spread thighs. She dragged her nails down his clothed back, pushing Rian deeper inside her.

"Where have you been?" he asked, dipping his tongue into her mouth. Danielle pushed back on his chest and rested her forehead on his chin. Rian kissed her before pulling her jaw up to face him. "Tell me."

"I was ill, my king." Danielle inhaled and slid her hands on Rian's neck, pulling him in.

"Did you not think to call on me?" Instead of answering, she wrapped her legs around the King's hips and smashed her lips on his. That would keep him quiet. Rian grabbed her and fucked his cock deeper inside her. Her hand slammed against the wall behind her for support. He put a palm over her mouth as she whined out for him.

"I'm not finished." King Rian pulled Danielle off her seat and spun her to face the door. Anyone from the reception might have heard him, but he didn't care. His wife could even have come to investigate where her new husband had wandered off to. Rian wasn't worried. If what her father promised was true, Rian suspected she would be too meek, too docile. He'd get to her later.

"Tell me again," Danielle whimpered, her face pressed against the door.

Rian grabbed her throat from behind and yanked her back to look up at him. "It doesn't mean anything." His long finger pressed into her cheek, forcing her plush pink lips into a pout. He slammed into her hard just to watch her wince. "Nothing is going to change." He flicked his tongue across her lips. "She's nothing to me," Danielle beamed. The door rattled when he slammed her back against it.

Danielle didn't linger when the King caught her eyes. Other men needed her attention. The sourness of shame filled his stomach. Shame for how he hurt Ivy. Shame for how he treated Danielle. Shame for how stupid he'd been. Cunt on principle still had a price.

"You alright?"

Rian snapped back into focus when Tristan spoke. "Yeah, I-" Rian struggled to pick up his thoughts. "Generalities only to any outside parties. Let's regroup. I want Torin on this."

"I'll send for him." Tristan slapped his hands on his thigh before he moved to get up. He couldn't wait on a nurse all day.

"A trusted and unmarked rider."

"In code?"

Rian nodded.

"I can't wait to listen to him bitch about his saddle sores." Tristan looked past his King. A young man approached in his uniform.

"Sir Tristan?"

"What is it?"

"We intercepted a Bloidarian messenger in the hills. He was bringing this." The soldier held out a piece of parchment sealed with the Bloidarian mark of two crows. He nervously glanced over at the King. When Rian looked up at him, the soldier's gaze darted away in fear.

Tristan accepted the envelope and shooed away the soldier. "Suppose you don't need the middleman anymore." Tristan handed the envelope over to Rian.

Rian broke the seal and scanned the words. "It's the chancellor. She wants a conclave."

"Will you go?"

"I think I will." Rian stood, his eyes still inspecting the note. "Still send for Torin. I should be back before he arrives. Hold steady."

A northern wind called Ivy and Luc out to the farmlands that resided at the center of Iosnos. There was a lightness in her chest. Sharing a truth, even a partial one, with Sophie had lessened the burden in Ivy's heart. For all the distance she'd put between her and Asmye, she'd yet to really leave it. Maybe this was a start.

Luc turned to put himself between Ivy and a wagon approaching on the south road. The farmer who drove it pulled back on his reins.

"Good afternoon," The man tipped his hat. A dog sat beside him on the wagon. Luc nodded and attempted to shield Ivy from the man's view. "Would you like a lift? I'm headed as far north as Taroti."

Ivy poked her head out from behind Luc's shoulder. "Thank you, that would be lovely."

"Oh! Is that Princess Ivy?" The man smirked.

"It is indeed." Her chest puffed with pride.

"You will address her as your Queen." Luc took a step forward as if to finish a fight no one started.

"Stop that," Ivy whispered. She recognized the farmer from the market some years ago. "And thank you for your kindness."

"Of course, Your Majesty." The farmer extended a hand but Luc grabbed Ivy instead. "Hop on up."

Ivy scratched behind the dog's ear. His head tilted in enjoyment. She climbed up into the back of the wagon and sat with her legs dangling. Luc jumped up and sat beside her. He adjusted the books Ivy had chosen in the satchel at his side. The wagon jolted as it started forward. Luc quickly steadied Ivy, letting his hand linger near her hip for the ride.

Moments passed without a word between them, rolling slowly on the road. Ivy looked over her shoulder to check that the farmer wasn't looking.

"What?" She looked at Luc's unchanged helmet.

"You are fearless."

"I don't think it's fearless so much as not having inherent distrust in people." The sun glinted off her smile. He grabbed her hand. Excitement sparked in her chest. "I trusted you as soon as I met you. You scared me, but I still knew." She knew he saw her through all the haze of her life. No clouds of wife, duty, or mother obscured her in his eyes. They couldn't shade her in any light as long as he knew her.

"I worry," Luc scanned the horizon, "that I won't be there when you need me."

Ivy laughed and recalled his words, "You've always got your eye on me."

It was hard for Ivy to focus on the book she held precariously above her face. Luc's hand gently ran through her curls as she lay in his lap under the Jacaranda tree. He twirled the strands, letting the curl wrap itself around his fingertip. The seclusion of nature allowed them more freedom in their affections. Ivy peered around the pages of her book to peek up at Luc. His own book rested in one of his hands and stole his attention. The light that cast through the purple blooms bathed him in a lavender glow. Ivy's eyes flicked back down to her pages. She couldn't find where she had left off and turned a page back.

"I don't think I'll ever finish this book under these conditions."

"Is it too warm?"

"Not at all." Ivy's cheeks creased as she smiled. "Too distracted by my man and how pretty he is."

"You think I'm pretty?" Luc closed his book and set it aside. "How would you know?" Luc rested his hand on her leg.

"I know what I see, and all I see is a beautiful man," Ivy sighed.

"Then why do you sigh?"

"I miss your eyes and have never seen them." Ivy reached up and slid her fingers under the edge of his helmet. Her fingers stroked his cheek.

"Querida, you-"

"I know, I know." Ivy pulled her hand away and pretended to regain interest in her book. "You can't because of your oaths. Your religion is very sacred." She wished the earth would swallow her whole.

"It's not something to be trifled with, Querida. There are consequences, and I do not speak of punishments dealt by men. Adievasinis is powerful." Luc rubbed his hand tenderly against her leg.

"There is magic in the world. I know that," Ivy sighed while the Jacaranda blooms fluttered. She felt the power of Adievasinis many times with Rian. Often, it felt like the intoxicating rush of love. She swallowed hard. "I understand that it is important to you, and you are important to me. I just - I don't trust that blood magick. It is misleading and thrives on violence and pain."

"Is there magic that you do trust?"

Ivy felt the smile in his timbre. "Magick is known by many different names," she smiled and lifted her fingers in the cool breeze. Luc clasped his fingers with hers, and Ivy brought both hands to her chest. "The wind is magic, but you might believe it is the breath of some god. Maybe it is the mountain's exhale. It moves our ships across the sea. Without it, we would have never met, nor would we be in this place now." Luc's leather glove was supple and worn. She pulled at the fingers to slide it away from his hand before kissing each finger.

"I would have swum across the ocean if I knew you were on the other side." Luc pulled his hand away, causing Ivy to whine, but her whimper changed to a moan when he softly squeezed her leg and pushed her dress to her knees.

"What makes the Jacaranda bloom delicate purple when every other tree is lush with green?" Ivy let her book fall to her side. "It could be magic or the bees or just how Ouraina made them."

"She loves beauty above all else." Luc's hand crept further up Ivy's leg.

"Where we came from, a seed or blood, or if we just stood one day as if we woke from a dream, it's all magick to me. I don't question the specifics. I only question devotion to the idea of knowing."

"What about believing?"

"Are they not the same thing?"

"No." His hand slid up her thigh under her dress. "Belief is trust, trust in a feeling." Luc skimmed his fingertips over her pussy.

Ivy let a soft gasp escape her lips. "What about trust in me?"

Luc brushed his gloved hand over his lover's cheek. How couldn't she believe he trusted her? "Often, we know nothing." He nestled his finger against her clit and drew achingly slow circles. "Or so very little, but it informs our beliefs."

"And what do you believe?" Ivy stared up into his faceless gaze.

"I believe in a God who saved my life because he knew I had something to live for, even if I didn't." Luc increased the pressure on his fingertips.

Ivy hummed in agreement as her lashes fluttered closed. "Luc," she whined.

"Yes, Querida?"

"Keep talking," Ivy licked her lips.

"The Gods take lovers." His finger slipped down along her folds, spreading her wetness. "Other gods and even humans." His wide finger pressed into her. He stared at her chest. Every breath and moan swelled it. Her neck stretched back. Beads of sweat gathered at her collarbone. "Chosen few are descendants of those affairs." Luc slipped a second finger inside her pussy. Ivy tried hard to suppress the moan that he coaxed from her. "Would you fuck a God, Querida?"

"Y- yes," she groaned out through heavy breaths.

"I am Adievasinis' body. That is what it means to be Adeshbu." Luc curled his fingers as he stroked them in and out of her.

Ivy's hand searched for something to brace herself. It found Luc's chest plate and gripped its edge. Her other hand grabbed at her breast, squeezing it tightly. Luc put his hand over hers, holding her there. He pumped his fingers harder.

"I fuck you with a God's body." His breath was heavy, panting. "But you, you are heaven in the flesh. So much beauty, lust, and pain tied up in you. You ache to be taken, harder, faster."

Ivy's hips bucked up and down to meet his motion, desperate to get more of him however she could. "Please,"

"Even now, you want to push it further. I can see it in your face." Luc pulled his fingers from inside her and rubbed his hand down her cunt. Her ample wetness had spread along her lips, down her ass, and the inside

117

of her thighs. When he dipped back inside her, she felt so much fuller. Three fingers stretched her. Her failure to mute herself was met with his hand across her mouth. Luc gripped her face tightly as Ivy screamed and moaned into his hand. Her body writhed against the grass as she came. Her dizzied eyes tried to fix on the purple leaves above her, but it was all unfocused as she came down in Luc's arms.

CHAPTER FIFTEEN

Pastoral life seemed luxurious for the horses in Iosnos' endless summer. The castle stables were quaint and mostly unoccupied, save the carriages stored there. The note Adne left Malcolm had specified the stables at midday but not much else. Malcolm wandered in lazy circles, pretending the fluttering in his stomach wasn't there. Boredom-fueled curiosity manifested in interest in the mundane. The well-used and worn bits of tack. A stack of buckets just slightly askew. A few carrots had fallen from a bushel. It was easy to imagine the hustle of first light. Stable hands working in stalls and filling wheelbarrows with sweet alfalfa. The midday lull was soft and quiet except for Malcolm's pattering footsteps. He glanced into one of the stalls; a petite mare and her days-old foal rested in fresh bedding. He hummed at the sweet sight, but it was not the soldier's flame that he so desired.

"It's cute the way you don't know what to do with idle time." Adne's croon made Malcolm jump.

Malcolm rattled. "How long have you been lurking?"

Adne leaned casually against a carriage. "Not too long."

"You Adeshbu love to sneak up on people."

"It's one of many skills we possess." Adne approached his prize and whispered, "People are most truthful when they shed the worry of being observed."

"And what truth did I reveal?"

"Nothing I didn't already know." Adne interlaced his fingers with Malcolm's. "Come. I've just been at the market."

Adne pulled Malcolm's hand toward a carriage. The wooden wheels creaked as they stepped inside. Malcolm was surprised to see fruit, cheese, and crab already arranged on one of the seats. A ripe mango was sliced and splayed. The vibrant yellow fruit was dusted with a deep red spice except where a bite was missing.

"Luxurious for someone with a measly allowance from the church," Malcolm remarked. "It's not the first time I've wondered about your deep pockets."

"Gold is easy to get when I need it." Adne fussed with a curtain over the window as they sat across from each other. "I have no desire to hoard it, but plenty of people do, and they are the easiest to lighten."

"What must you do to gain it?" Malcolm remembered Adne's familiarity with Endaya and swallowed.

Adne smiled, energy charging between his thighs, "Wouldn't you like to know?" He tapped Malcolm's chin, then stared through the curtain to ascertain they were alone.

Malcolm touched Adne's helmet and turned the knight's visor toward him. His lips parted with a sharp breath. Every dalliance only left him hungry for more. Adne slipped to his knees. His hands gripped Malcolm's muscular thighs. Malcolm pulled Adne's helmet off, uncovering the lust that glinted in Adne's eyes. It was easy to lose count of how many secret liaisons they fit between obligation and duty. Malcolm pulled Adne up into his kiss. Malcolm shuddered as Adne sucked on his bottom lip. Adne's long fingers pressed into Malcolm's cheek and neck as he held him close. Malcolm could taste the mango, sweet on Adne's tongue. Adne sank between Malcolm's thighs and took his cock in his mouth. As Adne attended his knight lovingly, Malcolm picked up the mango and sank his teeth in. When both had their fill, they ate.

"The food here is stunning." Adne licked his fingers for more than just mango juice.

"It's quite nice." Malcolm leaned back in his seat. "The whole place. Wouldn't mind coming back. Although, I think my perception may be skewed." He nudged Adne's leg with his foot.

"That does tint things quite nicely." Adne flashed his teeth in a laugh. "I hope we stay through winter. I wouldn't mind not freezing my balls off in that church."

"Do you know when we might leave?" Malcolm fiddled with his fingers. "I don't like to be away from my family for too long."

"As far as I know, there is no plan for the immediate future. Your King is making moves. The war is progressing, but beyond the ships, I don't know how Iosnos plays into it. So even if we're not here, I doubt we will go back." Adne scratched his nails through his beard. "There is enough trouble in Iosnos without outside influence. The problem with the raiders and pirates is deeply rooted in the island. I fear that it is a Hydra. Remove one head only to find two more pop up elsewhere."

"But you've got them running scared. I've seen what Baalestan and the new patrols have shut down based on your intelligence."

Adne waved his hand dismissively. "They'll just get smarter about outmaneuvering us. The work we are doing now is but a small skirmish in an ongoing campaign. The King must maintain a presence here for years to eradicate it. It's become quite clear that the other is a lame duck."

"You will weaken it," Malcolm reassured him. "What have you heard of John?"

"Ineffectual. Unfocused. Intellectually witless. Stuck in the past." Adne fingers counted the ways in which the King of Iosnos failed. "The way he treats his successor? He is a small man clinging to a legacy of failure."

"And my King?"

"Capable. Smart. Effective. Stuck in the past," Adne laughed. "Clearly, Asmye is a successful monarchy, but he wastes his reign on pettiness driven by religious extremism and a dead man's wishes."

"Religious extremism?" Malcolm laughed. "That's rich coming from an Adeshbu."

"I thought it was pretty clear that none of this," Adne gestured to his helmet, "matters to me."

"Then why do it?"

"It wasn't my choice. I was a thief by trade before. Ad Onondian was, too. Baalestan and the others, I don't know where they came from." Adne didn't seem to care either. "I was arrested, sold to slavers, and then, in turn, bought by the church. Men who survive the training are lucky, and once you're in, it's impossible to get out. If I could get out, I would, but it guarantees a full stomach and a place to sleep. Better than I was doing before."

"So you don't believe in Adievasinis?"

"No!" Adne let out a laugh, "It's a story to comfort the men who can't comprehend that their predisposition for violence is a character flaw. I'm well aware of my own flaws and that I'm not a good person. I kill because it's necessary, and I'm good at it. Fuck the gods."

"I thought you didn't have the stomach for violence."

"And you do? Enjoy it, that is?"

Malcolm stiffened, gripping his knee before turning to stone.

"Torture is different from violence. I don't get off on hurting people like some of you Knights. That Dieter, that's a sick fuck. Nice guy, but sick."

The butterflies turned into dust. Malcolm shifted. "Is there anything you don't know about the circles we run in?"

"Information is my trade, Knight. More valuable than almost anything in this world as long as you know the right things about the right people. There is an alluring power to it. Just having the knowledge that could tear worlds apart and crumble people. It's not that I desire to do so but the possession of that potential." The lust in Adne's eyes sparked again. "Most of it is just gossip. Fun for a laugh."

"Then tell me something that will make me laugh."

"Sir Torin. He's got a nervous tummy. Shits his brains out when he's stressed."

Luc waited outside Ivy's chamber door. A few minutes could feel like an eternity, but he practiced patience. His eyes and ears were keen to the comings and goings of servants. The bustle quieted in the evenings. When he was sure no one would see, Luc slipped into the room.

Ivy lay back in her chaise, reading by candlelight. The moon was far away, shining on other lovers who could relax in plain sight. Her eyes turned knowingly to the door, hips twisted, causing a comely fold at her waist. The lift in her expression beckoned him closer.

"I've missed you." Ivy reached her hand up.

"And I you." Luc helped her to her feet. "Even if it was barely half an hour."

"Too long for me," she giggled, looking into his visor. Ivy was quick to start removing his gloves. "We waste so much time pretending."

"It is to keep you safe."

Ivy exaggerated her pout. "I curse my safety, for it keeps me away from you."

"Don't say such things." He stroked her cheek with soft fingertips. "Adievasinis brought me to your side to keep you safe, and safe is where I'll keep you, even if it means away from me."

"Your god was the reason I was sold to that man."

"Two sides of the same coin."

"It seems I get less of you than when we were in Astrella." She loosened the cowl of his cape.

"Our circumstances have changed, and we now have reason to hide. We are no longer innocent in this," His tone shifted as he surveilled Ivy's body in motion. "Gods will forsake us for the sins we commit."

"Let them," Ivy smiled. "I only want you." Ivy blew out the last lingering candle flicker, thickening the air with darkness. She held out her hands until she found Luc's body and pressed against his chest plate.

"You say you are God's body." She pulled at the buckles secured over his shoulders. They were heavy as she lifted them away.

"This is Adievasinis' armor, forged in his temp-"

"No," Ivy cut Luc off. "Let me say this." Ivy pressed her palm flat against his chest. "This is a man." Luc held his hand over hers softly. "Not God's flesh, but his own. Not Adeshbu, not Ad Onondian." Ivy's hands held his helmet firmly as she lifted it away in the darkness. A whisper of fear in Luc's breath was suddenly apparent. Ivy held his face in her palms. "You are a man, Luc." Tears welled in her eyes. "Please. Let me know you."

It was then that Luc cursed himself, too. If not for his oaths, he would have kissed her face as it radiated in the sunlight as soon as he could. Ivy had been patient with him, pressing, yes, as was her nature, but she showed him more respect than God. He'd only killed for her, not because of her. He took one of his Queen's hands and pressed her fingers against his lips. He smiled as her soft sigh melted against him. He could not hide his desire any longer.

Luc grabbed Ivy around the waist, clenching her dress in his grip. She had looked so beautiful in the soft orange fabric. Sometimes, he wondered if she dressed as if it was an adornment of her body, her gift to him. If his body could be reborn as a sacrifice to Adievasinis, Ouraina blessed Ivy with beauty inside and out.

He drew Ivy closer, the sweet scent of lavender blooming in her wild hair. His heart thumped as Ivy glided her arms around his neck and rested her head against his chest. Luc hummed. Ivy sighed in his arms, locking her hands behind his neck, afraid to let him go. Gently, he unhooked himself and stepped backward.

"Trust me, Querida."

Ivy kept her arm outstretched, whining when her lover left her touch. After a few steps, she didn't hear anything at all. She gasped when something touched her face.

"I told you to trust me," Warm words whispered against Ivy's neck, followed by soft kisses and the playful nip between Luc's lips. After one more kiss, he tied a knot in the fabric around Ivy's brow.

"I already cannot see," she stood, unsteady without Luc to balance her. She tilted her head when she heard a stroke against metal, then another, and the hiss of a flame behind her.

"So I can gaze upon you. Too long I've suffered without beholding you to me." Luc dragged his fingers against Ivy's shoulder, pulling her sleeves down until her dress rested around her hips. She reached out for him, but Luc blocked her hands in, gliding his arms around Ivy's bare back, untying the knots in her stay until it loosened to where he could push the rest of the colorful fabric to the floor. Luc tried to hide his growl, exposing her body, silhouetted in the firelight. "You look beautiful, Querida."

A chilly breeze blew in through the open balcony door. Gooseflesh raised on Ivy's bare skin. Luc slid his tongue over his lips as he watched her try to cover herself.

"Don't, Querida. Let me look at you."

Ivy rested her hands at her sides, fingers brushing against the curve of her hips and the supple dips where they met her legs. A queen obeyed him: an orphan, a nobody. Luc stiffened. She shifted her weight from one foot to the other, waiting for further instruction. Patience was never a virtue she possessed, and he took pleasure in denying her. Luc purred as he gazed at the small lines on the tops of her breasts. Just like *hers*. Luc was silent

123

again, but his aura traced around Ivy like any motion she made would find her skin on his.

"Please," Ivy whispered, catching Luc's strong arm as he encircled her. "I need you."

Her desperation to uncover his body, to be close, thrilled Luc. Not even in his wildest dreams was her desire so needy. He finally felt some kind of power as he took in her soft, graceful shape. Luc lifted his hand to Ivy's cheek. The velvet of her skin nestled in his palm. He inched closer to her lips, and Ivy's breath sharpened with anguish. His lips were too far, if only a whisper away from her aching mouth.

"Pray for me, Querida." Luc's hand slid down to her pulse. He couldn't help himself as he tightened his grip. His words were soft, "On your knees."

Ivy sank before him, Luc's hand guiding her gently to the floor. She tapped her hand over her heart with a bowed head, just as she'd been taught. Her fingers intertwined in front of her chest.

She murmured, "Mi berain tu taliaire cept aline."

My heart is contented in devotion. Luc shuddered as he watched her, fire gnawing in his belly as she repeated one of the first prayers he had ever learned. He lifted her chin, and her words stopped. He skimmed his thumb across her full bottom lip.

"What comes next?"

Words slipped from between her lips, "Ai dulia mi Vass."

I serve my God.

Luc grinned and slipped his thumb between her lips. He pressed down on Ivy's tongue, opening her mouth wide. Spit smeared down her bottom lip as Luc pulled out his thumb.

"Keep your hands there," Luc motioned to Ivy's chest, although she could not see. She was obedient, mouth open and ready for him. Luc's cock throbbed as it slid against her tongue. Hollows sank into Ivy's cheek as she sucked. As he thrust quicker, her fingers dug into his thighs to steady herself. Luc brushed back the hair that fell on her face. Her beauty could challenge any rose that bloomed from Ouraina's own hand: soft, delicate, heavenly beauty. Her eyes. He wished to have them look upon him, confessing the longing they possessed through only his visor.

Ivy kissed the underside of the head, stroking his spit-soaked length with her hand. Her face tilted up towards him. The knot of her blindfold brushed against his fingertips. It tempted him. He could do it. It would only be a slight tug for it to slip from her eyes. She desired it so badly. There was a tightness in his chest. He squeezed his eyes tight. His fingertips moved away. His grip on her curls strained, and she whined. He pushed his cock into her throat, eliciting an involuntary gulp from Ivy's mouth. He held her there. A growl rumbled in his chest with a bull-like exhale. Her mouth watered around him, then he pushed back and released her. Ivy gasped for air.

Luc pounced, devouring Ivy's lips in a kiss like she were his prey, yanking her to him with brute strength. His hands tangled in her hair as he pulled her closer. Her hands gripped his waist, clinging to him and moaning against the bristles in his mustache. She pressed her chest against him, silently begging for his touch. With one hand at the base of Ivy's neck and another around her back, Luc swung Ivy until he could plunge her into her bed, sinking into silk and linen. It wasn't clandestine here. Not in this bed. Life fell away when he lifted her hips and pressed into her.

Luc drank in Ivy's whimper. She reached up, fingertips searching for the expression to match the hitch in his breath. Luc snatched her hands away. He leaned his weight into her wrists, pinned against the mattress. Ivy writhed beneath him. He never had a lover like Ivy. Her desperation met his. She burned like the sun.

"Fuck," Ivy's lips trembled when Luc sucked hard on her nipple. His grip on her wrists relaxed. Every touch of her soft flesh was heaven as his hands slid down her shape. Gentle pain ripped at Luc's scalp when she dug her fingers into his hair. It only spurred him to bite down on her breast. Ivy's breath sharpened, but she held him there. Luc smiled when he flicked his tongue over her hard nipple. It was only a tease before he sank his teeth into her again. Ivy's cunt clenched down around his cock. He could play with her like this for hours. She took her pleasure in all forms. The pain came again when she pulled him by his curls to her hungry lips.

Her breath was hot against the sweat tensing in his shoulder. Ivy clung to Luc's body as if she might fall if she loosened her hold. His bicep hooked under her thigh and pulled it higher. A gasp quivered in her lips as he hit inside of her just right.

"Don't stop." A blush rushed through her cheeks. His skin was tacky where her hands pressed into his back.

"Beg me."

She slapped Luc's back, urging him to take her. Luc fucked her harder, then clasped his fingers around her throat. Her mouth hung open, silently begging for air.

"Beg me!"

"God, please!" She squeaked, scratching her nails into Luc's back. In his groan, he loosened his hold, and Ivy gasped. "Please, Luc, please,"

Luc would have preferred *God*.

Her moans were quiet little secrets she whispered in his ear. His nose pressed into her cheek. Groaning, Luc squeezed his eyes tight as if he could control the rush. Ivy's feet flexed as his thrusts rammed her higher on the bed. Her fingers clenched the hair at the base of his neck. Ivy held back her scream when the first contraction hit her. Her sounds reduced to repressed, shaking breaths as she twitched. His chest heaved against her, rutting his body into hers, a god to a goddess. Ivy muttered his name as his length stroked her. Luc's face pressed deeper into her cheek, burying her voice into the darkest recesses of his mind. He clenched his teeth with restraint as he pulled out. He barely touched himself and came on Ivy's thigh and stomach. He collapsed on top of her, sinking her deeper into the mattress. They lay there a long while, sweat cooling them off in the candle glow. When Ivy was sure Luc was snoring, she untangled herself and made her way toward the shimmer of light she could see through the fabric. It took a few tries to extinguish the flame before she felt safe enough to remove the blindfold. Following Luc's gruff humming, Ivy climbed back into bed and wrapped herself around him, holding Luc's body tight against her chest.

CHAPTER SIXTEEN

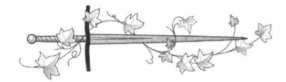

The warmth from the morning sun kissed Ivy's shoulder, waking her gently. Her body was still heavy from exertion the night before. A hum of soft sleeping breath filled her ears. Her eyelids shot open. Luc had always left before dawn but now slept beside her, unhelmeted in the morning light. His brown curls stared back at her. She couldn't deny the disappointment. If only he weren't turned away from her. She so desired to know her lover completely. To see his face. Still, she stared, admiring all the loops and waves of his hair. The little fold of his shoulder wrinkled from the position of his arm. His beautiful skin was marred with so many scars. The lines told a story about the person who wore them. The story Luc's skin told was about suffering. Ivy wished her touch might take the pain away from him. When she reached out with her fingertips, Luc's breath changed. Ivy shut her eyes tight, pretending only to have moved in her sleep. The bed shifted.

"Fuck," Luc groaned softly. Before he could lift himself from the sheets, Ivy lunged out to hold him from behind.

"Don't go yet." She brushed her lips against his neck. She could just open her eyes. She wanted to, desperately. All it would take was just a second. Luc would never even know.

"Querida, I have to. I shouldn't even be here now." Luc's voice was thicker with grogginess. Ivy's palm wandered down his chest and across the soft shape of his tummy. She hummed, deigning herself to obey the rules to keep her eyes closed.

"Don't you know what day it is?" Ivy tugged on his ear with her teeth.

Luc groaned, putting his hand over hers as she held him from behind. "I think it's the 17th."

"You're right," Ivy smiled. "that means I get what I want."

"And what is it that you want, Your Grace?" There was a playful smirk in his voice.

"You know." Ivy slid her hand beneath the sheets. She wrapped her fingers around his cock. Luc's breath hitched as she tugged on him.

"Do you ever not want that?" Luc laughed.

Ivy laid a benevolent bite on his shoulder while considering his query. "Not that I can recall." She let her hand drift back up to his chest, twirling her fingertips in the brown hair. "Why? Are a woman's desires so ungodly? So sinful?" Ivy smiled as her fingers landed in Luc's mouth. He sucked and flicked his tongue between her fingers. "I think it's natural." Ivy hummed as her grip found its way back around his cock. Luc stiffened as she stroked him. His breaths sharpened when she smeared a drop of come across the tip.

"We really shouldn't," Luc protested, but he made no genuine attempt to stop her. He gripped his hand into her naked hip behind him and tilted his head to look at the Queen. He stared as her mouth dropped open, but her eyes stayed shut. She was so beautiful, hair mussed from their romp in the sheets. He watched her, contemplating if there was time to take her again. Ivy moved faster, delighting in every quiet, pained moan from her lover's lips.

Ivy's body jolted when a knock rapped at her chamber door. She almost opened her eyes. Luc jumped from the bed, pulling on his britches and slipping his helmet over his face.

"Just a moment!" Ivy shouted. A rush of cool morning air hit her skin as Luc silently slipped onto the balcony. She threw blankets over his boots and armor that lay bedside. She carefully stepped over them and into her dressing gown to open the chamber door.

Malcolm stood patiently on the other side with a package in his hands. "Good morning, Your Grace."

Ivy held the door to block as much of the room from prying eyes as she could without stoking suspicion and smoothed her hair down at her shoulder. "Good morning, Malcolm."

"Where is your Adeshbu guard?"

Ivy sunk against the side of her door. "I'm sure he's around," she said breathlessly.

"You should be protected."

"Do you need something?" She rolled her eyes.

"Apologies for calling on you so early. It's only that I was given specific instructions to have this delivered first thing on the 17th."

Ivy's head cocked to the side as she gazed at the plain brown paper wrapped around the box. "Instructed by who?"

"The King."

Ivy's mouth went dry.

"He sent the package with me before we departed Asmye." Malcolm handed the box to Ivy. She kept her foot behind the door so it couldn't swing open as she reached her arms out. It was heavier than she expected.

"You've held it all this time?" She struggled with her posture.

"Yes, Your Grace,"

"But you didn't think to give it to me sooner?"

Malcolm only stared. Ivy knew she couldn't have expected Rian's Knight to disobey him. Not even if she thought they were friends.

"Thank you, Malcolm." Ivy nodded and closed the door, staring at the box in her hands. There was an immense desire to rip it open and learn what secrets it hid. It wasn't a trunk, so there weren't dresses he could send. What was it? She had half a mind to throw the box into the fireplace. Ivy took a deep and uneven breath as she glanced toward her balcony. The box could wait. At least wait longer than her lover.

Ivy closed her chamber door and hesitantly put aside the package in her hands. Luc came in from the balcony when he heard the latch click. His trousers hung low on his hips, emphasizing the curve of his tummy. Ivy only wished he wasn't wearing that damned helmet.

"Who was that?"

"Malcolm," Ivy's fingers lingered over the Garreau wax seal in the corner. It hurt to see more than the sigil on the flag.

"What did he want?"

"A delivery," Ivy sauntered closer to Luc, slipping her hands around his waist. "Nothing important."

"A delivery at first light seems like something important." Luc stared into her warm eyes.

"Isn't today about me?" Ivy rested her head on Luc's shoulder. She could feel his heart pumping under his skin.

"Isn't every day about you?" Luc smacked her ass. Ivy yelped when Luc gripped her thighs, lifted her off the ground, and tossed her onto the bed. Ivy stared up into his visor as he crawled over her.

"Since we were so rudely interrupted."

Ivy pulled open her dressing gown and bit her lip.

"Close your eyes."

Ivy pouted but obeyed. Her lashes touched, and she waited for him to kiss her, but nothing happened. Suddenly, something cold grazed her chest, and she yelped.

"What is that?!" Ivy slapped her hand over something as it slithered against her skin in a tickle.

Luc stifled a laugh. "Open your eyes and see."

"Is it going to bite me?"

"It won't. I might."

Ivy opened her eyes and looked down at her chest. A thin silver chain lay above her breasts. From it hung a single teardrop of amethyst sparkling in the sunrise.

"Luc, you shouldn't have- you can't afford something like this." Ivy held it to the light before Luc took it from her hand.

"Do you like it?" Luc clasped the ends of the chain around her neck.

"Yes, of course, it's beautiful," She smiled.

"Then that's all that matters." Luc grazed his fingers over the stone and lingered over her heart. "Ivy," he purred and brushed aside a curl that had fallen on her face. Her gaze was soft and warm. He hesitated, then reached for the fabric he used as a blindfold the night before. He paused before draping it over her eyes, hating to lose her. "I love you."

Ivy's cheeks rose with a smile. His fingers traced the shape of the lines that creased in them. Ivy wished she could look at him. She wanted to watch him say it, to make it real. She lifted Luc's helmet away from his face and kissed his face deep into hers. A wave of comfort rolled through her as she surrendered.

"I...I love you," she whispered against his lips. It was more of a struggle to say than she imagined. But it was true, wasn't it?

"Say it again, so I know this isn't a dream."

"I love you, Luc." Ivy kissed along his jaw.

She couldn't see the smile that stretched across Luc's face. His mustache bristled against her skin, tickling her as he sank down her body. Ivy giggled as he skimmed his lips over her hip, and she sank back into bliss.

The longer Ivy waited to open the package, the more fear stirred in her belly about what it might contain. Surely, he wouldn't send something bad today. It was too heavy for annulment documents. And those would all have gone to her father or Russell anyway. What did he want? Nerves fueled her hands as she ripped the brown paper away. Beneath it, a note.

My dearest, Ivy,

You are on the other side of the sea by now, and I surely miss you more than I could have imagined. I hoped we'd celebrate your birthday together, but alas, I find myself in exile by my mistakes. Perhaps one day, you'll see a path to forgive me. Until then, I humbly offer a gift that pales in comparison to your beauty.

I love you.

I should've said it before, a million times, every day.

Your husband,

Rian

Bitterness lingered on Ivy's tongue like his last kiss. His behavior soured every pretty word. She sucked in a deep breath to calm herself from the emotion swirling in her chest. Maybe the annulment wasn't coming after all. Her fingers navigated the clasps on the box and opened it. Inside, wrapped delicately in velvet, was a necklace of gold and emerald. Ivy's mouth hung open as she looked at the necklace, although it seemed an understatement. Intricate gold caressed the deep green stones with spires twisted into elegant shapes that flowed through the collar. Ivy closed the box, almost nauseous, thinking of its worth and how wearing it might cost her pride.

King Rian jumped off his horse, boots thudding in the sand. Gulls called in the distance, circling high above the shoreline. The Tolgeen shimmered crisp and green in the early evening sun. If there had been a boat, he might have chartered it all the way to Iosnos. Rian hated the idea of missing Ivy's birthday. A servant reached for the horse's reins, but Rian shooed him away.

"Bring him water here. I want him in my line of sight. Call for the ferrier. His back left shoe is loose."

The servant nodded and ran off for the supplies. Rian stared at his horse before patting him on his hindquarters. The black bear banner hung off his hip, and Rian pulled a tattered thread from it, wrapping it around his finger. The thread tightened around the tip of his finger, turning it a reddish purple. Rian pulled firmly and popped the thread with a clean edge.

"Your Majesty, the Chancellor is expecting you." A plump man with a wiry beard opened the tent drape to the side, motioning for the King to follow.

"I'm sure she is." With one look back toward his horse, Rian went inside.

The Bloidarian Chancellor, Gislina Alacade, outstretched her hand to greet the King. "It's an honor to meet you, Your Grace. I had the pleasure of serving with your brother for many years." Gislina surveyed the horizon. "You come alone? No entourage ready to cut off my head?"

"I can take care of myself." Although the thought had crossed his mind, Rian found no point in ruining the chance of subduing the Chancellor.

"I'm sure you can. Nothing can tear down the reputation of the great King Garreau."

King Rian glanced down. She wore three rings on each hand. Rian brought nothing of value with him except his marriage ring. "I've come at your request. Let's not waste each other's time with pleasantries."

"A show of goodwill isn't a pleasantry." Gislina stood eye to eye with the King, as tall a woman as he'd ever seen, with hair so blonde it was almost white. "You should consider yourself lucky we are willing to discuss terms at all." She gestured to their seats. "It took some persuading, but I've convinced our high council that you may be more amenable than your father."

"What would make you think that?" Rian sneered.

"You're a young man at the beginning of your reign." Despite Rian's attitude, Gislina remained unflustered.

"I've been the sole monarch of Asmye and all her territories for fifteen years."

"*Fifteen years ago,* you were tasked with the impossible: a grieving child without family suddenly in control of powers you only heard of." Gislina's eyes unnerved Rian. She looked at him without fear or admiration. "Now we find ourselves back in the trenches of your father's war."

"My father's war?" Rian scoffed. "Why did I find six Bloidarian assassins inside my home if it is my father's war? I have done nothing to you, and yet my wife, who is innocent of our shared history, had to wash the blood of her would-be killer out of her hair."

"That's a question better suited to a mirror," Gislina sighed.

"My intelligence informs me otherwise," Rian remembered Torin's discovery and a scrap of a torn Bloidar sigil in his findings. "Strength and power have no lack of enemies, but the poisoned blades of Bloidarian soldiers cut deeply, however unsuccessful they may have been. For that alone, you should consider yourself lucky you're not a head shorter on these shores."

"Perhaps you should consider the stability of the territories you already possess before you cross the Tolgeen with your threats. *My* intelligence tells me you seem to have your hands full with the Dureto."

"You say that as if Bloidar isn't bedfellows with the Dureto," Rian scoffed. "Perhaps your intelligence was gained as pillow talk."

"At one time, yes, that was the case, but now they find their funding with the heads of the underworld. They play a game outside of our purview." Gislina relaxed in her seat. "Many would benefit from the destruction of Asmye's economy. Your wealth gives you strength, but it places a large target on the Garreau line."

"Then why are you here? Why do you care if I fall?" Rian poured water into his cup from the carafe between them. "It would be to your advantage if I did." Rian sipped.

"This is where we differ. You lack the empathy to see that others don't hunger for the same things you do. Our high council wants stability and open trade in our corner of the world. I think Bloidar, Ilum, and even Lutrya should be safe to conduct our own affairs without the threat of Garreau's violence hanging over our heads."

"I don't threaten. I act."

"Yes, your military assembles, and they look the part." Gislina poured herself another glass of water. "Blood is spilled, and your God is worshiped. Tell me, Your Majesty, is that for your father's vanity or your own?"

Rian held back his anger. His fist tightened. "For all your knowledge and the fine things you choose to elevate yourself with, you lack actual wisdom. Posturing and insulting me as if I will submit simply because you fail to see the game I'm actually playing." Any day now, Rian expected word from Iosnos of how many ships were ready, how many men poised to fight.

"The *game* you're playing puts my people at risk."

"That's the price you pay for placing your aim on me. Every day, my ranks, my wealth, my power grows. You waste my time. You're afraid for your people. I understand that. So what will *you* offer me?" Rian tapped his fingers on the table between them.

"I do have an offer for you." Gislina sat straight to look into Rian's eyes. "A truce for at least the summer months. Both our forces can take a step back. Reassess where necessary. Continue your tiffs with the Dureto. It's no concern to us. But before you waste the lives of your men in a war you can't win, remember *we* only know what we're told."

Rian rubbed his fingers against his brow as if the pressure would help him see her intention more clearly.

Her lips curled into a smile. "You do remind me of him."

"My father?"

"No, you're surprisingly unlike him despite how you posture," Gislina laughed, "You're much more like your brother. Emeric was a good man. He would have been a great king. You still can be."

"That's not too tight?" Madeline tugged on the laces of Ivy's dress.

"No, it's good." Ivy stared at herself in the mirror. Her skin was darker even after a few short weeks in Iosnos. She ran her hand across her stomach. Embroidered roses and flowers brushed against her fingertips. Madeline secured the laces with a pretty knot.

"What's this?" Madeline eyed the elegant box.

"A gift from the King."

"Oh, really? May I?" Madeline gestured towards the clasps. Ivy nodded. "Wow. That's something spectacular," Madeline smiled. "It would be perfect for tonight."

Ivy rubbed her lips together.

"No?"

"I don't know. It's a little ostentatious for such an informal affair." Ivy anxiously curled her finger around the silver chain Luc had given her that morning.

Madeline made a face in the mirror and laughed, "Your Grace, no one on this island would consider your birthday an informal affair, especially not you." Ivy began to protest, but Madeline removed the silver chain, lifted the necklace from the box, and draped it across Ivy's clavicles. "That's lovely."

There was a knock at the door. Ivy gulped as Madeline answered it. It was only Luc, but what if it had been someone else? Ever since Luc left her this morning, Ivy imagined if other gifts might come, or worse, it might be Rian himself knocking. It was preposterous to even think of it. He would never come.

"I've come to escort the Queen." Luc poked his head in the door.

"She's almost ready. Wait here." Madeline motioned to the settee near the fireplace. It was too hot to light a fire now, but at least he could admire the masonwork.

Ivy lifted her hair as Madeline fastened the clasps down the back of her neck. The sheer size weighed Ivy's shoulders down. She swallowed hard as the cool gold wrapped high around her long neck and dripped down her chest. Green and gold suited her skin perfectly. The chain appeared to have been made specifically for her measurements. She hated how much she loved it.

"You look beautiful, Your Grace." Madeline petted Ivy's shoulders with affection. Still, it didn't do anything to calm The Queen.

"You'll come tonight, won't you?" Ivy grabbed Madeline's hand. She couldn't pinpoint why she felt so nervous. Something in her stomach was uneasy. Maybe she didn't want to spend more time with her father than necessary.

Madeline stumbled over her words, "I'm not sure I should. The other maids say King John doesn't allow staff in the events."

"Nonsense," Ivy waved her hand. "You're my guest."

"Your Grace, I do-"

"It's *my* party. Tell Janelle to come, too."

Ivy and Madeline stared at each other in the mirror.

"Please, Madeline?"

"It does sound fun." Madeline played with a piece of Ivy's hair.

"There will be chocolate."

Madeline stopped and stared into the mirror before she smiled.

Ivy rested her hand on Luc's arm as he escorted her to the dining terrace. Garlands of wildflowers weaved across the archways lining to draw guests toward the party.

"I wish you could dine with me tonight. I'd much rather look upon you."

"Shall I stand on the wall across from you, then?"

Ivy pouted, "You know what I mean." She had a pit in her stomach. Madeline and Janelle wouldn't be ready yet, but she was already late. "I wish I could replace my father with you at the table."

"It's his castle."

Ivy made a face to mock him. "Yes, his castle, his rules, his disdain for me. It's written everywhere except the stone." Ivy self-consciously touched the gift from Rian.

"I may not be at the table, but I'm always with you, Querida." Luc watched her hands tap the gold on her neck. "I hoped you'd have worn the necklace tonight," Luc spoke softly.

Ivy swallowed, "It was a gift from *the King*." That wasn't technically a lie. "My father is so particular about these things." Whether or not Luc believed her, he placed his hand over hers until they reached the end of the hall. Two castle staff opened the wide glass-paned doors and announced the Queen's arrival.

The sun had begun its descent, casting the dining table and its occupants in a warm glow of orange and purple. Waves sang in chorus with the birds as water crashed against cliff faces below them. This was something no other kingdom nor gold could buy. Asmye may hold a magnificent castle in Astrella, but Iosnos was always wealthy in beauty.

"There she is!" King John rushed over from his seat to Ivy, taking her hand from Luc and kissing her cheek. "My beautiful girl," He smiled warmly. "Come, come, we've missed you. Save us from another one of your Uncle's stories."

Ivy laughed. Luc sank into the background near the string and lute players.

Russell stood to greet Ivy along with his wife and children. The littlest, Arlo, reached his chubby fingers out for Ivy and grabbed onto her necklace. Russell's wife, Shella, tried apologizing, but Ivy shook her head and put the child in her lap. She unclasped the necklace and dropped it on the table so Arlo could play with it. After all, it was from Rian. What did it mean to her?

"It's a shame your husband isn't here." King John lifted his third glass of wine to his mouth. "It'd be nice to get him in a casual mood to talk." He always had an agenda, even if he was the only man in the room.

"We're so happy you're home, Your Grace," Shella smiled. Warm chestnut hair fell against her temple as she squeezed Ivy's shoulder.

"Please," Ivy held her hand. "You've known me as Ivy my whole life."

"I can think of a few things she's called you your whole life, darling." Russell laughed; even Ivy's father joined in as they compared nicknames they'd given Ivy over the years. Stubborn and Loud came to mind first.

"You have your mother's chin, Ivy. I see it when you smile." Russell nodded and took Arlo back into his arms. "She'd be so proud of the woman before us now."

Ivy blushed and held sorrow inside herself. *Would she?* Luc stood across the room, scanning every person who walked past him. Madeline and Janelle were yet to be seen. Sophie bounded up to grab Ivy's arm and led her away from the table to look at the view.

"I'm so glad you've arrived. I've been stuck listening to your cousin, Armand, preach about the merits of hypothetical city limits for the last twenty minutes."

"Cousin by marriage only."

"He gets a seat at the table, doesn't he?"

"So do you," Ivy laughed.

"It took you forever to show. Thought you might have abandoned me," Sophie leaned in to whisper.

"You know how much I love a party." Ivy twirled around, showing off the lavender linen draped against her tan skin.

"Yes, yes, especially one all about you." Sophie grabbed two glasses of wine from a nearby tray and raised hers.

"Lords and Ladies!" Sophie called out. Murmurs across the room stopped and turned their attention toward the railing, "or perhaps I should start, Kings and Queens?" The joke received a low chuckle from the crowd. "Twenty-six years ago, the shores of Iosnos were brightened by the birth of a lovely, beautiful, wonderful baby girl," Russell hid his smile behind his wife's shoulder as he kissed her. "and then three months later, our Queen Ivy was born to be that beautiful girl's dearest friend." Ivy laughed, snorting a little. King John pinched the bridge of his nose before downing another glass of wine. Sophie beamed out at the guests before looking back to her friend. "In all seriousness, Iosnos is made better every day that you step foot on her sands, and we are so lucky to have-"

A commotion at the terrace doors interrupted Sophie's speech with raised voices. Ivy turned to see what was happening. A familiar voice cut through the now awkward silence of the party.

"Excuse me," Ivy returned her wine glass to Sophie and rushed toward the commotion. Luc followed.

"We were invited!" Janelle's accent was more pronounced from her temper rising. Madeline's face flushed with embarrassment. She stood sheepishly behind Janelle in the green dress Ivy had given her all those months ago.

The doorman puffed up to loom over Janelle. "King John gave express orders that-"

"The Queen should like her own guests to be admitted to her party." Ivy's brow furrowed. "You will let them in at once."

The doorman stared between the women in front of him and then over his shoulder toward the rest of the guests. "I'm sorry, Your Grace, but I take my orders from your father. I'll have to have them escorted away."

"You will do no such thing." Ivy snapped her fingers, knowing Luc stood behind her. "Adon, please see that Madeline and Janelle are escorted to their seats."

"Yes, Your Grace." Luc stepped forward. The puffed demeanor of the doorman quickly wilted as the Adeshbu neared.

"Enough!" King John yelled, disregarding a room of friends and diplomats. Ivy didn't dare turn to look at her father. "Ivy, come now!" King John stalked away from the table. Ivy refused to hang her head in shame but followed after her father to a secluded corner of the terrace away from their guests. Luc tried to follow, but Ivy waved him off.

"What do you think you're doing?" John lifted his eyebrows when he looked at her.

"I'm giving a proper welcome to my guests at *my* party, Father."

John spied a glass left on the balcony with a splash of ale in the bottom. He sniffed, then took the final swig. "Your *guests* are servants. I cannot have a servant at my table."

"They are more than the job they have. They are my friends."

"But they're my friends," he mocked her. "Just because you invited trash doesn't mean I have to allow it. I already let the one drink my wine and eat my food. Shouldn't that satiate your appetite for the lowly dregs of society?"

"Sophie?"

"*Sophie,*" his voice went up in a nasal tone. "She's more of a handful than you are at times!"

"You're disgusting," Ivy grimaced. "I can't believe I'm related to someone so foul."

"Watch your tongue." John's lips curled into a snarl. "One more comment like that, and I'll-" His hand raised slightly, and Ivy took a step back, wishing Luc was with her. "You should learn the meaning of propriety if you desire the throne so badly."

"I have one, and I'll have yours soon enough." John's nostrils fumed at his daughter. "To speak of propriety as if you have any moral foundation beyond your self-righteousne-"

John's hand cracked across Ivy's cheek. She stood there, stunned and holding her palm where she felt the sting. "Perhaps you should leave if you can't behave like a civilized person. I can't imagine you speak to your husband in this manner and still have a head!"

Ivy stared at him, willing herself not to cry.

"Are we clear?"

Ivy stood silently. John rushed her and grabbed her by the arms, nearly spitting in her face.

"I said, are we clear?" His would-be scream only came out as a hiss. Ivy looked around, but no one could see her, not even her guard.

"Yes."

John let her go and Ivy stormed off towards the terrace doors. The crowd was seated at the tables inside. No one said a word. It only took a glance at Sophie for her to recognize that look. Sophie followed Ivy off the terrace and towards her room with Madeline and Janelle. Luc followed behind as he always did.

After the women filed inside Ivy's chamber, Ivy stayed outside to speak to Luc. He raised his hand to her reddened cheek, but Ivy pushed it away. "Don't."

"He hurt you."

She shook her head. "It's already done - just," Ivy took a breath, "my friends will be staying the night."

Luc nodded in understanding. He wanted to pull her in and kiss her face until it didn't hurt anymore.

"You should get some rest. You don't get enough. Let someone else watch my door."

"Are you sure you're alright?"

"I'm fine," she smiled to reassure him and nervously rested her hand above her breast. Her face scrunched when her finger tapped her neck. *Fuck.* "I left my necklace on the table. Can you-"

Luc lifted his hand. The gold and jewels glittered against his worn leather glove.

She sighed, relieved. One less thing to worry about. "Thank you."

He spoke softly, "Goodnight, Querida. Happy Birthday."

Ivy smiled but remembered herself before she sank back into her bedroom.

"Does he tuck you in at night, too?" Sophie said as she popped a cork from a new bottle.

Ivy raised her hand to her forehead, then plopped down on the settee. "Once when I was drunk."

Madeline laughed, "Well, we all know that's happened more than once."

"Usually, I can still walk, though." Ivy grinned proudly. "Rarely do I lose my feet."

"Unlike your father, it seems." Janelle lit a meelaflower cigarette.

"He's a boorish fool." Ivy sucked on her teeth. "Kings and their violent tempers. Might as well be children the way they pout when they don't get their way." It didn't matter which one she referred to. "If only we could yell and hit when we were upset. We'd simply be hysterical." Ivy rolled her eyes and gulped down the wine Sophie brought her.

"Well, I know a place where yelling and hitting are encouraged," Sophie smirked.

Ivy's eyes lit up. She knew what Sophie was thinking. "We could sneak out the way we used to when we were kids."

"What are you talking about?" Madeline asked.

"Come on, Mads, we can break a few more rules for a giggle." Ivy scrunched her nose. "Are you afraid of heights?"

"Oh no." Madeline looked nervously at Janelle.

Janelle smiled, "I don't even know what it is, and I'm in."

"We better change. We wouldn't want to ruin our *pretty dresses* climbing the lattice." Ivy headed towards her closet.

"The lattice?" Madeline's mouth dropped open, and she winced.

"Climbing down is the easy part," Sophie said. "I think we will really feel our age sneaking back in, but I guarantee it'll be worth it."

"What is it?"

"Fights in the Salt District, courtesy of yours truly." Sophie swigged more wine and then turned on a singsongy voice. "And Kal is fighting tonight."

"Kal?" Ivy poked her head out and threw a plain dress across the bed for Janelle. Sophie gave an evil smirk.

"Oh yeah,"

"What's a Kal?" Janelle took another hit.

"Ivy used to be sweet on him. Big motherfucker, just the way she likes them." Sophie leaned towards Janelle with a whisper. "Stupid as hell, too, but knows how to throw a punch. Nothing turns around this one's mood like being admired by a big dumb dumb." She nodded toward the Queen's closet.

"I heard that!" Ivy shouted, narrowing her eyes. "And he was sweet on *me*, not the other way around."

"Does it matter? You certainly had your fill of him on more than one occasion."

"Oh, he was always an occasion." Ivy's grin turned devilish as she emerged in a simple dress. "I recall an occasion where the brute broke the bed." She swallowed more wine and sank into the settee. The waves of her memories seemed like an eternity ago. Even though she hadn't left but a few months ago, would he still look like the same Kal? Handsome, tall, and thickly muscled. His hair was dense and curly like her own. Arched brows framed smokey eyes. Sophie was right; he was no conversationalist, but Ivy rarely spoke to him in their time together. She recalled stealing off into

Iosnote nights to fuck wild and fun in back rooms of taverns or on vacant rooftops. Once, he'd climbed the same lattice they were about to descend to fuck her over her balcony railing. That was a good night. The memory made her lips and her toes curl.

"You mean…you weren't?" Janelle asked with a curious face.

"Oh god, no!" Ivy giggled. "Rian knows that. I think he actually liked it. He doesn't have an appetite for virginal wilting flowers, especially with the way he likes to fuck." Pink warmed the apples of her cheeks. The memories of her husband were so much closer.

Madeline declared as she grabbed the bottle of wine from Ivy and finished it in one long gulp. "So, are we going to go to this thing or what?"

Sophie put her finger over her mouth to quiet her. "We wouldn't want her *guard* to hear and ruin all the fun now, would we?" she giggled. The girls gave each other one more look of trepidation, and then the energy lifted in the room. "Let's go."

CHAPTER SEVENTEEN

"Let me have a look at you," Endaya called out to Adne behind the dressing screen.

"It's a little big on me, I think." Adne pulled on the shirt. The burgundy tunic billowed loosely from his shoulders as he came out.

"It'll be better once you-" Endaya started fussing with the fabric, "-tuck it in properly." She glanced up at his face. "The color suits you." She tapped his side, and then Adne raised his arms.

"As much as it suited the man who wore it before me?"

"You should just be grateful to him for leaving it behind along with the others." The unorganized assortment of clothes she had collected over the years from forgetful patrons served well for creating Adne's disguise.

Adne glanced in the mirror. He ran his hand along the high waist of his trousers. "I look quite dashing."

"You act surprised." Endaya rolled her eyes and handed him a belt.

"It's not often I get a chance to see myself outside of an Adeshbu." Adne slid the scabbard for his dagger onto the belt and strapped it onto his hips. Endaya rolled the sleeves up around his forearms.

"You seemed familiar with that soldier the other day."

Adne didn't say anything, but he didn't have to. Endaya could read the twinkle in his eye.

"Still missing something." She rifled through the assortment of clothes she had collected for him. A dark shawl and hood would do the trick. She wrapped it around his shoulders. "There." She combed her fingers through his messy strands of brown hair until it was fluffed and pushed back.

"Not too much. I'm supposed to be a ruffian."

"Ruffians own combs," she smirked. "I'll keep your things safe, hidden away."

"Thank you, love." Adne grabbed her hand and kissed her palm softly. "If I'm not back in a week, sell it and get yourself something that sparkles."

"And what should I do if your *friend* comes looking for you?"

"Tell him the truth," Adne smiled, "That you haven't seen me since our last visit." He couldn't risk the young Knight following him. Adne pulled on his boots and handed Endaya a few gold coins. She slipped them into her pocket and tapped the fabric, considering the weight of them. Would it be enough if she were to get caught opposing Rex? Adne started toward the door but turned back to the madam. He held up a single gold coin. "Perhaps a kiss for confidence?"

Endaya's face scrunched in a smile. She stepped forward and stretched onto her toes to reach his face. A sweet, brief touch of their lips warmed Adne's complexion. Endaya pulled the coin from his fingertips.

"Good girl." His lips curved in a mischievous grin.

Endaya slapped her hand across his backside as he ducked through the doorway and onto the streets of Mermont.

There were plenty of dark corners for dark deeds inside the tavern of Port Cane. It was the first time Adne had crossed its threshold, despite his surveillance in the days since Endaya had given him the name. Candles wasted away on tables among card games. Adne sipped the wine a barmaid poured for him. He didn't let his eyes wander, but his ears were keen.

"Just let me talk to him, Freddie." The voice was thin and desperate. "I can explain why I'm short."

"Short? You seem like a tall motherfucker to me." The voice reverberated with depth. "Like you got taken for a couple of cranks on the rack," Freddie and others chuckled, "Certainly, you wouldn't be trying to explain why you are short on the Rex's cut? That would be mighty dim of you."

"There are more patrols now. I had to dump cargo to keep my head."

"You're worried about what the new patrols will do with you?" Freddie's laugh bellowed. Adne was certainly in the right place. He tilted his eyes to see the laughing man.

Freddie seemed to be almost as wide as he was tall. His head gleamed shiny and bald. The gruffness of his face matched his beastly appearance. Adne tilted his head to look a little closer. A snake was tattooed on his forearm. Adne squinted to make it out in the darkness. It curled around in a circle to eat its own tail. Adne dared not look any longer.

Couldn't be caught staring. He tipped back his wine to finish it. The barmaid was quick to refill. She leaned down to him, fingers twisting through the hair at the back of his neck.

"I've not seen you before. First time?"

"Mm," Adne roughened his voice and cadence. "Heard I might find work here."

"You can find almost anything a man needs here." She held out her hand. Adne was quick to pay her.

"Oi! Who's this pretty one you're talking to?" A scrawny and filthy man pulled out a chair next to Adne.

"Says he's looking for work." She tucked the coin in her apron.

"What kind of work do you want, pretty?" The man leaned in closer.

"The kind that pays."

"Well, a few here might pay to see you bent over," The thin man laughed. Adne took a breath. Opportunity had presented itself. He pulled his dagger from his sheath and held it under the thin man's jaw, knocking the full cup from the table.

"Then they'd like to lose a few parts," Adne growled. The tavern got quiet. Blades waited in darkness, ready to reach out and bite.

From the far corner, a clap broke the silence. Then Adne heard boisterous laughter from Freddie and the others. The thin man smiled, his yellowed teeth bared in the candlelight.

Adne caught the clapping hands retreating into the darkness from the western corner. Then a woman, fair as he'd ever seen with plaited fiery copper hair emerged. Her hips were hugged tightly by trousers, and a knife hung at her hip. Two massive hands landed on Adne's shoulders.

"Looking for work, you say?"

Adne only shrugged. He caught the snake tattoo in his periphery.

"What should we do with him, Siobhan?" Freddie squeezed Adne's shoulders tighter.

The redhead stopped at the table in front of Adne. "The Rex would like you to bring him three fingers. Come back when you have tribute, or don't come back at all." She had a deep voice, likely encouraging the men to take her more seriously.

"Does it matter who they're from?"

Siobhan gave him a half-hearted laugh. "No."

Adne twisted out from under Freddie's hold and threw an elbow into his jaw. He grabbed the back of his head and slammed it into the table. Adne caught Freddie's massive forearm, pinning it to the table. Freddie's crew had time only to stand back in shock as Adne quickly sliced through three of his fingers right at the knuckle. Freddie slumped into a screaming pile at Adne's feet as Adne collected the fingers.

"I have tribute."

143

Siobhan grinned with a closed mouth. "The Rex would be pleased to have your company." Adne scraped the blood off his blade on the edge of the table and put it back in its scabbard.

"You're going to let him do that?" The skinny man yelled after Siobhan. She ignored him and gestured for Adne to sit. Adne took a seat, and candlelight illuminated the Rex from across the dark table. His silver beard was peppered with black. It contrasted so beautifully with his warm olive complexion. Dark eyes smoldered under thick black eyebrows. Siobhan sat beside him, her hand landing casually against his mid-thigh. She relaxed in her seat.

"What do you call yourself?" Siobhan asked.

"Ed."

"Ed, Ed, Ed." The Rex repeated the name in a jovial melody.

"Well, *Ed*, clearly you're adept at the knife." Siobhan studied Adne with knowing eyes.

"Yeah, I like a bit of-" Adne scrunched his nose, "-wet work."

"Seems unlikely a man of your skill wanders into Port Cane and makes such a quick and impactful impression accidentally." The sharpness of her gaze could cut any man to bits. She leaned forward. A gold pin on her lapel caught the light: another snake, the same as the tattoo. Adne had seen it a few scattered times in Iosnos. It was everywhere, though. Men, women, and even children bore the symbol. Were they all connected? "Who have you worked for?"

"I did mercenary work on the Tolgeen for a few years under Clive Darby." Adne pulled the old pirate's name from deep in his memory. "Parted ways and landed on Iosnos only long enough ago to find out this is where the real work is."

"Captain Darby!" The Rex's shapely belly jiggled with his laugh. "I haven't heard that name in ages. I thought the fucker was dead."

"He might be. My loyalty to him ran out with the last of his gold." Adne sucked on his teeth. "I hear my loyalty could be endless with you."

"That's yet to be determined." Siobhan's tone was more serious. The Rex wrapped his hand around her waist, skimming his thumb over her side. Adne was careful not to stare, but he took note. Siobhan licked her lips as she turned to look at The Rex.

"He's bold." The Rex's dark eyes narrowed as he looked closer at Adne. "You just amputated three fingers from one of my top men. I should seek retribution."

"I think Freddie will seek that retribution himself," Siobhan interjected, "unless we say otherwise."

The Rex nodded right to left as he weighed his options. "I think handsome Ed here might be more useful than Freddie's now superfluous fingers."

"What is it you're interested in using me for? I heard you run the whole island under the King's nose."

"You see, Ed, what I'm interested in is...everything." The Rex scratched his fingers through the bristle of his beard. "And when you have an interest in everything, true currency is power. Power is obtained through loyalty, gold, and influence."

"Gold is easy. You can just take it," Adne chimed in, flipping a coin back and forth between his fingers. "Influence can be bought with the right broker at the right price, but currency isn't always gold."

"And loyalty, at least yours, it seems, is for sale." Siobhan's words were dry. The Rex's eyes crinkled with his smile. Adne could feel the energy between them. He read she was much more than lover, ornament, or muscle. Siobhan was his partner.

"And while the old man rots on his throne on the hill, my true competition is elsewhere." The Rex leaned forward to light a cigarette in the candlelight. "I don't succeed in a void." His cheeks puffed and hollowed as he sucked in smoke. "There are many who want to take what they think they deserve." Smoke ribbons drifted up from his lips. "What I need is an unattached man for the *wet work*. I invest in those friends who will get me there."

Adne sat in silence, prodding Rex to continue.

"The Farnum brothers. They run numbers on the fights at the Barricade." Coins scraped across the rough wooden table as Siobhan slid them toward Adne, enough to keep Endaya safe for years. "Twenty percent now. The rest will be paid upon proof of death. That's a 'getting to know you' price-"

"I'm much more generous with my friends." Smoke blew from The Rex's nose as a dragon's exhale.

"-Additional *friendliness* will be given if you can bleed information from them."

"How will I know them?"

"I'm sure you'll figure it out." Siobhan's soft features flickered wickedly. Adne saw her. She wanted to test him.

Adne pocketed the coins and stood. A dagger buried itself in the wall beside Adne's head with a loud thud.

"If anything should go sideways, don't bother to come back." Siobhan sauntered a step forward from her seat. She yanked the blade from where it was stuck in the wood and slid her tongue over her bottom lip. "I like to hunt."

The hood cast a dark shadow over Adne's features. The Barricade had an overflow of yelling men into the street outside its walls. Smokey exhales lingered in the air as empty bottles rolled against the cobblestone. Sound exploded from inside the club in cheers. Adne paid the doorman his fee and slipped inside, keeping close to the wall. Bodies crowded around the fighters brawling in the center of the room. The heat was thick. Sweat beaded on Adne's neck as he squeezed through the crowd.

He perched himself in the far corner. His eyes, concealed under his hood, surveyed fighters, sailors, whores. Money exchanged. A face he recognized was ringside: Sophie. She stood, shouting atop a barrel. At her side was - Was that The Queen? She may have removed all marks of wealth and status, but there was no denying she stood out in the crowd. The maids were there, too. Adne let out a quick whistle under his breath. That woman could make friends with anyone. Ivy beamed, raising her hands as broad men pummeled each other. She winced at the taller fighter taking a hit. Adne took a look around. There was no Ad Onondian, no guards at all lurking behind her. The thought of her fooling The Adeshbu's vigilant eye made Adne smirk. He'd be pissed if he found out.

A man with a thick black beard and the slinking look of a coyote pulled Adne's attention from the Queen when he palmed a scrap of paper from a fighter. He didn't even glance down. Quickly, he tucked it away. From the shadows, another man with the same features emerged. *Brothers.* One looked slighter older than the other. He was shorter, too, but the resemblance was undeniable. The younger moved through the crowd and placed a large bet on a fighter. Swings were thrown as the brawl between the two men commenced, but Adne kept his eyes focused on the brothers. Amongst the sea of cheers, a smirk creased the elder's cheek moments before a fighter took a weak punch to the gut and crumbled. Before the fighter yielded, the younger brother was already on his way to collect his winnings. Siobhan was right; it wasn't hard to figure it out. The Farnum brothers weren't slick in how they ran their game. Once they had their money, they crept toward the exit.

The brothers slipped through the backdoor of the Barricade. Adne hesitated, turning his eyes back to The Queen. Shouldn't he stay? It would put him in a better spot with Baalestan. She didn't seem in danger, but being among the common man wasn't exactly safe for royalty. Adne groaned, torn. He had his own duties to attend to.

It was quieter in the alleyway. Drunks stumbled about, talking and smoking among themselves. The brothers walked confidently with full pockets. They weren't hard to follow, nor were they hard to restrain once they had led Adne right to their home. The younger yanked against the knots securing his wrists behind his back. Blood crusted around the older's nose and dripped down his chin.

Adne lurked behind the brothers.

"Who are you working for?"

"We don't work for anyone but ourselves," The elder gruffed.

"Sure, and I'm just an ordinary thief looking for a quick take." His voice was calm and collected.

"We pay out the losing fighter. That's all!" The younger one whimpered.

"Shut up!" The older man shouted and attempted to jerk his body toward his brother.

Adne circled them to the table where they had counted their earnings from the night. Gold pieces and coins were counted into different piles. "I have no head for accounting, but it looks like-" Adne pulled out one of his knives. "I'd say about fifteen percent for the fighter who threw the match." Adne pushed the coins apart with the blade. "These two piles are almost identical. Twenty-five percent for each of you, and that leaves-" Adne knocked the neatly stacked gold pieces across the table. "-thirty-five for your boss."

"We just hadn't split it up yet, is all." There was panic in the elder's voice.

"You're not a very good liar. Wrong line of work for you, in my opinion." Adne pulled up his own chair and straddled it, leaning his head upon his crossed arms over the back. "So, why don't we make this easy? Tell me who your employer is and where, and we can all be done here a lot sooner."

The older brother spat on Adne's boots. Adne grimaced with disgust.

"No need to be foul about it." He wiped his boot clean with a discarded tunic from the floor. "I don't find torture very interesting, but since you've chosen that route, I have to change things every so often." Adne rubbed his finger down the cleft of his chin. "I might start with peeling the skin back on your fingers. You'd be surprised how hard you have to pull on human skin to peel. Losing an ear or an eye usually perks things up."

"Fucking do it, then!" The older brother shouted.

"I might go back and forth between the two of you. One screams while the other pleads." He waved his finger back and forth while counting off a list in his mind.

"I'm not going to tell you shit."

Adne bent at the waist and grabbed the scruff of the brother's neck. "I know a thousand ways not to kill you. By number five or six, you'll beg for me to end it." He squeezed tighter. "But I *will* force you to live until I get the information I want. So the choice is yours. Now or a thousand ways later?"

Sunlight crept up over the eastern horizon, although the sun had yet to appear. Too many drinks outside the pub gave way to lost time. Sophie reached down, grabbing Madeline's forearm to help pull her over the balcony railing. Madeline sprawled out onto the stone floor of Ivy's room.

"My God, you weren't kidding about the climb up," her voice was weak through pained panting and soft giggles.

"The view is gorgeous from down here," Ivy yelled as Janelle climbed above her. Sophie leaned over the railing to scold Ivy for being too loud. Janelle reached for Sophie's hand.

"Don't make me laugh! I'm going to lose my grip." She rolled over and crashed into Sophie's legs, then could only crawl to Madeline, lying on the stone.

"You're the one that suggested I go last!" Ivy pulled herself up, standing eye-to-eye with Sophie on the other side of the railing. "What are they going to say? The Princess has been caught sneaking into her own chambers? Oh, the scandal!"

"That's Queen, isn't it?" Sophie swigged from a bottle left on the table. Ivy stared at the golden necklace gleaming in the firelight beside it. She laughed and tapped her throat.

"It's nice to pretend you have no responsibilities."

"Well, if Kal saw you, the entire city would be raving about if they were possibly in the same room as you."

"Did you see his face? Do you think he'll say anything?"

"Everyone saw his face, Ivy." Sophie ripped at a piece of bread with her teeth. "He might as well have done a little dance in the middle of the ring right before he got his shit rocked by that sucker punch." Sophie sloshed the wine around at the bottom of its bottle before chugging it. "What's it to you if some pretty idiot still goes gaga every time he sees you? Last time I checked, *Queen of Asmye*, you're otherwise engaged."

"Is it so wrong for a queen to desire to be desired?" Ivy tapped her fingers over her stomach. "To look at someone and feel how they covet, how they burn to be nearer to you. As if the greatest prize for them would be to have you return their affection."

"It must be nice to have big tits," Madeline slurred, half-asleep.

They erupted in laughter.

"It is." Ivy grabbed her boobs, squeezing them together and looking down. "They are quite lovely."

"So, when can we do that again?" Janelle cuddled closer to Madeline on the floor.

Sophie perked up from where she sank on the settee. "The Evane Festival is only two days away. The tide has already started to shine."

Ivy groaned and slapped her palms over her face as she rolled into bed. "I have to do all the formal nonsense with my father." Ivy sat up straight and plastered on her royal smile, waving her hand gently. "Hi, hello, nice to see you." All the waving and the smiling, it could kill her with its dullness.

Sophie raised her eyebrows. "I recall many sunrises the morning after Evane with you."

"It depends. I might be getting too old for this." Ivy considered how she might pitch the evening out to Luc if he would even allow her to go. If she even wanted him there. Sophie rolled her eyes and disappeared behind the back of the settee.

"What's an Evane Festival?" Janelle whispered out. Madeline was already asleep on the stone floor. Janelle tucked a cushion under her chin and pulled Madeline closer.

"It's the easiest way to get The Queen naked in the water!"

"Sophie!" Ivy threw a pillow at her friend. It made a flat *thunk* when it met her face.

Laughter gave way to soft sleeping breaths as, one by one, they fell asleep. Ivy lay in her bed, somewhere between awake and asleep. A knock at the door startled her. She hadn't even slipped beneath her blankets. Her dress was rumpled and wrinkled as she attempted to straighten herself before opening the door.

"Luc!" Ivy slipped out of her bedroom and shut the door. "I thought you had someone else out here."

"Sorry to bother you so early." Luc's voice was soft, wavering as he touched her hair. "There was a message sent for you." Luc handed over the folded parchment. Ivy accepted graciously, lingering at the door momentarily, anxious for something more. There was no name written in, but she recognized the handwriting. The message simply read: *You will join me for breakfast.*

After going without it for a few hours, Adne's armor seemed to weigh more. He hated the uncomfortable cage he wore, even if it protected him from a cruel and violent world.

"Seems you've been busy," Adon nodded in respect to his fellow Adeshbu and the men who followed behind him.

"Just doing as duty, or at least how Baalestan dictates," Adne snarked.

"Odd how often the two are intertwined."

"Perhaps this will satisfy the old man enough to leave me be for a few days," Adne sighed and opened the doors to the dining hall to find King John at the head of his table. Queen Ivy sat to his right. She held her hand to her mouth, trying to hide a wide yawn.

"Forgive me for the early intrusion, Your Majesty."

"Out with it, then." John wiped his mouth with a white napkin.

Adne looked between the King and his daughter. "Perhaps it would be best if we excused the Queen as what I have to present might be considered quite…unsuitable for a lady."

"I shall be the judge of what is suitable for my own eyes and ears." Ivy straightened her back in her seat.

Adne nodded. "Very well. I have been working for some time to catch the threads of the criminals within Iosnos. I have made a bold move, but one I think will be the first to its unraveling." Adne snapped his fingers, and soldiers presented trays. Adne motioned for each cloche to be removed and a head was revealed. Ivy groaned, but her father seemed even more disturbed.

"Thayer Reid, the Rex," Adne introduced, "some whispers had called him the Pirate King."

"There is no king on this land but me!" John snarled.

"Yes, Your Majesty. Rex was simply order, enforcement, and distribution for pirated goods both on and off the island. His second in command, Siobhan Turney." Siobhan's copper hair was splattered and stained from blood.

"Tell me, soldier." John leaned forward, a red wine stain on his collar. "What did you plan to gain by carrying out this task, much less bringing its spoils to my breakfast table?"

"Daddy, he's just-"

John silenced her with a raise of his palm. Ivy leaned back in her chair and tapped her fork on her plate. She didn't raise her eyes.

"I didn't want to waste time. Before their early demise this morning, they provided me with information on their rivals, and I pulled another thread. The Farnum brothers." Their heads were presented on one tray; the older brother was missing both eyes. The younger appeared to have part of his scalp ripped back. "Sometimes a scalpel is more effective than the sword."

Ivy leaned forward, studying what was left of the faces. She thought she recognized them but couldn't place where. "And they were kind enough to give me information on their boss, Layre Noxx, head-" Adne stifled a giggle, "-head of a new company that calls themselves Vulous. It was little more than rigged gambling and intimidation."

Adne stood in silence, waiting for King John to speak. Instead, he took another drink. Ivy watched both of them. John picked up his fork and took a bite, pretending as if Adne wasn't there.

"Your Majesty," Adne said. Still, John said nothing.

"Father?"

"What?!" John slammed his hand on the table. "The boy did his job. Does he expect praise for doing what's expected?"

"Ad Nekoson has carried out a task you couldn't. He deserves something."

"What have we just discussed, Ivy? Do not embarrass me." His eyes narrowed toward his daughter. She didn't cower.

"You have done a great service to Iosnos, Ad Nekosen." Ivy stood and approached the knight. "You have done in a night what many have struggled to do in a lifetime." There was a sharpness in her tone that rivaled the blade at his side. She reached out her hands to take his. "I will see that you are rewarded graciously by both Iosnos and Asmye for your service." Ivy turned back toward her father. "Perhaps until we find an adequate honor for Ad Nekosen, we can provide him with an upgrade to his accommodations within the castle." Ivy motioned to one of the servants.

CHAPTER EIGHTEEN

King Rian laid back in his bed, staring at the ceiling, lost in his thoughts. Ivy nuzzled close to his side in the nook of his arm, staring at him. That beautiful, strong nose was like the highest peak of a mountain in his silhouette. She focused on the mole on his cheek right beside it. She loved how it sat in his smile line. He took a deep breath and let out a soft sigh.

"What's the matter?" she asked.

"Nothing, baby."

Ivy inched closer as if there was any space between them. "Tell me."

He caught himself in a smile. "I was thinking about the future." His voice was tender, soft, serene. Spring had turned to summer, and the castle was more alive than ever. Rian knew there was much to be done, more than he would let on to his wife. Ivy turned her head to look at the spot where his eyes were fixed, wishing she could see his thoughts painted on the ceiling.

"What's wrong with it?"

"Absolutely nothing." He turned to kiss her. He loved the way she looked in his bed every morning. Her hair managed to twist in every direction, sticking out wildly no matter what he'd done to her the night before. Her eyes barely opened, squinting for the first hour at least. He even loved how she would protest if he had to leave the bed for any reason. And he loved how her cheeks were softer and fuller when she first woke up. She'd yawn wide and crinkle her nose, and her husband thought she was the most striking thing in the world.

"Then tell me what it is," Ivy smiled.

"Would you like to know, Empress?" His voice was warm with a smile.

"Empress?"

"Yes. After we defeat Bloidar, we will own their land and harbors. It would give us control over the entire nation. From the western jewel of Iosnos, nestled in the teal waves of the Tolgeen, to the eastern coastal cities of Thaolor. I will rule until my dying day. I want you there as my Empress, and I-" Rian stroked his fingers through her hair. "-will be Emperor."

"Your Empire." Ivy stared at the ceiling, imagining all of what could be.

"Our Empire," he corrected her. Ivy smiled and played with his large hand in hers.

Rian knew Ivy's love was growing for him. He felt the same love in his heart. It was a feeling he had never really understood: to love and be loved. It was still strange, uncomfortable even for him. The last person he had said the words to was taken from him so brutally. Love. It filled him with terror as much as joy.

Ivy threw her leg over his hips, pulling him close to her. "Tell me what else you see in our future."

He grinned, gazing at her. "You look stunning, as always." He loved how she preened her hair as if her beauty was a given. "You'll hold our second boy to your breast as he feeds. His little hand will reach up to grab a strand of your hair." Rian gently wrapped a tendril of her hair around his fingers.

"Two boys?"

"And a girl between them. She's lovely and wild, just like you." He tapped his finger on her nose, pulling away when Ivy tried to catch it in her teeth. "Chaos breaks out whenever she enters a room. She's always covered in dirt from going on her little adventures," he laughed, "She's perfect."

"What about you? Where is my Emperor?"

"I'm there with you, happy. We could travel anywhere we wanted. Spend the worst winter months on the warm shores of Iosnos or stargaze in the forests of Ilum. Visit the largest libraries in the world in Lutrya!" He couldn't help but smile widely, imagining the whole scene. "Have you ever seen the Lutrya libraries?"

"No, I've never been." Ivy sank inside herself. "I never left Iosnos before coming here."

Rian cupped his hand on her cheek, soothing her. "They are brilliant: white shelves trimmed with gold leaf, three stories high, with books filling every wall. The ceiling is painted like a bright sky lined with soft, pillowy clouds. You'd adore it."

"Sounds like a beautiful place." Ivy's heart filled with butterflies, imagining the life she'd yet to lead, the world behind the doors he could open. He looked into her eyes, then brushed some of her wild hair away from her face. "Even if we never left this room, this beautiful place, I'd still be happy just to be with you."

Ivy beamed. "I'd be happy, too." She would be. The promise of the world was thrilling, but she didn't need much. This was more than enough.

He stared at her face, happy and full. "I want our portrait to be made. I've already been making arrangements with the finest artist in Asmye." Rian propped himself up until she was face to face, wrapping his arms around her.

"Really?"

"I always want to remember us like we are now. Even when we're old and wrinkled, we can look back and think, 'what a couple of beautiful young things.'" He grabbed her ass playfully.

"Look back?" Ivy pushed herself up on his chest. "Speak for yourself, old man. I will remain a beautiful young thing, even when I'm 100 years old."

"I'm sure you will." His mouth consumed hers again. Anxiety hit her like a punch in the gut, and she pulled away, resting her head on his shoulder. Her toes tapped against his thigh.

"What is it?" Rian asked, instinctively wrapping his arms around her back, hugging Ivy tightly.

"I need you to promise me something." Her words came out in a whisper.

"Anything you want is yours."

Ivy could hear the smile in his voice, the power. Good. It's what she needed. "I need you to protect her. Protect our daughter."

Rian pulled her jaw up to look at him. He puffed his chest and pushed his head back in the pillows as he met her gaze, giving him the most beautiful double chin.

"What are you talking about?"

Ivy closed her eyes and exhaled, praying she wouldn't start a fight. She reached out to hold his cheek, needing to feel connected. Comfort washed through her when he covered her hand with his.

"You have to protect her. It can be difficult to be a woman, especially one born into status and public scrutiny."

"Scrutiny? She can do anything she wants."

"She can't, Rian," Ivy sighed. "Men have it so easy. It's different as a woman. Her whole life will be someone telling her what to do or what to be. Anything that happens to her, she will be blamed for." Ivy sat over his hips, holding one hand while his other fell down her back. "I need you to promise me you will protect her, raise her to fight back. Stand up for her when the time comes. It has to come from you."

"Is that what it's like for you? Is that why you're scared?"

"Yes. It's terrifying," Ivy took a deep breath. "Sometimes I feel so powerless."

"You are the Queen. Everything in these walls is yours to rule." His hand squeezed her leg. He meant well, but he just didn't get it.

"I find these walls a prison."

Rian looked down. His gaze was on her stomach, but he didn't see her there.

"Are you so unhappy still?" He never looked up. Terror jolted in his heart, afraid of what she might say next. Ivy took both her hands around his and pulled them to her chest.

"I am happy, Rian. I am happy with you. You just don't experience the world the way I do. You don't hear whispers or walk in between guards, knowing they're your only chance if something happened and-"

"Ivy, do you think no one's attempted to take my life? They tried to take us together. You could've died, and I wou-"

"I'm not saying that at all." Why was talking to a man so frustrating? Could they ever just listen? "You broke that man's arm with your bare hands. I can wield a sword, but I have never been given one. Nearly everything in my life happens under circumstances. I don't get to choose my path."

He started to protest, defending the life he had given her.

"People who want to kill you want to be you, possess your power. People who want to kill me want to take something from you. They want to hurt you. They don't want me."

Rian's thumb squeezed against her finger. He would never really understand or feel what it would be like to be her. His life would always afford him advantages she could never have. He did empathize, at least.

"I will always do anything to protect you, to keep you safe."

"Protection isn't always high walls and swords," Ivy smiled. It was hard, but she knew he meant it. "Just promise me that you'll love our daughter the most. That you'll protect her with everything you have. She'll need it."

"Almost as much as you," Rian smiled.

Ivy shook her head. "More."

He kissed her again, tangling his fingers in her hair. Ivy rested her head back on his chest, falling with him as he lay back. Rian peppered soft kisses at the top of her head as he held her. They muttered whispers and promises of forever until she fell asleep in his arms.

Ivy woke with Rian's arms resting on her back. She smiled at the sounds of his soft snores. Ivy tilted her head to the side, kissing along his neck and shoulders. She didn't want to wake him. Ivy could worship him just as he laid. His body was beautiful underneath her; his freckled skin was soft and smooth, stretched over marbled muscle. Ivy ran a gentle finger over the scar on his temple and down his cheek, following the line down his chin and neck to meet it where his childhood scar sat atop his chest. Every imperfection in his features reminded her of his strength and power, everything he could overcome and outlast.

Ivy slid her hand down his chest and stomach and between her legs. She wasn't surprised that she was already wet. A dream of her and Rian back at the shore drifted in her mind during her sleep. He held her close amidst the waves. His touch in her dreams was nothing compared to the man resting in her grasp. Ivy tried to keep her moans quiet, but Rian's cock twitched below her.

There was no better way to wake up, he thought. His wife was a devious little thing, wanting pleasure as often as possible. Her desire was insatiable, like his, making him want her even more. Rian let his hands fall all over her skin, drinking her in with his touch before he even opened his eyes.

"Good morning," Ivy whispered, bringing her lips to his in a sweet kiss. Surely, it was past midday, but Rian didn't mind. He mumbled something resembling the same as he kissed her back. Ivy hated the tease as Rian pulled her hand away from her pussy, replacing it with his own. She pulled away, dragging her bottom lip out from his bite. She just wanted to sit back and look at him. As she rested her hand on his chest to prop herself up, she noticed streaks of crimson over her skin. Ivy blinked her eyes to make sure they weren't deceiving her.

"No!" Without an explanation, Ivy withdrew from her husband, rolling off the bed and running to the basin in the washroom.

Rian looked at his fingertips. Blood. His heart sank. He knew why her face had fallen in such despair. He wanted a child with her more than anything. Since their conversation in the greenhouse, she seemed to want it more than he did. Rian jumped up from the bed to chase after her.

Ivy drenched a cloth in water from the basin on the floor. She swiped it at her skin. Rian found her with her hands between her legs. Ivy pulled them away, and they were spattered with her blood. Rian watched her hands shake in fear in front of him.

"I'm so sorry." Ivy wiped away the blood. This was the first time she felt the need to conceal her body from him. Rian didn't care about that. He cared about her.

"It's okay." He tried to reassure her. The shake in his lip from the look in her eyes made him want to die. He took a few steps forward, wrapping his arms around her. "It'll come." He knew his words couldn't curb her grief, but he hoped she'd feel less alone.

Ivy covered her face, but he didn't want her to hide from him. Tears pooled in his eyes, but he held them back. Ivy needed his strength, and he would give it to her. Ivy grasped at his arms, shivering in her cries. Her legs gave out beneath her. Rian sank to the ground with her.

"I thought that wanting it would be enough. I've failed you again."

"You haven't failed me." He pulled her face back to look at him. "Ivy, you are enough."

Rian shot up in his bed. Instinctively, he reached to his side, but his wife wasn't there. She never would be again. The tent shook from the wind outside. He was covered in sweat, panting as a drop fell from his chin to his chest. It was more devastating each morning when Rian discovered he was alone.

Ivy sat at her vanity, staring into the mirror while Madeline pinned her curls behind a delicate tiara. She had been quiet all morning, silently cursing herself for the dream she had last night. It was the last time she and Rian held each other. The last time she believed in him. The last time she ever would.

The Evane Festival was set to start in just under an hour, and John, against his own desires, demanded his daughter accompany him at the traditional opening ceremony. They'd light the first paper lanterns, and the citizens would follow suit, sparking a thousand tiny points of light within Mermont.

"How long until you can skip out on the formal affairs?" Sophie sat on the settee, flipping through a book with her feet on the table.

Ivy shifted in her chair, wincing as a rumble of pain tinged between her hips. Madeline rested her hands on Ivy's shoulders.

"Are you alright, Your Grace?"

Ivy rolled her eyes and rubbed her stomach. "I'm fine." She squeezed her eyes shut and waited for the cramp to pass, then she stood to stretch once Madeline pinned the last piece of hair.

"Uh oh," Sophie gestured to the back of Ivy's dress.

"What?" Ivy pulled on her skirt. "Fuck!" Crimson stained the fabric where she'd been sitting. Madeline rushed away and then came back carrying a new gown.

"Little late, aren't you?" Madeline asked as she fluffed up the fresh skirt. She dropped Ivy's petticoat into the basin bubbling above the fire. Ivy glared at her, but she would know. After all, she did the laundry. Another wave rolled over her but was gone after a few seconds.

"I'm fine." And she should be. This meant the last of her connection to Rian was gone. She didn't have to wonder or worry anymore. She was done. She stared at the necklace hanging from her neck. The jewels glimmered in the mirrored reflection. The last time she bled, it hurt her deeper than she knew she could be wounded. Her memories reflected in her dreams so vividly. She relived that morning in her sleep last night. All that hope she had lived for was smothered out by the same blood that now pushed Rian's grip on her further away.

"Will you still be fine to sneak out?" Sophie asked. Ivy took a deep breath.

"Of course."

Sophie answered the door when there was a knock. She stared up at the blue-caped Adeshbu, who stood on the other side of the door. "It's for you," she called out to Ivy.

"Hi," Ivy sighed when she closed the door into the hallway.

"Are you alright? You look pale." Luc looked around before he touched her cheek. Ivy nodded and sank into his touch. "I will be away tonight. Natassa has called a special council."

Ivy perked up and then played into the pain of her period cramps. "You won't be at the festival?"

"I'm afraid not. I've let Malcolm know to be at post."

"How long is this council? Will you be back to sleep with me?"

"I don't know how long I'll be." Luc brushed his hand on Ivy's and squeezed.

"I'll just have the girls stay again. Will you mind?"

"Of course not," Luc lied. All he wanted was to be with her. It had been too long since he'd tasted her kiss.

Ivy's bedroom door opened, and Madeline leaned against the doorframe. She held up a few jewels for Ivy's hair. "I almost forgot about these. I need you back."

Ivy turned back toward Luc and gave a resigned smile. "Tomorrow?" Luc nodded, and Ivy shut the door behind her.

"I love you," he whispered to the wood.

Desert wind whipped a chill down Rian's spine like his nightmare lingered. The dawn painted the sky from purple to deep warm orange. The sun's heat had yet to reach the day as The King offered the latest batch of prisoners as a sacrifice to Adievasinis. With each slice of a throat, his thoughts clouded with different futures just beyond his fingertips, but for now, they grasped around the sword he was always destined to hold. He recalled dreaming of Ivy's blood that morning. He lied when he said he wasn't disappointed. Her blood brought shame   to his legacy. His sword, however, would not fail him.

The weight of Aternous vanished when it drew blood. The strain and ache in Rian's body were sure to come in the hours after he wielded Adievasinis' legendary broken blade. Still, while it was in his hand, nothing else came with extraordinary ease and ecstasy. All his pain, grief, and heartache channeled into strength as he drew it across another prisoner's throat—basin after basin overflowed with red. The men were little more than the thin flesh between him and the blood he needed. At least, that's what Rian told himself before he killed them.

The city of Mermont was awake like Luc had never seen it before. Paper lanterns of lapis and periwinkle hung over every street. His mouth salivated as he walked past a street cart selling spicy smoked meats and cheeses. His boots stopped. He could take a few minutes to eat, couldn't he? He paid the vendor and ducked into a dark alleyway. The kabob lived up to its enticing aroma. Fat and salt melted in his mouth.

"Fuck," Luc muttered to himself. Food was so often an afterthought to him. He wanted to shove the rest into his mouth, but he chewed slowly, savoring the bite as the heat tinged his lips. Children laughed as they ran by on the street with a ball. Music floated to his ears from some distant street. Luc found himself smiling. The Evane Festival was something special. No wonder Ivy had been so excited. He longed to share it with her, but Natassa had called for all the Adeshbu to join her for a special service. He licked his fingers, yearning for another bite.

Pop! Bang! Sound exploded from the street, followed by a loud whistle that made Luc jump to attention. His head whipped to find where the sound had come from. Another pop in the sky followed a rain of sparkling light that burst in the shape of a flower. The crowd gasped in astonishment. Some clapped. Luc pushed his helmet all the way off to watch from the darkness as another dazzling explosion of silver fluttered across the Iosnote night sky. He wanted to stay for the show, but his duty was to Adievasinis first.

The Iosnote church was next to nothing compared to the cathedral in Asmye. Luc wondered the first time he stepped inside if it was a restaurant or a tradesman's shop before it was converted. The pews were simple wood. No ornamentation or decoration to entice a passerby to look inside, yet the services he had attended were flush with people. The overflow of congregation would stand at the back just to glimpse the High Priestess of Adievasinis and her entrancing sermons behind her altar. Ivy was hesitant to go, and her newfound freedom gave her the power to say no. He hoped he could convince her one day soon.

But tonight, there were no lingering worshippers or curious onlookers. Ad Baalestan sat dutifully in the first pew with Ad Viena. Adne was nowhere to be seen. Luc sat beside the others.

"Decided to take a night off from your Queen, Ad Onondian? I would have thought you were too dedicated," Ad Baalestan casually chided.

"I am dedicated to Adievasinis and loyal to his faithful servants," Luc said calmly. "I take my charge as the Queen's protector with the same dedication that I do all my acts in service to Adievasinis."

Adne burst into the church. "Apologies for my tardiness. The streets were quite crowded."

"The rest of us managed to get here timely," Ad Viena noted.

"It's not like I'm late. She isn't even here yet." Adne plopped down next to Luc and leaned in to whisper. "Did you try some of the food?" he whistled, "Incredible stuff."

Luc only gave Adne a gruff sound of approval. He didn't need any more attention drawn to him in front of Baale. It wasn't long before Natassa emerged in her white gown. She was so fair and heavenly in appearance. If anyone had reason to be thanking the gods, it was her. Her pearl-like skin glowed even in dim candlelight. Waves of yellow hair were as gold as the jewelry she donned.

"For all their festivities, the Iosnotes have no idea why they celebrate." Natassa loomed over them from her makeshift pulpit. A wild light gleamed in her eyes. "A blue moon brings shining night waters, and they dance in the streets. Some think it is the island; others praise Rhyzden or the lesser gods." Her cold eyes looked over the Adeshbu. "I need one of you to bring me something of great value to Adievasinis. He calls for a sacrifice."

Adne leaned in, closer to Luc this time. "When doesn't he?" Luc chuckled in response but covered it with a cough.

"Quiet," Baalestan chided.

"Is there a question?" Natassa stopped midspeech, drumming her fingers on the wood under them.

"Tell us who, High Priestess." Baalestan shifted in his seat, sending a glare down to the disruptors. "We find our honor in serving Adievasinis." Natassa's eyes floated over each soldier. Candlelight reflected in their armor, waving against each breath.

"And do you serve Ouraina?"

Helmets turned toward each other and back to the Priestess. Their silence said enough.

"There is a ritual, one that can only be done under this moon. He who fulfills his duty will be blessed by God and achieve power beyond comprehension. I've prayed to Ouraina for weeks, begging Her to show me Her light. I will follow the path She lays for me, and I won't let anyone dishonor Her in my church or outside of it. Do you understand, Adeshbu?"

Ad Viena gave a solemn nod, and Ad Baalestan and Ad Onondian thumped their fists over their chests. Ad Nekoson sat back further in his pew, nodding when Natassa glared at him.

"A man preaches of Rhyzden while besmirching Adievasinis, Ouraina, and all of us that follow the true Gods." She clutched her skirt and took a few steps down, then called each man to stand before her. "He is called Marwyn. Bring him to me tonight, and Adievasinis will reward you."

Natassa reached to Ad Baalestan's hip to retrieve his dagger. Instinct led him to grab her wrist, but he let it go when she stared at him.

She cut her thumb and then slid the blade back into its hilt. Natassa's eyes stayed on him as she recited a prayer. "Adtinq perius turaine sabba soman belique." The blood from her thumb smeared against Baale's chest plate first. "You know what you have to do."

Baale thumped his fist over the marking and left the church. She repeated the prayer before each of them, the crude symbol marring the shining steel of their armor.

Luc stood on the street outside the church. Baale and Viena had already left to hunt their quarry. Adne came out and stood beside him.

"Is it even worth trying?" Adne sighed, scrubbing the bloodstain from his armor with a leaf from the ground.

"Baale probably already caught his scent."

"I'm going to look for this preacher near more food carts. Want to join?"

"No." Luc only wished to return to the castle and find comfort in his lover. Ivy should be back by now. The royals had to open the festival, but Ivy said nothing of other duties. It had been only three days since they'd been alone, but he wanted her. Maybe he could sneak her into the garden or his room.

"Your loss." Adne nodded to Luc and walked off toward the center of the festival.

The sand between Ivy's toes felt so right. Janelle hurriedly followed Ivy toward the beach. The endless ocean that stretched in front of her was broken by blue light. The waves would crash against the shore and glow in bright cerulean. Ivy didn't know if heaven existed but hoped it was as beautiful as this. Other islanders gathered on the shore, swimming and playing in the waves. Madeline had her skirt pulled between her legs, staring down as the otherworldly water rushed around her. Sophie waved her hand.

"Her Majesty has decided to grace us with her presence," Sophie laughed. "How'd you get away from your detail? He's pretty strict."

"As if I had a choice in the matter with you around." Ivy playfully nudged Sophie with her elbow. "Malcolm was tough tonight! I thought everything was smooth sailing when Lu-my guard said he'd be away, but even The Knights are on my ass!" Ivy crashed on the shore and leaned back on her hands. "Janelle was quick. Came in to 'bring wine and learn to play cards, and Malcolm just let her in. She's turning out to be more graceful than me to get down that lattice!" Off to the side, Janelle curtsied, then sank in the sand next to Sophie.

"All I heard was that Janelle brought wine," Sophie cackled and held out her hand. Madeline fished it from Janelle's bag, and they all took turns drinking.

Firelight lit up the sky, crackling showers of vivid colors reflected in the water. Ivy stood in admiration of the ocean's show for a few seconds. "I need to get in. I can't stand just to look."

"*As if* impulse control was something you ever possessed," Sophie scoffed.

Ivy lifted her dress over her head and threw it on the sand.

"Your Grace! Someone might see!" Madeline's voice jittered with concern as she surveyed the beach.

"Mads, you crossed an ocean, yet you're still stuck in Asmye! No one here cares. Look around." Tons of families and beachgoers laughed to themselves and watched as the ocean glowed. "We are all just children, playing the way we were always intended to."

Madeline glanced around the beach. People, young and old alike, bathed nude in the waters around them. "But-"

"I can't hear you!" Ivy ran into the ocean and dove under the waves.

Sophie took off her clothes and tossed them next to Ivy's. "You coming?"

Madeline stood on the shore with her jaw dropped.

"My love, there's nothing to be ashamed of here." Janelle stood on her toes to reach up to kiss Madeline in the moonlight. Madeline's stiffness melted against Janelle's pout. Madeline smiled with the folds of Janelle's skirt between her fingers, pulling her closer.

"Are you going to…you know?"

"I will if you will." Janelle's eyes twinkled in the moonlight as they walked hand in hand to the ethereal waters.

Madeline floated in the roll of soft waves. The laughter of those around her dipped in and out as the water muted her ears. She stared up into the black sky. It wasn't really black. It was its own ocean of the darkest blues and purples. The stars shone like a thousand points of light. Madeline exhaled. There was safety in a place like this, unlike she'd ever known in Asmye. Tears slipped from her eyes as she realized she could never go back, never hide who she was again.

CHAPTER NINETEEN

Natassa stood in a large copper basin. The temperate water lapped at her ankles. Jasmine blooms floated along the surface, wafting their scent into the room. Droplets dripped down her clavicle when she squeezed the cloth against her neck. Smoke curls thickened the air with the aroma of red clover and maca. She dragged the cloth up the length of her arm. She wanted the sacrifice to be pure and true. The water cleansed away the filth of mortality as she muttered a prayer. She didn't bother with a towel. A few moments in the warm Iosnote air would dry any lingering moisture. Footsteps echoed in the sanctuary. Natassa pulled a thin linen dress over her to greet her lucky guest.

Ad Baalestan stood at the center of the church, dragging Marwyn, the whimpering preacher, gagged with his hands tied behind his back. He looked like he might crumble to the floor if Baale wasn't holding him up by his elbow. Natassa smirked, pleased with Baale's performance. It had been barely two hours since she'd set his mark.

"You've done well, Ad Baalestan," she cooed. "I am not surprised it was you." The preacher's eyes went wide at the sight of the Priestess. He struggled and moaned against his gag. "Come, bring him back. The moon is high, and we shall not waste it."

The preacher struggled momentarily against moving forward, but Baale's grip tightened, forcing him into the Natassa's private quarters. She motioned to a large wooden table with rope straps. Baale made quick work of restaining the preacher against it. Tears streamed out of their prisoner's eyes and down the sides of his face.

Natassa pet Marwyn's hair as she leaned close to his ear and whispered, "Adievasinis will not take mercy on those who soil his name. You will die slowly; your soul lost to the seas of eternity, drowning in seawater, aching for relief from your Rhyzden's limited power. Your belly will twist with thirst, but you never know comfort or rest again." The preacher's lips trembled around his gag. Natassa wiped his tears. "You can pray now and beg for Adievasinis' mercy in your death, that He can use your blood to make something new and pure." The preacher closed his eyes and muttered a prayer into his gag. To whom he prayed was of no matter.

Natassa stood face to helmet with Baalestan and slid the thin straps off her shoulders. Her dress slipped down her naked body and pooled at her feet. Baale's visor stayed locked with her eyes while she outstretched her palm towards him.

"Your dagger?"

Surprised that she even asked, Baalestan pulled his dagger from its sheath at his side. Natassa gripped the blade, returned to the preacher's side, and cut away his clothes. Marwyn's ribs gutted out from his chest. Years of sacrifice to his powerless god failed him. Natassa dipped the blade's tip into his skin at the hollow above his sternum. No amount of cloth could muffle the preacher's screams. His fingers twisted and stretched, desperate to escape. Natassa's jaw tensed as the blade worked through the hard cartilage inside his chest. Blood seeped then splattered when the preacher thrashed, marring Natassa's pearlescent skin.

"Adievasisnis is pleased with you, Ad Baalestan," Natassa said matter-of-factly like it was a simple task she carried out. Baalestan took honor in the praise.

She kept her focus steady as she fileted the skin and muscle back on the left side of his chest. Marwyn struggled against his restraints, echoing wails reverberating off the stone walls. A warm puddle began to form around her feet as his blood ran off the table. Natassa dug her fingers inside his chest and gripped around the bone. She grunted when she pulled up and broke the bones away to reveal his heart. Its sporadic and quickened thumping matched the panic in the preacher's eyes. It was a wonder to Baalestan that he was still conscious.

Her lips pressed tight together as the blade began the more meticulous work. His screams dwindled to whimpers as Natassa cut out his heart. The last few pumps sprayed crimson across her face and chest. Natassa handed the dagger back to the soldier. She had no need for it anymore. Thick, waxy streams dripped down Natassa's forearm as she carried the preacher's heart to a metal basin. She doused it in oil, then chanted a melodic prayer, igniting the oil in a deep violet flame. A hum vibrated through the stone floor beneath them, slinking up into their skin like a calling from beyond.

"You are true, Adeshbu?"

Ad Baalestan stood tall. He was no stranger to violence. "I am Adievasinis reborn in mortal flesh."

Natassa turned back to the soldier, and her stained hand smeared the shiny finish of Baale's chest plate. His hand gripped hers, but she only smiled. With both hands, she led Baalestan's hand to Marywyn's still-spasming chest. She dipped his hand in Marwyn's blood and pressed it against her breast, holding it tight until their heartbeats matched.

"Do you give yourself to Him?" Natassa slowly dragged Baale's hand further down her body. Streaks of Marwyn's blood dripped from their skin, and he nodded. When Baale's hand pressed against Natassa's lower stomach, she stopped him. "Do you give yourself to me?"

Baalestan looked past Natassa's shoulder, avoiding her bewitching smile, and stared at Marwyn's limp body. Blood fell in streams from his veins, dripping and pooling onto the stone floor, inching toward them. The flames hummed as they enveloped his heart. It stirred something in Ad Baalestan, seeing Adievasinis' power before him. Natassa was such an alluring conduit of heavenly beauty and violence.

Natassa didn't wait for an answer. With a snap, she tore Baale's pauldrons from his shoulders. He stood, unmoving like God Himself trapped him in motion. A prayer-like chant fell from her lips as she undressed him. His chest rose up and down as he took in her movement. His arms stayed by his side, and his breath quickened as he stood bare-fleshed before the woman. Natassa looked him up and down. The Gods would be pleased. When she finished, she reached for his helmet with both hands. Baale pointed the tip of his dagger at her throat.

"I cannot remove my helmet in the presence of another." Baalestan's voice was low. Natassa pulled her hands back and bowed her head. She moved her hands to his chest, pulling his tunic open and revealing a muscled tone under warm olive skin. She dragged her right hand around his shoulder and started to walk around him. Bloody streaks followed her path.

"Do you hesitate to show your face to our God, Adeshbu?" Natassa whipped her long-flowing hair behind her shoulder.

"No," Baalestan's voice was smooth and unfazed.

"Am I not ordained by our God to carry out his mission?" She followed the line in his back up and down his shoulders.

"You are,"

"Then why do you deny me what our God has called me to see?" Natassa finished her circuit around him and pushed him to his knees. He sank easily, skin staining from Marwyn's blood on the floor.

Baalestan couldn't speak. Natassa rested her blood-stained hands on Baalestan's shoulders, her gaze peering through the visor of his helmet. A heavy weight seeped inside him as she lifted the last piece of armor away from his body, yet his eyes stayed fixed on hers.

A twinge of a grin curved in the corner of Natassa's pink mouth. She stared down at Baalestan. She was the first to look upon his face in God knows how long. He took a deep breath and exhaled, flaring his nostrils and flexing a strong jaw. Sweat-slicked chestnut hair fell forward on his brow above deep, striking eyes.

"Ouraina smiles upon you, Ad Baalestan. You are blessed with beauty." Natassa rested her palms against Baale's high cheekbones.

"As are you, Priestess." His voice hinted at a tone of restraint he would no longer need. Natassa took a step back and gave him room to stand. She took his dagger and laid it at the head of the table.

"Rise, Adeshbu. Tonight, you will give your body as a sacrifice. As will I."

There was no fear in Baalestan's eyes as he stood. His body felt stronger from sitting in Marwyn's blood. Natassa held his hand once again and dipped it into Marwyn's chest. She brought his palm to her face and ran her tongue from his wrist to the tip of his fingers. She threw her head back, flouncing her hair along her shoulders. Baalestan stretched his hand around her delicate neck and held it there, absorbing her pulse thumping under her skin. Natassa reached to scoop more blood on her hands and lifted it to Baale's mouth. Hungrily, he took his fill, blood staining his angelic mouth. His teeth were marked red at the points as he grimaced. This was not his first taste.

"Adievasinis grows stronger inside you, Adeshbu." Natassa looked down between Baalestan's legs. His cock twitched against her thigh as she gazed back at his eyes. Baale stepped forward, inching Natassa with her back against the sacrificial table. Out of the corner of her eye, Natassa noticed the flame still burned in a violet hue, whipping in the air surrounding them. A sickly sweet aroma enveloped them, drawing sensuality given directly from Ouraina.

"She calls for us, Adeshbu." Natassa closed her eyes and dropped her head back. The tips of her curling hair dipped into the blood seeping from Marwyn's still-warm body. "She desires power just like your God."

Baale reached his other hand to Natassa's back, pulling her body closer to him. He was close, she knew. Ouraina's siren call reached inside him, drawing the Adeshbu closer to his spirit. She needed more from him.

Natassa turned around, unwrapping the rope restraints, and, with all her God-given might, shoved Marwyn's body to the edge of the wood. His arm dangled over the side, blood streaking down his skin and dripping onto the floor. Natassa grunted and pushed again but was unable to move him further. Baalestan immediately pushed the body off the table, then lifted Natassa onto the wood. He climbed on top of her, forcing her to lay back in Marwyn's pool of blood.

"Have you studied *everything* your God has taught, Adeshbu?" Natassa smiled up at him while her golden hair haloed around her face.

"Yes, Priestess," Baalestan touched her body where it was soft. The blood inside him moved angrily, desperately. Natassa felt closest to Ouraina, then, more powerful against the strongest man. She reached above her head and drew the dagger gently across her chest. It pierced the skin above her left breast, drawing a thin line of blood from under her skin.

"What of his wife, did Adievasinis say?"

"That she yearned for power alongside him, to wield life inside her."

"I yearn for life inside me, Adeshbu." Natassa pulled Baale closer to her face and licked his blood-stained mouth with her tongue. Over her, Baalestan met her eyes, nodding slightly, agreeing to give himself to the Gods and his Priestess. Natassa breathed in the aroma of Marwyn's burning heart, her naked chest rising and falling with power. She grabbed Baalestan's shoulder and pulled him down to her side on the table. He groaned as she climbed on top of him, straddling his hips.

Natassa pulled Baalestan's mouth to her breast. His hands gripped her waist, and he bit her right where she had just cut her skin. Blood streamed over her nipple faster, and he rushed to lap it up.

"My body is the mother. Feast on me and give me the son of Adievasinis. Give him strength and fire, a descendant of truest blood. A true king born of pious servants. The world will kneel before him."

"Yes," Baalestan gave his final word. Natassa pulled him off her breast and pushed him down. He adjusted to lay flat on his back, Marwyn's blood covering his backside. His cock flexed against his marbled stomach.

"Soon, Adeshbu." Natassa slinked her body down and held Baalestan's wrists above his head. She ran her tongue over his jaw and whispered in his ear, "Ouraina has divined me to honor her. Fill me so I may be blessed."

Baale pushed his cock inside Natassa. Her wail lit up the room as she clung to his back. His hips thrust in time with hers as their Gods met once again inside their bodies.

Once all the bodies were drained and disposed of, Rian poured the oil Father Trevarthan had given him into the basin of blood. He wiped his temple and knelt in the dirt. Rust-colored dried blood emphasized the lines in his knuckles. He repeated his prayer.

"Adtinq valas berain tometerrian." The oil combusted. The flames boiled the blood beneath it. Steam and smoke curled up from the basin in noxious blooms. Ash clung to his sweat and smudged on his brow. Slowly, the liquid dissipated, and only a crude lump of iron was left. It surprised Rian how little a whole man emptied could yield. He carefully lifted the hunk of metal with pincers to quench it in a bucket of water. Steam erupted as it cooled. Rian's thumbs scrubbed at the rough surface to wash away the charcoal. The lump bore more similarity to a rock than a shiny piece of metal. Rian placed it atop the pile of blood iron he had collected. It would be up to the smiths to refine it and make Aternous complete again.

CHAPTER TWENTY

Saltwater had reinvigorated Ivy's curls and clung to her ringlets as she shuffled through the crowded tavern carrying two more bottles of wine. Sophie snatched one and refilled her cup before Ivy could even sit down.

"So much for patience," Ivy snarked.

"I have plenty of it, but I doubt that barmaid will if I don't take a chance at her soon." Sophie eyed the tall, plump honey blonde working at the far end of the bar. "And I need the courage."

"Sophie, you are, without a doubt, the boldest and most courageous woman I've ever met." Madeline poured Janelle's wine before she refilled her own. "How can you be intimidated by another woman?"

Ivy gave her a stunned look before she laughed, "As if I didn't hear all about how concerned you were if 'the girl at the party' might like you back."

Madeline blushed as Janelle leaned in and kissed her right on the mouth.

"Have you ever tried bedding a blonde after the witching hour? They are tricky pixies and sought by many." Sophie softened her eyes and gave a soft smile to the barmaid. The barmaid caught her eyes and smiled back. "And that, ladies, is my in." Sophie found her feet and made her way across the tavern. She looked so small compared to the portly man she pushed out of her way. The man stepped back, letting her by, and glanced at the table of women as he passed. He gave a menacing grin and shot the redhead a wink before joining some friends at the bar. Madeline averted her eyes from the man's stare but saw the crude and dirty bandage wrapped around his hand. The tattoo on his forearm made her grimace and turn away.

"What is it?" Janelle spoke softly.

"It's that snake again." Madeline shook her head and took a deep breath. "I feel like it's everywhere here."

"What snake?" Ivy leaned forward.

"The one that eats its own tail." Janelle kissed the back of Madeline's hand, clasped in hers.

"An Uroboros?"

"I don't know what it is called." Madeline's face was sour at the thought of it. "It was on a cheap necklace that bastard Torin tried to bribe me with." She shook her head. "I couldn't get it out of my head when he had me lashed. Makes me sick."

Ivy felt a stone plummet inside her stomach. That night, moments before her world was torn further apart, she had seen it: a gold snake set with emerald stones circling to eat its own tail hung on the beautifully pale neck of her husband's mistress. She called it a gift, but now Ivy knew from whom and the cost of obtaining such a trinket. An Uroboros didn't mean anything to Iosnos. It was a symbol of wholeness and infinity. Why was it haunting Madeline here? And what did it mean to Torin?

Riotous laughter burst from the end of the bar from the blonde barmaid. Sophie's arms were raised as she told a story with animated embellishments. She was captivating.

"Looks like Soph is making a good impression," Janelle's expression brightened, and Madeline seemed to shake off the uneasy feeling.

"She always does." Ivy pushed away the swirl of feelings in her chest. She would not let men across the sea ruin her fun. "She's a shiny person. People have always been drawn to her. I was."

"You sparkle, too, Ivy." Janelle's sweetness was genuine. "Especially away from that castle. Your father could never dull your shine; try as he might."

"Is it so obvious?" Ivy cringed.

"That your father is a pompous ass?" Janelle's tone was still so sweet, but Madeline gasped. "Yes. You are far too brilliant to be under his thumb. Don't let him squash you." Janelle lit a meela cigarette with the candle at the center of the table. "Men take up too much space in this world, not because they are smarter or more capable. It is only because they swing a bigger stick."

"I think you swing a pretty big stick." Madeline gazed at her with loving eyes, hanging onto Janelle's every word. Ivy couldn't blame her. Janelle was a woman that one would be lucky to love.

"I don't think a stick will do at this point. Maybe a battering ram." Ivy downed her wine, aching to keep the hopelessness at bay. "I will just have to wait out the slow decay of time with him." Her nerves were in retreat after three cups and she wondered how good she'd feel after the fourth.

The tavern was noisy with voices, murmurs, and laughs. Three men did a cheer at the bar top, clinking their glasses together. The portly man Sophie ran into nodded his head toward Ivy. That was nothing. She had made no attempt to hide her identity. She shouldn't be surprised to be a spectacle. She strained her ears to hear the conversation, but a hush fell over the room. Bodies moved out of the way, making a path right to Ivy, and when she turned, there was Luc. But he wasn't Luc then. He was an Adeshbu.

"Oh, fuck," Across the room, Sophie dropped the barmaid's hand and returned to their table. Each step she took brought her deeper into the pyre.

"We're leaving," Luc's voice was low, pointed only toward The Queen.

Ivy looked around at all her friends. The night had been so magical. "I don't want to leave," her words came out in a slur from the wine.

"I don't care." Luc pulled the glass out of Ivy's hand and nearly slammed it on the table. The echo filled the silence in the room as everyone stared at the soldier.

"We are just having some drinks. She's fine, I promise," Sophie protested.

"Now." This was a sternness Ivy hadn't heard from him in many months. It sent a chill down her spine. Ivy glanced at Sophie, who couldn't make eye contact. Madeline stared down at the table, rubbing her fingers over Janelle's.

All the joy had been sucked out of the room. Luc only had to point at the door before Ivy stood from her chair silently and walked out of the tavern without saying another word.

Luc was quiet, the kind of quiet that was deafening. Ivy walked the deserted streets with him back towards the castle. The remnants of the festival lingered. Voices drifted out from taverns and distant parties, but the roads leading to the castle were empty.

"Nothing happened." Ivy was finally brave enough to speak up once they were alone on the town roads.

"Doesn't matter."

Ivy covered her face with her hands like when Luc walked her home from the barn party in Asmye. So much time had passed since then, but there was still so much tension between them. "It's not dangerous here. No one is after me. Hardly anyone even came up to me in there. I was just trying to have a bit of fun."

"Ivy, you don't know that. People do want to hurt you, and if I'm not there to protect you, they will."

"Has anything happened to me since we've been here?" Ivy stopped and waited for an answer, but Luc kept walking. "No, Luc. Nothing ever happens here. I just wanted to feel normal for a few hours."

"You aren't normal!" Luc spun around quickly and grabbed Ivy's shoulders. "You're a queen. Even if there are a few who don't know that, there are people who'd bring harm to you for no reason other than that you're a pretty girl out all alone. I've sworn to protect you, and I intend to keep my oaths unbroken." He took a breath.

There it was. His *oaths*. The thing that he used to keep himself distant from her. Frustration flared inside Ivy's chest. "Why are you so mad about it?"

Luc relaxed his grip and drew a tendril of Ivy's hair between his fingers. "Ivy, you lied to me."

Ivy darted her eyes as she stood in the middle of the dark street. There wasn't a soul around. She resigned and looked back at her lover. "Luc, I'm sorry for lying to you. It was never to hurt you."

"Querida, I know that. I just-" he sighed.

"I know. You worry, but I'm okay. Everything is okay." That was a lie. "I just want to forget who I am sometimes, to be no one."

Luc nodded and reached out for Ivy. She took a half-step toward him but stopped. She was finally close enough to him to see.

"What is this?" Ivy drew her fingers across Luc's chest plate. When she pulled her fingers away, she saw the red streaks staining her skin. "Is this blood?" Ivy tensed and stepped back. She ignored the dull throb in her arm where Natassa had touched her.

Luc cleared his throat, "It's nothing." He reached into a pocket for a cloth and wiped it away. The last thing he wanted to tell Ivy about was some Adeshbu breeding ritual. He only wanted her to think about him.

"Are you alright?" Ivy asked once his armor was clean.

He embraced her in the dark street. "I was so scared. When I opened the door, and you were gone, I didn't know what to think."

"I'm sorry, Luc."

"You are mine. Don't deceive me." He squeezed her tighter, and she melted in his arms.

King Rian sat alone at his desk. The bustle of soldiers in the encampment was a distraction from the empty parchment before him. It didn't help that he didn't have the words to write on his own. He felt too much, and he wanted to share it all with his wife, but where to begin?

My dearest, Ivy

I wonder if you've seen your birthday gift or if you've only thrown it into the sea. If so, I wonder if I may hear its call deep in the waters - the same as I once was drawn to you.

It's been one more turn around the sun for you, and I am still less wise than you. I fear I always will be. Although I should not expect to hear from you, it pains me that I haven't, that it's been weeks since I've heard your voice or seen your name signed before me.

War rages on. I am in Suikar now, tired of fighting. Adievasisnis encourages me. I'm nearly close to halfway. I feel you in every strike.

Rian rested his head on his closed fists. What was he saying? Ivy wouldn't want to hear any of this except the compliments. He had a dozen floating around in his mind, but none compared to what she deserved to hear. He crumpled the letter and tossed it into the fire. Flames caught and curled the edges, leaving nothing behind but wasted time. Rian threw his head back and let it hang, fighting a scream of frustration.

Rustling flapped against the tent. Rian grinned when he saw his friend pushing aside the curtain.

"Torin." Grateful for a distraction, Rian stood to greet his knight. They grasped their forearms and embraced. "It's been far too long, brother."

"Long enough that you've grown that sorry excuse for a beard," Torin said with a snide. Rian laughed and scratched his fingers through his patchy facial hair. "It's good. Hides your ugly mug." Torin patted the King's cheek affectionately.

"Come, sit. We have much to discuss."

Torin pulled off his riding gloves and relaxed a few buttons before plopping down on the settee opposite Rian. "I heard you met with the Chancellor. How is Gislina?"

"She is a worthy opponent in conversation with a knack for a convincing argument." Rian poured wine for his friend.

"And has she convinced you of something?"

"An enticing proposal from Bloidarian High Council. Terms for a temporary truce."

Torin's brow raised as he pulled the glass from his lips. "Are you considering it?"

"I'm weighing it among my many options." Rian grabbed his cup with his right hand. Pain seared in his forearm, a wince flickering in his expression. "I admit it is very tempting. I am weary, and we've barely begun."

Torin sighed.

"Already you're vexed with me."

"I struggle to see why you would waste time. Delay what progress we have made." Torin's tone sharpened as he leaned forward, resting his elbows on his thighs. "I have ridden hundreds of miles across all our territories organizing your men, gathering information, and you would throw it away. Make us start again in three months. Are you afraid of the winter?"

"We need to reassess where our efforts are best spent. The Dureto are more organized and formidable than I was led to believe." Rian stole a glance at his advisor. "We need to secure Suikar. If our territories are unstable, how can we create the empire that my father envisioned?"

Torin looked deeply at the King. "It's not just Suikar, though. There's something else."

Rian looked away from his friend. "I am not well, Torin." He shook his head. "I have never been stronger with a sword in my hand, but I ache deep in my bones. I do not sleep, and when I do, I am haunted by my failures and grief. My faith brings me no comfort even as its power has never been clearer to me." Rian rubbed his fingers across his brow. "And I miss her."

"Who else have you told this?" His voice was low like he had already accepted defeat.

"No one."

"Good. Don't." Torin's face tightened. "Remember our discussion from months ago? In seconds, you'd destroy your reputation. A weak, love-sick fool they'd call you. We can't afford that." He ran his tongue across his teeth. "You can't afford that." Silence sat between the two men. "The Dureto are a problem."

"They have amassed a great host. It is far more than rebellious Suikarians. I cannot fight two wars." The words hung from Rian's lips when the curtain to his tent opened. A soldier stood in the entryway.

"The prisoners are ready for you, Your Majesty."

Torin looked to Rian, who unveiled Aternous from his sheath. "More executions?"

"Sacrifices."

Ivy's fingers tapped over her crossed arms impatiently while her father adjusted in his chair. He glanced up with an exasperated expression.

"What?"

"Did you not hear me, or did you simply choose not to listen?" Ivy's lips were pinched.

John turned to his advisor. "Russell, can you-"

"I am not speaking to Russell. I'm speaking to you."

"Ivy," John sighed. "Do you expect me to throw a parade for every man that does his job in Iosnos?" He waved his hand in her face like she was a fly pestering him. What happened to the softer presence she spent time with? What would it take for him to treat her like his equal?

Ivy smacked his hand away from her face. "Don't condescend to me." Her teeth clenched. Anger flared in her father's eyes. "I am not asking for frivolities. I ask for Ad Nekoson to be properly compensated for his service to Iosnos. It is an insult that you don't invite him to your council when he has done more for Iosnos in a month than," Ivy paused and looked at her father scornfully, "others have done in a lifetime."

"Everyone has duties. You should be more concerned with yours." John turned away from his daughter and back to his advisors. "Excuse her, you know irrational women can be."

Ivy spoke quieter, each word measured. "I am not irrational. I am here to help you. What was the point of me going to Asmye, becoming Queen, if it wasn't to help Iosnos? I'm capable. I just ask that you listen to me."

"Darling, you are hardly the most qualified person for these matters. Best left to those most experienced in such things."

"Perhaps I would have more experience if you allowed me a seat at this table." Ivy folded her arms and stared out the window, facing the harbor. Asmyian ships had arrived again. It hurt more every time she saw that flag with no King to accompany it.

"Even without a seat, you seem to have cost these fine men more than enough time with your little tantrum."

Ivy wanted to show him a tantrum. She wanted to rip out his tongue and claw out his eyes. Scream and yell for every insult he levied her entire life.

Russell broke the quiet tension. "Your Majesty, if I may, Queen Ivy has had quite a bit of experience in her lessons with me on many matters that are impo-"

"I think you should stay out of it." John's icy glare cut through his advisor. "Run along, dear; go play with your little Adeshbu." Gone were the days of Ivy's hopes that her father might ever respect her. "Invite them into your deep pockets that seem off limits from your actual family."

"If you allowed me in, I could see that funds are appropriately utilized within Iosnos." She was stone-faced. "I am the Queen of Asmye, the nation you are contract-"

"The marriage contract?" King John scoffed. "Is it even still valid? You have failed to fulfill the terms set forth."

"King Rian-"

"If you were a good wife to your husband, you wouldn't be here. If you cared about Iosnos, you would focus your energy on bringing your husband a son. I don't know how you intend to do that from here. When is your husband coming? Perhaps he hasn't come to collect you because you are as worthless to him as you are to me."

Ivy struggled to hold herself together. Her lips quivered as her eyes filled with tears. "He isn't coming. Iosnos is my home, and I am here to care for her. I brought funds but won't see them misappropriated on your vanity."

"The funds Iosnos needs would be delivered as you delivered your first son. But tell me, *Queen of Asmye*, how can you bear your beloved King Rian an heir with an ocean between you?" His thick brows raised when he muttered the condescending question. He spoke low so the room wouldn't hear. "Ivy, you should know better by now. I don't know why you insist on bringing shame to me. Same as your mother."

"Don't," Ivy muttered out through clenched teeth.

"Ivy, save yourself further embarrassment and leave."

Ivy flung open the council door, furious beyond belief. What she had to offer would never be enough in men's eyes. They always wanted something else from her. Luc's footsteps echoed behind her, another reminder of how she was kept, an object to own and admire rather than a person. Chattel to be traded at any given man's pleasure. His footsteps were pounding louder in her head now. Lines of succession. Legacy. Male heirs. Ivy hated men! Especially those they called King. She missed him. *Stop it.*

Ivy turned on her heel, almost running into Luc's chest as he had followed so close behind.

"Are you alright?" Luc brushed a hair from Ivy's face. She shook him off.

"Do you think I could have a little alone time today?" Ivy tried to be sweet, but venom pulsed in her veins. After all, he hadn't done anything but his job by being there. "I could use some time to clear my head."

"What's going on?" Luc looked around the room before he reached for her hand. Ivy simply shook her head. "We talked about this. You know I can't leave you."

More rules. "Hardly anyone even recognizes me here anymore. If anything, you'll draw more attention to me." Ivy tried to pull back on the sharpness in her tone. He had said all she had to do was tell him. "I just really would like to go on a walk by myself." Ivy looked down at his chest, then fluttered her eyelashes back open to look up into his visor. "Is that too much to ask?"

He sighed. How could she have so much power over him with just one glance? "I can give you some space, but I won't let you wander completely unattended. You won't see or hear me, but I'll be there." He reached to his side, pulling a small knife in a sheath from his belt. "You'll at least carry this, just in case." Luc knelt and lifted her dress just above her ankle. His glove caressed her leg while he slid the knife into her boot, ensuring it was secure. The confidence in his touch made her cheeks flush pink.

Blending in was easy if one wanted. Thanks to Madeline, Ivy's closet was filled with simple garments, nothing more extravagant than anyone else here might have in theirs. She wore no jewels or precious metals. No shiny silver man loomed behind her. She was just an ordinary woman walking through the city streets. It was nice to feel autonomous, even if she knew Luc was trailing behind, just out of sight.

Ivy wandered deep into the city. She was away from the vendors and the shops, tangled among the streets crowded with houses and apartments. Sunlight streamed through lanterns strung across canopies from last week's Evane Festival. Dark pewter and aged copper contrasted as they hung in chaotic lines, weaving back and forth in various sizes and shapes. How many times had she run up these streets as a child, untamed with a pack of other children, chasing mischief and adventure? Ivy scraped her knees from whichever new feat of courage Sophie had encouraged her to try. Now, the streets were quiet and lazy. There were no children kicking balls or mothers calling after them. Only a few people scattered here and there. Plenty of space for her and her thoughts.

Ivy loved the neighborhoods in Iosnos, but the walk wasn't for no reason. Ivy wanted to look at the city through a closer lens, find where the edges frayed and where she could make improvements, even if she had to do so through the voices of the Knights or Adeshbu.

Ivy followed a whiff of a foul scent coming from the southeast. *Always trust your nose.* Along the way, she noticed gutters backing up. Water sat stagnant in the street. Ivy lifted her dress to hop over a puddle. *The canals must not be flowing properly.* The stench was getting worse. She was definitely headed in the right direction.

Torchfire splashed warm light across the plains of Rian's face. Deep creases lined around pouted lips, stern with focus from each strike. Twenty-two souls were given to his God tonight. From the dark of night, guards brought forward the next prisoner. The ecstasy of Rian's kills vanished when Rian saw the last prisoner destined for the edge of Aternous. A boy. He couldn't have been older than ten. Rian's lip quivered as his soldiers began to fasten the bonds around the boy's ankles.

Rian whispered to Torin, "That's a child."

"You said *all* prisoners." Torin's voice was cold and unfeeling. "He is as guilty of treason as the rest of them."

Rian's jaw tensed as he clenched his teeth and sucked in a breath. Tears fell down the boy's dirt-stained cheeks, whimpering as Rian's soldiers secured his bonds.

"Have you no heart? A child can't be guilty of such a crime."

"You are the one who doesn't seem to understand." Torin's words tinged with a growl. He leaned closer to Rian's ear, turning his back to the other guards. "Mercy isn't a cost you can afford. The boy is a traitor who would have you strung up for the crows to eat your eyes rather than bend the knee."

Rian turned his face slowly to Torin. "I will not kill a child."

"And what if you don't? You dare to appear weak to the Chancellor, to your men?!"

"Find another use for him."

Torin kept his eyes locked on Rian's. He exhaled in frustration. The boy hung from his ankles like the other prisoners, preparing for Rian's blade. The corner of Torin's lip tugged toward his cheek. He pulled his knife from its sheath and quickly slid it across the boy's throat.

Rian stared at him. His hand clenched around Aternous' blade. Despite the sacrifices, he felt weak on his own.

"Now it's done." Torin wiped the blade on the boy's tattered clothes and slipped it back into its sheath. "For the safety of the crown."

Rian's lips tightened with anger. A wasted life. The boy's blood couldn't be used if it wasn't The King himself to carry out the slaughter. Rian dismissed the soldiers and fled to his tent.

The parchment creased under Rian's thumb as he folded it neatly. Red wax dripped from the candle he held over the seam, cooling as the heavy thud of his sigil embossed his mark onto the letter. He had written the words and signed his name, but it hadn't seemed like his decision was made until he saw his seal was dry.

Dawn's bright light ached in his sunken eyes. The camp was quiet as men ate their morning meal and sipped rich Suikarian coffee. It was a brisk walk to the officer's tent. Tristan held his fork in one hand and his coffee in the other. His cheeks were full with a hearty bite. The Knight and General stood suddenly when Rian entered, gesturing for the other men to follow. Torin barely looked toward the King from his seated position. Rian pushed the letter into Torin's chest.

"Send this to the Chancellor. We are to make good on her offer." Rian didn't wait for any opinions to be dealt.

Torin kept his eyes low. Underneath the table, he clenched his fist.

"Sir Tristan, keep your men occupied in Suikar."

"Yes, Your Majesty,"

"They can continue the effort against the Dureto as previously discussed. Hand it off to your next in command. You'll ride to Lund. He's to stand down with any Blodarian conflicts until I call on him."

"Rian, don't you think I should go to Lund?" Torin rose from his seat, dabbing his mouth with a napkin. "After all, it was I who pled to him on your behalf."

"You'll see to the men holding the western coastal position," Rian spoke in a no-nonsense tone. "No moves are to be made. They are only to watch and monitor."

"But, I-"

"You'll both join me in Astrella as soon as you've seen to your duties." Rian's back was straight, nodding when Sir Tristan agreed. Torin clenched his jaw and gave a resigned smile before sipping the last of his coffee.

"When should I transfer to Lieutenant Alexion?"

"Prepare him now. I leave at dusk."

CHAPTER TWENTY-ONE

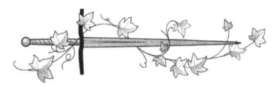

Pink and blue washed over the sky as the sun drifted closer to the horizon. Ivy turned back toward her father's castle. It seemed so small. How long had she walked? How far? She was almost to the eastern bay. Industry smeared its dirty hands on her beautiful island. Her father once said, "Progress demands sacrifice." Was Iosnos' future worth the sacrifice of its nature?

Luc hid in the shadows, nowhere to be seen. She was thankful for the space but still wasn't sure how he managed to do it. How could he always hide from her? She'd never been able to hide from him. There were no crowds to obscure him, only crude, artless buildings and iron fences. Oily-skinned sailors and grease-smeared workers lingered in the streets outside a rough tavern. No one paid her any attention but a nod. Perhaps she should turn back. Darkness would soon blanket the island, and an instinct of preservation stirred queasy in her stomach. She reminded herself she wasn't alone. She sighed and continued. She needed to know the island again.

Dark plumes of smoke billowed ahead, smudging out the blue sky. Birds circled above a tannery; pits sank all over the yard. An overwhelming stink wafted from the discarded corpses of livestock piled near an open well. *Foul.* Ivy looked over her shoulder at the houses nearby. She had heard children inside as she passed. This was no place to raise a family. She'd tell her father right away. It needed to be regulated better than it was, if it was at all.

Ivy held her hand over her mouth and nose, squinting to see through the iron gate. Workers were covered in soot and streaked with sweat. The whole sight was gnarled and blackened. A horn sounded in long beats. Ivy could hardly think; it was so loud. Putrid ash and rancid moisture filled the air while fires flicked in the pits. Skins stretched over wooden frames littering the yard. Ivy's eyes watered; she couldn't stand to be here any longer.

Ivy turned back and rounded a corner, ready to find Luc and go home. Big, gruesome men leaned against a wall in wait. The grease of sweat emphasized the ruddy complexions that clung all over their bodies.

One of them flicked a cigarette. "She's real pretty up close." The smallest of the men reached toward Ivy while the larger walked around. She stepped back, but a brick wall pinned her in. The man looked toward his friend. "Can't we have some fun? Seems a shame to waste it." Their stink was atrocious, breath hot and rotten through yellowing teeth. How did they sneak up on her so fast?

"Freddie said we had to be quick." He leaned in, blowing the last of his smoke in her face.

"Don't touch me!" Ivy frantically pushed away dirty hands, trying to see past the men. Luc had said he wouldn't be far. "Lu-"

The largest man's hand smothered Ivy's scream. "You're a hard little bunny to catch alone." The depth of his voice matched his mammoth proportions. Ivy pounded her fists into his forearm. His other hand slammed into her throat, thick fingers crushing her neck. Ivy tried to suck in air, throwing her fists into the man's ribs and stomping her heel into his shin.

"Oh, she's got a little fight in her!" He leaned in close, whispering in her ear. "I like that." His laugh thundered and was echoed by the other. They prodded and pulled her into the doorway across the street.

"Strolling a little far from home, aren't ya, girlie?" One cackled at her. The room was dank and dark. A small fire flickered in the corner, enough to cast horrible shadows over Ivy's captors. "You made it *real* easy for us. Where's your guard?" he laughed and swung her until she lost her balance.

Ivy hit the wall and crumbled against the floor. She curled her legs up to her stomach, making herself small, protecting herself. Ivy reached down to her boot, unsheathing the knife Luc gave her, then concealed it in the fabric of her dress. Where was he?

The smallest of them whistled at her, beckoning her to come like a dog.

"Come here, little bunny. Don't you want to play?"

"You sure this is the right one?" The small man sniffed.

"Oh yeah, I'm sure," The big man grinned at her and smoothed back dirty blonde hair. "Nice dresses. Big tits. Just like he described."

Another man burst through the door. His bald head was bleeding from the side, and he held up a hand with only a thumb and pinky finger. He limped toward The Queen, screaming to kill that bitch while the other men checked on him.

"Where's the tin man, Freddie?"

"Got him pinned down. Mory's gone." He dropped the bloody rag and reached a hand out for a knife.

"Do you need the head or just the helmet to collect that bonus?" The thin man laughed and handed over his blade.

"Go back for him once we have her down." Freddie wiped at his wound. "Take Mory's share."

"We was just talking about how down we want her," The larger man chuckled.

Ivy kept her position and closed her eyes. Was Luc dead? Footsteps plodded closer. The blonde man's stink worsened as he crouched down, grabbing her body. He pulled at Ivy to get her to turn around. She tucked tightly into herself, making it impossible for him to get a good grip.

"Stop fighting me, bitch!" he yelled as he pulled her around to face him. Ivy plunged the knife directly into his eye, then pulled it out and sank it into his chest. She yanked it out and slammed it back in, screaming while she did. His breath turned to gurgling as he choked on the blood spilling into his windpipe. Again and again, she used all of her strength to stab into his chest. His grip weakened as he frantically grabbed at her. When she felt satisfied, Ivy wrenched the knife from his heart.

The other men stared at each other before pulling up their sleeves. Marks gnashed over their tattooed skin. One started toward Ivy while the other drew a sword. The big man began to fall forward on top of Ivy, crushing her to the floor while she wriggled under his weight.

"Little bunny is tough," the smallest man chuckled. "More shares for us."

The door kicked in and the small man's head was lost from his shoulders seconds after. Luc stumbled forward into the room, burying the tip of his blade deep in Freddie's chest. He looked in disbelief at the blade impaling him. Still, he tried to fight back, spitting blood on the floor. Luc pulled out, slicing him again with a long stroke from cock to chin. It all happened so fast that they didn't even scream. The room was eerily quiet as Luc's sword cleaved through flesh. Blood trickled over the snake tattoo on Freddie's arm, pooling on the floor like vomit from the serpent. Ivy grunted and struggled to push the body off of her, flashbacks of the night she was almost killed flooding her mind.

Luc searched the now-still room, exhaling when he saw dark hair caked in blood. He dragged Ivy out from her underarms until she was free. His hands frantically roamed over her, checking for injuries through the blood and dirt staining her skin and clothes. This was the second time he saved her, and she vowed it would never need to happen again.

"I'm sorry, Querida." He hugged her tight, almost crushing her in his arms. Ivy couldn't stop the shake in her hands as she buried her face in Luc's shoulder.

"I want to go."

Luc led her around the bodies. Ivy had to step around the head, still wobbling on the floor. The sight made her queasy, but she focused her eyes on the back of Luc's helmet as he led her back into the daylight.

"We're at least a two-hour walk from the castle." Luc held her hand so tightly he could've crushed it. "Can you make it?"

Ivy walked behind him, eyes glazed, not even seeing the road before her. Luc surveyed their surroundings. The workers had gone home. There was no one around. Gently, he guided her into an alley.

"Querida?"

Ivy blinked back into focus, squeezing Luc's hand in hers. Tears welled up in her eyes and dripped down her cheeks. He hugged her again, never mind the bloody mess between them.

They stood there silently for ten minutes before Ivy finally broke out in loud sobs.

"I was so scared." She wrapped her arms around Luc while he held her tight to him. "I thought you were dead." Her words choked out through her ragged inhales. He counted her breaths out with her like he did the first night he killed for her. *One, two. One, two.*

"Querida," Luc purred, trailing his thumb down Ivy's back. "There's an inn, not fifteen minutes from here. Will you walk with me?"

"Okay." Ivy heard his words, but everything was kind of blurry, and disorienting. Luc wrapped his cloak around her. The blue fabric shielded her blood-soaked gown from wandering eyes. Ivy tried to focus on his hand holding hers, just putting her feet one in front of the other fast enough to keep up with him. *One, two.* Ivy counted her breaths. Staying on the run was hard, but she had to escape. Ivy broke down the last time. The last time led to more fighting. This was okay. She was okay. *One, two.* Sound came back to her as she crossed the threshold of a doorway.

"Back for days, and yet I have to call on you." Father Trevarthan breached the doorway of Rian's study in Astrella without knocking. Rian stood from his desk to greet his priest. He should have known he could only hide for so long. Castle head-of-household Colette was bound to let it slip that the King had returned once the wine needed to be refilled. "I worried you might have taken ill."

"Forgive me, Father."

Trevarthan took Rian's hand in his own. "It's quite alright. Adievasinis' strength is apparent. You've collected the iron, then?"

Rian felt like a child who hadn't completed his lessons, caught unprepared and empty-handed. "Only 112 men. I have brought their yield back with me."

"That's not even half." The old man's face creased with judgment.

"I know." Rian averted his eyes. "I needed to rest. I'll start fresh in a few weeks." His words clamored to make the priest's face change, to convince Father Trevarthan he was still a worthy pupil.

Trevarthan smiled and squinted his eyes as his lips turned straight. "Soon, then?" Rian swallowed and then nodded, suddenly sixteen again. "We don't want to keep Adievasinis waiting."

"Torin and Tristan have their orders."

"That Tristan is loyal to you. I see greatness in him." Trevarthan landed a heavy hand on the King's shoulder. "But you know what Adievasinis expects. Near 200 souls are left to claim. What of this war?"

"Gislina desires a truce."

Father Trevarthan's eyes went wide, and his breath came out in a huff before he exhaled and the color flushed in his cheeks. "I suppose she does, son. All the nations will tremble before they admit failure."

"You don't advise I consider it?" Rian's heart pumped a beat faster. He grew tired of war.

"I advise only what God has commanded. Asmye depends on you to grow her power, not cede it. The only way your strength will rise is if you take this seriously. God does not take chances. This is where your purpose lies. Do not lose faith."

"Torin goes in my stead. He waits for me in Tornbridge," Rian lied. He needed more time. "I will finish this."

"Good, Rian. Good." Trevarthan tilted his head toward the near wall. "May I see it?"

Rian nodded and presented a large chest wrapped in fine etched leather with a bronze locking mechanism. He carefully twisted the symbols into the proper combination and opened it to reveal the crude iron ore inside. Trevarthan picked up a lump; a smattering of ash dusted his palms.

"I'll send word to the Monastery of the Adeshbu in the Breovanian mountains. They'll have a proper smith for this." Trevarthan held up the blood iron. "Go. Rest now. You've done well."

A churlish man hunched over a corner desk, fiddling with some papers by candlelight. He looked up from his seat as a bloodied woman stumbled inside, followed by a striking knight.

"Heavens!" He fumbled the stack in his hand and tripped up toward the front. "Are you alright?"

Luc spoke to the innkeeper. "I need your most private room and a bath drawn immediately."

He looked back and forth between the two, debating if he were inviting trouble into his inn. Sympathy won out as he called for the porter.

A young man bounded into the room, gasping at the guests before him. The innkeeper, whom Ivy surmised was the boy's father, held his hand out to reassure him.

"One room or two?" The innkeeper stammered.

"One," Ivy and Luc replied simultaneously. Ivy didn't want to be left alone for a second, and Luc would never let her out of his sight again.

Ivy's eyes wandered around the inn as Luc spoke. It was simple but clean and well cared for. She already felt safer in these wooden walls, and Luc held her hand firmly behind the cover of the front desk. His grip tightened, and only then did she notice the innkeeper staring at her. Ivy looked down to see the front of her dress soaked with blood.

The innkeeper's eyes studied her, brow furrowing like he could recognize her but couldn't place her. "Excuse me, miss, but are you-"

Luc cleared his throat, "I need that bath readied *now*." He dropped gold coins on the desk. The sound of them clinking snapped the innkeeper's attention back to Luc. Enough money could distract anyone from the truth or at least make them ignore it.

"Right away, sir." He pointed at his son and then scurried away from the desk, leading them into the bathroom.

Luc grabbed the innkeeper's arm. He spoke low, "We require discretion and privacy. Are there other guests here?"

The innkeeper shook his head.

"Keep it that way. I'll pay extra. Are we clear?"

The man looked down at Luc's blood-smeared armor and raised his eyebrows. "Not a problem, sir. I'll have the water brought in straight away."

"And she'll need a clean dress," Luc called after the innkeeper, who was already barking orders.

Ivy sank into the tub. Her hands trembled as she fumbled with the soap and washcloth. The hot water felt comforting on her naked skin. She stared down at the red streams floating. How many more times would this happen? How many more attacks? Before Rian, she never had a care in the world for her safety. He was right. They only wanted her to get to him.

"Let me." Luc slipped off his gloves. In his firm, sure hands, the cloth lathered. The soap smelled of honey and thyme. He swiped softly at the splatters along her jaw. "Tell me if it's too much."

"It feels nice." Ivy let her eyes flutter closed. His tender touch swiped away the evidence of her assault. Her lips turned up as she pushed out her worry. Water trickled as he wrung out the cloth. Nothing could bring her a sense of ease quite the same as a bath. He delicately wiped away the stains from her palms as Luc kneeled next to the tub. He dropped his fingertips into the water to hold her hand. Ivy squeezed his fingers beneath the water. She was safe as long as he was close. How stupid it was that she wanted to be away from him for even a moment. Hot, soapy water let the last of the filth wash away from her before she raised the cloth to wash Luc.

The grand arching halls of Astrella should have been a comfort to Rian, but they were only empty air between their walls. If they were haunted, it would be easier to stomach than the eerie quiet of his thoughts. Regret blew through him like the summer breeze carrying lemon and lavender from distant fields. What would he have changed? He could have done so many things differently. He should have. It didn't matter now. She had tasted his poison enough times to know better.

"Rian."

The King spun toward the sound of his given name on a woman's lips. Elation waved over him. His wife was the only one to use it in months. His lips broke into a grin before turning into a scowl.

Danielle's long blonde hair hung across her shoulders as she approached. Pouty lips parted, and long eyelashes fluttered at Rian. His face dropped.

"Why are you here? You should be at the camp." Surely, there were men with more need for Danielle than he.

"Supplies," Danielle pointed toward the apothecary Ivy had spent time in. She was gone, but she was everywhere.

"I don't want to speak to you." Rian turned away from her.

"Why not?" Danielle scurried to cut him off in the doorway.

"You ruined everything."

Danielle scoffed as Rian pushed by her. "*I* ruined everything?! Please tell me how." She grabbed for his sleeve, but he shook her off. "Was it when I came when you called? Was it when I did everything you asked? Was it when you told me that you wanted no one else? Was it when I washed your wounds?" She stayed after him, pacing down the hallway. "I didn't ruin you, Rian. I saved you!"

"My *wife* saved me." Rian spun and leaned closer to Danielle's face, breathing her air.

"And where is she?" Danielle didn't falter. The long line of her back was straight and proud.

Rian stopped, forcing his hands to stay at his sides.

"I know she left. I thought it was only for a short time, but whispers speak a different truth. She hasn't been here in weeks. Does she serve Asmye? Does she serve you?"

He turned back, watching those glassy blue eyes gaze up at him, tempting his weakness, his loneliness.

"We don't have to fight, Rian. It could be like it was before. I miss you."

Rian looked toward the floor. What he missed would never come back.

"I thought your bed might be getting cold with all these lonely nights. I used to warm you, didn't I?" Her lips curved as she asked the question. Her beauty was breathtaking. It was hard to deny her. It wasn't a lie that Rian didn't plan on leaving her. He did not account for falling in love with his wife. Rian felt a longing in his heart to be touched tenderly. "Don't forget you needed me even when she was around. Now she's gone. So who is taking care of you?" Rian felt a heaviness in his eyelids as desire flickered in his chest. "Who helps you sleep at night?" Danielle reached out to touch Rian's cheek.

He grabbed her wrist, pushing her hand away. "We're not doing this anymore." Exhaustion weighed heavy on him. Too many restless nights clouded his mind.

"I can see so much burden on you. In the camps, inside these walls, you hold onto it all, carrying your grief across every mile, every hour. Let me take it from you. Talk to me. We used to talk."

Rian didn't push away her hand when it brushed his. Danielle swayed her hips in her skirt, presuming she'd made some progress.

"Rest first. You need your strength." Her fingers squeezed his bicep, dragging her thumb over the muscle.

It took everything for Rian not to slam his ex-lover into the wall. He settled for squeezing the arm outstretched toward him and yanking it away. "Why didn't you tell me?"

Danielle's eyes shifted nervously as she suddenly felt small. "Tell you what?"

Rian lowered his voice, ensuring no staff could hear. "About the baby."

Her expression fell, and a swallow dropped in her throat. A glimmer of a tear ghosted her left eye before she blinked it away. "And what would you have done differently, Rian?" Danielle stood, silently staring into Rian's eyes. Her raspy voice had once allured him, but its honey had turned sour. He didn't have an answer. She yanked her hand away, accepting her fate. "You'd still be standing where you are, and I'd still be exiled from your life."

Rian swallowed. Torin had been right. That baby couldn't exist. It could threaten the Garreau line for centuries. Danielle was nothing, a nobody. A pretty necklace wouldn't change that.

"See to your duties. Attend to them well, but I can't bear to see your face or hear your voice."

"Rian-"

"Don't make me say it again." His lips snarled as she reached for him again, but the king was already out of her grasp.

Chapter Twenty-Two

The suite the innkeeper had provided was nicer than Ivy expected, although the bed was all she had eyes for. The linens smelled fresh as she collapsed on them in her robe. A pink dress hung beside a large mirror leaning against the wall. Luc nervously paced around the room as if some new threat might suddenly emerge. He stopped at a small table under a window where parchment sat next to a vase of frail, yet comforting flowers. His fingers lingered over stationery as he considered sending a message to Adne. Ivy pulled a pillow under her head, folding it into the right shape to support her neck.

"Come lie with me." Ivy reached her hand out toward her guard.

Luc double-checked the locks on the door, then slid a large chest in front of it as a second line of defense. He stuck his head out the window. It was sheer wall. The window was four stories up, impossible to climb. He started taking off his armor. Ivy watched through half-closed eyes at the meticulous way he removed it. It was only for her. No one else would ever get to see him this way.

As soon as he laid down, Ivy curled against his chest as he wrapped his arms around her. It felt normal. No secrets, no hiding. Listening to his breath gave away so much. It wasn't even; she could hear it wavering. Ivy looked up into the face of his helmet. She couldn't see it, but she knew he was crying.

"What is it?"

He put his hand on her chin. Luc's words pushed around a lump in his throat.

"Querida, I almost lost you."

"You didn't," Ivy tried to comfort him, although she suspected he should be comforting her, considering she was attacked with next to no defenses. "I'm okay."

"There's no excuse. I shouldn't have let you wander so far in front of me. I let myself get distracted, lost in a daydream." He shook his head. "I wasn't ready when they came for me. I fought like hell to get back to you."

Ivy had wondered how far behind he was but had only attributed his distance to stealth. She didn't dare ask. He'd been hurt enough, too.

"I would never forgive myself if you were hurt. What would I do without you? I'd be so lost." He held his heart out to her without hesitation. Ivy nuzzled her cheek closer to the bruise on his collarbone and pressed her lips against it. It felt like forever since they'd had any intimacy. A knot formed in her stomach. That had been her fault. She traded nights with Luc for sneaking out and drinking. He deserved better.

"Tell me to close my eyes," she smiled.

"Close your eyes, Querida," his words came back in whispers.

Ivy pulled off his helmet. Holding his face in her hands, she kissed him deeply. Luc rolled Ivy onto her back. She could feel his tears fall onto her face as he pressed desperate lips against hers. He pulled open her robe. His hands were everywhere, holding her, touching her, feeling her. His grief turned to ravenous hunger. Her hands slid up his back, feeling his strength and tension. Ivy pulled his shirt off over his head.

"Luc, never leave me," she whispered as he kissed her neck. She fought back tears.

"I won't. I can't." His hands went to the inside of her thighs. With a forceful grip, he spread them wide. Her cunt was exposed: hot, wet, and throbbing for him. He put his cock inside her, thrusting hard.

"Oh, fuck!" she cried out. Hopefully, the room was private enough that no one heard. Luc pressed his forehead against hers. He kept his jaw tense, fighting back his own lust. He fucked her slowly, savoring her tight cunt. Ivy held the back of Luc's neck, gliding her fingers over the corded muscles in his shoulders as he moved further down her body. She bit her lip to hide the sound he elicited inside her.

"You're so good for me, Ivy. You don't need to be quiet here." Each thrust slammed her deeper into the bed. Her entire body was pushed forward. Her head dipped off the side of the bed. "Let me hear how good I make you feel."

"You feel-oh fuck, keep going." Ivy covered her mouth with one hand. "You feel so good." His teeth nipped at her breasts. Luc's tongue teased her nipple before he sucked it between his lips. Her head arched back as she tried not to scream. Her eyelids fluttered open. Ivy looked into the mirror. Her face was flushed, her mouth hung open, gasping for breath. Ivy could see the top of Luc's head, the shaggy brown curls, and his massive, tanned shoulders. Beyond that, the yellow blooms next to the window seemed to perk up, as if they felt the energy in the room. A delicious distraction, Ivy moaned when Luc's hand climbed up her body until his thumb landed in her mouth. She sucked on it graciously, watching herself in the mirror before she closed her eyes again.

Luc pulled her back towards him. He twisted her hips, putting Ivy on her side, kissing everywhere from her temple to her ear to her shoulder. He pushed her legs apart so he could mount Ivy again.

"Fuck, yes. You feel so fucking good." His moans were almost angry, primal. He leaned down with his face right above hers. Ivy loved how his words growled through clenched teeth, "You're mine." Ivy twisted her face into the pillow, biting down on the fabric as Luc slammed his hips against her. "Say it," Luc reached for Ivy's hair, gripping it near her scalp. He dragged his tongue over the salt on her cheek.

"I'm yours." Ivy reached back, supporting herself on his stomach. His hand gripped her ass tightly when he leaned down to kiss her, forcing a moan into her lips.

"Oh, you like it a little rough, don't you?" He pushed her leg up further, getting a deeper angle. Ivy cried out with every thrust. Ivy grabbed his arm, squeezing it tightly.

"Luc, I'm going to come. You're making me-" Ivy screamed as it shook through her. Her pussy clenched tight around his cock.

"That's good, baby. Scream for me." He brought his hand down on her ass, smacking it hard as he continued to fuck her. Ivy shook underneath him as another wave came. "Come here." Her muscles were still weak as he turned her body, repositioning her so she was on her stomach. He lifted her hips to his, sliding his come-soaked cock back into her.

Her face hid in the mattress. Her head felt light. "Luc, please come in me. I want to be yours."

"No," he growled. His hips rammed into her faster.

Her stomach dropped. "Please, Luc, I wa-"

"Be quiet," His hand smacked her ass again. He sated her, though, testing Ivy as his thumb breached another tight hole while he fucked her pussy, pushing her over the edge one more time.

Ivy gripped the sheets tightly. The edge of pain blurred into pleasure as her cunt pulsated with sensitivity. It surprised Ivy how good it felt to have him in both her holes. Ivy pushed her face into the mattress to scream as aftershocks rolled through her. Luc pulled out of her, stroking his cock quickly until he came on her ass. He collapsed on the bed beside Ivy, panting. He rubbed her back with his rough hands until they caught their breath.

Luc hummed in the afterglow. "You did so good. Are you okay?" He kissed along her shoulder. "Do you need some water?" Ivy smiled at his sweetness while he wiped his come from her ass with a towel.

"Water, please." She turned her face away, too weak to dare to look at him.

He kissed her hair before he rose from the bed. Ivy heard him pouring the water from across the room, but then there was silence.

"Luc?" Ivy picked herself up and balanced against the headboard. Ivy kept her eyes closed, just in case, but there was nothing. No sound came from anywhere until he rested the cold glass against the bare skin on her chest.

"Luc!" Ivy thrashed back into the bed, trying to escape him. It was too late. Ivy already made him laugh. What a beautiful sound.

"I had to do it."

"Are you satisfied?" Ivy laughed, too, rubbing her palm against her breast.

"I am. I'm sorry." His words dripped with honey. Luc took a step forward and leaned down to kiss her ear. "Can I make it up to you?"

With her eyes closed, her eyebrows raised. "Maybe," Ivy scooted to the side of the bed and tapped the pillow beside her. Luc only chuckled and grabbed her hand and put the glass in it.

"Ivy, you didn't think I was done with you yet, did you?"

The Queen smiled and shook her head.

"I'll have you all night, Querida. We can stay right here."

Ivy reached for his hand, sighing when he brought it to his lips.

"Drink, Ivy. You need it."

Ivy misjudged the distance and spilled water onto her bare chest. She shook at the cold temperature against her skin.

"I can put my helmet back on."

"Don't." Ivy took another sip, more carefully this time. "I prefer you without it, even if I can't look." She handed him the glass.

"Well, I am looking." His finger skimmed along her bottom lip. Ivy gasped quietly as his tongue lapped at the water she spilled on herself. "I just wish I could see your eyes without the helmet. Feels like I'm missing the best part."

"Tell me about it." Ivy laughed at him, and then there was a moment of silence. "You know, we coul-"

"No, Ivy." Luc pulled her down until she laid back on the bed with him. Ivy turned to him, resting her ear against his chest and ignoring the disappointment. What would it take for him to show himself to her? Ivy opened her eyes, gazing down at his body. She put her hand on his tummy and moved her fingers lower in the trail of plush hair that grew between his hips. She could spend the rest of her life in the afterglow with Luc. Embarrassment hung in her belly. She didn't want to ask, but she had to.

"Why won't you come inside me?"

"I don't want to lose this with you," he paused, "If you get pregnant, especially now that you're away from him, I'd lose you. I'd lose the baby, too. I can't go through that again."

"You don't have to worry about that," Ivy buried her face deeper in his chest, "I don't think I can get pregnant."

Luc squeezed his arm around Ivy's shoulder. "You don't know that."

"We've been trying for months and nothing." Tears sprang up in her eyes. Her hand immediately twisted around her bare finger.

"That doesn't mean *you* can't. Better to keep you safe." He stroked his hand across her back. "If you were caught with child by another man, he could have your head."

The thought made her queasy. Rian never learned to share. *Wait. He said, "Again."* "Again? You can't go through that again?"

Luc took a breath. The rise of his chest lifted her head. "I told you a long time ago that I suffered loss before I became an Adeshbu. I did lose everything: my wife, my son, my home."

Her stomach twisted in her gut. Ivy never asked him about his life. Ivy hated herself for the jealous pang in her stomach as he spoke of a wife, a woman before her. *Like you're any better. You're still married.* Ivy pushed the thought away to focus on Luc.

"What happened?"

"Greed is a hungry beast that consumes all. They just happened along its path. I couldn't protect them."

Ivy shuffled in the sheets. "I'm so sorry, Luc. I didn't know."

"How could you know? It's not something I like to talk about. Sometimes I try to forget," he sighed, and Ivy held him tighter. "These days, I can't stop thinking about it—the fear of losing you, of going through that again. I couldn't endure it. At least now I can protect you, protect what I love."

Luc's love was whispered all over her skin, dark marks that wouldn't let her forget. "You've always kept me safe."

"I think you are why I was reborn."

"Reborn?"

"When I became Adeshbu-" Luc intertwined his fingers with hers. "-it was harder than I can put into words. Brutal at times. Death would have been easier, less painful, but Adievasinis was there." Ivy kicked her foot from under the sheet into the cool air. "He fed me when I was starving. He sheltered me when I was freezing. He paid the slavers and liberated me. The strength, the faith that He would lead me to the life I needed."

Ivy swallowed. She had never known a life like that and had hardly met anyone who experienced it. She was so adamantly against Rian's god. How could she not be, considering everything he put her through? Her resistance to it only hardened whenever she was told to have faith. Faith was something she buried so deep. If she gave in, she might lose what little control she had in her fate. She took a deep breath and let his words into her heart.

"If I am His body, then you are Hers. 'Beauty that would make the stars jealous of how She shines,'" Luc recited from ancient texts. "The power to grow life from the earth. Compassion and love, both bound inside a Goddess that walks the fine sands of Iosnos. I would lose my Heaven if you fell from my grip."

Ivy's fingers dragged along Luc's stomach as they lay there in silence for a while. "You don't have to worry about losing me, Luc." She propped herself on her elbow, leaning in with her eyes closed, feeling around for a soft kiss against his lips.

"You are married to another man, a King no less. I could never give you all the things he can."

Ivy swallowed, "I don't wear his ring." Luc grabbed her hand, interlacing his fingers with hers. "Whatever he can give me, I don't want."

"What do you want, Querida?"

"I want you." Ivy kissed his chest. "I want your fear," another kiss, "I want your cock," she giggled as she wrapped her fingers around his neck. "I want your mouth," Ivy brushed her lips against his. His inhale sharpened. "I want your doubts," Ivy kissed him. "I want to know you, own you," Ivy could feel him start to get hard against her thigh. "I want your love, and I want the morning never to come."

"You have all of me, Querida."

"All of you?" Her lips drew nearer to his.

"Yes," he whispered. She knew it wouldn't be true until he showed her his face. Why would he promise forever without trusting her? One day, it might not matter so much to him, and she would be waiting. His lips brushed against hers. Ivy couldn't get any closer to him. She could practically hear his heartbeat in his chest as she kissed him. Her hand rested against his cheek, desperate to memorize every curve of his skin.

When Ivy had enough romance, she bit his bottom lip and pulled back on it, inhaling as he moaned.

"Thank you," she whispered.

"For what?"

"Loving me, letting me love you." Ivy kissed him again.

"I love you," Ivy felt his smile spread across her lips. In the same instant, he flipped her on her back. "I will love you all night."

"What about after tonight?" Ivy asked as his lips brushed over her collarbone.

"I will love you then, too." He started to trail kisses down her body. Her nerves were still on edge, and she tried to deter him from touching her aching pussy.

"Are you hungry?"

"Yes, but I don't wanna leave this bed." He was getting closer now.

Ivy wanted him. She just didn't know if she could take it. "We could probably get the innkeeper to bring us something as long as he's properly motivated." Ivy was breathless as his lips skimmed over her hips.

"I think I can hold myself over for a little while with what I have right here." He nibbled at her thigh.

"Luc, I think-"

"You're too sensitive right now?" He kissed the inside of her thigh deeply.

"Yes," she moaned. She hated to admit it, but it had been quite a day. Fatigue ached through her bones.

"Don't worry, I wasn't going to touch you there."

"What do you-" He turned Ivy onto her stomach. He left her in the bed, and all she heard was fabric ripping. *Great.* It was so hard being blind all the time. Ivy never knew when or what his next move would be. She especially didn't think it would come in the form of his tongue sliding against her backside.

"Luc!" Ivy lifted onto her elbows. The fabric wrapped around her eyes. Luc fiddled with tying it behind her head. He kissed her cheek and tapped it with the back of his fingers.

"Lie down," he murmured. When she didn't immediately obey, he pulled her legs down until her arms were above her head, and her head hit the pillow. Luc's shoulder pushed between her thighs until she was spread apart for him. "Do you love me?"

"Yes, Luc,"

"Are you going to do as I say?"

"Yes, Luc," she was nervous but loved him. He would never hurt her. His lips kissed their way up one leg, then the other, and met her right in the middle. Ivy moaned when his tongue slid over her slit and up.

"Luc?"

"You can always tell me to stop." His hands gripped her ass firmly, then slid down her legs.

Ivy hesitated, "No, I want to."

Luc couldn't hide his excitement. His hands massaged her calves as his tongue lapped around her hole. It felt so good. He tickled her with ecstasy. He pushed his face into her, moaning as he licked and kissed her. Every moan vibrated against her. He pulled her ass cheeks apart and dove in deeper. Ivy writhed in the bed, pushing her hips back to get more. Ivy relaxed into the bed when Luc's weight shifted. He positioned himself on his knees, hovering over her. He kissed her shoulder and pet his hand down her back. His fingers slid over her ass, rubbing his spit around.

"I'm gonna touch your pussy, Querida."

Ivy couldn't speak. She just nodded and moaned desperately for any touch. Luc's hand slid up the length of her pussy. Ivy shuddered at the contact. He pulled his hand away, covered in her slick. Luc pumped the head and length of his cock, soaking himself with her come. His free hand gripped her hip to keep her steady. He laid the head against her. Ivy tensed upright as his cock breached her.

"Let go, relax. Let me." Luc squeezed her ass and pushed in an inch deeper. Ivy bit into the pillow, trying not to make any sound to discourage him. It didn't hurt, not really, but it was different. He paused as he felt her tension.

"Why did you stop?" she asked.

"I don't want to hurt you."

"Keep going," She always wanted more of him. Ivy pushed her hips back, feeling him spread her slowly.

"You're doing so good, Querida." Luc's voice praised her as his hands caressed her. He pushed in deeper. Ivy let out a low moan into the pillow. His voice hummed. "You feel great." His words only made her want more of him. Ivy pushed back again.

"Oh, fuck!" she cried out at the sensation.

Luc's breath was shallow as she tightened around him. Ivy felt tingles in her cheeks as she relaxed.

"More," she whispered.

Luc pushed in deeper and then again. Ivy teetered on the edge of it being too much. Her breath shook as she adjusted to the sensation.

"Baby, you're amazing." Luc bent forward. He kissed her shoulder. His hand grabbed her throat, softly caressing the curve of her jawline. Ivy tilted her face back to him.

"I love you," Ivy whispered to him.

Luc eased himself inside her fully. Her eyes rolled back, and her breath hitched. Ivy had never felt so full. Her fingers tapped on the sheet next to her face. There was so much nervous energy inside her. All she wanted was to please him.

"Are you okay?" His hands slid all over her body, giving her goosebumps. Ivy nodded and reached her hand back to him. He grabbed it and squeezed before he started rocking his hips against her. He moved slowly, taking care of her. Ivy moaned as his pace increased. Ivy blew her breath out against the bed. He filled her so well. Her pussy leaked between her legs. Ivy had never wanted him so badly.

"Luc, fuck me," she begged. Luc bucked his cock in and out of her tight little asshole. Every stroke earned a moan from her throat. It started to feel so good. Why didn't Rian do this with her? Ivy bet he would feel amazing stretching her out this way. *Fuck, stop thinking about him.* Luc's cock knew how to bring her back to the present. Ivy arched her back, letting him get even deeper. It hurt, but it was a good hurt.

"Does that feel good, baby?" His hips slammed into her.

"Yes-s-s-" Ivy could barely think coherently, let alone speak. The only thing her mind focused on was *baby*, on being loved.

"I can feel you open up for me. You're such a good girl." He buried himself as deeply as possible, muttering how good she felt around his cock. He leaned down and kissed her back. Ivy turned her face back toward his, hoping he could reach her for a kiss.

"Querida, I want to see that pretty face of yours while I fuck your ass." He pulled out slowly. Ivy focused only on her breathing, trying to stay relaxed. As soon as he was out, she wanted him back in. His body leaned over hers as he wrapped his hand around her jaw. Her neck cracked as he pulled her in for a kiss. His tongue fought against hers as he grabbed her shoulder and threw her onto her back. Ivy spread her legs under him and rolled her hips up to meet his.

"You want it so bad, don't you?" He grabbed her ankles in his hands and lifted, "You're so desperate for it."

"Yes, Luc, please." Ivy grabbed her legs, bending at the knees and stretching them as far back as she could. His deliciously thick cock pushed into her hole again. This time, he slid in with ease, forcing little moans from the back of her throat. Luc said he loved her as Ivy took all of him in one long thrust. Her jaw dropped. Ivy wanted to cry out in pleasure but couldn't find the sound. Luc leaned forward to kiss her while he fucked his cock in her ass. Finally, the sound returned as she moaned loudly into his mouth. His body pressed right against her throbbing pussy in this position. Tears sprang in her eyes as she shook and released under him. Her arms wrapped around him, and she bit down into his neck, a welcome side effect from the exquisite torture of this pleasure.

"You want all of me, Querida?" He just kept going.

"Yes, Luc."

"I'm going to give you all of me," He fucked her harder. "I'm going to come inside you."

"Please, Luc, come inside me. I want you."

Luc kissed her, and she came again. As she thrashed underneath him, she felt it. He came deep inside her, letting her have him completely. His moans pressed against her lips as his breath quivered, whispering praises in her mouth.

CHAPTER TWENTY-THREE

Rian threw open the door to his chamber and then slammed it shut. This was the only place he felt he had any control anymore. He stared at his freshly made bed, pillows arranged above fine linens. It was so empty without Ivy. His whole life felt empty without her.

He stomped to his wine cabinet, retrieving the first bottle he saw, and downed nearly the whole thing. It was bitter and did the job just perfectly. He glanced at the label, hardly reading it before throwing it against the wall. Glass shattered and whatever wine was left dripped over the floor. Rian grabbed another and pulled the cork out. He didn't want to be here. He didn't want to be anywhere she wasn't.

Rian twisted the knob and walked inside his wife's chamber. He remembered sending Ivy to sleep in her bed soon after they married, even calling for Danielle when she was gone. Trevarthan promised Rian's strength and legacy in Adievasinis, but he never felt weaker. He would have to leave soon to complete the ritual. It was either that or admit his weakness. Rian covered his face with his palm, digging his fingers into closed eyes. He wished to open his eyes to find her standing before him.

But she was gone. The bed was empty. It had laid untouched for weeks in Ivy's absence. Rian dragged his fingers over her pillow, pulling at a stray hair she had left behind. What else was left? He rummaged through her things, starting in the closet. All her formal gowns hung neatly, freshly pressed. He stopped when he saw the midnight blue dress she wore the night of the banquet. His fingers stroked the velvet, the thick weave melting beneath his fingertips.

Mats and tears muddled over the luxurious texture that rough brushes could not clean. Colette has said his wife returned filthy, but he had attributed that to the storm. He should've searched for her and brought her into his warm bed no matter how angry she was. He remembered her face before she stormed out. It was the last time she had touched him.

He bunched the skirt in his fists before moving on to the drawers. Something glimmered in the light and caught his eye underneath a piece of scarlet ribbon; the same Ivy wore in her hair at the ball the night she was attacked. His eyes flooded when he saw her wedding ring tied inside. Rian couldn't remember ever seeing her without it. He picked up the golden band, holding it between two fingers. It looked so tiny in his grasp.

I find these walls a prison. Ivy had escaped. Was this the shackle she left behind? He held the ring in his fist tightly and then lay in her bed, burying his face in her pillow. He inhaled, desperate to catch any scent of her. There it was: the smell of lavender that always lingered in her hair.

He breathed in deeply, closing his eyes. He imagined pressing his nose into the waves of Ivy's hair, holding her close. He wanted her so badly, needed to feel her touch. She'd unlace his shirt while she looked upon him with those eyes, her eyes: the rich coffee that sparked with golden fire. Ivy gave him everything he didn't know he needed.

He reached down, unfastening his pants to pull out his cock. He was half-hard just at the thought of her. He spit in his palm, wishing he could spit in her mouth. He touched himself. She'd like it. Rian stroked his cock, smiling at the thought. He wanted to look down and see her face, watch as her lips wrapped around him. He twitched, thinking of how wet she'd get while she pleasured him.

"Fuck," he moaned, stroking himself faster as he imagined how Ivy would ride him, sinking onto his cock. How big she'd make him feel as she gasped for air the deeper it went. Her cunt would squeeze him while her tits bounced in his face. Rian opened his mouth to pant. His hips thrust to meet his hand. Ivy had wanted every part of him: licking up his blood, sucking on his fingers, pushing him to feel everything: pain and pleasure in equal measure. So good, so greedy for every bit. She was astonishing, forcing him to the edge, devouring him. He fucked his fist harder. His hand flexed, remembering her life in its grip. His power over her was only an illusion compared to the power Ivy held over him. He craved her with his whole body. Ivy was his: his Queen, his wife.

He moaned. He was so close. Her lips tasted her own come off his kiss. His expression tightened. Rian came hard all over his chest and stomach with a guttural groan. He fell asleep in her bed, dreaming of her tongue sliding across his skin.

Rian didn't go back to his chamber for days. Trevarthan called for him, but he stayed in Ivy's bed sheets. He clung to them, wishing the fabric would turn into her skin. In his deep sleep, images of her flashed in his mind.

Dark hair fluttered in the wind. Ivy was back, their family together at the beach. She stared at the sea as her daughter was swimming in the waves.

"Don't go too deep!" Ivy shielded the sun from her eyes. "Rian, make sure she doesn't hurt herself."

"She's your daughter. Do you think she'd listen to anything I say anyway?" He caught her smile as he threw more kindling on the bonfire. Their girl was so much like her: adventurous, stubborn, knew how to crack a joke. Rian watched her eyes follow his path. Ivy held their son against her hip.

"Do you want me to take him?" he asked, reaching out his arm.

"No, I've got him." Ivy swung her around to the other side to see the shore. Rian took a step closer, wrapping his left arm behind them. His family. He rested his right hand on her stomach. It was swollen with-child. Like a wave breaking over him, Rian felt happy. But, as the joy retreated, fear was left in its place.

A flutter.

Ivy's arm went limp, falling against his. He caught their son under his elbow and pulled him to his chest. In the same instant, Ivy's legs gave way underneath her. Their son turned to salt in his arms. Rian reached for Ivy but couldn't catch her before she fell back, sinking into the sand.

Another flutter.

Ivy lay in her husband's bed, Rian at her side. She hadn't opened her eyes in hours. The only reassurance Rian had that she was still breathing was her chest's soft rise and fall and the barely there warmth of her hand under his palm.

The doctor's voice was distorted.

"There is nothing left to do." The doctor's mouth kept moving, but there was no sound. Rian understood the choice was his wife or his child. He didn't have long to decide.

"It wasn't like this with the others."

"Every pregnancy poses new risks," the warbled sound returned, "These things do happen."

"I need more time! I need more time!" Rian kept shouting, but the room's chaos clattered around him, unaffected by his screams. The doctor pulled

horrifying metal instruments from a boiling pot of water. The hot steam was thick in his lungs, clouding his eyes.

Rian stood at the head of the table, leaning over her. "It's going to be okay, baby. I won't lose you." Rian stroked his fingers through her hair and kissed her forehead. His every movement taxed him, weakening him by the minute.

When the knife slid into her skin, Ivy shot up, screaming and thrashing to get away. Rian struggled to restrain her. His arms were tired and heavy. Ivy whimpered in pain, "Please stop, please stop, Rian," Ivy pleaded through a pained expression. "Have mercy on me," Ivy screamed. Rian closed his eyes.

Rian sat up in her bed. The last thing he heard in his dreams was the sound of her agony. What was this? A premonition? Was that her future if she came back to him? His fingers clutched her pillow. He only foresaw the future once, when he was a boy. He would not lose what he loved again.

CHAPTER TWENTY-FOUR

A soft grey mist thickened the forest air. Luc could only see maybe fifty feet in any direction. Orchids bloomed, and mushrooms grew from the moss-covered bark of the trees. He looked up; the peaks of the trees were hidden in the same wispy fog. If this wasn't the same path home he'd taken thousands of times, he might feel the danger of being lost. He picked luscious brown mushrooms from a tree stump that had fallen years before. He lifted the biggest cap to his nose and sniffed deeply before tucking it into his bag. The slow roll of far-away thunder echoed above the treetops. Rain couldn't be far behind. He flipped the hood of his cloak over his head and began jogging on the path. Just a mile or two more, he might be able to make it.

Eulalia added another log onto the hearth to keep the tiny home warm. She could sense the cold snap of winter coming. They'd been here since their son was born, hidden away from the world, protecting him from his parents' mistakes. The flames caught the wood, and the flickering warmth popped and hissed, letting off its orange glow.

"Don't get too close, Mateo." She crouched beside the small boy playing beside the fire and brushed the brown curls away from his forehead. With those soulful brown eyes, he looked just like his father. She tapped his nose, then returned to the counter and pulled her long black hair into a loose bun tied to her head. She chopped potatoes and carrots from the garden, adding them to a pot. She'd try to stretch them as far as she could. The rain started to fall loudly against the roof. She peered out the window, setting the pot out to catch the freshwater. Nerves fluttered in her stomach. Why wasn't he home yet?

The long arm of the war had reached the borders of Bloidar. With it came uncertainty for the life Eulalia had hoped for, a life uncomplicated by the harsh realities of the world. She had felt safe here, their hideaway tucked deep in the forest of Emrata, miles from any town. Now she prayed they'd stay hidden, unnoticed by the outside world.

Eulalia jumped when the door opened, but her shock washed away when she saw his face. Luc. He carried in the nearly full pot of water from the porch. Mateo jumped up from the floor and ran over to him. Luc kneeled to hug the boy, holding his tiny body close to his chest. Luc pushed back the wet hood of his cloak, unveiling disheveled curls that clung to his skin.

"I've brought you something, mijo."

"You have? What is it?!" Mateo preened in his tiny voice.

Luc reached into his bag and pulled out two wolves carved from wood. "I brought you two. Wolves need their pack, their family."

Mateo held one of the wolves in his tiny hands, inspecting the new toy. "Thank you, Papa!"

Luc looked at the wolf in his own hands. "Ah-woooo," Luc howled to Mateo, who joined in with his own small howl. Luc smiled at his son and handed him the other wolf.

"And what did you bring me?" Eulalia raised her eyebrow with a smirk on her face. She leaned into her hands on the counter behind her.

Luc looked at his wife, her lovely dark eyes and beautiful golden skin. He rose from the floor and softly kissed her plush mauve lips. "I brought you bread," He kissed her again, "and this." Luc reached into the bag and pulled out the mushrooms he'd harvested earlier.

"You really know how to win a girl over." She smiled, taking them from his hand.

"Well, I brought more than that. It's not good." His brows turned upward in a melancholy expression. Her smile faded.

"There were men in town. Unfamiliar men asking questions."

"No," she muttered. Eulalia turned back to her cooking. "They could be anyone. He couldn't have tracked you here."

"A man like that doesn't forgive debts. You knew when we ran away, when we gave up that life, that he would seek retribution for his loss."

Eulalia whipped her face to look at him. "You didn't take anything from Shurvie but yourself."

"And I made him more money than any of his other thieves," Luc sighed. "He won't stop until he has what he believes he's owed, and we have nothing to pay him with."

She nodded her head. They had talked about this, the moment they'd have to abandon their home in search of safer shores.

"We don't know yet." She chopped the mushrooms and added them to her stew. "They could just be passing through. Lots of people are moving with the war. Some towards it, others from it."

Luc sighed, "We can't hide forever." His hand touched the small of her back. Eulalia nodded, understanding with sorrow on her beautiful face. "I want you to be safe." He slid his hand around her tummy, yearning to feel the steady heartbeat of a new life, and hugged her from behind. "Keep our future safe." He kissed her neck and squeezed her tight in his arms.

The pounding on the door jolted Luc out of their bed.

"What is it?" Eulalia asked, tugging the thin sheet up to her chin.

"Stay quiet," Luc whispered, "Get Mateo and go out the back, just like we talked about. Do you remember?" Luc looked into her frightened eyes.

"They're here, aren't they?" She asked, pulling on her cloak.

"I don't want to wait to find out." Luc grabbed his only weapon, a large hunting knife. He crouched down and kissed Mateo's forehead. The loud pounding thundered against the wood door again. "I'll find you. Go now!"

Eulalia quietly creeped out the back door with Mateo as Luc shouted toward the front door.

"I'm coming!" When Luc cracked the door open, twenty men held torches, illuminating the black night. The man at the door sneered through a beard peppered with silver and black.

"What do you want?" Luc asked, trying to hide the fear in his voice with gruffness.

"We're looking for a man." The man looked at Luc through narrow eyes. "A friend of a man we're in business with."

"There aren't many out here. Next town's a ways that way." Luc pointed to the left. "You might make it before sunrise if you start now."

A gruff hand caught the door before it hit the frame, and a knowing smile crossed the bearded man's lips. "I think we took our directions well the first time. We paid Shurvie out to collect on his old debt."

Luc's eyes went wide for only a second before he cleared his throat. "Never heard of him. I don't know about anything like that." Luc tried to shut the door again, anything to give Eulalia more time.

The man's hand blocked it from closing. "I think you do."

The black-bearded man dragged the head of his axe along the ground as he stepped forward. The metal shrieked in a low, eerie tone. He forced Luc back into the house, brandishing his torch close to Luc's face. "What a lovely little home." The man looked around. He spotted the wooden wolves on the floor in front of the smoldering embers of the fire. "Ah, yes." He picked up the toy. "Where have you hidden them?"

There was a moment of silence before Luc swallowed hard. The man looked around the tiny house and spotted the back door.

"Or have they run?" He stared Luc down, reading his face for the lies and truth. The man turned and yelled to the men outside. "They ran out

204

the back! Find the-" The man groaned sharply as Luc plunged the knife deep into his stomach. Luc didn't hesitate as he pulled the knife from the man's gut, spilling blood onto the floor.

The man swung his axe. Luc dodged it, and the axe's head buried itself into the wood floor. The man weakly pulled the axe from the floor. He swung again, spitting up blood as he demolished a chair in his path. Horses whinnied, hooves thundered, and men shouted. Luc ran out the back door.

"Eulalia, run!" he yelled as loud as he could, and then something hit the back of his head. He stumbled as his vision doubled. Luc tried to steady his balance but was hit in the stomach, doubling him over. He took two more unsteady steps and fell to the ground. He tried to open his mouth to yell again, but nothing came out but a weak whisper.

"Eulalia."

The cold, grey morning light crept in through the trees, the fog settling heavier over the dirt. Luc blinked open his eyes as water poured over his head. He felt like he was choking; he tried to cough, but his mouth was stuffed with a gag, and his arms were tightly bound with thick rope.

"Thought you might want to see this," one of the men laughed. The man yanked Luc up from the ground and turned him to face his home. "You will catch a pretty penny at the market. They weren't worth what it costs to feed them." Above Luc, Eulalia and Mateo hung from a tree. Luc went wild, thrashing to break his bonds, but they only grew tighter. He sobbed, choking on the gag. "Maybe if they hadn't run, if you hadn't killed one of ours, I could have shown them mercy and sold them for a few pennies."

Heartbreak or something worse rumbled inside Luc's chest. Eulalia's feet and legs were covered in mud. Cuts and scrapes from branches had torn through her skin as she ran. She never had a chance. The man leaned down to whisper in Luc's ear. His breath stank through rotted teeth. "Your wife, though, I don't think I've tasted anything sweeter. Tsk, tsk, such a waste."

Luc whipped his head, smashing the man's nose. Luc tried to stand but was clubbed across his back and fell into the mud. The man wiped the blood away from his nose with a chuckle caught in his throat.

"Burn the house."

Tears stung Luc's eyes. Two men threw torches into the house, and slowly, smoke billowed out. They pulled Luc to his feet. He tried to turn back to look back for some hope, but that was all gone. His life and family went up in flames, just like his home, as they dragged him, stumbling behind their horses.

Luc stared out the window of the inn. The sun had cast its first golden light over the sea as he finished his story. Ivy held him from behind, her cheek pressed against his back as she listened to Luc's story. Tears glossed over her eyes at the pain he <u>had just</u> unraveled before her. An orphan turned thief. A thief turned father. A father turned slave. A slave turned Adeshbu.

Luc squeezed Ivy's fingers around his waist before bringing them to his lips. He held back the haunted shudder under his chest. It had been a long time since that fateful night, yet he dwelled in each piece of the memory, preferring to remember his wife for her last smile than anything else.

"Close your eyes, Querida." Luc rolled over in the bed, taking in Ivy's beauty as she lay before him. Her lashes fluttered with anticipation before he reached his finger under her chin and pulled her in for a kiss. He relished how familiar she looked to him. Ivy had the same hair, the same nose, the same glint in her eye when she had a dastardly plot. Luc was grateful Adievasinis had given him Eulalia again. Only this time, he would never let her go.

Luc didn't object when Ivy started taking the long way home. It was a much more scenic route than cutting through the city. Instead, they were able to walk through a rolling expanse of pastures. Sheep and goats grazed as she walked beside Luc. It wasn't totally secluded, but she didn't feel the gaze of prying eyes as they walked together. Ivy couldn't decide if it was safer to stay off the main roads or to be surrounded by people. Whichever was true, she knew no harm could come to her with Luc at her side. She looked at him, her Adeshbu, her savior, time and time again.

A bumblebee flew past her face. Ivy smiled, following it down to a patch of overgrown lilac. Luc bent down, picked a long, thin leaf blade, then pulled off his gloves before taking her hand.

"It won't fetch a price in any shop, but it isn't worthless." He began wrapping the leaf around her third finger. "I'll have to replace it every day, but you will know it means the same to me every time I put it on your finger." His fingers gently tied the leaf into a ring. "I am yours." Ivy smiled at her hand, the little strip of green against her skin. "If you'll have me."

Ivy stared down at her hand. It had been months since anything marred her skin. She waited for the uneasiness, for the weight in her stomach to creep in, but there was nothing. She was free. Ivy looked into Luc's visor, wishing to meet his eyes. It was hard to contain her smile. She bit down on her bottom lip and took a deep breath.

"If you can catch me." Ivy took off running across the field, smiling back at him. The sheep ran, panicked, blocking Luc's path to her. Ivy laughed, watching him struggle. She headed straight for a small group of trees as fast as her feet could take her. As she reached their shade, she felt his hand at her waist. They tumbled to the ground laughing. Twigs and leaves caught in her hair as she play-fought him until he pinned her to the ground.

Luc's voice buzzed, "I love you, Ivy."

Ivy closed her eyes and lifted his helmet to kiss him. These feelings were so overwhelming. The unease finally broke through, settling in her chest. She had fallen for him, but Rian wasn't gone. He was still her husband. No ship could take her far enough away to dissolve that truth.

Ivy broke from his kiss and dropped his helmet down. "I don't know if I should accept this."

Luc's breath stopped.

"It's not you, it's me." Ivy pushed herself up from her elbows to sit straight. "I haven't been honest about everything that's happened. I know you don't like talking about him-" Ivy had to divert her eyes from the line of his visor. "-but we need to."

His helmet turned away from her, and he threw his arm over his knees. "I want you to feel comfortable talking to me." He turned back to her. "Even about that."

Ivy took his hand in hers and held it against her chest. "You have me," Ivy smiled. "I need you to understand what happened. I wanted to be a good wife." Luc shifted his weight but held Ivy's hand in the cool grass. "I tried and I tried and it was getting somewhere. I thought we were happy."

"But he hurt you."

"He did," Ivy looked at her feet and dug her heels into the earth, "and I forgave him. I thought he was getting better. At least he made me believe he was." Her breath started shaking. Ivy missed Rian so much. And even though Luc was right there, he still wasn't her husband. "You can imagine how I felt like an idiot when he told me of a mistress." The lump rose in her throat.

"I'm sorry."

Ivy recalled Luc's lecture about the castle gossip. "Did you know about her?"

Luc shook his head.

"You don't have to lie for my sake." Ivy waited for an admission but Luc only shrugged. "I felt so humiliated walking those halls. That's why I took off his ring. I couldn't stand being his for a moment longer. He put a ring on my finger, and I became defined by him completely." Ivy looked around the hillside at her island. Off in the distance, she could see the castle construction near completion. "He still defines me. Now, that definition includes 'fool.'"

"You are your own, Ivy."

It took everything in her not to laugh. How could he not see? "I have always been someone else's. My name passes from one man to another. A footnote under Crestieene, now a footnote under Garreau."

"Querida, you don't have to wear it," he sighed, determined to hide his heartbreak. "I just wanted you to know that you have my heart, that I'm yours. I don't want to define you. I only want to be with you."

Ivy felt pink flush through her cheeks as she began to smile. The sun shone over his armor. She remembered the light glinting over him during her wedding. Something inside her drew her to a man she had never seen. Ivy fiddled with the grass around her finger. Finally, peace settled over her. It had been months since she felt this content. How silly that she hadn't seen it before. Her soulmate stood at the altar waiting for her on her wedding day. Ivy didn't know it wasn't the groom, yet it was the man in the mask.

"I know forever isn't promised to us. I can't see past my fingertips, but I will still dive in." Luc lifted his helmet and leaned in to press his lips against Ivy's. "Querida, you are worth the risk. I'd burn in hell for all eternity for one more kiss."

"Only one?"

He covered her eyes and kissed her again.

CHAPTER TWENTY-FIVE

An angry trumpet sounded at the palace gates as Ivy and Luc approached, a swing in their step. They'd dropped hands nearly a mile behind them, wary of wandering eyes. Within moments, Russell rushed toward her. His arms wrapped around Ivy too tightly.

"We've been so worried."

She tapped him gently on the back as he squeezed all the air from her lungs. Her eyes darted around the castle. There was an anxious energy in the air. Her presence had suddenly jolted it to a standstill.

"Are you alright?" He pushed Ivy back by her shoulders, turning her to and fro.

"I'm fine."

"Three men were found dead, gutted on the outskirts of town. You never returned home. Some witnesses saw a woman covered in blood. We didn't know where you were."

Ivy opened her mouth, but it took a second for anything to come out. She debated lying, but what good would it do? She turned her face toward her guard. "The Adeshbu killed those men. They attacked me."

"Are you hurt?!" He studied her once more, searching for any hair out of place.

Ivy's skin was clean, and her new dress showed no sign of distress. "I'm alright, Russell, really." Ivy couldn't hide the fear in her voice.

"Did they hurt you? Why didn't you come home?"

Luc interjected, his voice calm and assertive. "It was late. I didn't think she should be traveling back after dark. She stayed in an inn. I guarded her."

Russell breathed a sigh of relief and then reached out his hand toward her guard.

"Thank you for keeping her safe." He shook it, then ushered her inside. "Come, you must be exhausted. Your father will be so relieved to hear you're alright."

Ivy took her breath in a sharp inhale. Her father? Relieved? It took everything in her not to laugh, but Russell distracted her.

"Did they say anything? Were they going to use you as ransom? What happened?" Russell fretted, hurling question after question at her.

"I-I don't know. It all happened so fast." Ivy closed her eyes and pushed the image of a man's head rolling near her feet from her mind. *One, two.* It didn't matter. It was over. The incident at the ball with Rian drew nearer in her head, painting a perfect picture of his vow to protect her, yet he pushed Ivy away and forced her here. Ivy supposed she could catch her death anywhere, with or without him. "They mentioned a bounty on the Adeshbu."

"Did they recognize you?"

Ivy swallowed. An image flashed of the two men and their leering eyes, calling her pretty. She shook her head, choosing only to be grateful nothing worse happened.

"We're grateful for your safe return." Russell stopped in the hallway and rested his hands on his niece's shoulders, looking at her once again before he pulled her into a gentle hug. "I'm so happy you're home. I love you like you were my own daughter, I wouldn't know what to do if-"

Ivy squeezed her arms against her uncle's waist. "I love you, too."

"Reckless girl!" King John bellowed, "Where were you?!"

Ivy attempted to keep her tone reasonable. "I was surveying the city."

"What for? Planning on giving tours?" His sarcastic tone slid through her. Russell put a hand up between them.

"Let us all be grateful The Queen has been delivered home safely to us."

John only sneered at his advisor.

"Daddy, you know what for. I'm tired of the affairs of my country being hidden from me!" Ivy bunched her fists in her skirt in frustration; she decided it was less childish than stomping her foot.

"How many times must I tell you-"

"What? That I needn't concern myself with it? Someone should!" Fire shone through her eyes as her father rolled his own. "You miss things right under your nose while you busy yourself with choosing upholstery!"

The king's face whipped around until it was right next to hers, forcing Ivy to flinch. "Girl! You speak with far too much confidence." His piercing eyes burrowed into her. Luc stood a few feet behind, hand quietly moving toward his dagger. "You think an education entitles you to so much.

I should have paid for etiquette lessons instead of tutors; would have been more useful."

Fear flickered in her. Even as a grown woman, he still scared her. Ivy thought he might hit her. She had to remain collected. If she let her tone rise or fall, he would find weakness. "I seek only to do what's best for Iosnos."

"What's best for Iosnos?" Rage flowed through his veins as he grabbed her arms and squeezed. "You think you know what's best for Iosnos? What would happen to Iosnos if an accident were to befall you and end our alliance with Asmye?!"

"You're only concerned about my life because of my marriage?!" Ivy winced.

King John exhaled and composed his voice as he watched the silver-clad guard take two steps forward. "No, no, that's not what I meant."

"That is exactly what you said! Every single day since I've arrived, you've only concerned yourself with my husband. I am your daughter!" John took a step back, raising his hand dismissively, and began to walk down the stone hallway. Ivy ignored Luc's urge to escort her to her room and chased after her father. "I'm your blood, and you cast me aside for your political ambition. Why?!" Ivy would not let him see her cry. She wouldn't.

"You're bending my words, darling." All at once, the facade was lifted again. "Russell, tell her to calm down. She's mishearing things." Ivy looked at Russell. He stared at the floor. He wouldn't defend her father's words, but he couldn't openly defend Ivy without risking his position. His cowardice had always been apparent to her. When she looked back, her father was gone.

Ivy's chest heaved. Her vision blurred with the tears she fought back and whispered to herself, "he was right," and walked out of the room.

He was right. He was right. Rian was right. All through the halls, Ivy stomped her feet and ignored the silence, moving only a few steps behind her. Her father had once been a warm man. He had to have been. Not all her memories could be fabricated. Like all fathers, he dealt out punishments and lashings, but he wasn't all bad. He couldn't have been. Her mother had loved him and encouraged Ivy to do the same. How did he become this way? Now, he was just an old man poisoned by his greed and insecurities.

"Heard you'd made it back." Malcolm walked up the hall toward Ivy and Luc.

"What is it now?" Ivy wasn't even sorry for being rude. She could hate the Knights and everything they stood for, especially how they reminded her of her husband. But not Malcolm. He was the only one to treat her as more than his king's property.

"I've got something for you." He held up a stack of letters. Ivy's name was inscribed in Rian's handwriting on the front of each. Without a word, she took them, ignoring Malcolm's expression that he, too, was glad she was safe. The letters weighed heavy in Ivy's hand. Her fingers grazed over the texture of the parchment in her grip as she shuffled through each to count them as she walked back to her room with Luc beside her. There must be more than twenty. Was the room spinning, or was she going to pass out? Her heart pounded in her ears. *What did Rian write?* When she got to her doorway, Ivy turned to Luc.

"I'm feeling a little tired." Weariness melted her strength and fortitude. "I would like to lay down."

"Of course, Querida," He brushed his hand across her cheek. She tensed at the touch. "You need it. You look a little pale." He stood there looking at her expectantly. Ivy wondered if he wanted an invitation. She opened her door, poised to escape from the world.

"I think I'll go in alone." Ivy held her breath and looked only at the far wall of her chamber.

"Do you need anything?" His voice wavered with worry.

Ivy pushed the door open further and slipped inside. Too much had happened. She needed room to breathe, to think. "I'll call for Madeline if I do."

"I'll stay right here."

"Thanks."

Luc drew himself up tall and dropped his hand. He couldn't lose all they had gained overnight. "Get some rest." His words were soft as he reached for her arm. "Will you do something for me?"

"What is it?"

"Please don't read his letters."

Her brows drew near each other, creating a V in her forehead. Ivy hadn't expected such a bold request from Luc. "What?" She turned toward him for the first time since they'd entered the castle.

"Please don't read his letters." Even with a 'please,' it didn't sound like he was giving her anything other than a command.

"Why?"

"What do you mean, 'why?'" he sighed. "I thought we were past this." A grave whine.

Ivy stared at the wooden door before her. Try as she might, she could never be *past him*. Even as the sun rose and set, she would always know him. "Luc, I don't-"

"He just, he-" Luc couldn't put it into words. He sounded more irritated than she thought she'd ever heard him before. "He's not worth your time. He'll try to guilt you for being here." His voice softened. "And here, here is good. It's you and me."

Without a word, Ivy shut the door behind her. After Ivy laid the unopened letters on the side table, she simply sank into her bed. She was tired. Exhaustion chased her like every confused feeling running through her body. Ivy looked at her finger at the little blade of grass tied around it.

Rian's letters called out to her, whispering that she should open them, but she was too scared. Whether his words were kind or cruel, it wouldn't matter. Ivy rolled over, closed her eyes, and buried her face in the pillow. *Go to sleep, Girl. Go to sleep.* Easier said than done. Everything tangled together in her mind until she was physically uncomfortable. How long would she be able to run away from Rian? How long could the hope of a new life last?

Ivy lay there with her thoughts even less clear than they were before. Hours drifted by while she tossed and turned, adjusting and readjusting her pillow countless times. If looks could start fires, Rian's letters would have been ablaze.

The bedroom door opened with a creak. *Luc.* He was sneaking in before daylight to sleep beside her. His presence might make it easier for her to sleep. Ivy didn't open her eyes as his weight sank into the bed behind her.

"Luc?"

"Querida? I didn't mean to wake you." His hand stroked her hair softly.

"I couldn't sleep. I've been trying for hours," Ivy groaned, turning towards him. All that time spent thinking hadn't yielded any other option for her than where she was, what she had before her.

"You can open your eyes. It's too dark to see anything."

It was harder than she expected to open them, knowing he was there without his helmet. Ivy finally fluttered them open to see...nothing. There were no beams of moonlight, no ambient glow from a dying fire. Nothing but blackness and the shape of Luc in shadow lay before her.

"Hi," she whispered, looking at him. He leaned forward and kissed her. Her restlessness started to melt. She felt badly for how she left him this morning. "Can we go to the west shore in the morning to pick meelaflower?"

"Of course." His naked body slid under the sheets. "I like the west shore." There was no hiding that devious smile in his voice.

Ivy hooked her leg around his hips, pulling him closer to her. If she couldn't see him, then he should at least let her touch.

"You're a fiend."

Luc slid his hand between her legs and sighed deliciously, "I'm a fiend? You're already wet." Ivy was glad he couldn't see her blush. Her insomnia had led her to purge sexual energy with her fingers, but to her dismay, thoughts of Luc's touch were joined by the memory of Rian's. After she came, imagining one above and one below, Ivy was left with more unease than before. Luc wrapped his arms around her, bringing her right to his chest. Ivy touched the tip of her nose to his. She still couldn't see him, but she was looking at his face. She couldn't be sure, but she thought she caught a glimmer of light in his eyes. Ivy tasted his lips again as tears pooled in her eyes. "It can't last forever."

"Hush, Querida." Luc's hands touched her cheek. "Stay with me now." He kissed her again. Luc's hands were so tender, sliding over her skin with a gentle grip.

Her hand drifted up the back of his neck and into his hair. Ivy pulled his kiss deeper into hers, hungry for his everything.

"Luc, please, I-"

"Ssh, I know." His lips crushed against hers. Fervently, he touched her, roaming his hands all over her body, worshiping soft, folded skin until he was on top of her. There was so much she needed to say to him, but she didn't care. At least, not right now. He was the one who was here. He was the one who protected her, that saved her, even when it was from herself. Ivy loved him.

Instinctively, she raised her hips to open herself to him. Luc slid his cock right into her, eliciting her to moan into his mouth. It only sparked his flame. His hands trailed up her arms until he had grasped both her hands. He pushed them into the mattress above her head, where his fingers intertwined with hers. Ivy loved how his tummy pressed against hers as he rocked his hips back and forth. With her eyes closed, Ivy tried to paint the picture in her mind and memorize every feeling. She whined as his kiss left her lips, but they felt so good drifting down her neck. Ivy softly panted as she suppressed her moans. Luc's teeth grazed her skin as he thrust harder. It took a feat of strength, but finally, she got enough leverage to pull his hand towards her face. Ivy only wanted to kiss his palm, to show him something tender compared to how he wrecked her.

"Tell me you love me."

"I love you, Luc," she whispered.

He brought his face to hers. Ivy didn't open her eyes, but she felt Luc's stare. "Tell me again."

"Luc,"

His cock pulsed inside her as Ivy spoke his name. Ivy reached up, searching for the side of his face under her fingers. It was harder to stifle her moans now. "I, I love you."

Luc's mouth crashed into hers. His breath shook as he kissed her. The lingering soreness in her body was reawakened with his fervor. It was like they just started, like they'd never touched each other. Something sparked inside her chest and shot through her body like a flame. Luc must have felt it, too, because he wrapped his arm under her back and hugged her tight. His lips pressed gently into her, nipping and biting at her lips. Time slowed for Ivy as he touched her and their bodies melded. His every exhale was her deep breath in. Ivy gasped as his cock throbbed. His movements were deliberate, pulsing inside her pussy like it was the last time he'd ever have her. Ivy wrapped her arms around his shoulders, pressing her fingertips into his back. She felt around for the scars on his skin. Ivy needed him. His skin was warm, and his scars rose and fell in scattered patterns under the pads of her fingers. Ivy silently wished that summer could last forever. She wanted nothing more than to live out this moment for the rest of her days.

"Luc, I need you."

"Tell me, Querida,"

"Please. I love you. I need you." Suddenly, her cunt throbbed against him, squeezing and tightening around his girth as she came. Luc thrust his hips against hers, pressing deep into her cervix. Ivy pulled away from his lips when she felt it. Luc's stare blazed against her body, and he held himself up like he didn't know what to do. Without meaning to, she started to cry.

Luc couldn't take his eyes off the curl cascading down the back of Ivy's long, elegant neck. It was hot enough that she had pinned her curls up. A rare occurrence for the Queen, who always preferred her long dark hair to be as free as she was. It was a becoming look on her. It was not how it had been tightly styled in Asmye for a time, pulled and restrained. This was softer, the shape of her curls still full-bodied and wild, but it was directed up into a lovely mess away from her face. Her petite ears were uncovered but decorated with gold and framed short wisps of hair that fell from the pins. And that one curl must have fallen after her maid had left. It trailed between her sunkissed, supple shoulder blades, enticing him as he walked behind her. In a gown of white linen that draped and twisted around, her womanly shape had never looked more like heaven on earth. Ivy turned her face to look back at him. Sunlight caught in her amber eyes, igniting the twinkling gold fire within them. Her plush mauve lips held back a smile, and Luc had to have her right then.

Luc glanced around them. No one was around, and the stables were just off the path they were taking toward the western tide pools. Luc hooked his arm around Ivy's waist, twisting her against the wooden wall. She giggled.

"We should be more careful."

"How can I be careful when you look more divine than any goddess?" Luc's fingertips traced the shape of her ear and down her neck to the amethyst necklace he had given her. The jewel hung delicately at the center of her chest.

"Flattery will only get you exactly what you want." She danced her fingers over Luc's chest plate, squeezing her thighs together. "We should go in. The horses will be all turned out, the stable hands gone with them."

"As you wish."

Luc pulled open the stable door just wide enough for them to squeeze through. Midday light hovered above from the high windows in the hay loft. It was quiet and empty, as expected. Luc took another look around before pinning the queen against a stall door.

"Reminds me of when we met." Ivy pulled him closer by the fabric of his tunic. Their first words to each other had been in the stables outside Astrella. What was supposed to be a tour for Ivy to familiarize herself with her new land, a simple conversation had changed her life completely.

"I would have liked to do this then, too." Luc's hand slid down her body and squeezed her breast. Ivy lifted her leg to hook around him. Her lips shuddered as she stared into his visor. Luc reached up to lift it.

"Clo-"

Ivy gripped his wrist. "Keep it on."

Luc's helmet tilted in a nod of approval, and he pushed her dress up around her hips. His thumbs pressed into the soft flesh of her thighs. A creak. Ivy held her breath. Their motion stopped. Luc guided Ivy's leg to the ground as his helmet scanned the stable. Another creak. Luc pulled his dagger from his belt and walked silently toward the carriages at the opposite end of the stable. Ivy's hands trembled. Anxiety flooded her mind, pounding in rhythm in her chest. She tried to follow, but Luc held his hand behind him in a wordless motion to wait. Luc stepped forward, peering around the corner of a stall toward where the carriages were parked.

"What is it?" Ivy whispered, clinging to Luc's bicep. It had only been a day since she'd been ambushed, and her heart might not make it if it happened again.

Luc cursed the helmet that separated him from reassuring Ivy with a kiss. Instead, he squeezed her hip and hid her inside an empty stall as he went to investigate.

The curtain was drawn in the rear window pane of the furthest carriage. The dark fabric momentarily went flat against the glass as something pressed against it. Luc crept around to the carriage door. His heartbeat didn't quicken. His breath was quiet and even. His body was conditioned and instinctual, ready for the kill. After a quick look back to determine Ivy was nowhere in sight, he pulled the door open. Luc paused at what he saw. Malcolm's shocked expression mirrored Luc's own. A man of brown hair and pale complexion kneeled between Malcolm's legs with wide eyes.

"I'm sorry, I -" Luc fumbled with the door and took a half step back. His eyes caught something shiny in the seat—a helmet. Luc widened the door—a crimson cape pooled at the man's knees.

"You motherfucker." Luc grabbed Adne by the front of his shirt, pulled him from the carriage, and threw Adne into the wall. A crash reverberated through the stables as he hit collars, bits, and reins hanging from the wall. The soldier grimaced as he caught himself before he fell.

"Wait, b-" Adne held out his hand in an attempt to keep distance between himself and Luc. Luc rushed Adne and tackled him to the stable floor. The carriage jostled as Malcolm stumbled out with a hand holding up his britches.

Ivy pulled the knife from her boot. She couldn't yet see, but she dared not risk Luc fighting anything alone. Her grip was sweaty as she took a timid step forward. *One, two. One, two.*

Luc had a knee pressed into Adne's hips, pinning him down. His fist hammered as Adne tried to block the blows. Malcolm grabbed at Luc, trying to pull him away. Luc flung his arm back, and the steel of his forearm bracer cracked against Malcolm's nose and mouth. Malcolm stumbled. Adne used the distraction to twist out from under Luc. Blinding pain shot through Luc moments after Adne landed a hit to his left kidney. Adne flipped Luc onto his back.

Adne slammed his knee up into Luc's crotch. He leaned down to Luc's helmet to whisper. "We wouldn't want to be hypocritical now, would we?"

Tears fell through Ivy's lashes when she saw Luc pinned to the ground. Ivy rushed toward the brawling men. Malcolm caught her and knocked the knife from her hand.

"Don't. You'll be hurt, Your Grace."

"Malcolm?" Ivy stared at the half-naked soldier before her, then startled as Luc screamed.

Luc's groan came out as a growl. "Do you hold nothing sacred?!" His words ignited a force inside him. He threw Adne off his body and pinned him to the ground, pulling Adne's knife from its sheath and holding it under Adne's sharp jaw. Luc's teeth clenched with the effort against Adne's grip, pushing the knife away. Heavy breaths rumbled between them.

When Malcolm saw the knife at his lover's throat, he lunged. Luc crashed under him while Adne scrambled to his feet.

"No!" Ivy shouted. Her head was spinning with confusion. She stepped forward. Adne held his hand out toward the Queen.

"Stay back, Your Majesty."

Ivy recognized the voice from the shouting back and forth but couldn't quite place this face. She squeezed her eyes shut when she remembered a passerby. A stranger who had caught her eyes for a moment in a crowded room. The fights at the barricade. Had he been following her? Was he behind those orchestrated attacks?

Luc threw Malcolm off his back into a haystack, littering the cobbled floor. He tackled Adne and took to his knees to pummel the man

217

over and over. Spittle mixed with blood, smearing over the soldier's face, dripping onto his collar. Ivy spied the red cape fluttering against the carriage wheel. *Adne*. She couldn't believe he might have conspired against her.

"Luc!" Ivy lurched toward Luc, tugging at his arm when he groaned and tossed her back on the floor. Dirt and dust fluffed in the air as Ivy skidded on her ivory skirt. The clasp of her necklace snapped. Her wrist caught her fall, but the momentum pushed her to slide further, and the stone scraped her skin up to her shoulder.

Luc rose from his knees. He pulled Adne up from the ground with him. Adne's legs wobbled beneath him. He gripped Luc's forearm for support. Ivy groaned as she pushed herself up from the floor. Luc's attention was pulled from Adne's bleeding face.

"Stop this," The Queen beckoned.

Malcolm stood and drew his sword from inside the carriage door, blocking Luc from Ivy when he realized what he'd done. From inside his helmet, he widened his eyes as he watched Ivy fumble over her skirt to right herself back on two feet. Luc took a step forward. Ivy winced as she gripped her elbow and stepped back behind Malcolm. Luc looked down at Adne's collar, bundled in his left fist.

"So, Luc, is it?" Adne managed a wink under the split in his left brow. Malcolm held the tip of his sword under Luc's helmet. Adne pushed Luc's grip away from his shirt with a gentle shove. He slid his tongue over the blood caked over his lip. Ivy's heart stopped as she heard her lover's name on Adne's lips. Luc's faceless gaze locked onto her.

"Seems I'm not the only one getting intimate," Adne smirked. Luc wished to lunge again, but Malcolm's blade threatened any movement. Rage bubbled inside him. He wanted to scream.

"Control yourself, Adeshbu." Malcolm forced Luc to take a step back from Adne.

"I'm not the heretic here." Luc looked between Adne and Malcolm. "What business would a blasphemer and a naive knight have here that wouldn't leave them a head shorter?"

"I could ask you the same question." Adne pulled a piece of straw from his hair.

"I asked him to bring me," Ivy interjected. "I wanted to see my old mare." All three soldiers looked at her. Malcolm stayed silent and lowered his sword, but Adne caught his knowing gaze. Luc only cleared his throat.

"Hasn't she been turned out with the herd, Majesty?" Adne rolled the straw between his fingers before biting into it. "Only storage here since the newest foal left." He gestured to the nothingness that decorated the stalls.

Ivy swallowed. She should've known it was a poor excuse.

"Don't worry, my Queen. We all have secrets. It's an honor to share one with you." Adne bent forward in a shallow bow. Luc kicked dirt on the soldier. Ivy's heart raced. No matter what Malcolm or Adne may think she had done, if it got back to her husband, each scenario would sign her death warrant.

"Malcolm," Ivy's voice wavered on the name. "Please take me to my chamber." Malcolm nodded.

"Your Grace," Luc reached toward Ivy. She flinched, and he realized she was afraid to have his hands on her again. Luc's voice fell as he looked at her fearful eyes. "I ask your permission to deliver Ad Nekoson to our priestess for his sins."

Ivy couldn't look at him. "You may as long as you can do it without further beatings." Ivy turned away to leave.

"Follow orders, Adeshbu," Malcolm strained when Luc gripped Adne's shoulders.

"Take her to her chamber and nowhere else," Luc barked after them as they left.

Adne wiped his nose against his sleeve while Luc pulled a length of rope off the wall. "I do understand the appeal, Luc."

"Shut up," Luc huffed as he pulled Adne's hands behind his back. Luc wrapped the rope around his wrists.

"It's all starting to make a bit of sense, Luc. I love when that happ-" Adne's words were cut off by his groan when Luc looped the rope around Adne's neck. He pulled it taut and secured it back to his wrists. Adne's back and neck arched.

"Walk." Luc pushed Adne forward a step.

CHAPTER TWENTY-SIX

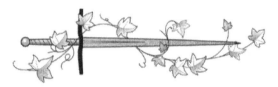

Ivy argued with Malcolm until they reached the castle. The halls were quiet. The air between them was quieter. She winced as she tugged on the doorknob and remembered the scrape on her skin.

"Are you sure you're alright, Your Grace?" Malcolm pushed the door open, giving it a quick scan. A still steaming pot of tea sat on the desk near the vanity.

"Yes," Ivy assumed he only meant her arm. That's about all that was fine.

"Goodness!" A voice shrieked inside the room. Malcolm yanked Ivy back into the hall and drew his sword once more. Even after a quarrel with the Adeshbu, his orders from his King superseded all. Rian wanted Ivy safe.

"I'm sorry!" Madeline threw her hands in the air and dropped the linen she had been carrying from the bed.

"Are you alone?" Malcolm raised his blade. Madeline squealed that she was. Malcolm scanned the room once more before Ivy pulled at his shoulder.

"It's alright." Ivy strode into the room and sat at the vanity. "You're dismissed, Malcolm." The soldier nodded reluctantly but shut the chamber door behind him.

"I didn't know you'd be back so soon. I'm sorry." Madeline resumed her fussing over tidying the room. It was barely midday. "I try to get these things done while you're out. You needn't worry about your linens when you have more important matters on your mind."

"It's quite alright, Madeline," Ivy exhaled with exhaustion. "Things so rarely go as we plan." Ivy inspected her palm and picked a tiny pebble from her scrape. It stung. Madeline took notice of the injury as Ivy inspected it in the light from the window.

"What happened there?"

"I fell," Ivy swallowed. "Tripped over my own feet."

"Should I call for a nurse or a doctor?" Madeline fussed over Ivy.

"No, no." Ivy shook her head. "It's not that bad. I just need to wash it." She wondered how long Luc would be gone as Madeline carefully rinsed the abrasion. She wondered if Adne would come back. Luc had once said there were dire consequences for an Adeshbu who went without his helmet. Her thoughts were bleak as she instructed her maid to mix a simple salve of honey and calendula.

Madeline took her time prying each dirty speck from The Queen. It had done her no good to ask any questions, for Ivy wouldn't answer any beyond reassuring her maid that she was fine. After the warm bath of bloomed jasmine and lavender, Ivy blew off the steam from a fresh pot of dandelion tea. She sipped silently, thinking of nothing but Luc's rage at Adne, Malcolm, and her. The cut on her arm was superficial, but it stung in the water and again when her dressing gown sleeve brushed over it. Ivy sat at her desk, looking out the window. It was a beautiful day.

"I saw these earlier and meant to ask-" Madeline picked up the thick package containing Rian's letters from Ivy's desk. "What are these?" Ivy widened her eyes and commanded Madeline to put them back. She didn't imagine Madeline for a snoop, but that was a conversation she couldn't stomach.

The redhead bit her lip and laid the bundle back where she found it. "Is there anything else I can do for you?" Madeline's hands landed on her hips.

"No." Ivy only wanted to be left alone. It was too early for bed, but what else was there to do? She downed the rest of her tea, yearning for the burn of wine running down her throat. She peered at her empty cup. "Actually," she called to Madeline, who rested her hand on the doorframe.

"Will you have some wine sent up?" Ivy fluffed her skirt in her fist and aimed to lie in bed.

"Of course," Madeline drummed her fingers on the metal knob. "You know, if there's something you'd like to talk about, I'm always here to listen."

Ivy softened her expression. She knew it was true. Madeline was as close of a friend as she had in Asmye; these last few months had only brought them closer. Unfortunately, she had already spilled enough secrets today. She shook her head. "Just the wine, please. And make sure it's from Asmye."

Once Madeline had gone, Ivy picked up the letters. She thumbed through the stack. Her name was written in different moods, the pen strokes varying from clean, elegant loops to short, quick scrawl, but all by the same hand. The parchment was soft as she placed it on her bedside table. She closed her eyes and flopped her head back on the pillow, the braided hair thudding on the sheets.

The late afternoon sun shone directly in her eyes, beating warmth against her skin until it woke her. Ivy opened her tired eyes, and the first thing she saw was Rian's letters stacked on the bedside table. *Please don't read his letters.* Luc's voice echoed through her head until her stomach turned sour. She'd seen him fight, seen him angry, but she'd never seen him so hateful. Who was he to tell her anything?

Ivy did want to read the letters. They wouldn't make her change her mind. There was no apology nor pretty words Rian could give to call her back to Astrella. Although...she still wanted to know. Maybe it was the actual business of the crown. It would be her duty as Queen to open them. Yes, that would be enough. Ivy pulled the letter from the top of the stack, sliding her finger against the paper to break the seal.

My darling, Ivy,

It felt like a punch to the gut.

I wish you would let me explain and hear me. You have this habit of making up your mind. It's something I-

Fuck that.

Another letter:

Please let me know you've arrived safely if nothing else. You are still my wife. I won't let a silly ring stand for the vow I made. You must-

Nice try.

Another letter:

I'm sorry.

What was that?

I'm sorry.

Ivy sat back on her bed, staring only at the two words. Sure, he'd said it before, once or twice, but now it was written. It was like he meant it.

I'm sorry. I know what I've done to you is wrong. I know there's nothing I can do to take it back. I don't think it's fair to say that either of us knew how much I would love you. I don't assume you would say it to me now, but I don't care. Ivy, you are my wife, my chosen, and I will choose you every day, even if you never come back with me. I wish to-

Ivy put the letter down. It was too much. She couldn't read his words. She could only sit there and stare at the wall until the thundering pain in her chest withered into a dull throb, and finally, she was hollow.

A rhythmic melody danced on the door. Ivy pulled it open just enough to see Sophie with a tray of food and a bottle of wine.

"You going to let me in? This is starting to get heavy."

Ivy stepped aside and Sophie stepped past her. Ivy gave a casual look into the hallway. There was no one there.

"I could only carry one bottle of wine, but-" she reached into her shirt pocket and pulled out a cigarette of meelaflower, "-this should supplement nicely."

"Fuck, yes," Ivy grabbed the cigarette from her and rushed over to a candle to light it. Ivy inhaled deeply, pulling the smoke into her chest.

"That bad, huh?"

"Yes," Ivy blew out the smoke and took another draw on the meela.

"Well, damn. I only brought one!"

Ivy handed the cigarette over to Sophie. She pulled on the cigarette and blew out a perfect ring of smoke. Ivy looked at the tray of food she brought. It was full of fresh fruit and plenty of cheese. Ivy tore into a baguette with her teeth. It seemed she only got hungrier the more she ate, and it wasn't the meelaflower.

After an hour or so of gab, with Ivy strategically navigating the conversation away from her day, there was a knock at the door. It startled her enough to choke on her apple. Sophie hit her back as she walked past her to the door, but her breath stopped cold when Luc was on the other side of the door. Ivy's face flushed a deep crimson when he stood there, gesturing toward Sophie, although she was sure he thought it was Ivy behind the door.

"I didn't realize you had company, Your Grace," his tone was even and calm. It didn't at all match the pounding in her chest. She wasn't ready to see him yet. The vision of him standing there made the pain in her arm throb. "Madeline said you called for wine." He held up a basket with two bottles.

Sophie howled and raised her fist in the air, hinting that her small frame had already absorbed the influence. "We needed this! I only brought the local stuff." She held the basket handle over the crook in her elbow and fiddled with the bottle cork.

"Do I need to escort you somewhere?" Luc kept his gaze only on Ivy.

"We're staying in tonight." Ivy pointed her foot toward the bottle of wine on the table. There was no mistaking the sharpness in her tone or how she swallowed when she turned away.

"Yes, Your Grace," Luc bowed and turned around, positioning himself on guard.

Sophie shut the door behind Luc and whipped her head around so quickly that Ivy wasn't sure that she didn't hear Sophie's neck crack.

"You really don't care if your head stays attached to your shoulders, do you?" She sauntered back to the loveseat.

"What are you talking about?"

"I'm talking about you-" she sank in the cushion and took a quick swig from the bottle, "-fucking your guard."

Ivy blinked and stared at the floor while Sophie poured the Asmyian wine to mix with what was left in her glass. Sophie was always brash, and Ivy loved that about her. However, she had no business saying *that*. "I beg your pardon, Sophie. I don't think that you-"

"Oh, I know exactly what I saw. Wow," Sophie reached for her glass and took a long drink. Each sip she took made her toes tap under her skirt. "It's amazing no one's caught on."

After the stables that morning, Ivy wasn't sure about that anymore. She had a choice: tell the truth...or lie and let Sophie read her face. Ivy took a breath in and-

"I knew it. Oh, goddamn." She rested her forehead on the back of her hand as it held the glass.

"Sophie, you-"

"I don't care that you're doing it. Just admit it."

Ivy's face froze as she looked at Sophie. Her heart fluttered under her ribs. She thought she might vomit.

"Ivy, I won't tell anyone. Besides-" she looked back toward the door and crossed her legs, "-he has an alluring voice."

Ivy unfurled her fingers from the fist she held in her lap.

"Does this mean you've seen him without the helmet?" Sophie's eyes opened wide in anticipation. Ivy just shook her head.

"Really?" she asked. Ivy nodded her head up and down this time, finally taking a breath. "Hmm. I suppose *I* don't care that much." She pointed her finger over the rim of her glass. "I only care that you never get caught. The King would have your head in an instant, and it takes entirely too long to break in a new best friend."

"Sophie, you can't sa-"

Sophie groaned and drew her hands to cover her face. "I just have to ask. Do you realize how stupid you are?"

"I know that it's...not right." Ivy couldn't form the words. She loved Luc too much to say it was *wrong*.

"You're married to a king! A handsome king," Sophie reminded her. "A handsome king known for cutting down entire villages of people and burning them like a bonfire! What do you think he'll do to you? Or to him?"

"He doesn't know." Ivy sank back in her seat.

Sophie squinted and curled her lip. "Of course, he doesn't know. You'd be long dead if he did, and he might burn us down with you."

"He did it first!" Ivy stood. She couldn't help it. Sophie couldn't judge her now. Admitting it only made it hurt worse. There was no soft touch from Luc to ease her ache, no reassurance. Ivy just had to stand there and think about it.

"How do you know?" Sophie's tone was softer.

"He told me. Look." Ivy grabbed all of the letters from Rian and dumped them in Sophie's lap. Sophie carefully unfolded the first and read. Her eyes scanned over the words while Ivy crossed her arms across her chest self-consciously. Sophie rifled through the rest, probably reading more than Ivy ever would.

"Wow," she sat and stared into space, "that takes guts."

"Excuse me?" Ivy snatched the envelope from Sophie's hand. "Did you say it takes guts to cheat on your wife?"

"No. It takes guts to tell your wife you cheated. It takes guts to apologize." Sophie read on. "It takes guts to grovel like this. Isn't this guy supposed to be scary?"

"He did it for six months of our marriage." It destroyed Ivy to say it. "Six months of lies to me." Why did he have to do that? Why wasn't she enough?

"And how long have you been schtupping your guard?"

"Sophie," Ivy whined. Could anything go right today?

"What? We're being honest here. How long?"

Ivy had to let it settle. "It's really only been since we've been here." That wasn't a complete lie.

"Okay," she took another drink, "let's say I believe that. How long did you want to before?" Sophie's eyes narrowed at her friend.

Ivy pursed her lips and slid her tongue over her teeth. "Nearly since I met him," Ivy recalled how close he got to her in the stables the first time they spoke. Then she remembered this morning, how everything went wrong.

"Uh-huh," Sophie groaned, "how long have we known each other?"

"What?"

"How long have we known each other? Answer the question."

Ivy made a face and threw up her hands. What a foolish question. "I don't know. Forever?"

"Exactly. And in all that time, have I ever betrayed you?"

"No," Ivy sighed, praying those days hadn't ended.

"No. I haven't," she paused. "I won't tell anyone."

A breath of relief washed over Ivy. "Thank you, Sophie, I-"

"But you have to do something for me."

Ivy stared at her. *Blackmail?* "What is it?"

"I won't tell anyone-" Sophie stopped to take a long sip. "-but you have to stop. Now."

"What?"

"Ivy," Sophie picked herself from the sofa and neared her friend, raising her hands to rest on her friend's shoulders. "You have to stop."

"I'm your Queen. You can't give me orders." Ivy regretted the words as soon as they left her lips. She had never pulled rank on Sophie, not even as girls. Sophie stood there, shallowly nodding her head. Ivy didn't say

225

anything else, not even an apology. Sophie just crossed her arms, hoping it would come one day.

"You have to."

Ivy's words came out in a whisper. "I don't think I can."

"Yes, you can. You know it's not right. I can see it in your eyes."

Tears welled up almost immediately. Sophie was right. Everything Ivy was doing was wrong. And she only did it because of how much Rian hurt her. Ivy buried her face in her hands and rested her elbows on her knees. But she loved Luc. Truly, she did. If this were another life, they'd be together without fear, without consequences. Her father wouldn't take out his rage on her, demanding something Ivy didn't know if she could give. It would just be her and Luc smiling in the sunsets, sleeping together every night. Maybe she'd make him her lemon cake.

"I didn't mean for it to happen like this," The words stuttered out in whispers. Sophie sat by her side, wrapping her arms around her.

"Will you answer me something else?"

It was all Ivy could do not to roll her eyes. She waited.

"Do you love Rian? Or care about him at all?"

That was when Ivy started to cry. Long, hollow sobs that she'd held back ever since she told him she was leaving. The kind of feelings Luc would shun if she ever admitted them.

"Have you written him back?"

Ivy picked her head up. Sophie dragged her thumb over her cheek, picking up her tears.

"No," Nothing else could she say between sobbing breaths. "I don't know what to say."

"It's a letter. Just talk to him."

"But I've-" Ivy tried to hold her sobs back. "-fucked it all up." Sophie let Ivy weep into her shoulder, running a comforting hand across her back. "I'm sorry," Ivy cried.

"I know."

They talked for a little while longer. Ivy revealed everything. She told Sophie about the blood god, how he made Rian act insane. She told her about Rian's injury, how she was so afraid to lose him. She confessed how it hurt worse when he admitted his nurse was his lover. And she talked of Torin and how the bastard hurt Madeline.

"I don't even know him and I hate that guy," Sophie balled her hands in a fist. "I better never meet him."

"I doubt you will. He stays wherever Rian is, and obviously, he's not coming after me." Ivy wiped away her tears.

When the fire died down, Sophie kissed her cheek goodbye, then slipped past Ivy's guard without even looking at him. Once she left, Ivy laid another kindling on it, just enough to illuminate her desk. She lost herself in her thoughts. Maybe Sophie was right. Ivy did have a duty, at least for now.

Without even thinking, Ivy grabbed a pen and parchment. It took nothing for her to scribble out her husband's name, but as soon as the quill touched down, she had nothing to say. Every time her heart softened for Rian, something inside her reminded her of what he did. What response could she give? What was left? If she went home now, it would be with her tail between her legs, and she wouldn't allow that. Her stomach hurt.

She tapped her pen against the paper. Sophie was wrong. Ivy couldn't forgive him.

CHAPTER TWENTY-SEVEN

Ivy sat on a chair on her balcony, surveying the dim city with a blanket wrapped around her shoulders. The night seemed blacker after midnight. The wine had long been drunk, the meela burned to ash, and she held her thoughts at bay with nothing to protect her. Tightness lingered on her cheeks where her tears had dried. Her eyes fell shut at the sound of her chamber door opening behind her, merely waiting for the knife to slice through her back. She listened to the soft thudding of boots and sighed.

"It's coming undone," she whispered toward the sea.

"We will manage." Luc kneeled in front of her chair. He laid his helmeted head on her lap and held onto her legs. "I'm sorry, Querida. It got away from me." His voice was heavy.

Ivy held him there with a comforting touch between his shoulders. No longer was she afraid of him. "And what of Adne?"

"He is in the custody of Baale at the church. His fate is to be decided tomorrow."

"Does he know?"

Luc looked up at her. "Not enough to save himself."

"So it is death then?" Her face and stomach soured at the thought.

"Do not weep for him." Luc touched her cheek. "He would use what little he knows for whatever advantage it offered him. He is as ruthless as any Adeshbu under that charm. His quick end will protect you."

"Sophie knows." Ivy had to push the words out. "She knows."

Luc's breath caught. His tone roughened. "Knows what exactly?" His hand squeezed hers under the blanket.

"Everything." Even more than Luc knew about The Queen.

Luc's body stiffened. "Did you tell her?"

"She guessed it, and I tried to deny it, but she knew." Ivy rushed the words out as her tears returned. Luc stayed silent, but his body went rigid. "What are we going to do?"

Luc pulled his gloves off to hold Ivy's hands in his. "We will go about as normal as if nothing has changed."

Ivy looked down at his hands. His right hand was bruised and swollen across the knuckles. "Luc, your hand."

"It's fine." He flexed his fingers. It wouldn't ease her ache to learn what else Luc had done to Adne before he handed him over to the church. "We will need some time before we can do anything."

Ivy looked at his injuries closer. "You haven't even washed the cuts."

"We will need money."

"Money?" Ivy looked up from his hand. "Money for what?"

Luc cleared his throat, "Food, room and board, passage on a swift ship."

Ivy's stomach flipped as she heard the words. "Where are we going?"

"Anywhere you want. So long as it is away from here." His right thumb stroked a soft line along her jaw. "A chance to do things right. A new life." The one they had would soon end if they did nothing. "I'll sell my armor. We'll change our names. Forget it all, and we'll buy a little piece of land-" Luc's voice shifted from anxious to hopeful as he waxed poetic about the possibilities. "And we could be married, properly married."

Ivy's heart had already stopped listening. "Sell your armor? You'd show me your face?"

The question hung in the air. Luc nodded. "I'll leave it all behind."

Ivy kissed the broken skin of his knuckles to her lips. It was too late to think, to talk anymore. "You are hurt. Let me tend to you."

The drapes rustled as Colette pulled them open wide. Light spilled across Ivy's bed. The King groaned and rolled away, covering his face, much like his wife had done each morning. She pulled another set open, and more light brightened the dreary room.

"How did you find me?"

"I know everything that goes on in my castle." Colette stepped over Basker, who was stretched out on the rug.

"Your castle?" Rian opened one eye, squinting in the sunlight. Colette stood before him, hands on her hips.

"I've been here longer than you have."

Rian rolled onto his back, massaging his temples with large fingers. The orange blanket that covered his chest slid to his stomach as he moved. One foot poked out from the side.

"How can you be so cross this early?"

"You're in my way." Colette threw the King's discarded britches at his chest.

"In your way?" Rian pushed the undergarments aside and stretched his arms up above his head.

"Yes. I need to clean the room."

"There's no need. Leave it all as it was."

Colette huffed. "Perhaps there might be a need for new linens." Her eyes trailed over The King's naked body. A lingering odor perfumed the room. "The reek of your desperation is starting to linger in the hall." Rian's cheeks did not give way to his understanding as Colette opened the balcony door. The late summer's warm air drifted into the room. Rian stared at the ceiling.

"Go to her." Colette looked out over Asmye from the queen's balcony.

Rian turned his face toward Colette but said nothing.

"Go to her." She turned back to look at Rian.

A knot formed a pit in his stomach. "I can't." He could practically feel Colette's eyes roll.

"Never once have I seen you so weak." Colette huffed and resumed her tidying.

"I could have your head for that," Rian grumbled as he lazily pulled up his britches.

"Watch your mouth. I would hope that all my effort to raise you with a bit of decency would have given you some manners," she sighed with frustration and shook her head. "There's nothing you can do to me that your father didn't."

"He let you live."

"Long enough to see his son fall prey to his schemes, to follow the same path. He let it get the best of him." Colette dropped her hands from her sides. "He loved your mother, Rian. Before it all turned to madness, he was so devoted to his wife."

Rian said nothing.

"And you love yours, don't you?"

He sat on the edge of the bed, hunched over and covering his face with his palm. "It doesn't matter if I did. She'd never have me again."

"She loves you. She always did. You were too stupid to see it." Colette sat beside him. "Don't live the rest of your life in misery because of your pride."

"She left me."

"What reason did you give her to stay?" Colette touched him under his chin to bring his eyes to hers. "Pray about it."

A message arrived early the following day from Natassa asking for the Queen of Asmye's presence. Luc was gone before the sun had risen, leaving with a kiss in the dark and a nudge for her to consider his offer to run away. Ivy had only turned to her side, facing the wall, saying nothing until the messenger arrived.

Ivy spread a fresh, thin layer of her salve over the scrapes on her arm before choosing a dress with billowing sleeves to conceal it from prying eyes. She had Madeline scour every inch of her room, looking for the amethyst necklace Luc had given her, to no avail. Ivy pressed her fingers against her eyes. What if she was called to the church because Adne had used his information? What if this was the dress she died in? *I'm fine. Everything is fine.*

As Ivy quietly walked beside Luc, words longed to break through her lips. Fear tightened them. She cleared her throat.

"I cannot find the necklace that I was wearing yesterday." Ivy kept her eyes forward. "Perhaps it fell off when I-"

"I will check the stables when we are done at the church." His voice was as warm and even as it had ever been. Whether he knew the meaning of her summons, he did not let on.

"Thank you." Ivy glanced over at him. He was still hers. That kindness was there, hidden beneath his armor.

Ivy swallowed hard before Luc opened the door to Natassa's church. Adne turned his head toward them as they strode into the room. He sat in the front pew with his hands bound in his lap. His tunic was still covered in dirt and blood, but his face had been cleaned. They had allowed him that dignity. Purple and gray painted the hollow of his eye. Cuts split his brow and lip. As they approached, Adne stood in respect for the Queen before he bowed, fiery eyes blazing through her.

"Good morning, Your Grace," Adne's cheery voice unnerved Ivy. His face was so foreign to her, yet that melodic cadence was familiar. "Looking lovely as-"

Baalestan shoved Adne by his shoulder before dipping in his shallow bow. Ad Viena appeared from a back room, followed by Natassa.

"Welcome, Your Grace." Natassa's bright smile shone towards the Queen. Her blonde ringlets bounced off her back. "As unfortunate as circumstances may be, having you in our modest church is an honor." She dipped in a low curtsey.

Ivy swallowed and bowed her head. "Thank you, Priestess."

"I imagine you don't know why I asked you here today." Natassa held out a hand towards Ivy. "Come. Let's speak in private." The Queen paused, considering the last time the priestess had touched her, then slipped her hand into Natassa's ivory palm. No ache pulsed in her arm.

The quarters behind the church were beautifully appointed. The room was plain, but Ivy could see the care Natassa had put in to make the quarters feel soft, luscious, and elegant. An office of sorts was decorated with a desk and a table near the hearth. Sheer curtains hung across the room, separating what looked to be her living space. Ivy sat across from Natassa on a plumply cushioned settee. The Queen studied the room while she waited for the priestess to speak.

"Are you familiar with the ways of the Adeshbu?" Natassa's angelic voice pitched up.

The question was pointed. Ivy readied her defenses. "My familiarity starts and ends with one being my guard."

"I've read about them since the time I was a child." Natassa relaxed in her seat. "My favorite heroes in the old stories: Adievasinis' strength and skill given to mortal men, warriors fighting for their God. I was fascinated. But there wasn't much to know as their order was so hidden from the world." Ivy nodded her head. There was so much she didn't know herself.

Natassa danced her fingers over the back of the couch, twiddling her fingers in the sunlight that streamed through the small window. "My father told me they were nothing more than legends and that no one had seen an Adeshbu for hundreds of years. I didn't care. My faith never faltered. I loved Adievasinis because of the Adeshbu." Her gaze became unfocused and wistful. "A God who would give His power and love to those devoted to Him-I wanted that for myself. I poured over my texts, and I became a priestess, one of only a handful across these lands. That's when I learned of Ouraina."

Ivy furrowed her brow. "You didn't know of her before?"

Natassa simply shook her head. "It's silly, isn't it? How the Fathers and their men hide beauty and love, even from their own." Ivy stared at her shoes, wondering how far they might take her if she had to run. There was nothing to suggest the priestess had any ill will toward her, but a deep ache pulsed and her teeth clenched in irritation. Ivy made an effort to loosen her jaw as Natassa spoke.

"I was surprised you had already heard Her name before I told you. That husband of yours must want you learned."

A weight settled inside Ivy's chest as she tucked a piece of hair behind her ear. "My Adeshbu told me." Natassa's eyes gleamed.

"That is interesting. How much did he say?"

Ivy shrugged. "I suppose only the beginning, just of her love and loss." Natassa reached for Ivy's hand, ignoring the tremor in her fingers.

"And what of the life?"

Ivy's eyes met the Priestess' and found nothing sinister. Instead, she found sisterhood.

"Creation, you mean?"

Natassa's eyes crinkled as she drew her lips wide. "A man might tell you that. Ouraina did create the world we live in, even created us in Her image. If you ask me, I think She did well designing you and me." Natassa tossed her fluffy hair back with a laugh. "But it's everything. Everything born comes from Ouraina, everything with an opportunity for survival. It's Adievasinis that takes life away."

Ivy sat back on the cushion, unsure what to say.

"If I wanted to learn more about Ouraina, I needed to learn more about Her mate. I made a pilgrimage to the Temple of Adeshbu." Natassa's eyes sparkled with wonder. "It was a truly holy place. The air was thick, as if the power of the Gods was something you could pluck right out of the sky. There, I was able to read about all the ways of the Adeshbu, and I was able to meet them. I should have been terrified, for they were terrifying. But I was drawn to them just as I had been as a girl."

Ivy nodded. Even before she knew Luc as a man, something had called out to her to inquire more. Those early days in Astrella's library gave inconsequential information. She kicked herself for not seeking out Natassa sooner. "What happened there?"

"I read their sacred texts. I watched them. I saw how they trained, how they spoke. Something occurred to me. They were touched by Adievasinis, but they had to sacrifice something so precious to the nature of man."

"What did they sacrifice?"

"Themselves." Natassa leaned forward. "Their names. Their faces. Their hearts," she smiled at Ivy. "When you take everything away from a man, he is hollow. He has lost his humanity. Adievasinis filled the void. A warrior who is nothing but their God is mighty. I believe in that power that is Adeshbu. Although, I have to admit they have their faults."

"And what does this have to do with Ad Nekoson?"

Natassa put on a serious air, the first Ivy had ever seen. "Ad Nekoson removed his helmet. An offense of the highest degree to Adeshbu. Have you ever considered why?"

Ivy said nothing. She couldn't admit all she'd learned was a restriction of her lover.

"They have mortal bodies. They must eat and drink at the very least, and they can remove them to do such things in private, in the darkness. The offense isn't really in removing your helmet, then, is it?"

Ivy waited.

"It is in being seen. When you are seen, you are taking back your sacrifices. You regain that humanity, and you are no longer the infallible warrior of God. You become what I saw in those mountains, only a man."

233

Was that all Luc was concerned about? Fear of being seen as a man?

"It is an act of heresy in the eyes of the Adeshbu. To me, it is simply a man without faith reclaiming something he lost. If I were not here, Ad Nekoson's fate would demand a head as is Adeshbu custom. But I am here, as are you." Warm eyes met Ivy's gaze.

"If I am honest, I am not a woman of any faith." Ivy shook her head. "I never have been. Why would my presence interfere with Adeshbu custom?"

A smile appeared once again from Natassa. "Holy Father Trevarthan gifted these four Adeshbu to you on your wedding day. As it is, they are yours to command as you see fit, including dealing out their punishments."

Ivy opened her mouth, but nothing came out. No one ever let her decide anything.

"I would not supersede your authority in these matters, regardless of your faith. So it is yours to handle as you wish, Your Grace."

Adne leaned back in the pew, staring up at the ceiling. He pressed his lips together, pushing them apart to make a soft-smacking noise. His fingers tapped anxiously against his thighs. He sighed, then started to mutter a melody:

I'll dance a floorless gig when I hang from his rig
And when my lover comes knocking
They'll find me stiff and well worth the dig

Baalestan slapped his hand across the back of Adne's head. "You never could shut your mouth."

"It's a talent, really," Adne smirked and looked toward Luc. "What's more surprising is what I don't say."

"They should have cut out your tongue before you ever put the helmet on," Baale growled.

"I'd have found a different way to irritate you. It's simply too fun."

Natassa emerged with the Queen, pulling Adne's attention from the cross-armed stance of Baalestan. The Priestess stood beside her pulpit to address the Adeshbu. An empowered Ivy remembered who she was as she stood tall with her back straight and chin high.

Natassa gripped the wood before her. "Ad Nekoson-"

Ad Baalestan dragged him up by his bonds and shoved him into the church aisle before his Ladies.

"-you have removed your helmet in the presence of another. For this, you will be stripped of your armor, position, and rank in the order of the Adeshbu," Natassa spoke firmly.

Baalestan's weight shifted as he listened, eager to have a reason to clean his blade.

"Ad Nekoson was pledged to the crown of Asmye. That crown has decided what punishments it sees fit."

Baale looked toward Ad Viena and Luc. He stayed silent, but his body tightened, and his hand fell to the blade strapped to his waist, counting down until he heard the order.

"You will be excommunicated from the church of Adievasinis."

Baalestan took a step forward, leaving Adne kneeling behind him. "Excommunicated?" His tone grumbled as he stared at the Queen. "He has broken our oaths. He should be put to death."

Ivy's eyes did not falter. She did not hesitate. "My orders have been given."

"You do not command the Adeshbu. I do!" Baale turned his head to the man before him, unsheathing his dagger. Luc caught his hand before it passed his shoulder.

"Our Queen has spoken." Luc disarmed an incredulous Baalestan and then bowed toward his Priestess.

Natassa hardened her voice. "Any attempt to deal out your own punishment will be viewed as an act of treason to the crown of Asmye on pain of death." Natassa looked to Adne. "You're free to go."

"Seems like I'm done here then." Adne lifted his bonds in front of Baalestan's helmet. "Do you mind?" Baale's chest heaved, but he did not move. With Baale's knife, Luc sawed through the thick rope. Natassa and Ivy moved from the pulpit.

Adne rose and rubbed his skin. He leaned close to Baale. "Do be careful. I wouldn't want the blade to slip and have you acquire a count of treason." Adne flaunted his dashing smile as the bonds fell from his wrists.

Adne bowed low before Natassa and took her hand. "It has been, as always, lovely to see you." He pressed a respectful kiss against her fingers. "I suppose our paths won't cross again, but if they do, I will find myself humbled by your beauty and devotion as I am now." A dimple sank in her cheek as the corners of her soft lips raised.

Adne stepped toward the Queen, but Luc blocked his path. "I only wish to express gratitude for Her Majesty's merciful decision."

"Do it from here, then."

"Let him pass," Ivy scolded, extending her hand to Adne.

"Your Grace, you have my deepest gratitude."

"A fair punishment for your offense." Ivy tried to hide the fear in her eyes and hoped this would not be a mistake.

"Indeed, very fair." Wrinkles creased at the corner of his dark eyes. "Queen Ivy Garreau, the just and fair ruler of Iosnos. A woman of the people."

"You forget who holds the crown on these shores." If her father had been here, he would have been angry that his time had been taken even to consider sparing Adne.

"I did not forget." His bright smile made pink flush her cheeks. "And I hope that you trust I will return the fairness." Adne kissed her hand and turned on his heels to leave the church.

CHAPTER TWENTY-EIGHT

The sun had yet to rise, but the blackness of night faded away. Luc had dressed and started a fire to warm her room. Summer began its slow wane to autumn with crisp, cool nights. Ivy was barely awake, grateful that she had even fallen asleep next to Luc. He hadn't said a word when he sneaked in. She listened to the sound of him moving around the room. There's no way he got more than a full hour's rest with all his tossing and turning. If he wanted to start a conversation, he could use his words. Ivy opened one eye to look at him. He walked toward her desk.

"Are you going to steal some more of my books?" Ivy whispered from the bed.

"Maybe," his voice was warm. Ivy sighed as sleep beckoned for her. Maybe they'd be okay. Luc's helmet tilted down at her desk. Ivy realized her letter to Rian was still laid there, unfinished, unstarted, really. Anxiety twisted in her chest.

"Were you writing to him?" His tone was low, dragging out of his throat in the early morning.

Suddenly, she was very awake. "I thought I might."

He opened her desk drawer without permission, rifling through her things. "And his letters? You read those, too?" He pulled them out of the drawer. Their seals were broken, and the pages unfolded. "I told you not to read these."

Ivy pulled the sheet up around her chest as she sat up. "You *asked* me not to read them. Last I checked, I'm a grown woman-"

"Are you this stupid?"

Ivy stared at him. He had never been so brash. "Excuse me?"

"He will tell you whatever you want to hear! He'll manipulate you for his own benefit. Don't you see that?" Ivy had never heard him speak to her like that before. It was shocking.

"Don't you think I'm smarter than that?"

"You didn't see it before. You forgave him before. You went back to him once. What am I supposed to think now that I find you were writing him back!" Luc slammed the letters down on her desk. A few of them scattered toward the floor.

"I didn't write anything," Ivy lied.

"His name is on the page!" Luc kicked the desk leg with his boot. "Tell me something, Ivy. If I did not find them, would you have told me?" He stalked toward the bed, hovering over her. "Would you?"

"You don't trust me."

"You haven't given me much reason. Deceiving me when it suits you. Adne, Sophie - it's like you want it to fall apart." The condescension was evident in his voice.

"If I condemn an Adeshbu for death for removing his helmet, how will I ever know your true face? I saved him for us!"

Luc's words stayed sharp. "Until he runs his mouth and starts a rumor that could kill us both."

"I had a decision to make. I set a precedent so you could be free of the Adeshbu. I won't apologize for doing what I thought was right."

"Maybe I don't want to be free of it." Silence.

Ivy felt a flutter in her chest. The sun began its rise over the oceanside cliffs. "You don't mean that."

"It's all I have, Ivy."

"Yet you say we will leave and start a new life. How could we when you fear letting the Adeshbu go? Are you so afraid of what you are without it?"

"Without it, I am nothing!" His anguish trembled his words. "I am a failure. A powerless man who couldn't even keep his family from starving. They died because of what I am without that helmet!"

"It's just a helmet!"

He turned, stomping back to her desk. His fists clenched as he grabbed the letters, crinkling them in his hand before throwing them into the smoldering embers of her fireplace.

"Luc, stop!" Ivy threw herself out of her bed and charged at the fireplace. Ivy fell to her knees as the flames started to catch. The paper curled while it charred.

"Get out of my room," Tears fell as she whispered. Fury thumped through her veins. Ivy bent down to the fireplace, trying to pull the letters out before engulfing them in flames. Luc just stood there. "Get the fuck out!" Ivy didn't care who might have heard. This was cruel. He deserved whatever he got.

Luc left the room wordless, leaving her kneeling by the fireplace, trying to recover what she could. The letters were lost in an instant, torched into burning embers. Ivy winced as the fire licked her palm as she reached in. Only a few words were salvaged. *Hear me—every day—I'm sorry.*

The wind whipped through Rian's hair as he rode south. The black of night retreated into warm purple as dawn approached. Basker kept pace with long strides. Colette was right. He couldn't hide away from his responsibilities forever. Torin had sent word that he was still occupied in Tornbridge. Rian urged his stallion forward up a steep incline. As he reached its crest, the sun broke over the eastern horizon. Tangerine skies filled his eyes, so bright and warm he could almost taste the citrus. Clouds cast in shades of magenta and indigo were as royal and proud as the dawn. His black cape caught a gust like a sail, pulling it west. From here, he could barely make out the western coast and the Thraxian sea glittering beyond it. Did his wife watch the same sunrise? Rian closed his eyes and whispered a prayer. His heart thumped like the ticking of a clock. Time was not his to regain. Could his blood still keep her warm on their coldest nights? Some breaks were not meant to be mended. Rian squeezed his legs and loosened his reins. His horse leaped forward at a gallop.

"I would like to call on Priestess Natassa." Ivy couldn't look directly at Luc as he stood outside her door. Three days had passed since they'd spoken. Ivy hadn't left her chamber. She only left her bed at Madeline's insistence that she bathed. Once her body had been cleaned, Ivy wanted to cleanse her heart. Her gaze was needlessly distracted as she fussed with her skirt. "I'm ready to leave now."

"Yes, of course, Your Grace."

His voice. How could she ever hear it and not feel something for him? The words were nothing, a formal exchange in public between two people who had thrown the most painful words at each other in private. Not once had Luc tried to apologize. That stubborn man was more exhausting than worth it sometimes. But Ivy had hope. That pain of loving each other wore thin and vulnerable as reality crashed through the summer.

They walked through the streets of Mermont, but no words were exchanged between the Queen and her guard. As they approached the church, Natassa stood outside, shaking hands with her parishioners. Ad Viena stood a few feet away, watching dutifully. The faithful crowd's attention was pulled from the Priestess as the Queen approached. Luc stepped forward to block them from rushing Ivy, but she tossed her hair toward him and extended her hands to greet her people.

They all bowed their heads. Some fell to their knees. Rough hands brushed her palms, gnarled from lives' worth of work. She had never considered herself so delicate, so unworn, but in harsh contrast, she had turned soft since her wedding. She remembered Torin sneering at her, torturing her for being unlike them. Now, she was unlike her people. Who was she now?

Natassa's sky-blue eyes lit up when they fell upon The Queen. She fluffed her skirt and nearly leaped from the crowd to offer a curtsy before her. Ignoring her remaining parishioners, she ushered the Queen into the church, with Luc following close behind. Ad Viena held his position at the door to bar anyone from entering.

"I'm so delighted to see you back in our church, Your Grace."

"Could we speak in private?" Nerves jittered through Ivy as she squeezed her hands together.

Natassa extended an arm to show Ivy back to her quarters. Ivy took a seat on the overstuffed settee just as she had before.

"Can I get you anything?" Natassa asked. "Water? I can put on a kettle for tea. Wine?"

"Wine, please." Ivy fidgeted with her hands in her lap.

Natassa poured two glasses and handed one to Ivy. Ivy tipped the glass back and swallowed more than half in the first sip. Natassa smiled and drank with a similar enthusiasm.

"I'm not surprised you came back."

"Oh?"

"I saw something in you the other night, an unsatisfied curiosity."

Ivy cleared her throat. She couldn't be that transparent. "I wouldn't call it curiosity. I am seeking something more. Answers."

"And what is the question?"

A frustrated sigh escaped Ivy's lips. "I find myself at a loss. I had no faith for most of my life. When I was taken to Asmye, I-" Ivy considered the word "-converted to the Church of Adievasinis against my will. I didn't object as it was expected of me, but there was no devotion in my heart to any God."

"It is often the providence of women to bend to the faiths of their husbands."

That felt like a punch in the gut. Ivy had bent for Rian in more ways than one, yet still couldn't satisfy him. What would have been enough?

Natassa reached for her Queen's hand and gave it a gentle, encouraging squeeze. "Go on."

"I hear Father Trevarthan preach, and at times, his telling of Adievasinis is repulsive to me. It makes me sick to hear of the depravity like bloodlust is the only admirable quality in His followers. But I feel the power. I felt it in my husband. I feel it in my Adeshbu. You speak of Ouraina and Adievasinis as equals, and I find myself...."

"Curious?" Natassa flashed a knowing grin.

Ivy sank back in her seat and nodded. "I don't know what comes over me. It's this thirst that's insatiable. I fear once I give in, I won't be able to stop. It makes me wonder what I believe in anymore." Ivy swallowed the last of her wine.

"Belief or not, the power of Adievasinis is real. A preacher is only a conduit for their God. Father Trevarthan is a power in his own right."

"He has his own power?"

"Of course, Your Grace. We all do. His well of knowledge is deep, but his methods are old. Older than even him," Natassa smiled wide and chuckled. "Although his interpretations of the holy texts may not be-" Natassa paused as she considered, "-evolved as they could be, they seem to have served your husband well."

Ivy couldn't talk about Rian. Even thinking of him hurt too much. "What about Ouraina? How could She ever love a harbinger of death and violence?"

"There is a delicate balance between life and death. Death and decay feed life, and life cannot exist without death. A life without an end would ruin us. Fucking, eating, loving, all those beautiful things would all cease to please us, and our grief would be unrelenting. That's what love between Adievasinis and Ouraina is - the balance."

"I don't know how to accept it."

"May I?" Natassa took Ivy's hand once more. She turned her palm upward and traced her finger softly over the scar Rian had made on her wedding day. "This was your first act of sacrifice to Adievasinis, a pain that shows dedication, a mark you will wear forever." Ivy stared at the mark on her hand. Scar tissue sat in the center of her palm. Despite folding and bending her hand daily, healing hadn't taken much time. Could it have been her husband's magick? "When it bled again, I took it as a sign that you were one of the chosen."

Ivy remembered that morning in the hall after she arrived in Iosnos. Natassa had been so excited to meet her again. All Ivy had wanted was to shoo her away. Ivy decided it wasn't fair how closed off she had been to the Priestess. Natassa could have been the easing presence she never felt in Asmye or anywhere else. She never gave her the chance to try. "Whom do the Gods choose?"

"Adeshbu are chosen. They must pass a rite to earn their armor. Then there are some faithful others."

Ivy stared at the door, wondering if Luc could hear. "And Priestesses?"

"Yes. I believe I am one of Ouraina's conduits." Confidence punched through every word that fell from Natassa's lips. It wasn't arrogance or conceit. It was assuredness. "I believe you are, too."

"Me?"

241

"Yes, My Queen. Those strong in faith are drawn to each other. Those couplings are more powerful than either by themselves."

"What am I supposed to do? I am hardly allowed to make any decisions that could make a difference." Ivy considered how similar her husband and her father were. Maybe it *would* be better for her to run.

"Ouraina will make Her needs known to us in Her own time. You'll know it when you see it. For myself, I took an Adeshbu as my lover as Ouraina took Adievasinis."

Ivy furrowed her brows in a pinch. "How? I thought Adeshbu couldn't.."

"Ouraina encourages love in all forms, Your Grace. It's Her Divinity we're called to." Natassa touched her hand to her stomach. "I have obeyed, and I have been gifted new life of the purest kind: life created and consummated by faith."

Ivy watched Natassa's hand slide over the gossamer skirt covering her belly as the information clicked. "Which Adeshbu?" She recalled the mornings that she woke up without Luc.

"Ad Baalestan, of course."

A wave of relief washed through Ivy. "Did he remove his helmet?" The words fell out of Ivy's mouth before she could catch them.

Natassa nodded.

Ivy was aghast. Her head felt faint. Luc was so angry at Adne for removing his helmet for a lover. Ad Baalestan took the helmet off for his. Why couldn't he do it for her?

Natassa studied The Queen's reaction. "It is no love match, but our faith and ritual brought us together under the right moon. I sacrificed to create life just as Ouraina wanted me to."

"How did you know he was the right one?"

Natassa stared at the wall momentarily with a smirk as the memories of her encounter overwhelmed her. "I was drawn to him. It was a thought I couldn't purge from my mind. I prayed to Ouraina and sought Her guidance. I asked him to complete a task to be sure of it. I must admit, I was more pleased with him as a woman than I should have been as a Priestess." Natassa held in a glinting smile. "When I took his flesh, he was Adievasinis, and I was Ouraina."

Ivy had no words.

"I understand it is a sensitive subject, and perhaps my enthusiasm for your presence in Iosnos made me overzealous in my approach." Natassa met Ivy's eyes and bowed her head.

"What does it mean for me?"

A sudden knock rapped on the door. Luc stuck his head in the door. "I beg your pardon, Your Grace. We should get back before the sun sets."

Ivy stared at him, recalling her father's request as they'd left the castle, then turned to Natassa with an apologetic nod.

Natassa squeezed her hand once more and planted a kiss on each cheek. "You are on the correct path, Your Majesty. You do not need to fear."

As Luc closed the door to allow the ladies a few moments to finish up, Ivy wished to confess, to take reassurance that all she had been through, all the pain and confusion, had led her where she was. She took a breath, choosing to trust in Natassa, to put her faith in love.

Natassa spoke softly, "Ouraina is all our mother, and She gave us that same power—the power to create life. You would not be chosen if you could not create life. She will give you a child. Have faith."

The walk back to the castle was primarily in silence. The Queen had much on her mind. Reconciling that a second Adeshbu forgoing their helmet sent fire into her veins. But then, there was the consideration that Natassa encouraged Ivy to continue this path. Luc said he would sell his helmet. Either way, she wasn't sure how much patience she had left. She ate dinner with her father, ignoring his remarks about her less-than-jovial attitude, then slipped away after dessert.

The knock on the door was soft. When Ivy opened it, Luc stood there with his head bowed in defeat. She leaned against the door, waiting for him to do something.

"Can I come in," his words were soft. "I just need to speak to you for a moment."

Ivy stepped back allowing her door to open enough for him to slip inside.

"You've ruined me, Querida."

"It is my fault then?" Ivy's eyebrow cocked.

"No, no, that's not what I meant." There was a sincerity in his tone that lowered her walls. He reached for her hand. "I can't control myself."

Ivy bit her tongue to not let her truthful thoughts slip out. He was trying. She wanted him to try. She needed him to.

"I've never felt this way before." He fell to his knees in front of her. Not a strong knelt proposal but a pathetic display of begging. "I promise I'll be better." He looked to the ground as if the next words were unbearable. "The only thing worse than knowing you lov-," he stuttered, "-loved him, is living through another day not knowing you." His visor found her eyeline. There was no stutter or waiver in his voice when he said, "Forgive me." He placed a ring in her hand, twisted from a tiny gypsum flower. The little white buds served as diamonds along the band.

You're on the right path. Ivy recalled Natassa's encouragement. There was no other path but Luc. Ivy picked up the ring and put it back in Luc's hand.

"You have to trust me."

He nodded his head in understanding, waiting for her to drop the axe. His shoulders slumped until he looked up at her outstretched, empty fingers.

"If you want me to wear your ring, you should put it on me yourself." Carefully, he slid it over her third finger. A smile curled across her lips as she stared down at it. It might be the closest she could have to wearing his mark, at least for now. She grabbed him and pulled him to his feet. She backed him up until he fell onto her bed. He had nothing to do but watch her blow out the candles.

"Luc," Ivy whispered, petting her fingers against his stubbled cheek as she rode him deep and slow. Her other arm stayed draped over his shoulder. Ivy relaxed every part of her body except her cunt, giving one last squeeze as she straddled him. Luc sucked in a breath and came. His hand gripped her hip, where he rolled to lay his weight on her.

"I'm sor-"

"Don't!" she laughed, reaching up to kiss him. "It feels good. I want this. I want you."

His lips met hers again. He had given as much of himself to her as he could. Ivy wasn't afraid. If it happened, it happened, and she'd deal with it. Ivy loved him. He was hers. If Natassa was right, this is where she was always to be, who she was meant to be with. Perhaps every drop of blood that marked her failure with Rian was Ouraina's grace to keep that part of herself for Luc.

Luc kept his cock inside her as long as he could before he was too tired and rested on his side. His fingers trailed over her breasts, twirling around her nipples, dragging down over her stomach and back up again. After a few moments in the afterglow, that old familiar body ache sank inside her. *Guilt.*

"I need to tell you something," Ivy had to clear her throat halfway to speak.

"I love you." He couldn't keep the words inside.

Warmth spread in her belly, reaching all the way into her tippy toes. "I love you," she murmured as she rolled to face him. Either his come or hers, or maybe a mix of the two slipped out of her pussy and slid down her leg. His hand covered hers in front of their chests, and she adjusted her head on his forearm. "You're right. I think we should run away." There was a palpable change in the air.

His lips curved into a smile, and Ivy saw the tiniest glimmer of straight, white teeth. Ivy kissed him and dragged her tongue across them, tasting him and embedding another piece of him. One day, the puzzle would be complete.

After he pulled away, he rested his forehead against hers. "Whenever you want to go, I'm ready." With those words, Ivy had never felt so weighted down but simultaneously so free. How would it work?

Where could they go? The only place she knew to run away to was where they already were.

"Okay," Ivy couldn't say anything else about it. For tonight, there was no need to run. Here, she was safe. Here, Luc could lie right beside her and hold her in his arms all through the night, or what was left of it, anyway. It wouldn't be long before the morning rose over the coast, but she would take whatever moments she could get tonight.

"You come to the porting of every ship?" Adne questioned as he and Endaya watched sailors move cargo into tenders and towards the shore. His room and board was conditional on him earning his own keep. Endaya wouldn't have cadgers within her walls. Adne had suggested he earn it, "the same as the other girls" but Endaya thought his skills were better put to use in management.

"Not personally," Endaya chuckled. "It is good business practice. Sailors are often on the prowl to make their own port as soon as their boots hit dry land."

"A woman of enterprise." Adne watched as the beautiful young women and men of various skin tones and sizes waved and flirted with the sailors. Playful touches of fingertips against chests, subtle leans, whispers in ears, well-timed giggles. Endaya had trained them all well in the art of seduction.

"I'm just meeting the needs of the free market," she smirked. "Why shouldn't it be my pockets they fill?"

"One day you will be the richest woman in Iosnos."

"Maybe I already am." Endaya bummed her luscious hips against Adne's thin ones. "You see that one?" Endaya pointed to a tall dark-haired beauty who seemed indifferent to the men trying their hand at her. "She earns three times as much now that we adjusted her strategy. We curl her hair so she favors the Queen's likeness just enough and they pay her more the meaner she is to them."

"And she enjoys it?"

"She's never been happier."

"Lovely."

Luc's hand touched Ivy's lower back, ushering her down an alleyway. Every time he touched her, she ached for him. The tender torture of never being able to see or touch him meant that every peek of skin, every brief touch, awakened lust. Ivy spied a little alcove for a doorway deep in the alleyway. She grabbed Luc's hand and pulled him into it. Ivy smiled and pulled off his gloves. Soon, she would look into his eyes and see the love he confessed written in his gaze. She could wait a few more days, a few more weeks until they had made their arrangements. Perhaps, one day, they'd cherish this time. All the secrets and lies they shared now would pave the way for their freedom.

Luc pushed back the hair from her face. His necklace hung around her neck. The broken clasp was repaired with delicate finesse. He would never be so careless again. Her eyes. Dark as coffee, warm as the sun. To be seen by her. Luc put his hand to his helmet. Ivy's thick lashes fluttered closed.

"No."

Everything stilled for a moment. Ivy looked up at him. Luc lifted his helmet just above his lips. Wonderstruck, Ivy's lips parted. His square jaw was peppered with dark hair streaked with gray. The crease at the center of his bottom lip accentuated a natural pout that sat under his mustache. Ivy shuddered as she studied every bit of golden skin he allowed her to see.

"Close your eyes, Querida."

He loved how her face glowed when he said that word, how her cheeks would flush. He loved the flutter in her lashes as they closed and the taste of her lips when he tilted his helmet up. They were on the precipice. Luc waited too long to run once and wouldn't wait again. He sensed her hesitation, her fear of that path. He was afraid, too. He pulled away from her lips, letting his helmet slide back down.

"Open."

Ivy slid her hand around his lower back, feeling his body through his tunic. She pulled him closer, lifting her leg, and her dress slid up her thighs. His hand followed the curves of her body up to her hips. She kept her eyes on his helmet. She wanted more. She unfastened his pants, pulling them open just enough to pull out his cock and position him against her slick. He pressed in, watching her face as she took him inside. Her jaw dropped open with a shaky breath. Ivy tried to hold in her moan as he began to fuck her, but it escaped her mouth involuntarily. His palm covered her mouth, muting her moans.

"Quiet, Querida."

Ivy nodded her head, keeping her eyes locked onto his visor. Ivy kissed the center of his palm. Tightly, she gripped the back of his tunic in her fists as she felt herself closer to the tipping point.

"Come in me," she whispered. He increased his speed and lifted her leg higher. Ivy felt tingly as her muscles stretched.

"Fuck!" She clenched around Luc's cock, pulling him to his peak. He grunted, and she felt him bury himself deep inside her. His chest rose and fell heavily against her as he stuttered out curses of his own. He tilted up his helmet and kissed her neck, tasting the dew of her skin. Ivy just wanted to hold and hug him as close to her as she could.

Luc picked up a small apple from an overflowing basket at one of the market stalls. The skin had been painted in dappled layers of yellow and red. He bounced it between his hands, then off his shoulder in an attempt to impress his lover.

"You know what?" Luc held the apple out in front of her face. Ivy reached for it, but Luc snatched it away in jest.

"Hmm?"

"Henry would absolutely destroy this."

Ivy laughed at him, recalling his horse's comedic nature. "It is unfortunate you had to leave him behind in Asmye."

Luc examined a few more before choosing two. "I'm sure he'll serve some other knight well." He held out two coins for the vendor.

"Here," Ivy reached for her purse. "I can get that."

He put the coins in the vendor's hand, thanking him as they started to walk away from the booth. "Querida, I *can* buy you an apple."

"I know, but-"

"I don't have much, but whatever I do have is yours." He handed Ivy an apple, green and tart.

"It's plenty enough for me," Ivy smiled. "Do you think we should bring horses with us when we leave? Go out and collect my mare from the herd?" She wiped the apple across the soft fabric of her blue flowing skirt before she bit into its crisp skin. The sweet flesh made her hum as she chewed. A bit of the juice ran down her chin. If she weren't in public, she'd wish Luc to lean over and lick it off her. Ivy reached out her hand to hold his. The market was crowded enough that no one would notice if their hands touched, just for a moment.

"Hard to say. I suppose it depends on where we will go. Who we will become. "

"Perhaps then we should go see the herd tomorrow. Pick out a horse of your-"

An unexplainable chill ran up the back of Ivy's neck like there was a shift in the wind. A voice called out from over the crowd.

"Milady!"

CHAPTER TWENTY-NINE

Ivy snapped her hand back close to her body, turning to see a vicious sight in Torin as he walked toward her. His face was as smug as ever, cropped blonde hair hugging his pale scalp. The fierce gaze of his blue eyes locked on The Queen as his black cape hung over his shoulder. Ivy's stomach dropped as she reached her hands behind her back and snapped the blade of grass from her finger. She felt like she could faint. *Why was he here?*

"Lucky me!" Torin reached for the Queen's apple and took a bite. "I get the honor of escorting you to the King."

"I don't need you to escort me to see my father."

"Milady," he droned between chews, "I was referring to the *actual* King." He walked closer, circling her. Her heart twisted in her chest as she backed up right into Luc's chest plate. It was all she could do to not reach for him and seek his comfort.

"*His Majesty* arrived two hours ago. He sent all of us to look for you." His venomous smile made something in her stomach turn sour. It might have been the news that Rian was *here*. It might have also been that she was fucking Luc twenty minutes ago in a shadowy alleyway while all the Knights of Garreau were searching for her. She couldn't fathom if they'd been caught.

"What did you say?" With her vision going blurry, her head felt a little loose from her neck as she thought of the consequences. *One, two.* "I'll have my Adeshbu escort me." Ivy turned away from Torin. She was outside, but she needed more air. The world she deluded herself into thinking existed crashed as an invisible noose tightened around her neck. Luc had his knife out instantly as Torin's hand grabbed her wrist.

"Easy there, Adeshbu, nothing worth getting your helmet fogged up over." Torin raised one hand and shot him another smirk. Ivy yanked away her hand.

"Stop acting like children. I'll go." Ivy was sick of posturing and competing egos. *Men.* Was Luc only being protective? Or did it only fuel their constant cock-measuring?

Luc dropped his knife. "Yes, Your Grace."

Ivy tried to calm her breathing, but it didn't matter. Everything was ending. *One, two. One, two.* Her heart thumped heavily in her chest. *Had Rian discovered them? Why else would he show up if he hadn't? Who told him? She was in trouble. Why else would he come? Did Sophie tell? She wouldn't. Adne said he would honor her secret. How much did he know? Who else could've found out? Would Rian execute them right away or drag it out? What did he know? How did he get here so soon?*

Ivy shot a worried glance at Luc as Torin led them out of the market towards her father's castle. It was like she was sixteen again, summoned to receive her punishment for being out too late. Ivy marched to her own gallows with Luc trailing behind her. He felt more like The Adeshbu and less like Luc whenever he followed her. *Would she have to watch him die? Rian was cruel. Torin was worse.* Madeline's face flashed in her mind. Torin seemed so pleased to break her heart, reasoning why he tortured her. How much joy would it bring him to kill Ivy himself? Ivy dropped her head, fighting back tears. Now that she was outside the dream, what would the real world look like?

Once they reached the castle gates, Ivy froze. She couldn't see him. Not yet. Luc's come was still wet between her thighs.

"I need to go to my room."

"The King called on you. It will do you no good to dawdle." Torin reached for her, sliding his hand up toward her shoulder. "Come, it's time for a happy reunion."

Ivy thrashed her arm away from Torin's grip and adjusted her skirt. "As delighted as I am, I need to change first."

Torin looked her up and down, whether agreeing that The Queen did appear unpolished or if it was worth it to have her piss off the King. "Hurry up."

Ivy all but ran toward her chamber. Luc stayed outside and guarded the door. Madeline sat at Ivy's vanity with her head in her hands but jolted as The Queen entered. Ivy ran toward her and hugged her.

"What is happening?" Madeline whispered. Ivy simply shook her head.

"I didn't know he was coming." It didn't matter which "he" she meant. One wouldn't go without the other, and they had both hurt Madeline. "Are you alright?"

Madeline brushed away frustrated tears. "I only saw Janelle for a moment once I saw the Knights arrive. They strode right in while we were carrying your clothes," Madeline took a deep breath. "I'm so sorry. I saw him, and I just came here. I didn't want him to see us together."

Ivy threw her arms around her maid again and inhaled a shaky breath. She promised Madeline she'd never have to deal with Torin again. "I'll have a guard assigned to you."

"Really?" Madeline's eyes widened.

Ivy nodded. "Anywhere you go, with Janelle or without, I'll ensure you're not alone. Just stay here until I get it arranged."

That seemed to placate Madeline, even just for a minute. "What are you doing here? Shouldn't you be at dinner? I heard the other staff talking about it."

Ivy covered her face with her hands and groaned. She pulled at her skirt and gestured toward the closet. "I couldn't let him see me like this."

"I can get you dressed." Madeline hurried around the room, ready to perform her duties. She pointed toward the fireplace. "No time for a bath. There's fresh water in the basin for you to wash up quickly." Ivy was grateful and quickly ran the cloth between her legs while Madeline was distracted.

Ivy flopped in the seat in front of the mirror but couldn't make eye contact with her reflection. She stared at the jewels on the counter, at the necklace Rian sent for her birthday. When Madeline reached for it, Ivy felt nothing. It wasn't until the clasp was locked that it felt like the metal burned against her skin.

"Madeline?" Ivy finally looked at herself in the mirror.

"Yes, Your Grace?"

"I want to wear the blue dress." And finally, she smiled.

Neither Luc nor Ivy said a word as they walked down the corridor. Only in front of Madeline did she ask Luc to call on Ad Viena. Ivy stopped and reached for the stone wall as the laughter inside her father's dining hall uneased her. Rian's distinct voice echoed against the walls. Her heart dropped into her stomach. It had been so long since she heard him speak. Wait, was he laughing? What was so funny? King John's voice rang over her husband's. Were they laughing at their success? Plotting her execution? Enjoying that neither would have to deal with Ivy any longer? The page at the door announced her arrival.

Rian rose from his seat as soon as he saw his wife. His hair was longer than she'd ever seen, and his cheeks were scruffy with stubble. Ivy's father stayed in his seat, following Rian's gaze until his eyes fell upon her.

Time seemed to stop. Rian's sea-glass eyes met his wife's. Her lips parted after she swallowed a dry breath. Her face went pale as she stared at the man in front of her. He looked taller than she remembered, stronger, too. His gloved hands squeezed each other as he looked back at her. He reached for her hand to greet her. She reached out her left hand and nearly gasped when she remembered the ring she left at home. Their hands were inches apart when Ivy thrust her hand behind her hip and simply bowed. Rian opened his mouth to speak, but Ivy heard nothing but her own heart beating in her ears.

"Oh, hello, darling! Come, sit! We've been waiting for you." King John gestured toward a chair at the table where a cheese and fruit plate had already been picked over. "Your husband was just telling me all about his travels."

A servant pulled out a chair for Ivy. Surely, the whole room could feel her nerves. Rian's eyes never left her. He didn't sit down until she did.

Ivy avoided looking at him, instead choosing to stare at the glass of wine before her. It was a shame that, when emptied, all she could see was his form through the glass. Finally, Ivy looked up. His eyes were soft and wide like he was happy to see her. His lips turned upward in the subtlest smile. Her father sat at the head of the table just to her left.

It was interesting. Rian never sat anywhere but the head of the table. In the earlier days of her marriage, she sat across from him, generally ten seats down on the other side. It had only been since he had healed that he asked her to start sitting at his right for the ordinary day, more than a special occasion. Her hands trembled as she sat there, wishing she was more covered. The draped and plunging neckline of her midnight blue dress made her feel exposed and vulnerable. She thought she could play a power game of her own, but she was losing. Ivy crossed her arms over her chest like she could hide behind them.

King John droned on throughout the dinner. His words began to slur as the wine flowed without interruption. Rian and Ivy offered words here and there, but mostly, they stared at each other. Rian appeared earnest, hanging on every word. Ivy was too afraid to look away. King John took another swig. "It'll be good for her that you're here. She's been moping around without purpose. What's the point of a sad wife? They aren't even pleasant to look at when they constantly scowl." Ivy finally looked down.

Ivy could barely pick at her dinner. Her stomach was still too unsettled. She made a point to keep her left hand turned palm up if she had to expose it to eat or drink. It seemed more trouble than it was worth to hide, but panic leads to stupid, awkward decisions. While her father hardly even glanced at her the whole meal, Rian's eyes checked in with her constantly. *Is he flirting?* The unease of her entire body started to unwind the longer she sat there. She shook her leg, tapping her heel against the cool stone in wait. *Why is he here?* Ivy thought she knew, but this certainly didn't seem like

251

the precursor to her execution. Rian's foot reached under the table and just barely touched hers. Ivy pulled away in shock as her cheeks flushed. Unfortunately, she couldn't help herself, and she smiled. She didn't know what to do. It had been months since she'd seen him and he was beautiful. Her smile faded as the pain tinged in her chest. Missing him hadn't changed what he'd done.

Rian nodded at her father, rubbing his left hand with his right. Ivy could tell he was getting tired. Her father wouldn't stop talking about the *improvements* to his castle since she left.

"Ivy, what do you think?" Rian asked her.

Something about him directly addressing Ivy extinguished her lingering nerves. The words came quickly like she'd been waiting for a moment to let it all out.

"I think the money would have been better spent on some less exciting investments." Ivy shot a look at her father, daring herself not to slouch. "The irrigation infrastructure needs to be updated. A weak rain season could destroy our farms and orchards. We can't sustain our economy without healthy exports. There are industrial practices that need to be better regulated. Drainage in Mermont has backflow. We also need to maintain the Southlands. There are too ma-"

"Irrigation?" Her father laughed at her. "My dear Ivy, you lack imagination." He reached for the bottle to refill his wine. In his drunkenness, he knocked the bottle over, spilling it on the table.

Ivy immediately began wiping the spill, dragging her napkin under the bottle.

"Daddy, be careful."

Rian coughed, "I think updating the irrigation system sounds like a wise investment, John. Something that would pay back tenfold for years to come. You'd be smart to listen to your daughter."

"Ha! I'll listen to her when I need advice on which beaches are best for nude sunbathing." His eyes cast toward her. Ivy didn't miss Rian's glare. "With that, I think I must be off to bed." Her father's words mumbled out as he stood. "Good to see you, Rian. It's about time we have some forward motion here." He shook Rian's hand aggressively, then squeezed his daughter's shoulder uncomfortably tight and planted a wet, wine-soaked kiss on her cheek before he walked by her chair. "Come see me in the morning, Rian. We have much to discuss." he ambled, trying to hide his unsteadiness, and then his guard followed him out.

"Beaches?" Rian raised an eyebrow.

"In the afternoon, the west shore tide pools are lovely." Ivy smiled at Rian, not letting her father's slight bother her. It was hardly the most insulting thing he said to her, even this week. A servant filled her glass and left them alone at Rian's insistence. They sat quietly for a long while, neither willing to speak first. Ivy's fingers danced around the rim of the glass as she glanced at the door, hoping that Luc had followed her instruction to help Madeline feel safe. Ivy didn't want to say anything. What was there to say?

"Hello," Rian said with a smile. "I feel like I didn't get to say that earlier."

"Where's Torin?" Ivy asked. "I would have thought you would be surrounded by your entourage."

Rian cleared his throat. "I thought this dinner should be more casual." He took a sip of his wine. "I liked your idea about irrigation. It seems like it may serve your father if you were allowed more than a word or two."

"Yeah, he tends to dominate every conversation." Ivy reached for her wine but did not drink it.

"I noticed," he laughed.

Ivy took a breath. "Why are you here?" The question had burned inside her for hours. The waiting and agony spilled out of her stomach and into her chest. Would she die tonight?

"I wanted to see you," He leaned forward on his elbows, and Ivy resisted matching his posture. After all this time, he finally chased her. "But other business called me here, too." He got up from his chair and walked around the table to sit closer to her, the head of the table where he belonged.

"I thought you were coming to get me, to punish me for leaving."

"Darling, no, I-" He reached for her hand, but she pulled back. She didn't know if she could give herself to him. Not yet. "I'm just happy to see you, is all. You look well," he stuttered over his words as his eyes grazed her body, taking a long moment to admire the necklace he'd gifted her around her throat.

Ivy smiled, "You look like shit." Rian was taken aback, but a sudden jolt of confidence had Ivy lifting her hand to touch the stubble on his cheek, sliding over his mustache, "You should take better care of yourself." He closed his eyes as her fingers ran over his skin, but she felt herself being too close to him. "What's the business you came here for?" Ivy sat back in her chair and laid her hands across her lap. It wasn't fair how he could do this to her.

"I wanted to see our progress with the ports and the new defenses." He took a moment to consider his next words, "and your father reached out for supplementary funding."

"What?"

"It would seem he spent your dowry with zest."

"All of it?" Ivy was shocked. It had been less than a year. Ivy knew he wasn't great at these things, but she'd never expected him to be so reckless. Did he completely ignore Russell?

"Yes."

Ivy put her face in her hands, rubbing her forehead and eyes anxiously, and forgot about her left hand. She knew something was wrong.

The projects he had boasted about were utterly useless, but she hoped he wouldn't be so careless. What about his new tower? How could he do that without taking care of their people?

"A nicer chair, right?" Ivy laughed in a defeated voice.

Rian looked down at the table, trying to swallow his own words. "I'm sorry I ever said those things. I was-" he searched for the right word, "- scared-" he swallowed hard, "-scared for you to know about me, and I said things I didn't really mean."

"It's not that you said them. It's that you were right." Ivy took a deep breath in and stared at her still-full glass. It appeared that Torin's return wasn't her biggest concern. Today was too much. "I think I want to go to bed." They were halfway to the door when he spoke.

"Can I walk you to your room?" He smiled at her, trying to lift the tone. Ivy looked back at him, sinking into those hazel eyes.

"Okay."

Rian walked with her. Silently, Luc trailed a few steps behind. Ivy couldn't imagine how he must be feeling.

"Did you bring Basker?" Ivy asked.

"Of course," Rian laughed. That man loved his dog. "He's in my room. You'll have to take him to that west shore you discussed. You know how he loves the water." Sure. It was the shore part of the conversation that he remembered.

"He should be thrilled while you stay here."

"I think we both will be." Rian's tone was so bright and warm. It snapped her right back to where she was before she left, the happiness she felt in her highest highs with him. "You're welcome to stay with us. I overheard a maid say that side of the castle faces the moon shining over the sea. I bet you'd look lovely in the moonlight."

It had been weeks since Ivy saw light in her room at night. It might be nice to see. *No.* Ivy clenched her fists in her skirt to keep her hands from reaching out for his and dug her fingernails into her palm to keep them there.

Rian stopped at her door. "Adeshbu, leave us." He gestured toward Ivy's guard but also at Ad Viena, who stood watch at Ivy's door.

Ivy shot her eyes towards Luc. Panic throbbed in her chest again. Her heart began thumping loudly. Her fear was not for her life or safety now but only for Luc's feelings, having to leave Ivy with her husband. Ivy gave Luc a slight nod.

"Yes, Your Majesty." Luc walked away from her, down the hall, until he was out of sight. The silence hung in between them as Ivy looked up at her husband.

Madeline and Janelle emerged from The Queen's chamber as Ad Viena swiftly knocked at the door. The redhead's eyes widened at the stature of The King before them. Ivy quickly reached for their hands and kissed Madeline's cheek before giving them a reassuring nod as Ad Viena escorted them back to their room.

Rian raised an eyebrow as the ladies squeezed past him, their backs to the wall. They wouldn't even meet his gaze. Rian cocked his head and watched them scatter down the hall. He didn't feel he should be surprised that his wife had kept her word about them. Ivy hoped to reassure them soon, but now, she stood alone with only her husband's attention.

"Did you get my letters?" Rian's brows gathered in the center of his forehead. He lifted one shoulder higher than the other.

"Yes," Ivy looked down at her hands at her sides.

"And what di-"

"They're in the fireplace."

"Oh," Rian looked toward the ground. His mouth opened like he had something to say, but he shut it quickly, not daring to meet her gaze.

"Thank you for sending them. For apologizing." Ivy stared up at him through her eyelashes, feeling guilty about his words that had been turned to ash. Ivy wished she'd been able to read them all. "I, I -"

"Ivy, you don't have to say anything right now."

Ivy sighed, "I just wasn't expecting any of this."

"You didn't think I would come after you?"

"You never have before." It hurt her to say it as much as it hurt for him to hear it. Ivy stared at his chest as it slightly heaved in front of her. It wasn't her fault that it was the truth.

Rian fluffed his hair from one side to the other with his hand. "I would really like for you to come to council tomorrow. Your knowledge would be invaluable." She considered if his flattery was only a tactic. Probably. But at least it would get Ivy in the door. "Will you come?"

Ivy lit up at the opportunity. "I would very much like that, Rian. Thank you."

A smile made his cheek dimple. *Fuck.* Feelings were cracking through the walls she had put up. She shouldn't even look at him. Ivy dropped her eyes to the floor, desperate to push down the rising tide of emotion.

His voice was soft, almost a whisper. "I want you to know that I meant what I said." His ill-timed *I love yous* echoed in Ivy's mind. Rian's fingertips pushed back her hair from her face and tucked it behind her ear. She looked up at him. Her warm, wild eyes met his. "Ivy, you are still the most splendid thing I've seen." The soft pout of his lips made her want to abandon everything right there, to touch him, kiss him, let him know everything she was feeling since the moment she heard his voice in the hall.

"Your Grace,"

Ivy whipped around to see Luc standing there. Rian's hand stayed pressed against her blushing cheek.____

"King John sent me with a message for you." Luc lifted the folded paper in his hand.

Rian stood there awkwardly. "I'll see you tomorrow," He gave her another warm smile, and Ivy nodded.

"Goodnight." Rian walked away, passing Luc. He approached slowly, waiting for Rian to be as far as possible before handing her the paper. Ivy opened it, but there was nothing written on it.

"Really?" Ivy crumpled the paper and threw it at his chest, then slipped behind her door. Luc tried to speak, but she didn't care. That was a new low. Ivy pressed her back against the wood and closed her eyes, listening to Luc's footsteps fall until they landed outside her door, taking position to guard her.

It took everything in her not to stomp to her bed. Even though he was viciously jealous, Ivy had fallen so madly for Luc. However, she couldn't erase the stir that brewed deep inside her heart for Rian. Ivy didn't want to forgive or take him back, but finally, he was doing everything she'd ever asked. Ivy didn't want to give Luc up. His arms felt more like home than any other place she'd been. It should have been easier to hate Rian, but she didn't. She related to him: the loss, the abandonment. Luc had been through so much, too, yet his heart was still so open. Without even bothering to undress, Ivy plopped herself down onto the mattress. The scar on her palm trembled. What a mess she'd made.

Ivy closed her eyes. Fuck, she was tired. Then she heard the door open. *Luc.* Ivy sat up. He just stood there.

"You shouldn't be in here. It's too dangerous." Ivy rested her head back on the wall.

"How long have you been writing to him?"

"I haven't."

His quieted voice rasped with anger. "Don't lie to me!" His body stalked toward her on the bed.

"I'm not lying." Ivy stood to confront him. "I had no idea he was coming!" she whispered, but she wanted to yell.

An exasperated sigh came from his helmet. "We should have left weeks ago." Tension hung in the air. "I'm sorry, Querida. I prayed this day would never come."

"I know." Ivy pulled his glove off to hold his hand. She wanted to reassure him. She wasn't sure of much herself, but maybe the touch could comfort them both. He was so still. Ivy squeezed his hand with hers. "Luc, I want to-"

"We could still leave."

Ivy's heart beat faster. "It's not that simple. I'd put everyone I love in danger, including you. We are safe, at least right now."

"But what about your husband?"

"What about him?"

Luc didn't say anything. He couldn't. Ivy didn't know what to say either. She exhaled and pushed herself against his chest. No matter what, nothing could take him away.

Luc sighed, "Even if it's selfish, I think we should go." He looked away from her.

"Look at me." Ivy pulled his helmet back to her, running her thumb over it like he could feel her through the metal. "If there is one thing I do know, it's that I love you," Ivy swallowed hard. "We just can't be so careless now. You can't come in here. I don't even know when we'll be able to talk after tonight."

"What will we do?"

"We'll just wait."

"Close your eyes."

Ivy smiled knowingly as she heard him shifting. The soft pout of his lips pressed against hers. Ivy opened her mouth to taste his tongue. He hummed but pulled away to whisper, "One more night, Querida?"

"You can't stay." As much as Ivy wanted him, it wasn't right. His hand made a convincing argument as it tried to persuade her, reaching inside the neckline of her dress.

"An hour?" Her heart thumped heavily in her chest as Luc kissed down her ear and neck. His deft hands slid around her throat, lifting the golden chain and Ivy heard the soft clack of metal as he laid his gift on her bedside table. Ivy remembered asking for an hour of her husband's time.

"No, we can't." Ivy wanted to convince herself as much as Luc. "It's too-"

Her words were cut off by his tongue flicking across her nipple. Luc's hands bunched her skirt until it was up around her hips. *Fuck it.* Ivy pressed her lips together, focused only on not moaning.

His voice drifted to her, "I just want a kiss."

"Okay, a kiss." Ivy waited with closed eyes to feel his lips on hers. Ivy clasped her hand over her mouth as Luc dropped to his knees and kissed her cunt. That was certainly not what she was expecting. Her knees buckled as he licked and sucked on her clit passionately. Ivy reached down, twisting his hair around her fingers as his lips focused on that perfect spot. God, he knew her so well. Her cheeks tingled.

Luc started to pull away, but she gripped her fingers in his hair and pushed his head back against her pussy. Luc moaned loudly and grabbed onto her thighs. Ivy felt weak in her knees as he continued to kiss her. Keeping quiet was proving to be more than challenging, but thankfully, it wasn't long before she felt herself coming against his face. Luc's strong arms held her up as her thighs quivered.

When he felt the final pulse in her pussy, he pulled away. He stood. Even with her eyes closed, she could feel his face right in front of hers. He kissed her sweetly.

"I love you, Ivy."

"I love you, Luc," Ivy whispered back. He squeezed her hand gently and then pulled away, leaving her to wait until she heard the door shut softly and she could open her eyes. The room was empty. He was gone.

CHAPTER THIRTY

The next morning, Ivy lay in her bed with her eyes wide open and only one thing stuck in her mind. Today, she would join Rian at his side for council. It had been a long time since she'd been taken seriously, since she was given the respect she deserved. Even with her reservations about sitting at her husband's side, she still felt hopeful. Ivy sat up from the bed, stretching her shoulders. It would be a good day, and she needed to prepare for it.

Green. Bold. Present. The color that just felt the most like her. Ivy dug through one of her trunks. She was positive she had brought it; she just didn't quite know where she had packed it away. Ivy hoped she might have some use for her more courtly attire while she was here. Unfortunately, that hadn't been the case until now. Ivy rolled her eyes and sighed, thinking of every single time her father dismissed her.

Ivy pulled out garment after garment, and there it was: sea green, sleeveless with structured shoulders and an uncharacteristically conservative neckline. It was one of the dresses Rian had sent her before he had been wounded, from the first time he fucked up. Ivy unfastened the buttons at the top of the collar above the delicate gold brocade that framed the open back. She looked at herself in the mirror after pulling the dress over her hips and shoulders. Ivy flashed herself a serious expression and then smiled. *Perfect.* She reached behind herself to fasten the tiny buttons and bit her bottom lip as she concentrated on trying to loop the first button from this odd angle. *Got it.* It took her an unreasonable amount of effort to get most of them buttoned, but there were still two more to loop. This was a dress where getting Madeline's assistance would have been helpful. Ivy sighed, cursing herself for not calling for her maid in the first place. She just needed to put on the finishing touches first. Three pins decorated with gold leaves pulled her hair back from her face, a berry tint dotted across her lips, and she tapped jasmine oil behind her ears. *There.* Ivy caught herself in the mirror again. Only this time, a Queen looked back at her.

Ivy opened her chamber door and saw Luc's cape. His broad shoulders were capped with silver pauldrons, and in her vision over them, Rian stood across the hall. He was waiting for her. The man who waited on no one was waiting for her. Luc stepped aside, letting her into the hallway.

Before Ivy could say anything, Basker jumped up on her chest. The giant grey dog happily panted and wagged his tail while she greeted him with head pats and scratches. Rian stepped forward.

"You look incredible."

Basker jumped down to sit obediently next to Rian.

"Thank you. Actually, I'm not quite done. I need to see Madeline quickly to get these last buttons." Ivy grinned, but Luc was still there. She didn't know what to do with them in the same space. "I hadn't expected you'd be here."

"Here, I can get them for you." Rian stepped behind her. Ivy lifted her hair away from her back, and as she turned to peek at him over her shoulder, she caught the angry gaze of Luc's visor instead. Rian was surprisingly adept and gentle, fastening the tiny buttons. "I wanted to escort you to council, but then I realized I probably need you to escort me." Ivy swallowed hard when she felt his fingertips graze across her exposed skin as he secured the final button.

"Well, if there is one thing my father thinks I'm qualified for, it's giving tours."

Rian was utterly in his element. He led the council with authority and efficiency, and he looked incredible. He had tidied his facial hair since the night before. His hair looked more coiffed and neat. He wore no crown, but it didn't matter. Ivy could feel the power he radiated just being near him.

Rian called everyone to the table, pulling the chair out for his wife. Ivy sat to his right, opposite Torin on his left. Ivy didn't care. She was beyond thrilled to have a seat at the table. Her father looked like he wanted to object when she walked in, but Rian never even gave him the opportunity. He studied the court members.

"Weren't there four of you?" Rian gestured to Ad Baalestan. Ivy's heart thumped in her throat. *Adne.* With all the hubbub from yesterday, she'd hardly spared a thought for the dismissed soldier.

"Three, now," Baalestan folded his arms over his chest, nearly glaring through his visor at The Queen. If he had any more harsh words for her, he did not let on. Malcolm and Ivy shared a look. The King huffed.

"Malcolm," Rian leaned back in his chair, "you've been surveying the coastline. What are your opinions on securing the rural areas?"

"Here and here. The cliffs are so high and steep, there's no way to make landfall efficiently." Malcolm went over the map in great detail. Rian listened intently, marking where they would install more pikes on the map. The Knights hadn't been sent to spy on her as she had once suspected. They were diligent in gathering information and assessing how best to protect Iosnos. These assholes were doing better than her own father.

Ivy had an idea. She was nervous to speak up, but Rian could sense the words hidden behind her lips. He looked at her with reassuring eyes and gestured for her to have the floor.

Ivy pointed to the map. "The cliffs here are steep, and it would be impossible to move large amounts of men or goods in or out. Malcolm is right about that." She nodded toward the soldier, still hesitant to interact with him after the stables. "There is hardly any population, maybe one or two farmers. But if a ship travels south, they could go virtually unnoticed for hours, maybe even days, if they used skiffs to cut through a small tunnel passage. It's, um-" Ivy grabbed the quill from Rian's hand, leaning down and marking the map, "-here. You won't see it on maps, but it connects to the river here. They could smuggle in and out without raising any suspicion. If we could put a seafort here and build a beacon system across the island, we could prevent them from sneaking in."

"Let's put a barricade in the tunnel. Good idea," Rian smiled, "Tristan, Malcolm, arrange for the builders to assess whether we can put a seafort - about 100 feet from the coast, right-" He made a mark on the map, "-here."

"Excuse me, Rian," King John interrupted.

Torin popped up, correcting him with a "You mean Your Majesty." It took everything in Ivy to not let her jaw drop. How many times had he disrespected her title? Now, he presumed to correct her father. Her father's eyes narrowed, but he continued.

"Your Majesty, it seems a little far-fetched to think smugglers might know of such a small-"

"That's what smugglers do. They find the smallest weakness and exploit it. I've seen it." Rian shut him down. He didn't need to raise his voice or make a show of it. He didn't come here to argue with an old man. He came here to lead. "Now, let's talk irrigation. Kieran, were you able to dig up any plans for the city's water system?"

Kieran came forward with some scrolls and laid them out.

"Thank you," Ivy took a deep breath and looked at Rian. Her stomach fluttered when he gave her the go-ahead. "We have sewers overflowing in the southeast quarter of the city..."

After council had adjourned, Rian asked Ivy to have a private lunch on the castle terrace. She accepted. While they waited for their plates to be served, Rian stood at the edge, looking out over the sea with Ivy beside him.

"Does it ever make you feel alone to be here?"

"Alone?" Ivy sauntered up to the balcony but kept a few feet of distance between them. "I have many friends in Iosnos, both in and out of the castle."

He smiled, and she spied that little sharp canine of his that she always had a weakness for. "I didn't mean it quite so literally. But alone, trapped in the middle of the sea. Nowhere to go."

"No. I quite like it." She leaned against the railing, pushing her chest up out of habit. "I'm surrounded by so many things that I love. I could never feel trapped."

He stared at her, transfixed by the sun glinting on the dew of her cheek. "I haven't spent enough time here. Since you're so adept at giving tours, perhaps you can show me your island."

When their plates arrived, they sat across from each other under dripping blooms of wisteria.

"I have been traveling."

"How else would you have arrived here?" Ivy teased.

"Before I sailed here, I had been in the southern territories."

"I assume Bloidar has advanced their position." Ivy took a bite of her roasted vegetables.

"Not quite." Rian took a sip of wine. "We've had some difficulty maintaining the peace in Suikar. An uprising that calls themselves Dureto."

"That complicates matters significantly." Feigning disinterest was difficult. Ivy yearned for any information outside of the island.

"Yes, but I have managed to arrange a truce with Bloidar for the time being." Rian's cadence dropped with the heaviness of his feelings. "Father Trevarthan encourages me to continue my efforts, as does Torin."

"Neither of them could make a convincing argument to me," Ivy snarked to lighten his mood.

"We don't need to speak of such things over a meal. I have another council scheduled tomorrow with Sir Tristan regarding matters of Asmye and the war. I hope you'll join me for that as well."

She nodded her head and pierced the fish on her plate. "I appreciate your inclusion."

"It took me far too long to realize what an asset you are," Rian spoke plainly. Ivy nearly dropped her fork. "I blame my pig-headedness." Eyes locked between husband and wife. The latter couldn't breathe. "I've made plenty of mistakes, but I try not to repeat them. Especially that one."

Ivy had to look away. She couldn't put words to the feeling. She managed a polite gratitude before fixating on her plate. "How's Colette?"

"A tyrant," he smiled. "The best women always are."

"A truth in any part of the world."

He raised his glass to that, and she returned the gesture.

"I'd like to spend the day with you. Where should we go after lunch?"

She laughed when the King licked chicken grease off his fingers. "The Mermont market is always an adventure."

Ivy walked with Rian and Basker through the city. She'd like to say he was learning about Iosnos, but his eyes hardly ever left her. He seemed fascinated and entranced by every word that left her lips. It was proving more difficult to keep the topics superficial with every glance at her husband's gorgeous face. Luc stayed behind, making up some excuse to run an errand for Natassa.

"Hi!" Sophie popped out of the marketplace crowd and made her way toward Ivy. Rian reached for Ivy and shielded her with his arm, and the Knights that trailed behind them instinctively reached for their weapons. Ivy ducked under Rian and wrapped her arms around Sophie, pushing her a step back.

"Damn, that's a lot of metal," Sophie whispered to Ivy as she waved them down. "Are you gonna introduce me?"

Ivy swallowed and cleared her throat, "Rian, this is Sophie. She's been my friend sinc-"

"Since forever." She bowed dramatically. "Your Majesty," her words were over-enunciated, mocking the formality of it all, "pleased to meet you."

Rian darted his eyes between the women and sheathed his dagger at Ivy's insistence. "I'm pleased to meet you, too. Any friend of The Queen's is a friend of mine." Strangely, it made Rian smile. He was never like this with anyone else they ran across in town at home. Ivy narrowed her eyes, waiting for the lie to fall through.

Sophie looked Ivy up and down and gave a look that spoke volumes between friends. "You've made an honest woman of our girl here."

Ivy dug her fingernails into her best friend's shoulder and plastered a smile on her face. "What are you doing out here?"

"I'm on my way home to clean up before work." Sophie batted her eyelashes, and Ivy noticed that Sophie came from the direction of the tavern. She wondered if Sophie and the barmaid had met again. "What are you doing here?"

"I asked her to show me the island," Rian interjected and looked around as if he had studied every vendor they'd passed. Sophie clicked her tongue and gave an approving hum.

"Iosnos is quite beautiful, Your Majesty. We produce much of the world's wonder, wouldn't you agree?" Sophie bumped her hip into Ivy's thigh.

"I'd be inclined to agree," Rian bit his lip and stared at the wonder that was his wife.

Ivy reached for Sophie's elbow and leaned in to whisper, but Sophie cut her off.

"He's very hot."

"You're not helping!" Ivy said through gritted teeth. She loosened her grip.

"Sophie, would you accompany us? We've hardly made it halfway through the city."

Ivy's eyes widened at her husband. She turned back to her friend. "Didn't you say you were going to work?"

Sophie took the hint as she gave a once-over to the rest of Rian's Knights. "I'm actually on the run. Some vendor is trying to dick me out of a case of wine for tonight's matches."

"Matches?" Rian asked.

"Oh! Ivy, you should come, it's going to be a rowdy one! Kal's coming back."

Ivy widened her eyes at Sophie and looked back at Rian.

"Sophie runs some fights down in the Salt District at the Barricade. Pretty brutal stuff." Ivy flashed back to a night when three men had to carry someone home because he broke so many bones. And he wasn't even the loser.

"Oh yeah, it's intense. It can be easy money if you've got more brains than brawn. Some of these guys don't know when to quit! It's delicious," Sophie smiled mischievously, "I gotta get going." She started to jog off. "I'll save you some seats."

"Bye!" Ivy waved to her before she ducked down some alley. Ivy sighed and turned back to Rian, who had an amused look on his face. "We don't have to go."

"Do you like going?" Rian asked, resuming his pace through the market.

Ivy looked around and shrugged. "Yeah. I used to go all the time."

"Then we should go. The Knights would love it," he paused, "I'd love it." He grabbed her left hand, holding it softly in his while they walked. He didn't even mention her bare finger.

"Really?"

"Of course."

The room that made up The Barricade was dark. All the light came from torches that lined the ring—bodies crammed in as they watched the match. The crowd whooped and hollered as one fighter knocked the other into the ring of mud. The fight was far from over, though, as they began wrestling, fighting to force the other to yield. Sophie stood on top of a barrel and yelled. She was working, exchanging bets hand over fist and making marks on parchment on the wall behind her. Stale ale wafted up from the dirt floor and stank up the room. The crowd erupted as the fight took a turn. Covered in mud and his blood, the fighter who had fallen was suddenly on top of the other. His fists landed heavily across his opponent's face. The sound of bones being cracked under the pounding blows somehow cut through the room's noise. A man jumped in, pulling the fighter off the other. He bent to the man lying unconscious in the mud and motioned to Sophie.

"We have a winner!" She yelled over the men. The crowd was a mixture of cheers and groans as coins and trinkets changed hands. The winning fighter was handed a big pint, and the loser was dragged from the ring.

"Next, we have -" Sophie saw Ivy near the entrance, huddled behind her husband. A behemoth of a Knight she didn't recognize stood before them, surveying the crowd. "The King and Queen of Asmye!" The crowd turned towards them. Maybe for the first time, the Barricade went silent as they dropped to their knees. Ivy felt self-conscious, bringing the event to a standstill. She'd been there so many times and no one paid more attention to her than the ring. Rian acted as if it was to be expected. Sophie waved them over. They had brought quite the party: Rian, herself, the Knights, and Luc. Sophie's eyes widened like she didn't think they'd actually come. She pointed to a couple of men seated ringside and walked toward them.

"Excuse me, gentlemen, could you kindly get the fuck out? I need these seats." The men started to put up a fight, but once they saw the King over their shoulders, they sidled away. Once seated, the crowd stood and began murmuring again, but now more quietly.

Sophie's voice boomed loudly, "I invited the King and Queen personally, and I promised them a good time, so don't get shy on me. They came to watch a show, and you better put on a good one!"

The crowd erupted back to its previous self. Sophie announced the next fight with men striding around the ring for a few minutes while bets were placed. Once the bell rang, they slammed into each other.

Malcolm's stomach twisted as he recognized the handsome fighter in the ring. Ivy recognized him, too. They shared a worried glance, but Ivy's nod encouraged Malcolm to stay silent. Adne dodged every punch his opponent threw, His fair, sinewy build on display as he moved with elegant, fluid motion. The other fighter could barely keep up as he chased Adne around the ring, throwing big, ineffective fists. Adne ducked low, then, with calculated precision, landed a combination of jabs and hooks that toppled his opponent into the mud. The man rolled to his side and coughed, spitting up blood.

"Don't give up so easily. I've only just started," Adne snarked. He raised his hands toward the crowd and skipped around the perimeter, beating his chest until his opponent was ready to fight again.

The match continued similarly for a few more minutes. Adne toyed with the other fighter until the man couldn't stand and yielded. Adne strutted around the ring, moving his arms with a flourish as the crowd cheered and applauded the showmanship. After Sophie hung a ribbon around his neck, Adne bowed low before the King and Queen.

"Your Majesties, it is an honor as always."

"I'm glad you've found uses for your special skills." Ivy reached her hand out. Adne took it and laid a soft kiss against her skin.

"I'm thankful for the opportunities Iosnos has presented for me." Adne glanced over to Luc with a smirk and a nod.

Malcolm watched Adne with hungry eyes, desperate for his former lover to look toward him. Adne's dark eyes found the knight. Adne flashed his charming smile, then retreated out of Malcolm's view. They hadn't spoken since that day in the stables. Word got back to the Knight that Ad Nekoson had been spared, but he had disappeared after that.

"Friend of yours?" Rian asked, familiarity with The Queen not lost on him.

"I suppose," was all Ivy could say.

Sophie hopped down from her barrel and started towards Rian and Ivy's seats, her arms filled with bottles of wine. Torin stepped in front of her, blocking her path and looking at her with disgust.

"Excuse me." She looked up at him, annoyed.

"Let her through," Ivy commanded, and he stepped aside with that sick smile of his.

Sophie handed Ivy a bottle. "What's his problem?"

"Everything? Being born grotesque and with such an ugly face seems to have soured him towards, well, almost everyone." Torin's annoyingly handsome face looked unamused by the delights of the unwashed masses.

Sophie laughed and looked to Rian, "How about you, Your Majesty? Should I have them fetch you a chalice, or can you drink from the bottle with us ruffians?"

"My wife didn't tell you? That's how I prefer it," Rian smiled at Sophie, and she handed him a bottle. Rian pulled the cork out with his teeth and began to chug.

Sophie looked back at Ivy and shot her a wink. "Have I mentioned that I like him?"

Ivy rolled her eyes.

"Where are Mads and Jan?" Sophie searched the crowd. Ivy shifted in her seat.

"They didn't want to come."

"I thought Janelle liked the fights."

"I'll tell you later." Ivy gave a look of warning and then looked toward Rian, who was caught up in a conversation of his own.

"What about all these fine specimens?" Sophie gestured towards the Knights, who were standing in a circle around Ivy and Rian. She thought she had counted another helmet amongst the group, but one was missing. Oh well, what did it matter? A man was a man. "Any of you willing to ditch the armor and go a round or two in the mud?" She pointed at Luc. "What about you? Would love to see what a real Adeshbu is capable of."

"Adeshbu don't fight for sport." Luc's tone was serious, and his voice was low. There's no way he was having any fun. Ivy felt awful.

"Boring." Sophie made a face and then turned to Tristan. "What about you, big man?" She fluttered her eyelashes. "I bet you can do some real damage even without this." She ran her finger over his chest plate. Rian's General had never looked so soft and giddy as Sophie brushed against him like a purring cat. Ivy tried to suppress her smile as Sophie flirted shamelessly with Tristan, but that was Sophie.

"Tristan, you should have a go." Rian took another big gulp of wine. "Show Sophie what you're capable of."

"Maybe I will." Ivy saw Tristan crack a smile at Sophie. She giggled, then grabbed his hand, leading him away from their seats.

Ivy had never seen Tristan without his armor before. Bare-chested, he was just as massive and intimidating. Rian placed a generous bet on Tristan. The odds quickly shifted in Tristan's favor as he paced back and forth, sizing up his opponent. When the round started, he made quick work of it, beating the man unconscious with a few blows.

"What a knockout!" Sophie raised her hands, encouraging the crowd to cheer. "We hardly got to see you play." Sophie put on a pout and looked up at Tristan. "What do you say? Want to go again, big man?" Sophie cooed to him.

Tristan was absolutely smitten, his gaze soft and smiling at Sophie. "I'm ready."

"Does he mean he's ready for the round or for Sophie?" Ivy leaned in close to Rian.

"Who do you think would win?" he laughed and squeezed her hand.

It was nice just to be able to talk to him. Ivy didn't move her hand away.

The Knights cheered and whooped. It wasn't long before Malcolm and Dieter were stripped down, ready for their own matches. Rian was delighted, smiling wide and drinking. His hand landed on his wife's thigh. Ivy thought of watching the jousts by his side in the early days of their marriage. It really wasn't that long past, but so much happened in the interim that it felt like lifetimes ago. He was excited, happy. Ivy felt it, too. He leaned in to whisper into her ear during the matches. Feeling his breath that close made Ivy warm in her core.

Malcolm breathed deeply. His bare chest puffed.

"Give them a show, Knight." Adne ran his tongue over the split in his lip as he leaned over the railing. "I know how impatient you can be."

"Why don't you stay and watch?" Malcolm stared at the twinkle in Adne's eye. His heart quickened. "After I win, you can teach me how to make a spectacle of it."

"I'll be studying your form." His eyes drank in the knight's bare chest and shoulders.

Sophie pushed Malcolm to the center of the ring as the crowd cheered. After the bell rang, she scurried back to Tristan, casually preening in his lap with his arm draped around her hip. Malcolm stretched his shoulders. He made a meal of taunting his opponent. He could have taken him down in a few strikes, but he played with him—quick jabs built to big hooks. Malcolm smiled when he landed a powerful uppercut on his opponent's jaw. The man crumbled, and Malcolm swiveled to see Adne's reaction, but he was gone. Dieter grabbed Malcolm's shoulder to whoop and hollered at his win.

After his third victory, Tristan walked around the ring with his arms out, riling up the crowd. They cheered for Tristan. His left eye was swollen and bruised, but that was nothing compared to his opponent's injuries.

"Looks like your leg healed up nicely," Luc's voice cut through the cheers as Tristan walked back toward their group. "Surprised an old man like you can even walk after a scuffle with an Adeshbu." Ivy glanced up at him from her chair. She shot daggers at Luc, but she couldn't see anything back. That wasn't fair. Luc only hurt Tristan because she needed to see Rian after he was hurt.

The crowd loved the Knights. They cheered wildly when Dieter entered the ring for his match. Sophie came over mid-way through the absolute pummeling Dieter was giving. "So, Your Majesty, you want to join in the fun?"

Rian looked at Ivy. "Should I-"

Ivy cut him off before he could even ask, "Go!"

Rian grinned. "Wish me luck?" He squeezed her thigh.

"You don't need luck," Ivy smiled at Rian, keeping her eyes on him as he followed Sophie into the ring.

Sophie stood on her barrel and bellowed, "Ladies and gentlemen, The Knights of Garreau were only your first taste. We've got a real treat now. King Rian Garreau has agreed to one match." Rian walked out into the ring, reaching his arms over his shoulders. He gripped his tunic and pulled up. His torso was thick and defined as the fabric lifted away. Every woman in the room must've been salivating, just like Ivy.

His sides were tight, leading up to his broad, muscled shoulders. Ivy caught a glimpse of the black hair under his massive arms as he pulled the shirt over his head. He shook his hair back. His elegant curves and angles of his neck and jawline led up to that beautifully brooding face. His pants were just low enough that she could see a few flecks of black hair on his stomach. His shoulders were broad and framed his massive chest. Ivy saw his scars. The ones she helped heal. *Fuck.* Ivy hadn't seen him in any state of undress in months. She bit her lip.

"Anyone out there think they're a match for him? Think you could get him on his back?" Sophie riled up the crowd. "Who wants to hit the King?!"

Ivy's hand shot into the air. Rian looked at her, shaking his head and smiling. He waved two fingers at her, almost daring her to square up.

"Well, I know *you* can," Sophie sighed. "Okay, does anyone *besides the Queen* think they can take on King Rian?" The crowd laughed, and Ivy dropped her hand, shrugging her shoulders.

The crowd started to part to reveal a man who nearly matched Rian's size. His skin was darker, and he didn't have the same plethora of scars that Rian did. He wore his long dark brown hair tied back. His fierce eyes were dark and smokey.

Sophie eyed Ivy's old beau up and down and pinched her brow before she tossed a look toward Ivy. "This will be interesting," she mouthed, then called out to the crowd, "Looks like Kal, the undefeated, wants to take on the challenge. Time to make your bets!" Ivy saw the frenzied crowd murmur and trade currency. Ivy knew Rian was an incredible fighter but couldn't help worrying. Kal had never met his equal in that ring. Rian jumped up and down, warming himself up. Kal watched him and cracked his neck from side to side.

Sophie stood between them. She looked so tiny between the two behemoths. Ivy overheard her, "Don't kill each other. It's not worth it." Kal sniffed deeply, furrowing his brow as he stared at the King. Rian focused and took a deep breath.

"Don't worry, Sophie," Kal growled. "Wouldn't want to upset our Queen."

Sophie cleared the ring, and Kal charged at Rian, trying to grapple him. Rian dodged the attack, ducking low, landing his fist in Kal's side. Rian stepped away and squared up, eyes studying his opponent. Kal grunted deep and slammed his fist against his chest. Rian's boot shifted against the ground before he took a step forward. Rian's fist split open Kal's cheek, but Kal's was pushing Rian's whole body back. Ivy clasped her hands over her face. She'd never seen Kal take a hit like that.

Rian repeatedly landed hits to Kal's sides. The crowd jumped out of the way as the two men barreled out of the ring. Rian's back crashed into the wood wall. Ivy thought she could hear the wood crack behind him. She covered her mouth with her hands, wincing like she took the hit, too. Then she heard Kal yell when Rian pulled Kal's chin into his knee. Rian grabbed Kal's hair and dragged him back into the ring.

Kal got back up to his feet. Rian stood, waiting, then gave a little shrug, beckoning Kal to come at him again. Kal threw a big right hook that Rian dodged easily. As Rian closed the distance between them, Kal landed a jab on Rian's mouth. Rian's lip trickled a little blood, but he didn't care. He landed body blow after body blow to Kal's torso. The uppercut to Kal's chin clearly rang his bell. He staggered back for a moment, trying to shake it off. Rian's breath was heavy, but he was focused, a warrior skilled in combat. Kal grunted as he bear-hugged Rian to get him to the ground. The men hit the floor with a thud.

Rian managed to twist his body and pull away from Kal's grip. Ivy stood up as Kal wrapped his arm around Rian's neck and squeezed. "What a pretty wife you've got," Kal said low enough that no one else could hear. "I remember how much fun she could be." He licked his lip and turned his gaze toward The Queen.

A rush pulsed in Ivy's stomach. She shouted to her husband, afraid for the first time. Kal blew her a kiss. Ivy swallowed and ignored him, queasy and wondering what she ever saw in him. She met Rian's eyes and gave a slight nod. Rian hammered his fist backward into Kal's face. Kal's hold around Rian loosened instantly. His nose poured blood into the mud. The crowd screamed in amusement. Rian rolled onto his knees and threw another punch at Kal's jaw. Rian stood.

"What were you saying about my wife?" Rian's dark eyes bore into his opponent.

Kal was desperate. He grabbed Rian by the leg, pulling him back into the mud. Rian stomped his boot onto Kal's bicep.

"You should yield." Rian looked down at Kal.

Through the blood and the mud, Kal grunted, "No!"

Rian shrugged at the crowd. "You want a show?!" Rian smiled as the cheers rang out. He grabbed Kal's hand, then yanked upward. Kal's arm snapped under Rian's boot. Kal's screams of pain were drowned out by the crowd shouting, "Rian! Long Live the King!"

Rian dropped Kal's limp arm as Sophie declared him the winner. Rian found Ivy and walked straight toward her. A calmness washed over her as she studied the way his body moved. There couldn't be anything seriously wrong with the solid and heavy steps he took.

"Congratu-"

His dark gaze transformed into a smile before Rian grabbed Ivy's face and pressed his lips against hers. The tip of his nose pressed into her cheek as the crowd cheered him on. When he pulled away, he laughed softly. His eyes scrunched from his smile. Everyone else in the room blurred like they were the only two there. A familiar ache called out inside her as she looked at his face with forgiving eyes. Sure, he won the fight in the ring, but a battle was brimming inside her. Ivy knew Luc was somewhere. Was he watching? Rian's thumb skimmed over her cheek as he kissed her again, deeper. Maybe it was the wine. Maybe it was the energy in the room. Maybe it was just how good he looked, and fuck, did he look good. Ivy didn't care anymore. She wrapped her arms around Rian's neck and pulled him in closer. Let the whole town see.

CHAPTER THIRTY-ONE

Adne's cheeks warmed as he watched his sweet knight fight. He was disappointed to leave him behind, but their separate worlds tore them apart. Maybe a goodbye could be the promise of another sweet night. Adne noticed Sir Torin leaving the Barricade, shaking his head and peering over his shoulder before he exited. Disappointment washed over Adne as some core instinct told him to follow him. With one last glance at Malcolm, Adne slipped out the side door.

Adne followed Torin closer than he would have liked, but Mermont was still thick with early evening crowds. Adne squeezed through people to keep his eyes on the King's right hand. A chill ran down Adne's spine when Torin turned down the street toward Port Cane. That was a place he could not follow. Adne peeked around the corner, and hands grabbed the front of the shirt, shoving him down a thin, dark alleyway.

"Why are you following me?" Torin pressed Adne against the brick wall.

"I saw you at the Barricade and thought you might be interested in something I have to offer." Adne sweetened his voice, ready with a lie about whoring.

"Who are you?"

Adne searched Torin's icy eyes for any sign of recognition. "I'm anyone you want me to be," Adne deflected and glanced down at Torin's wide, pale lips. He had learned a trick or two from the brothel.

Torin pushed the man and let him go, scrunching his nose. "I don't fuck men."

"I saw how you looked at the King, but maybe you're just moon-eyed for his specific affection." Adne wore dreamy eyes, playing his part.

"He is a fine specimen. I'm sure he treats his concubines well." Torin slammed his hand around Adne's throat.

"Shut your whore mouth." Torin's nose nearly touched Adne's. "I'm Advisor to the King."

Adne coughed and stroked his hand across the front of Torin's pants. Torin's cock stiffened against his will. Adne struggled through the grip, "Does he need much advice? Long nights and all?"

Torin spat in Adne's face. "Keep your hands off me." He let go of Adne and walked down the road towards Port Cane.

Adne yelled after him, "Come find me when you change your mind." He wiped the spit away. Their dance had only just begun.

The walk back to the castle made Ivy feel like a teenager, like she was given a night off from the real world. Torin left early. Praise Adievasinis for that small mercy. With his three wins and Sophie on his shoulders, Tristan led the pack as they walked home. The Knights hung off each other's shoulders, singing victory songs and swigging from...how many wine bottles did they take? Ivy would have to get the bill from Sophie. On second thought, she'd stolen enough from The Queen. Luc trailed far off behind them. Ivy consoled herself that it was better to play the loving wife than the adulterous whore.

"What did you even win?" Malcolm laughed at Tristan's boasts.

Tristan turned around as Sophie straddled his head. "I thought it was pretty obvious what I won." He slapped Sophie's thigh playfully, and she raised her arms in a victory of her own. "Plus, The King gave me everything he won on bets."

"Then, what's my prize?" Dieter asked, scratching his fingers through his dark beard.

Rian shouted a few steps back, "You got your winnings!"

Sophie gripped her hands in Tristan's hair. "I can think of a prize for you," she smiled devilishly and sent Dieter a wink.

"I have to share?" Tristan tilted his head back to look up at Sophie.

She leaned down to give him a soft, sensual kiss. "Not if they can't catch you."

When Sophie pulled away, Tristan took off running towards the castle with Sophie giggling on his shoulders. Malcolm and Dieter chased after them.

Rian walked next to Ivy, setting the pace for a perfect distance in any direction so it could feel like they were alone. Even Luc had dropped back somewhere. The moon hung high in the sky, illuminating the road ahead.

"So, how did it feel?" Ivy asked.

"How did what feel?"

"Tonight? Being with everyone?" Ivy nudged him with her shoulder. "Having a good time?" Ivy watched Rian's smile spread, revealing that one tooth she loved nearly as much as the man himself.

"I won. I feel great," he laughed. "Your boyfriend didn't fare so well, though." Ivy cringed, remembering Kal's swollen black eyes and the horrible sound of his bones cracking. She couldn't believe that, even for a moment, she had doubted who the victor might be.

"Impossible man." In her haze, Ivy rested her head on his shoulder as they walked. A shiver from her shoulders had Rian draping his cloak over her in the chilly air. His arm fell to her back, holding her closer to him. It was nice to walk like this, to be touched in a public space. There was no fear, no hesitation. Her left hand felt light, missing a weight. A single pang stung in her stomach. Surely, Rian noticed she hadn't worn it since he'd seen her. What he didn't know was right where she left it, hidden in his home, back where she'd never see it again. Maybe one of the maids had found it by now. Ivy snapped back to reality when Rian's lips pressed against the top of her head as they passed through the castle doors.

It didn't take any thought for Ivy to enter Rian's room. It felt like the most natural thing to do as they continued their conversation. She hardly even realized where she was until the door closed behind them. It was awkward as she stood there, watching Rian stoke a fire. The flames danced around in his eyes, igniting the spark that had been burning between them all night. That kiss in the ring, the way his lips felt against hers, it wasn't enough. Ivy rested Rian's cape on a chair and shifted on her feet. The man in front of her was her husband, and she didn't know how to make a move on him.

"Are you just going to stand there?"

Ivy snapped up, eyes meeting his. She guessed he caught her staring. But, thankfully, Rian had no qualms about taking charge. The wine buzz still beat her brain as she walked to him. His hands were on either side of her as she looked at his eyes. Ivy bit her lip as she trailed her fingers over his chest, pulling at the laces of his tunic.

"You're filthy," she laughed as he pulled his shirt off—anything to distract the anxiety in her stomach.

"I thought you liked that."

"I do," she smiled as her fingers skimmed over his bare chest. "Still think you can go a few rounds in the ring with me?"

"I can go a few rounds. Just not in the ring."

Her lips parted as she looked at him. There was a bit of blood caked in his facial hair. A sheen of sweat covered his neck and shoulders as they stood in front of the fire.

"You should let me clean you up." Her hand brushed his cheek. There was a basin of fresh water near the fire. Ivy took a small cloth from the table and dipped it in before walking back to her husband's side. "Sit."

One of his eyebrows raised at her, but he obeyed. Ivy pressed the cloth over his skin in small dabs. He'd taken a few hits. Surely, his muscles must be sore.

"Does it hurt?" Ivy asked as she sank to her knees, trying to see better in the firelight.

"You feel nice." Rian reached out for her hand as her balance wavered. His grip on her tightened, but it felt so good. Ivy used her right hand to continue swiping at his skin.

"Is this your blood or his?" She pointed to his chest. Rian looked down and ran his fingers through it. There was a small clot cinching his skin.

"Does it matter?"

"No." Ivy pulled Rian's hand closer to her mouth, dragging her tongue over the pads of his fingers. Ivy watched the twinkle in his eye turn to hunger. Rian stood, pulling Ivy to her feet. His hands gripped her biceps for leverage as he crushed his lips onto hers. His tongue slipped into her mouth, tasting the blood that lingered.

"Rian," Ivy whispered, digging her fingers into his neck. She couldn't get close enough. Rian apparently thought the same because he lifted her thighs around his hips. Ivy moaned into his mouth as he pushed her back against the wall. Her fingers were in his dark, tangled hair, and the rush of wine flowed in her blood like a waterfall. Rian nuzzled his nose under her chin to get his lips on her neck.

Fuck, he felt good. He always knew the right spots to make her weak. The friction between her legs was growing needier by the second, literally growing. Ivy dropped her head back down to meet his lips. The cut on Rian's lip split open when she tugged his kiss between her teeth. His blood tasted divine as the drop hit her tongue. Ivy pushed her chest closer to his as she leaned her head to the side. Ivy couldn't hide her moan as she exhaled, drinking him deeper.

Rian's hand nearly covered the width of Ivy's back as he slid his hand under the fabric of her dress. He bucked his hips into her core as he readjusted her weight. The jostle pushed his teeth into her tongue, eliciting a moan from her lips into his mouth. His other arm slid up her thigh, around her hips, and up her back until he was wrapped around her. The buzz waned as her heart thumped louder in her chest. Her husband whispered her name as he pulled her body closer. The kissing stopped, and he just held her. It had been so long since she'd been in his arms like this, where it meant anything. Ivy dug her face into the crook of his neck and held him.

"I love you," he said at last, setting Ivy down on her feet. She leaned into him to hide the shudder in her breath. Why did he have to say that? Ivy didn't want to cry. She loved him, too, but everything was so fucked up. What if she told him the truth? Could they just forgive and forget?

"I need to go back to my room."

"What?" Rian pulled back but kept his hands on her. "Why?"

"This is wrong." Ivy took a breath and a step back, remembering the fated lover Natassa spoke of. The chosen. The Adeshbu.

"What is wrong?"

"This. Us. We're wrong." Ivy couldn't bear to look at him.

"Why are you saying this? I love you. I came for you." He reached his hand out to brush her cheek. Ivy couldn't meet his eyes.

"I don't trust you, Rian." Why should she trust him? Ivy couldn't even trust herself anymore.

"Is this because of Danielle?"

Ivy didn't think she'd ever be able to get that image of her in his arms out of her head. Then, she had tended to him the same way she had. It was more than just a fuck. "Don't," she held her hand up to his chest. "Don't say her name to me ever again."

"That's long over. I told you that."

"How do I know it's true?" Ivy blinked back tears as she turned away from him. "How do I know you just don't want anything from me?"

"Because I'm telling you!" He was desperate for Ivy to believe him, his voice strained. Ivy looked up at him. Seeing his eyes, the same eyes that had hurt her, how could she trust them? Every time she let those sad eyes win her over, it ended in pain.

"Your word doesn't mean anything to me, Rian." Neither did hers. It was killing her. If she made him angry enough, maybe he wouldn't want her anymore.

"When will you end my exile?!" He grabbed Ivy and pulled her close. His eyes bore through her. What was he searching for?

"I need to go." Ivy felt winter's chill in her blood as her eyes turned away from him.

He held Ivy for a minute more, silently begging her to stay. It didn't matter. It was already over.

Her voice was cold. "We shouldn't see each other anymore. It'll only hurt. Russell is more than capable of assisting you with Iosnos."

His grip released her. Gently, he skimmed his thumb over her skin as she pulled away from him.

"I'm sorry," he whispered as her hand twisted the knob.

Ivy couldn't look at him as she opened the door.

Luc stood outside. Ivy nearly bumped into his back as she hurried out into the hall, away from Rian. Guilt overcame her as she walked in silence. There was nothing to say. Ivy wanted to get in her room, in her bed, and forget she even existed.

Ivy clenched her fists as she stalked down the hall to her chamber. While trying to close the door behind her, she heard it catch on something. Turning around, she saw Luc's hand around the edge of the door. Ivy watched as he finished slamming it for her.

"Did you have fun tonight?"

Ivy whipped around to face him, exhausted and desperate to cry alone. "Do you not care if you're killed? If I'm killed? You can't be in here."

"I asked you a question." Luc stalked toward her.

"Does it matter? I'm trying to survive, and you seem hellbent on us losing our heads. Antagonizing the knights, 'Adeshbu don't fight for sport.' That's not even true!"

Luc caged Ivy against the wall. "So what then? You're spreading your legs to save my head?"

"What did you say?"

"You heard me. What is it? He bigger than me?" His hand flexed against his gloves. Ivy could hear the leather crackling.

"Luc, you can't be in here." Ivy was so tired. She didn't want to deal with this. Her husband was mad at her. She didn't need it from her lover, too.

"Ivy, you told me you loved me." His voice sounded so hurt, so angry.

"I do lo-" Ivy reached for Luc, pushing him a step back.

"You told me to trust you and he's back for one night, and you're already fucking him?" The hurt was vanishing. He was seething.

"We didn't. Luc, I di-"

"If it was just fucking, I might be able to stomach it, but the way you look at him..." The words caught in his throat like it was painful even to consider.

"He's my husband!" That hung in the air. It was the unavoidable truth. It was hard to fathom what to do now. Luc looked away from her. Ivy reached out to him, laying her hand softly against his neck. Her fingers stroked along his jawline under his helmet.

He turned his helmet back to meet her eyes. Ivy heard a shuddering breath, "You're mine."

"Yes, Luc, I-"

"Swear to me." He took a step towards her. His hand gripped against her hip. Suddenly, she felt like the quarry he had cornered.

Ivy nodded at him.

"I told you I would never stop." He took another step. His body forced Ivy backward into her shelves. His breath sounded more like growls.

"Luc, we can't-"

His hand clasped over her mouth, and his thumb pressed into her cheek. Ivy tried to speak, but her words were muffled against his palm.

"Quiet." The hardwood of her bookshelf pressed against her back. He yanked her thigh up, forcing her skirt around her hips. "Wouldn't want your husband to hear."

"Luc," the word didn't go past his hand.

"Pull out my cock." Obediently, Ivy dropped her hands to his waistband, trembling over the laces as she tried to pull him out quickly. It was better than fighting. He was deliciously hard as she rubbed her finger over the tip, smearing his pre-come across his head. Luc's breath sharpened at her touch.

Her heart already raced. Ivy positioned his cock at her slick, and he was inside of her instantaneously. Ivy couldn't help it; she moaned loudly. She'd never admit to Luc that it was Rian who had aroused her this way. Luc's hand slapped back over her mouth, stifling her moans.

"Do you want to get caught? You want him to know you're such a whore?"

Each of his thrusts slammed her back against the bookshelf. Pain shot through her bones, where bruises would soon form.

"I hate to see him even look at you." He tilted his helmet back in the dark and leaned his lips into her neck. "I hate knowing that he's touched you!"

Ivy grabbed his shoulders, bracing herself as he pounded into her.

He took a long, deep inhale. "I can smell him on you."

Ivy screamed curses into his palm as he split her open on his cock.

"You're mine," he growled. He fucked Ivy harder. The fabric tore as he yanked her dress off her shoulders. Her thighs quivered. *I came for you.* Her eyes watered. *You are the most splendid thing I've seen.* Ivy turned her head away and closed her eyes. *I love you.* She didn't want this right now. Ivy thought she did, but it was too much. It was all too much. She felt sick. She worried about Rian being wrong, but Luc was a sin.

"Wait, Luc. Stop. We shou-" Ivy tried to plead with her eyes, words distorted under his hand.

"He will not take this from me!" The words Luc growled into her ear filled her with guilt, not lust. Her hands reached to his chest to push him away, but he took them both in one hand and held them tight. She couldn't move. She felt Luc's cock twitch inside her. He pressed his thumb into her neck, cutting off her whimpers as he pumped his cock in and out of her. He didn't feel good anymore. He felt rough and painful. Ivy attempted to press him off her shoulders, but his body pinned her against the bookshelf as he emptied himself inside her.

Luc relaxed his hand from her mouth, but Ivy couldn't look at him. The moon sat high in the sky as she stared out the window. Ivy had never seen it shine in her room. It was always dark, safe for Luc to take his helmet off. Now, she was thankful he couldn't. Luc stroked his fingers across her cheek as he tried to turn her face to look at him.

"Querida-"

Ivy pulled away. "You should leave." She felt a shiver in her voice. He groaned as he pulled out of her and stepped back, then fastened his pants.

"I jus-"

"Go. Please." Her breath shuddered, but she wouldn't cry. Not in front of him.

He hesitated for a moment before he walked out, shutting the door behind him. His come dribbled down her thighs. Ivy wanted just to shake it off as she put her face into her hands and screamed.

"Fuck!" Ivy sobbed and crumbled to the floor, wiping him off her with what was left of yet another tattered dress. What else could she do? Any move she made would be dangerous for the other. *Stupid girl.* What a fucking mess she'd made.

CHAPTER THIRTY-TWO

Luc relaxed his hand from her mouth, but Ivy wouldn't look at him. The moon sat high in the sky as she stared out the window. Luc stroked his fingers across her cheek as he tried to turn her face to look at him.

"Querida-"

Ivy pulled away. "You should leave." Luc felt the coldness in her tone. He fucked up. Blinded by his jealousy, he had hurt her. The thing he was always terrified would happen to her, he did himself. He groaned as he pulled out of her and stepped back, then fastened his pants.

He wanted to apologize, to try to make things better. "I jus-"

"Go. Please," her voice quivered with pain.

Self-loathing flooded through Luc as he walked away from her chamber. He mindlessly went through the motions, handing off her guard duties to Ad Viena for the night. The maids were safe in their room.

His mouth felt parched and metallic with every passing minute. His lungs were tight like he couldn't pull in enough air to breathe. When he passed into his tiny chamber, he pulled off his helmet and opened the window. He tried to suck down the cool air, but only shallow breath came back to him. Water, he needed water. It dribbled down his chin as he gulped straight from the carafe as much as he could. Luc threw the carafe at the stone wall, shattering the glass. His chest rose and fell with heavy breaths.

Luc unclasped his armor, letting it clatter against the floor, and kneeled in front of his trunk. Everything he possessed fit in the partially empty box: a few books he loved, an unstrung bow and quiver of arrows, a few changes of clothes that looked identical to what he wore right now, and a small wooden wolf. Buried at the bottom of the chest was the leather grip of his flogger. He pulled it out and laid it on the bed. Luc pulled off his tunic. He prayed silently, holding the leather whip in his fist.

"Forgive me." Luc struck his back over his shoulder. He grimaced at the pain. Streaks of pink flesh were left in its wake.

"Forgive me." He gritted his teeth. He didn't know if he prayed to Adievasinis or to Ivy.

"Forgive me." Luc's back rose and fell with heavy breaths.

"Forgive me." The leather lashes split his skin.

"Forgive me." Tears fell from his eyes as he saw Ivy's pained face in his mind.

"Forgive me." The flogger drew blood.

"Forgive me." Sweat collected on his brow.

"Forgive me. Forgive me. Forgive me…"

Luc collapsed with exhaustion on his bed. The pain didn't absolve his guilt, nor did it lessen hers. He would never forgive himself for what he had done.

Ivy lay there on the floor, awake most of the night. She couldn't force herself to get up. Two men, twice the pain. Nerves made her stomach flutter. It was sickening what he'd done to her. Ivy hated that she hurt him.

With a knock at her door, Malcolm came to escort Ivy to her meeting with the canal builders. Luc apparently hadn't returned, but she didn't want to see him anyway. Rian must be off somewhere, fixing one of her father's mistakes. Shame slid down her spine as she walked down the hall. It wasn't supposed to be like this.

"So," Ivy tried to lighten her mood. "Did you catch them?" She remembered Malcolm and Dieter chasing after Tristan. Her friend could be very friendly.

"Yes, Your Grace." His tone was polite and serious, but he smiled, a far departure from the rowdy, drunk young man Ivy had seen the night before. He had a cut across the bridge of his nose and purple under his eyes.

"I'm sorry for everything," Ivy stuttered. "-with Ad-" Malcolm drew his shoulders up tall.

"We don't have to talk about it. You saved him, and that's all I can ask."

"I wish there was more I could do." Neither knew what more could be done for Adne. If he chose to spend his nights at the Barricade, at least he wouldn't starve.

Voices shouted down the corridor, distracting her. Sophie was usually never quiet, but this was something else.

"Wait here," Ivy spoke to Malcolm, then turned in the other direction. He hesitated to let her go, but she raised a swift hand, and he obeyed. "I can handle it."

Around the corner, Sophie stood across from Torin with his ugly face sneering down at her. Tristan emerged from his chamber, covering himself with only a sheet wrapped around his waist.

"Tristan, if you needed a deal on some two-bit pussy I could have had my friend Fred make some arrangements for you."

Sophie looked furious. Her usually cheerful face scrunched in anger.

"Or maybe you like this," Torin looked Sophie up and down. "Whatever *it* is. I always suspected your lid was a bit thick. First, Rian returns with an island mutt, and now this one's poisoned you, too."

"Torin, stop this," Tristan's voice boomed.

Sophie stood in shock. "This is Torin?" The two men looked at each other, unable to discern where her vitriol came from.

Sophie spat in Torin's face. She jumped forward, her arms outstretched like she would claw Torin's eyes out. Tristan hooked his arm around her waist, preventing her from attacking him. Sophie struggled against Tristan's arm as he tried to carry her back into the room. "Let me go!"

Ivy ran forward, wedging herself between Sophie and Torin. "What's wrong with you?!" Ivy stared up at him defiantly.

He pulled a handkerchief from his pocket to wipe Sophie's spit from his cheek. With a wicked smile, he said, "Nothing that couldn't be solved with a few swift cuts." He leaned down, his face uncomfortably close to hers. Ivy grimaced the closer he got. "Are you frightened of me? Where is your guard dog?" His eyes searched for her Adeshbu. "Must have run off in the night. What a pity he leaves you unattended, so vulnerable."

Hatred burned in her stomach as Ivy slapped his hand from tugging on her hair. She wanted to bite his face, rip his throat out with her bare hands, and leave him screaming and bloody on the floor.

"How sad you must be, Torin." Ivy chose a weapon of a different kind. "Lonely, bitter, always second. How dark it must be in Rian's shadow, especially when he doesn't even like you best anymore."

Torin narrowed his eyes; his bottom lip twitched with anger. His eyes darted over Ivy at Sophie's disturbance against Tristan, then back to her.

"Is that it? Are you jealous? Did you want to hold his hand last night?" Ivy's sneer matched his. She cut him off before he could protest. "Just find someone else to fuck and get over it."

"He certainly found someone else to fuck, didn't he?" Torin lowered his voice and leaned in so the others couldn't hear. "Hmm, maybe *I'll* fuck Danielle again. She's fantastic. I see why Rian keeps going back."

Sophie pulled the sheet from Tristan's waist, distracting him just enough to break free of his grip. She pushed past Ivy, grabbing at Torin's face. Three long red gouges trailed behind her fingernails. Torin yelled, pushing Sophie off him, and he drew his knife.

Tristan, completely nude, stepped forward to protect Sophie.

"Get out of my way," Torin yelled at Tristan. "I'm gonna gut that little bitch like a pig."

"The fuck you will." Tristan pushed Torin back against the wall with one hand. For all his exertion last night, he hadn't lost an ounce of strength. "You won't touch her."

"Tristan, I'm just looking out for you. I only don't want you to catch fleas." Torin pointed his knife directly at Tristan's cock. Having enough of the bickering, Malcolm rounded the corner and made his way toward the lot of them. Tristan stepped back as the sharp point of the blade pressed against him.

"Bare-assed and unarmed, I could still beat you to death."

Torin grinned, "Even if you did, I'd take a few of your prized possessions with me."

"God! You're all so fucking exhausting!" Ivy yelled. "Torin, go the fuck away."

"Milady, you can't command me."

"For the last time, I am your Queen!"

"Last time I checked, the Queen bears the King's son and wears his wedding ring. You do neither." Ivy was suddenly aware of the unsheathed blade in his hand. Ivy swallowed hard. *Fuck it.*

"Aw, is your jaw sore from sucking him off since I left?"

Torin raised his hand, and Ivy braced herself to take the hit. She wouldn't cower or run. Fuck giving him the satisfaction. Malcolm caught Torin's arm and raised his dagger to protect Ivy.

Everyone yelled. All the voices blended in her ears.

"You are a spineless cunt."

"Bitch!" Torin pushed Malcolm off and raised his hand again. Tristan grabbed Torin's wrist and threw him to the ground. In the motion, Torin's blade drew a thin line across Tristan's chest.

"Torin!" Rian's voice boomed from behind her. *Shit.* Tristan stood at attention for Rian. Ivy had seen him stand that way hundreds of times before, but this was the first time she'd seen him do it nude. She stared between his body and Sophie. *Good for him. Good for her.* Torin stood up, more relaxed.

"I'm only speaking with your wife. You know how dreadful a task that can be."

Rian glanced down at Ivy. Instantly, she recognized the fire in his eyes. *Fuck.* That primal, terrifying blaze that Ivy had felt the wrath of a time or twenty. She felt a throb between her hips.

283

Rian walked right up to Torin with Basker at his side. His voice was low and angry. "You are on very treacherous ground. Do you think I haven't been paying attention? I will not tolerate this." Torin began to protest, but one lift of his finger shut him up. "For your sake, get the fuck out of my sight and stay the fuck away from my wife."

"Rian-"

Rian grabbed Torin's throat. Torin's cheeks turned red as he struggled for breath. "Open your mouth again, and you'd better be prepared for eternal fucking silence." Torin's feet barely touched the ground. Basker's hackles stood on end, teeth bared as he growled. Sophie grabbed Ivy's hand as Rian threw Torin against the wall like he was weightless. "Leave Iosnos. Go back to Tornbridge and prepare for my arrival." Rian's eyes checked in with Ivy, but her eyes darted away. The King dismissed himself from the group, ordering Malcolm and Tristan to meet him at the terrace within the hour. Basker licked her hand before trotting away with Rian.

Torin pulled himself up from the ground. Malcolm stood in front of Ivy, blade drawn, ready to strike. Torin nodded at Ivy as he passed, "Milady."

"Fuck yourself." Ivy didn't even turn to look at him. Ivy heard the flex of his glove, but he kept walking.

"Are you okay?" Sophie asked, more concerned for Ivy than Tristan, who seemed relatively unphased. He looked down at his chest and wiped the blood away with the sheet that had fallen to the floor.

"Hardly the worst I've gotten."

For the first time, Sophie frowned, getting a sense of the pain her friend experienced in Asmye. "Doesn't make it better."

"I'm fine," Ivy faked a smile. "There does seem to be a man over there who could probably use your help more than I."

Sophie turned to see Tristan standing. He didn't seem scary or menacing. He was more like a puppy patiently waiting. She looked up at him with starry eyes. A big, goofy smile stretched across his face.

"Big man," She stepped away from him. walking backward until he followed her, "Looks like you need some assistance." Giggling, she turned away from him and ran back into his room. He chased behind her with a low grumble of laughter. The sight made Ivy smile. At least someone was having a good time.

The castle kitchen was humid. Ivy's curls were swept up from her neck and cascaded out the top of an orange silk headscarf. An apron was tied at her waist, protecting the vibrancy of her teal dress. Butter simmered in a pan, and Ivy sprinkled fresh-picked herbs into it. The fragrance bloomed as the ingredients melded. A bead of sweat slipped down her temple. Ivy grated nutmeg over the pan and sprinkled in her spices. Sophie arranged oysters on a platter.

"I can't believe you are cooking for a man." Ivy poured the sauce over the oysters.

"I'm not, you are." Sophie bumped her hips into Ivy's thigh. "I'm just assisting, but I'll be sure to take all the credit."

The Queen was grateful for the distraction and something to keep her hands busy. Ivy looked over the arrangement of shellfish, portions of pasta, and vegetables. "This is entirely too much food for two people."

"Have you seen the size of him?" Sophie slid her knife through a lemon.

"Yes, I have." Ivy widened her eyes and bumped her hip back into Sophie's waist, nearly knocking her a whole step over.

"Well, I want it to be special." Sophie carefully garnished a plate with her lemon slices.

"Oh, you like him, like him." Ivy's lips curved into a wide smile.

"Shut up!"

"Nope, this is one for the island historian. I'll write him: Sophie Unstred liked a boy on September 30th." Ivy wiped a sauce splatter away from the edge of a platter of scallops. "Better get this out to the terrace before it gets too cold."

"Wait, wait," Sophie took off her apron and tussled her hand through her short hair. "How do I look?" The dark sage green of her dress suited her complexion. Ivy fluffed up the ruching on the off-the-shoulder sleeves.

"Turn around."

Sophie obeyed, and Ivy inspected the ties around her back, ensuring the bows were even and secure.

"Perfect."

"Yeah, I know." With a high, confident chin, Sophie grabbed a platter in each hand and walked toward the terrace.

Ivy nodded her head, and a few others from the kitchen grabbed what plates Ivy could not and followed Sophie out.

By the time Ivy reached the terrace, Sophie was mid-twirl in showing off her dress to Tristan. The Knight was dressed in his finest tunic, a deep red with embroidery on the shoulders. When Sophie turned back towards Ivy, Ivy noticed Rian standing beside Tristan. Ivy's mouth went dry. She hadn't seen him since yesterday when he ordered Torin away. There was hardly time to talk to him, as Ivy's father hated to let his meal ticket out of his sight.

"You see, it won't be too much food," Sophie smiled at the Queen. "I hope you don't mind. I wanted to surprise you."

"Certainly." Ivy was anything but certain as she put down plates and untied the apron at her waist.

"You look radiant, Your Grace." Tristan took her hand and leaned down to kiss it.

"She always does." Rian pulled out the chair at his side for his wife and reached out his hand for her to hold while she sat. Ivy took it but glared at her friend. Sophie shrugged her shoulders and blew a kiss toward The Queen.

Sophie and Tristan filled the air with chatter. Rian kept Ivy's fingers in a soft grip. He leaned down with his own soft kiss and then stared at Ivy through dark lashes.

Rian cleared his throat, signaling the servants to fill their wine glasses. Ivy reached for hers and downed nearly all of it in one swig. She didn't wait for someone to refill it; she just reached for the bottle herself. Tristan gave a concerned look toward the King. Sophie kicked her under the table. Ivy kicked her back, blaming her for the mess in the first place. She hadn't seen Luc since the incident, hadn't breathed a word of it to anyone. If she were being honest, she might have enjoyed this evening by herself, holed up in her room. It was the only time she didn't have to lie.

"Your father has requested your presence in the throne room." Luc stood on the other side of the door. Ivy hardly opened it more than a crack once she saw the helmet and blue cape.

"Oh, has he? No more empty notes?"

"He has." There was sorrow in his voice. Ivy felt his sincerity.

Ivy hadn't spoken to him since that night. If she wasn't with Rian, Malcolm had been guarding her for two days. However that had worked itself out didn't matter to her.

"I'll just need a few minutes to get ready. Thank you." Ivy started to close the door.

His voice was soft, a whisper. "Querida, I'm sorry, I-"

"I know." Ivy knew he regretted it.

"I never meant to hur-"

Ivy cut off his whispers. "I'll be out in a moment." Ivy shut the door and sniffed deep, drying the tears welling in her eyes. Ivy loved him, but all of her feelings were tangled together in misery. Love had never done anything but hurt her. Even now, she craved the safety of his embrace, but it wasn't safe, not for her, not for him.

"Come here, Darling." Her father motioned Ivy closer to where he sat on his throne. The room was nearly empty. Ivy asked Luc to wait outside.

Only a few of her father's guards stood around his throne. Russell wasn't present. Cautiously, Ivy put her hand in his as he reached for her. Lack of affection from him seemed more normal than this. "I wanted to have a private discussion with you. Seems my adoration for you has been overshadowed by our disagreements these past months."

"They aren't disagreements. You refuse-"

He raised a finger to stop her. "I don't want to get into another political debate with you. What I want to discuss is a bit more straightforward."

"And what would that be?" Ivy was so tired. Whatever he wanted, he just needed to spit it out. Ivy could smell the rat.

"You."

"What about me?" Her heart pounded. Did he know? Sophie knew. Adne probably knew. Her father surely knew her just as well as Sophie did. What would he say to her now?

"Clearly, your husband is quite fond of you, yet I wonder why you do not go to his bed."

Ivy dropped his hand and clasped her own behind her back. The red fabric at her waist belted around a soft yellow skirt. True, she and Rian hadn't shared more than a kiss since she left his room three days ago. Even at dinner last night, he was more than charming. Ivy couldn't detect anything false about him. She almost asked for him to escort her back to her room. After Luc...she just needed time. "That's none of your-"

"Ivy, you withhold from him. You don't hold up our end of the deal."

"You are my father." Surely, he must understand how invasive this conversation was.

"Then obey me, daughter." Nothing. Nothing at all. Ivy was chattel to be traded at his pleasure, an X on a dotted line.

"My marriage is not up for discussion." Ivy shook her head.

"Oh, but it is, Darling. You will go to your husband's bed with humility and serve him." His words dripped with the confidence of a mediocre man. Ivy rolled her eyes. "Then you must secure the funding I require." His enunciation punched every word. "He gets you. I get the gold. That's the arrangement."

"How dare you make such a request."

"I've been very patient with you over these months, but it-"

"Have you?" Ivy interrupted. "I seem to only remember your constant nagging about-"

The back of his hand struck her cheek, cutting off her words.

"It's not a request, Darling. You would be wise to learn your place from me rather than him."

Ivy held her palm to her cheek. Tears gathered in her eyes. Would these men do nothing but abuse her to get what they wanted? It seemed Rian

287

was the only one who cared for her these days. Ivy straightened herself up, pulling back on the emotions that might threaten to make her look weak in his eyes.

"I will do no such-"

He struck her again, harder. This one seared her face with pain. Ivy could feel the welt forming across her cheek. John took another sip from his chalice.

"Are we going to have to keep doing this, or are you going to learn to respect me?"

Ivy was disgusted. "Respect you? What is there to respect? You're just a fool in a King's hat, in a King's cha-"

He grabbed her arms and stood closer, leaning his face into hers until she could smell the stink on his breath. No one else in the room moved. No one dared to cross the King.

"I would choose your next words carefully. I am not as tolerant of your behavior as your husband."

Ivy looked up at him. His grip twisted her arm painfully. Ivy did choose her next words carefully. "Fuck you."

He threw Ivy to the ground. The hard floor was unforgiving, and the ache shot deep into her bones. That was too far.

"No, Darling. Fuck *him*. Provide him with an heir and secure my coin." He casually sat back on his throne as Ivy picked herself up off the ground. Without even looking at her father, Ivy turned and walked out. Luc was outside, waiting at the door for her. Had he heard everything?

Ivy walked right by him, not pausing for even a moment. She refused to cry. She inhaled deep through her nose, drying her eyes as she walked. Luc's footsteps were soft behind her. Even if he recognized something was wrong, it would be too bold of him to ask here. Ivy didn't want him to ask. Truthfully, she didn't want to talk to him at all.

Kieran and Dieter stood guard down the hallway. They stood aside as Ivy raised her hand to knock. It was only a moment before the door opened. Rian's face was half-covered in a thin lather of shaving cream. He noticed his wife's face, red cheeks, fallen hair, and misty eyes, then stepped aside to let her in. Rian wiped away the cream with a towel, revealing his bare face. Ivy stood there, tapping her toes against the stone.

"What happened?"

The moment Rian asked, her facade fell. Tears brimmed over her eyes. He closed the distance between them and pulled her against his chest. He didn't try to stop her crying; he let her sob against him. His hands held her, softly stroking her hair as she let it all out. Ivy didn't even have to think about it. He was just where her feet took her. With a stuttered breath, Ivy pulled herself back from him. His hands shot over her face, wiping away the tear stains from her cheeks.

"What happened?" Rian asked again when Ivy flinched as he touched her cheek. He was so gentle. His thumb lingered over her lips, rising and falling with every open-mouthed breath she took. Ivy couldn't even look at him. She felt so stupid. Why did she come here? Rian didn't deserve this, to have to deal with her. Ivy exhaled like a pufferfish, blowing air over her husband's thumb. He didn't remove it, though. If anything, she felt him stare at her harder.

"I'm sorry," Finally, she looked up at him. The tide of emotion was starting to die down. His sweet face was calm as he looked at her: all puffy and with red eyes. "My father, he-" Ivy found herself at a loss for how to explain it to Rian. "-he wanted me to get more money from you."

"I'm not surprised." He tried to hold back an eye roll as he tilted Ivy's chin up with his finger and thumb. "Is that all?"

Ivy didn't have anything to say but the truth. "I refused and he hit me."

A calm rage washed over The King. Rian's brow furrowed. His nostrils flared, and his breath was suddenly heavier. He took a step back and looked down at her.

"Are you hurt?" He restrained himself, pulling back on his anger. He dropped his eyes from hers, searching her shoulders with his hands, looking for anything that may tell him where her father hurt her.

"No. No. He just hit me like-" she sniffled, "-like I was a disobedient child. He told me to 'provide you with an heir and secure the coin,'" she said with a sneer, "that I was breaking the terms of our marriage." That broke her heart. Ivy had been trying and lying for so long that she didn't know which way was up. "He just scared me. I'm sorry. I didn't mean to come here and cry."

"Ivy, you have done nothing wrong." Rian planted a warm kiss on her temple.

Guilt twinged in her stomach, but it wasn't something she was at liberty to admit.

His hand cupped her cheek, reassuring her. It took everything in her not to fall at his feet. Ivy pushed her face into his chest and held him tight.

"This whole time, I've been trying to help, and he refuses me at every chance. I just want to do what's best for Iosnos, and he treats me like I'm incompetent." Rian motioned for Ivy to sit as her tears waned. Rian just took her in. By listening, he made Ivy feel resolute and confident in herself. Her father had been demeaning her worth since her arrival. No one defended or stood up for her, not even Luc - not even in their private moments. Rian bolstered her self-assuredness. It took so long, but he finally made her feel seen as the valuable, intelligent, and necessary woman she was.

"I must seem weak, coming here in shambles after a few hits."

"No." He squeezed her hand in his. "Don't let the cruelty of the world make you think otherwise. Not even me."

Ivy watched as Rian stood and reached her hand out for him. "Where are you going?"

"To speak with your father."

"You can't!" Ivy jumped up out of her seat and followed him toward the door.

"I most certainly can."

"Rian, I-"

"I won't let anyone hurt you."

"This isn't your battle."

Rian grabbed her hand in his and brushed her hair with the other. "I would go to war with anyone for you." They stood and stared at each other, then embraced.

"I've made you soft," Ivy smiled, poking him in his stomach.

He jumped a little as her finger tickled him. He grabbed her hand gently. "Not that soft." He grinned wide after he leaned down to kiss her forehead. "There is fresh water in the washroom. Take a moment. Wash your face. Catch your breath. Just stay here."

"But I-"

"Stay here, Ivy. I love you."

Something in Ivy realized that Rian's way of dealing with her father might include more violence. "What are you going to do?"

He pulled her hand to his cheek to feel her skin on his. "You don't need to fear him anymore."

"John, we need to talk." Rian's voice boomed through the throne room. Russell turned to look behind him. The younger King demanded their attention, interrupting their conversation.

King John looked up, annoyed. "Sent you to fight her battles, has she?" Her father gestured towards Ivy behind him. Rian looked over his shoulder and noticed Ivy quietly standing by the doors. She tossed a look and shrugged her shoulders.

"I come on my own account." Rian turned his attention back to his father-in-law.

King John leaned forward in his seat, studying Rian. "I suppose she is your property now. I may have overstepped by reprimanding her, but she is a disrespectful little girl, and I won't tolerate it." He leaned back in his chair. "She probably left out that all I asked for were grandchildren, an heir to your throne, Rian."

"She told me of your demands." Rian raised an eyebrow. "You are not to lay hands on her again. You'll show the Queen respect-"

"She hasn't earned it." John's voice was irritatingly matter-of-fact as he slapped his hands on the chair's arms. "She comes here, and she thinks that she knows things and can tell me how I should run my kingdom. Well, it's still mine!" He slammed his fist down. "What does she know besides getting herself into trouble? Too much like her mother. I had to break her spirit, too."

"Don't talk about her!" Ivy yelled, stalking right toward him. Ivy only stopped once she stood in front of her husband.

Ophelia. Her mother. She always had Ivy out of the castle. Off on little adventures. Digging in sand or climbing trees. Making little crowns from braided flowers. Her perfect days with her mother were her refuge. Ivy had never thought it was to escape his cruelty or avoid his drunken temper.

John ignored Ivy and sipped from his cup of wine. "I figured you'd do the same, but you're weaker than I assumed. Your reputation must be overblown if my only child, a disappointment-" he looked closer at his daughter, "-a silly girl, has you soft. Why should I fear you if you can't even stand up to her? Perhaps I should marry again. Maybe a young new wife would provide me with a suitable heir." John tipped his glass at Ivy, then drank the rest of it.

"You are relieved of your position," Rian's voice wasn't raised.

"Excuse me?" John chuckled softly.

"Our agreement gave me rights. Rights I abstained from to see your rule," Rian paused as he walked forward, "uninterrupted because it was what my wife would have wanted."

"This is outrageous. You can't remove me." John was flustered. "I am the King. My line has ruled here for two hundred years!"

"I can." Rian's voice was firm and confident. "Don't worry, John. The Crestieene line rules on with our Queen."

"Russell, say something!" John was flustered, yelling.

"The marriage contract clearly states that Iosnos is now a territory of Asmye. King Rian can replace the existing monarch at any time. You would know that if you read what you signed." Russell's voice was collected, unemotional. "He is well within his rights to replace you. He *should* replace you," Russell sighed, finally brave enough to speak his mind. "You've been failing your kingdom for years, John. When was the last time you even left the castle? You have no head for this."

"You've squandered the resources I've provided, neglected your people in favor of vanity." Rian took a deep breath. "I am not a perfect man nor a perfect king. Yet you've squandered the greatest resource you ever had: her." Rian outstretched his hand and Ivy took it, two hearts beating as one. "My wife is much more than a silly girl. She's smart and compassionate. She's kind and ferocious, stubborn to the point of frustrating." Ivy couldn't help the grin that widened her cheeks. "She is not a disappointment. She is the rightful heir, and I have the power to remove you and give her home back."

John's eyes narrowed. "High compliments for your whore. I'm glad you enjoyed your purchase. Do you think she'll stand for you removing me by force? She always cowered before me, begging for every scrap of my approval. Do you think she'd stand against me now? Betray her own father?"

"Remove him." Ivy's voice did not waver.

Everyone in the throne room whipped their heads to see Ivy standing tall.

"Excuse me?" The look on her father's face should have filled her with fear, but with Rian's support, she stood firm.

"I may be your daughter, but I am a Princess of Iosnos and the Queen of Asmye. I will be treated with respect and dignity," Ivy commanded the room's attention. Their eyes fixed on her as she walked forward. "I don't need your crumbs anymore. I am the wife of the most fearsome warrior this world has ever seen. He restrains himself on my word." Ivy touched his shoulder. "Rian, remove him."

Rian grabbed John by the back of his shirt and pulled him from his throne, tossing him at Ivy's feet. Her father groaned as he hit the ground.

"Guards! Guards!" He called out, but no guard stepped forward.

"A lifetime of beatings and unkind words. I realize now I idealized you and thought the best of you, even when you were horrible, but you are a small man. I thought I missed you, that I missed it here, but you were always selfish. That's why we struggled. You let this beautiful place fall apart, and when you finally had the means, you took it for yourself. You are a fool." Ivy grabbed the crown from his head and put it on hers. "I am your Queen."

"Delusions of grandeur. If you're going to overthrow me by taking my crown and beating me, you had better take your swing, *Princess*, for Iosnos has never knelt to a Queen."

"Then I'll be a King and I'll take what's mine." Ivy paused, looking down at her father. He was as pathetic as he was cruel. "Rian," Her husband flipped his hair around as he looked forward to her. "Swing."

Rian's fist hammered down across John's face, the familiar sound of flesh hitting flesh, the distinct crack of bone against bone.

"What a lovely pair you two make," John spit blood from his mouth onto the floor. "A thug and a whore-"

Rian kicked his side hard, cutting off his words. Her father rolled onto his back. He winced at the pain that radiated from his broken ribs, clutching his side. Rian leaned down and landed one more fist blow across John's cheek. Rian stood, shaking out his hand. His knuckle had split open.

"Russell, see to my father."

Russell motioned to two guards. "Yes, Your Majesty. Pick him up. Take him to his chambers. I'll send for the doctor."

John groaned as the guards lifted him from the floor. Russell crouched down over the small puddle of blood that had spilled from his mouth and picked up two teeth.

"We have much to discuss in the coming days, Uncle. I look forward to putting Iosnos on the right path with you." Her words hung heavy in the air. The shift in power was nearly tangible.

"Certainly, Your Grace," he smiled, then dipped in a low bow.

"Out. Everyone else, out," Rian's low voice demanded. The few that had lingered scattered as Ivy walked towards her father's throne. The new wood was stained dark. In the dim light of the room, it looked almost black. The wood was carved to look like the intricate swells of waves were lifting the seat from the ground. The tufted blue-green cushion curved up the high backrest into an arch of curling driftwood toward the ceiling. Ivy dragged her fingers on the arm, feeling the smooth finish against her fingertips.

"It is a nice chair, isn't it?" Ivy sat herself down in it and looked at the empty room. Rian was her only subject. His black coat was unbuttoned; the white undershirt hung open around his neck. The warm island air hadn't gotten him to abandon his aesthetic completely, but this was different. He pushed his long hair back from his face and walked toward her slowly.

"It suits you completely, Your Majesty."

The words from his lips sent a pulse through her. Her lips parted as she sat. "Say it again."

He stood right in front of her throne, towering over her. "A new King of Iosnos?" Ivy raised her eyebrows and smiled. Slowly, he dropped to one knee. "But would she still be my Queen?"

Ivy bit down on her lip and nodded.

"You look beautiful-" the other knee dropped. Rian reached for her foot. "-on your throne, Your Majesty."

He slid her dress up her legs and leaned down to kiss her foot. Ivy held back a moan as his lips pressed against her ankle.

"What's this?" Rian spread Ivy's yellow skirt at her knees, tracing his fingers to her thigh where a leather holster concealed the knife Luc gave her. Ivy nearly snapped her legs shut, but Rian held her open. He brushed his thumb over her copper skin and waited for an answer.

"It's just something to help me feel safe." Ivy hadn't told him about the tannery. The threat was vanquished.

Rian pressed soft, yearning kisses over Ivy's leg as he rested her ankle over his shoulder. Deft hands unbuckled the sheath, and he gripped the blade before it could clatter.

Ivy watched Rian drag the blade over her skin. She basked in the cool metal, lighting a flame inside her. Knowing eyes followed her motion, every hitch in her breath, every flex in the fingertips gripping the arm of that throne. Rian nicked Ivy's inner thigh with the dagger, drawing a drop of blood. He leaned in and started to suck.

293

"Rian, what are you doing?" Ivy squirmed in pleasure.

"I kneel at my altar," His eyes flicked up, "worshiping my queen on her throne." His tongue stroked along her skin as his hands slid further under her skirt and up to her hips. He lifted his head. "Your Majesty, may I?" His fingertips squeezed at her hips. This was it. If Ivy took one step now, she would fall off the cliff. Ivy looked down at Rian's pouting lips, that whispered breath of "please" as his lips brushed against her leg.

"Yes, Ria-"

Rian tugged firmly until her whole body shifted in the seat, and her ass teetered on the edge. He wasted no time shoving her skirt up to her stomach. He pushed her legs apart and dug his face into her pussy, nose first. His tongue lapped all over her lips as his hands slid around her thighs, holding her in place while he devoured her. From sheer force, Ivy leaned her back against the throne and scratched her fingernails against the armrest. She could hardly do anything but try to keep her voice down under Rian's control.

Rian flicked his tongue up and down over her clit. The warmth rushed deep into her pussy and spread like wildfire through the rest of her body. Ivy grabbed his hair with her right hand, shoving him closer. His breath hitched as he drank her in. His hands slid over the tops of her thighs and up her body until he palmed both breasts. Ivy bent her head down and grabbed one of his hands. Emotion flooded through her as she brought it to her mouth and kissed it. Ivy needed to feel close to him like she was grounded, like this was all real. Rian must have thought it was real enough. Using two fingers, he pulled her jaw down and shoved his thumb inside her mouth. Ivy moaned on his skin as she sucked on his thumb. He twisted his hand around to run his first two fingers over her tongue all the way back to her throat. Ivy felt the vibration from the sounds he made on her clit as she gagged.

Rian pulled his fingers from her mouth with a trail of spit dripping down over her chin. He didn't wait at all to fit his fingers inside her pussy. Ivy let out a whimper and jerked in the seat as her husband filled her up. Ivy leaned forward over him, trying to adjust to the size of his fingers. The hand over her chest pushed her back to give him a better angle. Fuck, he felt good.

"Rian," Ivy mewled as he pushed her closer to the edge. Rian pulled his mouth off her and looked up. Her juices glistened over his lips and chin. Ivy wanted to lick it off him, but his fingers curled up into her before she could move and hit that perfect spot. Her jaw dropped, and she tossed her head back as her orgasm built. Rian leaned right back in and sucked her clit between his teeth. Ivy couldn't hold back how good it felt as she moaned and groaned. He went back for more, ignoring his wife's pleas as she shook her hips to twist away from his grip. It felt good, but it was too good.

"Please," Ivy fought his hands and pushed him away. She leaned forward, resting her forehead on his. Her hands slipped up over his shoulders, and they just stayed there. Ivy didn't pull him tighter or push him further away. He was right where she needed him to be. Her breaths slowed as she felt his hands squeeze the folds where her waist met her hips.

Ivy brought her hands up to his and pulled his mouth in to kiss her. This time, she controlled the game. He would only be hers if she chose it. She would only be his if she chose it. His exhale into her mouth and the soft whimper of his "please" cinched the deal for her. Ivy arched down further into him and hugged her arms around his neck. She needed him. He made her feel so good, asking nothing in return.

"You are-"

Ivy didn't care what he said. She lunged forward from the throne without letting him finish and pushed him onto his back. Straddling his hips, she leaned her lips down to his and kissed him. Her chest smashed against his as she forced her body on him.

"Touch me, Rian," Ivy dragged her teeth down his jaw to his neck. Her hips bucked over his, urging him on. He took her cue and flipped her onto her back, his hand behind her head before he slammed her into the ground. Rian crushed his lips over hers and kissed her like he was dying, and her lips were the only thing that could save him. He reached his hands inside his trousers and pulled out his throbbing cock. All Ivy felt was the wide head slipping inside, stretching her out before her moan caught in his kiss as she pressed her nails into his back.

Her back slid against the stone floor as her husband pushed his way into her. His arms wrapped behind her and pulled her up into his lap. Ivy cried out and leaned forward into him, balancing her weight across his hips. Ivy rocked her hips back and forth against him, savoring his cock sliding in and out. He felt amazing. She could feel every ridge and vein under his skin as it pulsed inside her.

"Rian," she whispered as she nibbled on his earlobe, running her hands down his back and pushing her chest closer to his. Ivy grinned and ran her tongue up his neck as he growled into her ear. His grip tightened around her, carrying her up as he stood. How it was so smooth, she'd never know. Ivy whimpered as the jostle shoved his cock deeper into her cunt.

Her nails dragged on the back of his neck as he shoved her back against the wall. Her arms reached around to brace herself on the stone. Rian held her by her hips and fucked his cock into her pussy, moaning and groaning with every thrust.

"Look at me," Rian said. Ivy hadn't realized she'd been keeping her eyes closed. *Habit.* She looked deep into Rian's golden-green eyes, and something in their chests connected. He picked up his speed and pounded her into the wall behind her. Her fingers grasped at whatever they could find to brace herself. Something soft in her grip stretched with her as Rian pulled her closer to him. Ivy clenched her fist tighter and heard fabric ripping. The tapestry behind them fell to the ground with a clatter. Ivy didn't care. Fuck this castle.

"I love you," Rian whispered, pulling Ivy away from the wall. He held her, fully supporting her weight in his arms. His hips rocked up as he kept fucking her. His pace quickened as her dripping cunt squeezed down around him. Ivy whined as her orgasm took over her. Her tits bounced in her dress while Rian kept going. He fucked her through it, finishing not far behind her. Even when he was done, he didn't let her go. She didn't want him to.

CHAPTER THIRTY-THREE

"Where are we going?" Rian asked as he struggled to walk across the sand in his boots.

"I want to show you one of my favorite parts of Iosnos." Ivy had taken off her shoes miles back. "You would do better if you listened to your Queen and would stop being so stuck in your ways."

"How are no shoes better than boots outside?"

"Because you're on a tropical island. Look at yourself!" He looked down. His boots were ankle-deep in the sand of the dune. He was sweating, still wearing all the cumbersome layers of black clothing that were part of his daily dress.

"Isn't it autumn in this part of the world?" Rian complained. Ivy only stared and put her hands on her hips.

He laughed, falling back onto the soft sand. "Okay, you win." He started unlacing his boots.

"Of course, I win. I always do." Ivy bent down to kiss his cheek.

He unbuttoned his coat and removed it, leaving just his undershirt and pants on. "Satisfied?" he asked.

"Never, but it's a start," Ivy smiled and started walking ahead of him again. "We're almost there." She breached the top of one last dune, and there it was: a vast sandy beach with tall patches of grass scattered along. The waves gently rolled against the northern shore. Rian reached her side, and she pointed down the way. "Look."

A herd of wild horses stood grazing. They were smaller than the horses in Asmye, dainty even by comparison with delicate features, long graceful necks, and petite frames. The herd showed every variety of color and markings: paints, appy spots, white, black, red, even a palomino with a coat of shining golden yellow.

"I think I see my mare!" Ivy held her hand to her brow to block the sun from her eyes. She grabbed Rian's hand and pulled him down the dune towards the beach. "Come on!"

At the bottom, Ivy put her fingers to her lips and whistled. The horses all turned their heads to look. Ivy heard a whinny. Pushing her way through the other horses, she saw a fiery red chestnut with white freckled spots on her hindquarters and a white stripe down her face. Elira whinnied again when she saw Ivy and started running straight towards her. Rian tensed and stepped forward between Ivy and the horse running her way.

"It's okay. Relax," Ivy reassured him.

Elira came to a halt right before her, pushing her head into Ivy's torso to nuzzle her. She snorted as Ivy stroked her cheek.

"Her name is Elira. I turned her out with the herd when I left for Asmye."

Rian reached his hand out to stroke her neck. "She's beautiful."

"She is." Ivy looked up to see the rest of the horses walking towards them, following Elira. "They are all quite friendly. Just don't fuck with the stallion." Ivy pointed out a paint that lingered at the back of the herd.

The other horses started to swarm around them. Rian smiled as he laid hands against their coats. "Are they all wild?"

"Some are. Some are just retired. We don't keep horses the same way you do. They aren't tools for us. Certainly, we use them when we need them, but they are more companions than workers. We let them roam free for the most part."

"But you're such a good rider. How?"

"Have you ever tried to ride something half-wild?"

"You," he laughed.

Ivy shoved his chest and laughed, too. "You know what I mean. You can't break a horse like this. You have to earn their trust and give them your trust in return. You can't just dominate them. You'll never win." Ivy leaned her cheek against the velvety soft nose of Elira, feeling her warm breath against her skin. "Would you like to see?"

Rian laughed as a pushy bay forced him to scratch behind his ear. "Yeah, I do."

"Ready, girl?" Elira snorted, which Ivy took as a yes. Ivy started to run down the beach at full speed. Elira took off after her. Rian's black hair caught the wind as he whipped his head to watch. When Ivy matched Elira's pace, she grabbed her withers and leaped, pulling herself onto her back. Her fingers gripped her mane as she found her seat. Ivy felt the wind fly through her hair as she looked forward between Elira's ears. Water splashed on her legs as Elira ran through the waves. She slowed to a trot when Ivy clicked her tongue. Ivy pressed her leg into her side, and Elira turned back toward the herd and Rian.

His smile was so wide Ivy could see all his teeth. Her heart was fluttering as Elira trotted back to the herd. "Do you want to try?"

"Desperately."

"Try the palomino." The horse was standing right behind him. Golden coat, white mane, and socks. Bigger than Elira. "He's been out with the herd for a few years, but I've ridden him a few times. Don't tense up. He'll sense it."

"Don't be tense while riding a wild horse with no bridle or saddle. Easy," he sighed as he held his hand out for the palomino to rub his nose against.

"Take your time. Get to know him."

"What? I should introduce myself?"

"Yeah, exactly," Ivy smiled at Rian.

Rian looked slightly embarrassed to be talking to a horse, but he listened to her. Rian spoke so softly that Ivy could barely hear him.

"You seem nice. I promise I'm not trying to hurt you. Just want to go for a ride." Rian worked his way down the horse's body. His hands ran over the muscles, following their curves and natural lines.

"Keep going. You're doing great." Ivy pushed him closer to the horse. Rian looked over his shoulder and pointed for Ivy to leave them alone.

"You're a handsome guy. If you promise not to buck me off, there is a bucket full of carrots I'll have brought to you." He leaned in closer. "I'm trying to impress my wife, and I'd rather not fall off in front of her." Ivy pretended she couldn't hear him, but hearing Rian talk that way made her glow.

"Okay, I'm just gonna hop up here." Rian kept his hand against the horse as he jumped up and pulled himself onto its back. The horse started walking as Rian found his balance. "Good boy, good boy!" Rian praised him generously, rubbing his neck and shoulder. The palomino began to trot, and Rian smiled, looking up at her.

"Argus would never be so relaxed." Rian adjusted on the palomino's back.

"Who is Argus?" Ivy strode up beside Rian.

"My horse back in Asmye."

Ivy made a face.

"What is it?"

"I never knew your horse had a name." She couldn't help the way it made her start to laugh.

Rian scrunched his brow in earnest. "Why wouldn't he?"

"I've never heard you say it before." Ivy whooped loudly and pressed her legs into Elira's side. "Do you think you can keep up?" She took

299

off at a gallop. The entire herd began to run after her. Elira weaved in and out of the herd until water splashed around them. Ivy looked back at Rian; his hands clenched into the white mane of palomino. He started to relax, finding that connection of trust between him and his horse. His body relaxed with every passing moment. Ivy closed her eyes and dropped her hands from Elira's mane, and felt the air whooshing around her. Nothing felt as free as this.

Rian's grip on the palomino's mane loosened. He watched as the horses galloped around him with their bodies uninhibited by any man-made contraption. Their flow was smooth and elongated; their pace was set only by their desire to run. Ivy led the herd deeper into the waves. Their gait slowed, but they whinnied, happily splashing in the water. Ivy laughed, turning back to see Rian. The paint stallion charged toward him, nipping at the back of the palomino who bucked. Ivy gasped as Rian fell back into the water. The herd of horses side-stepped to avoid him. Ivy turned Elira sharply to ride back to him. She slid from Elira's back, landing beside him in the water.

"Are you hurt?!"

Rian looked up at her. He was happy, soaking wet, but happy. "Only my pride." Ivy hugged him, almost pushing him back into the water. "That was incredible. Thank you."

"Are you sure you aren't hurt at all?"

"I'm okay." They stared at each other briefly before he said, "I have something for you." He reached down beneath the waves. He pulled a completely drenched velvet pouch from his pocket, "I found this in one of my weaker moments." He opened the pouch and pulled out her wedding ring. The sight of it made Ivy gasp. "I gave it to you. I also made you promises on that day, some I didn't keep. Vows I broke, but I swear to you now that I honor, cherish, and love you with every fiber of my being for now and the rest of my days or until the world crumbles beneath our feet."

Ivy stared down at the ring in his hand through blurry eyes.

Ivy leaned her forehead against his. "Take me home."

His shoulders dropped. "I'm really okay. We don't have to go back to the castle. I want to try to ride again."

"No, you impossible man," Ivy laughed, "I mean *our* home. Take me to Asmye. I want to go home with you."

"You do?" Her favorite little askew tooth peeked out through his smile.

"Yeah, I do." Ivy held her hand so Rian could slide the ring onto her finger.

His wet palm touched her cheek and brushed a tear away. Ivy looked into the sea-colored glass of his green eyes and kissed him softly, tasting the salt water that clung to his skin.

"Let's go home," he said as he kissed her again. "But first," He took off his wet undershirt. "That palomino and I have unfinished business."

"Your Majesty, this just arrived." Dieter handed over a stack of parchment. Rian let go of Ivy's hand and broke the seal of the first letter. The seal of Gislina Alcade. His face soured. He unfolded the next report from Tornbridge. He slammed it down, eliciting a jump from everyone in the room.

"What does it say?" Ivy leaned forward in her seat.

"The Chancellor's promise of a peaceful truce is short-lived." Rian stood over the table and drew his fingers across the map of Asmye in the council chambers. "Bloidar is on the move. They'll try to take Tornbridge since we moved half our legion to Suikar." Tristan was focused, intently watching as Rian explained his strategy. Ivy's eyes darted back and forth between them. "I need you to go Suikar and pull our men back to the western coast. Bloidar's sheer size boasts an infantry with twice the men as ours. We need to have a strong show of force." Rian looked up, placing his hand on Tristan's shoulder. "Go as quickly as possible. I'll meet you in Tornbridge in two week's time."

"I'll make arrangements for the ship immediately, Your Majesty. I won't fail you."

"I know you won't." Rian's face reflected his respect for his brother-in-arms.

"Rian?" Ivy rested her hand over his. "I thought we were going home."

Rian cradled his wife's face in his fingers. "We will. I need to take care of this."

Ivy's eyes wandered over the map across the table. The ache inside her would swallow her if she were to be away from him again. "I'm going with you."

Rian tilted her chin up and pressed his lips against hers. "Please. I need you by my side." Ivy's eyes lit up. "I will need your diplomacy skills dealing with these wolves at our door."

Ad Baalestan and Ad Viena strolled in the council room, trailed by a blue-caped soldier. Ivy's swallow caught in her throat.

"Majesties," Ad Viena bowed. Luc stood silently while Baalestan folded his arms. Rian gestured for them to sit.

"Malcolm, I'll need you to take the new fleet and patrol the Tolgeen." Malcolm nodded his head.

"We have forty ships and crews ready to set sail," Malcolm confidently said. "I'll need three days to secure the stock and supplies."

"Good, good. Ad Baalestan, the island is secure?"

"Yes, things have been running smoothly. The captain of the guard has things under control," Ad Baalestan replied.

"Ad Nekoson surely helped with that." Ivy glared toward the Adeshbu.

"Then the Adeshbu will accompany me and the Queen to Tornbridge."

"Your Grace, perhaps I could stay on here," Luc interjected. Ivy tried not to look at him. "See that things don't backslide."

"Nonsense, we have a force of fine Iosnote men trained by Adeshbu. They can hold the island." Rian dismissed the request. "You may not need to guard the Queen day in and day out, but I will need the strongest men at my side in the coming months."

Ivy kept her eyes focused on the parchment in front of her. She could hardly ask Rian to allow Luc to stay behind, but a pit formed in her stomach, knowing he'd be forced to watch her with Rian again. She swallowed and looked at her guard. Natassa had told her that he was the one for her. What was she supposed to do?

Strategies were discussed, plans laid, pieces set in motion for some time when Rian finally dismissed the council. He held Tristan back.

"Ivy and I have spoken about it and once we've secured the coast, we want you back here as the Guardian of Iosnos."

Tristan's face lit up. "Thank you."

"Thank *you*." Ivy smiled warmly at the General. "Iosnos will be honored to have such a fine man at the head of its defenses."

Rian smiled and patted Tristan on the back. "The women of Iosnos are worth crossing oceans for, aren't they?"

"They are," Tristan smiled widely, glancing at The Queen.

"Do this for me and then come back to her." Rian turned to look at Ivy. "Make a life with her. You've earned it." Once Tristan was gone, Rian shut the door behind him.

"Worth crossing an ocean?" Ivy smiled at him.

"I'd sail across all the seas, the sky, through the stars for you, my love."

"Thank you. Thank you for doing that…for him, for Sophie, for Iosnos." Ivy pressed her lips against his fingers as they brushed over her face. He held her hand in his. Her wedding band was cool against his palm.

"Iosnos is important to me. You've shown me just how beautiful it really is. I want to protect that for you."

"For us." Ivy kissed him.

"For us."

"We should go. I need to take Russell's oaths if he's to serve as Steward of the Throne while I'm in Asmye. We have only a week left, and I intend to get as much done as possible before we leave."

"Lead the way, my Queen."

EPILOGUE

It was near dawn when Ivy and Rian made their way to the church, their last duty before they boarded the ship to Asmye. Natassa wouldn't let the King and Queen leave without a blessing. Ivy's reluctance towards the priestess had vanished. A deeper understanding bloomed between the women and bonded them. Women in a man's world, in a man's job.

Natassa led them to the altar. A statue of Ouraina smiled upon them. Natassa took Rian's black cloak from Ivy's shoulders. The Queen of Iosnos knelt with her husband. Rian's britches rested low on his hips as he faced her. Ivy wore only a slip, as Natassa had instructed. Incensed ribbons of red clover and maca twirled from the hearth. There was some other scent, too, one Ivy couldn't quite place, but that mouth-watering aroma enticed her.

Ivy held her hand with her scarred palm up. Rian's own met hers. His eyes, hazel and dark, stared into hers, brown and full of light.

Natassa read from her book, "Berain sept tulaine tan carrdemonique es tu Ouraina. Berain sept ulaine tan carrdemonique es tu Adievasinis. Toues et perius merree samma tan adtinq." The unfamiliar words rolled around them in a chanting haze. Ivy didn't resist as a foreign feeling stirred in her. It wasn't foreign, though. She'd felt it before, felt it when Rian took her, but held it at bay all these months. Now she let it reach deep inside of her, let it become her with trust and faith.

Ivy's palm tingled and warmed. A moment of sharp pain and then elation as her woundless palm bled against Rian's. They repeated the words after Natassa, pledging their love and devotion. Rian pulled Ivy's palm to his lips. He drank from her, crimson staining his full lips. His eyes stayed fixed on his wife. He outstretched his bleeding palm to her. Ivy gripped her hand around his long fingers. His blood was warm and thick as it filled her mouth and ran down her throat. She closed her eyes and moaned.

The world fell away as she felt Rian's soul burst inside her. His heart beat inside her chest. His love, warm and true, enveloped her. Blood dripped down Rian's chin and onto his bare chest as the flow rushed into his mouth. A buzz settled deep in her core that was neither her nor Rian. The streams of blood that slid down Rian's skin turned green and grew as vines crawled across his body. Leaves unfurled, and flowers bloomed. Rian's blood glittered like diamonds on Ivy's body, spilling down her chest and dripping to her thighs. Ivy pulled her hand away from his mouth, sinking her fingers into his raven hair. She wrapped her other hand around his neck and flew into his arms, consuming his lips. Their blood mixed between their mouths, dribbling from their lips and growing into beautiful, twisting life.

Ivy pulled away. There was no doubt of her own power now. For the first time, she had true faith. Her eyes were soft and dreamy as she stared at her husband. This was an intoxication of a different sort, warm and comforting all over her body. Red stained their lips and chin. Ivy drew her bloody finger over his heart. The symbol was crude, but Ivy made all the marks Natassa had taught her.

Natassa poured hot water from a kettle into the basin beside them, instructing them how to complete their ritual. Jasmine perfumed the air as the heat consumed the flowers. Rian reached down into the steaming basin. He wrung the cloth out before swiping it delicately over Ivy's skin. The cloth washed away the blood. As Rian washed away her doubts, Ivy wondered if she could ever really, truly be clean.

THE STORY ENDS....

RUN FROM ME

IF THE
MORNING COMES

COMING SOON

ABOUT THE AUTHOR

Cristiana JaNell is the combined talents of Marissa Cristiana Mortati and Rachel JaNell Cox. After meeting in 2020, they quickly became friends and soon after collaborative creative partners.

Born and raised in Southern California, Marissa Mortati found solace from the trials and struggles of growing up in stories. As the daughter of a liberal and free-spirited librarian, she indulged in books, movies, and TV of any genre and subject matter. Marissa wrote short stories throughout her schooling but left college to own and run a record label, The Redwoods. During the pandemic, she found her love for writing again.

Rachel Cox grew up in Kansas City and has traveled all over, including most of the States! Writing always was a piece of her, achieving an early Master's Degree in Creative Writing and worked in production in Los Angeles for several years. She's always making up songs to sing to her dog Cinnamon (who couldn't care less) and is the biggest Swiftie you'll ever meet. Follow her on Instagram @Racheljanell04

www.cristianajanell.com
@cristianajanell

ACKNOWLEDGMENTS

Cristiana –

"Last book, voodoo, proved that we was fuckin' brutal."

To my mom Anna Lynda, your unwavering support has kept me afloat in my worst times and enriched me in the best ones. I couldn't do any of this without you. You put art in my hands before anyone else and created a creative. Thank you for giving me that.

To my sister, Marlaina, thank you for holding my hand even though we are thirty-something-year-old ladies. You are an inspiration and a force of kindness & love. I couldn't be prouder of the person you've become. Also, thanks for doodling this book cover, I guess.

To Melissa & Marissa Two, thank you for being my chosen family.

To the Molari, thanks for letting me be the little weirdo living in your backyard. Your love and support have helped me through the toughest times while writing this book even if you didn't know it.

To all my friends that exist in my headphones, you have influenced & inspired me in countless ways.

To my co-author, my soulmate, and my favorite, Rachel, thank you for being just as insane as me and making it all feel like genius. You showed me colors I never saw and now we speak a language all our own. I love you and still, most importantly, thank you for fixing all my commas. Okay, but what if...

JaNell -

Uhm, wowsies, a whole nother book, huh?

The first thanks goes to my mommy (not mother?) Lynnette for her unwavering love, even though I am a very difficult (yet entertaining) daughter. Whatever you do, never read this series. You are too precious for it. To my father Dennis, I hope I made you proud and that you think the degree is finally worth it. To my brother Jared, thank you for supporting who I am and encouraging me, even when I feel like I don't belong. You also can't read this book.

To Katrina, my most supportive and dear friend, thank you for your random acts of encouragement and your earnest desire to see me succeed. Your friendship means so much to me and I am so grateful to share one brain cell with you. If our podcast doesn't work out (@Boosandboobs on Spotify and Patreon, y'all!!!) then we can keep trying to make it on a game show. I'll never forgive RuPaul for not picking us for Lingo.

Once again, Taylor Swift, thank you for allowing your heart to remain breakable (but never by the same hand twice) and sharing your words with me so I can sort out my own thoughts and feelings. I'm so grateful to have "known" you for over half my life and you have always and will always inspire me.

Last but never least, Marissa, you are my best friend and I am so so so lucky to have found my soulmate and safest place, even if it was via Tiktok. Thank you for knowing me and still choosing to stick around. You are the second funniest person I know and the most beautiful human the world has ever seen. I'm so proud of what we've accomplished and I will always love you. Long live all the mountains we moved. I had the time of my life writing novels with you.

To the Inner Circle, Aly, Celestina, and Emilie, we're so happy to have this wonderful group where we feel safe and comfortable enough to be our truest (and Rachel's most annoying) selves. Your friendships and book recommendations are what keep us alive. Belief means a lot - just ask Tinkerbell. You are the respite in an unrelenting world and make our hearts golden.

For Christine and Pam, thank you for sticking with us on this journey. We hope the evolution of what was once just *Ivy* and is now *Run From Me* has been half as joyous for you as it is for us. Your feedback and support mean the entire world and we are more than lucky to have you as friends.

Thanks for reading!

Join our mailing list to
keep up to date with our latest releases
and exclusive content!
www.cristianajanell.com

Please add a review on Amazon
and let us know what you thought!

Made in the USA
Columbia, SC
31 July 2024

39335196R00172